when stars rain down

a novel

ANGELA JACKSON-BROWN

When Stars Rain Down

Published in Nashville, Tennessee, by Thomas Nelson. Thomas Nelson is a registered trademark of HarperCollins Christian Publishing, Inc.

Interior design by Emily Ghattas

Thomas Nelson titles may be purchased in bulk for educational, business, fundraising, or sales promotional use. For information, please email SpecialMarkets@ThomasNelson.com.

Scripture quotations are taken from the King James Version of the Bible. And from the Good News Translation in Today's English Version—Second Edition. Copyright 1992 by American Bible Society. Used by permission. And from the New International Version®, NIV®. Copyright © 1973, 1978, 1984, 2011 by Biblica, Inc.™ Used by permission of Zondervan. All rights reserved worldwide. www.zondervan.com.

Publisher's Note: This novel is a work of fiction. Names, characters, places, and incidents are either products of the author's imagination or used fictitiously. All characters are fictional, and any similarity to people living or dead is purely coincidental.

Library of Congress Cataloging-in-Publication Data

Names: Jackson-Brown, Angela, 1968- author.
Title: When stars rain down : a novel / Angela Jackson-Brown.
Description: Nashville, Tennessee : Thomas Nelson, [2021] | Summary: "Award-winning author Angela Jackson-Brown delivers a moving coming-of-age story about a summer that changes a young girl's life, told in a distinctive Southern literary style"-- Provided by publisher.
Identifiers: LCCN 2020045148 (print) | LCCN 2020045149 (ebook) | ISBN 9780785240440 (paperback) | ISBN 9780785240457 (epub) | ISBN 9780785240464
Classification: LCC PS3610.A355526 W47 2021 (print) | LCC PS3610.A355526 (ebook) | DDC 813/.6--dc23
LC record available at https://lccn.loc.gov/2020045148
LC ebook record available at https://lccn.loc.gov/2020045149

Printed in the United States of America

21 22 23 24 25 LSC 5 4 3 2

In loving memory of M.C. Jackson, Ellena English,
Gwendolyn English, Judith Brown, and Craig O'Hara

"And the stars in the sky fell to earth . . ."

Revelation 6:13

A Note from the Author

Dear Reader,

Racism in the 1930s was rampant throughout the country, but especially in southern states like Georgia. Because my goal as a writer is always to strive to be historically accurate, there are occasions when characters in the book, who are members of the Ku Klux Klan, will use the "N-word." My intent in using this word is not to shock but to punctuate the fact that racism was brutal and still is brutal nearly eighty-five years later. I have been a target of the hate that word gives, and I want the readers of this book to understand the full weight of a word so powerful that it is now referred to by its first letter. The white people who were actively participating in the racist behavior found in *When Stars Rain Down* were ordinary, and this word is a necessary reminder of the hate that lived in the hearts and minds of some of the white citizens of Parsons, Georgia, whom everyone in the community knew. Even when "that word" was not being spoken out loud, many of the white characters illustrated the power of the word through their actions. My hope is that a day will come when that word and other derogatory words are no longer part of our lexicon, but the way we ensure that happens is by staring back at our collective history without blinking or flinching.

Sincerely,
Angela Jackson-Brown

*T*he inside of Miss Peggy's house was hot like the End of Days the preachers preached about during summertime revival meetings. My pastor, Reverend Perkins, said just this past Sunday that if this heat was a clue of how hot hell was going to be, we should all be lining up to get rebaptized. This type of heat was new to all of us and had some of the End of Days crowd prophesizing that maybe this was the sign of the end. I didn't know about that but I knew one thing: this heat made everything unbearable to do, especially cooking and cleaning.

I was naturally thin, and usually when everybody else was soaked with sweat, I was walking around with a sweater on. But this day, I felt like somebody had drenched me in water. We'd been experiencing unseasonable weather since the middle of April. Tornadoes had been hitting all around us, and it only got worse as the days went on. Now we were in the middle of one of the worst droughts to ever hit the state of Georgia. Lou Zoller, on WSB radio, said 1936 would go down as one of the deadliest years when it came to the weather. It most surely felt like Mother Nature was on a warpath, and we were her targets.

Of course it didn't help that I was stuck cooking in the kitchen like it was the day before Christmas instead of the middle of June. I would be eighteen in a few days and I had planned on spending this day shopping in Atlanta with my cousin Lucille. She and I were going to look for outfits to wear to Founder's Day in a few weeks, a celebration that had been going on in Parsons, Georgia, since before Granny was born. Everybody, young and old, Colored and white, wanted to be at Founder's Day dressed in their best outfits. Yet here I was, cooking and cleaning at Miss Peggy's house instead of gazing at dresses made out of tulle, taffeta, and silk. I wasn't planning on buying one of those off-the-rack dresses; since I was pretty handy with a needle and a thread, I planned on making the dress that I liked and saving some money.

I had asked for the day off weeks before, and Granny and Miss Peggy had said yes, but when Miss Peggy told me Jimmy Earl was coming home on the same day as my trip to Atlanta, I knew I had to stay and help her and Granny get ready. Both of them were too old to try to cook and clean in all this heat. I was sad that I had to give up my trip to Atlanta, but I would have just spent the day worrying about Granny and Miss Peggy.

Jimmy Earl was coming home from the University of Georgia to visit for the summer, and Miss Peggy wanted all his favorite foods waiting on the dinner table when he walked inside the door. Ordinarily, on hot days like this, we didn't even cook. I'd make some sandwiches or a tray of vegetables or fruit, and that would be about all. But Miss Peggy was bound and determined that Jimmy Earl get the king's treatment when he returned from school.

I leaned against the counter. I was so hot I could hardly breathe. The windows were all open, and I had a little fan sitting in the windowsill that wasn't doing much more than circulating hot air. I filled up my mason jar with some of the spring water I'd stopped for that morning. Miss Peggy had indoor water and a Frigidaire she kept it cool in, but water straight out of the faucet just didn't taste the same to me, even though the water came from the well my grandfather had dug for Miss Peggy and her husband when they first built this house.

I mopped the sweat from my face with the dish towel on the counter and looked around the kitchen. There wasn't a single spot that wasn't filled up with a pot or pan or serving tray of Jimmy Earl's favorite foods. The menu for his homecoming consisted of baked ham, short ribs, fried chicken with gravy, dressing, collard greens, stewed okra and tomatoes, potato salad, apple dumplings, buttermilk biscuits, and German chocolate cake. Most everything was already done except for a few things like the biscuits and the gravy that I planned on making right around the time Jimmy Earl arrived.

It was four thirty, and Jimmy Earl was sure to be home any minute. Miss Peggy tried to help me earlier after Granny had to go home on account of her gout acting up, but Miss Peggy was getting feeble her own self, so it was up to me to make sure Jimmy Earl's homecoming dinner was everything his gran wanted it to be.

"Opal, I swear you done got to be as good of a cook as your Grandma Birdie," Miss Peggy said as she walked into the kitchen taking slow, measured steps. Miss Peggy used to be a big woman like my granny, but she'd lost a whole lot of weight over the last few months. And on top of that, her movements were getting slower. A sign of age, she had said. I'd wondered if that was really the case, but I didn't dare ask. Even at the age of nearly being an adult, I still understood my place when it came to Granny and Miss Peggy. Some things they just wouldn't discuss with me, and their health was generally something they only talked about with each other in hushed tones.

Miss Peggy made her way over to the stove where the pot of greens was still cooking. She stuck the big metal spoon into the pot and dipped out some of the pot likker. She blew on it and then took a sip. I watched her as she closed her eyes and moaned.

"Lord, chile, this pot likker is better than any I've ever cooked. You're gonna make some lucky man a good wife someday."

"I'm not looking for no husband," I muttered. But even when I said the words, I knew I wasn't exactly being honest. I was almost eighteen. No, I didn't necessarily have a boy in mind to marry since Granny wouldn't even let me keep company with a boy yet, but I did wonder who might be the boy I would someday marry and start a family with.

"Every girl is looking for a husband, honey. Some just look harder than others. But never mind all of that. When do you think everything will be ready? Jimmy Earl should be home any minute, and his mama's been napping all afternoon. Hopefully she won't get in one of her moods today," Miss Peggy said.

Jimmy Earl's mama, Miss Corinne, was a bit touched. As far

as I knew, she'd been that way most of her life, but especially after she had Jimmy Earl, or at least that's what Granny told me. She said some women never overcame the stress and strain of childbirth and that Miss Corinne suffered more than most, especially since her marriage to Jimmy Earl's daddy, Mr. Earl Ketchums, didn't work out. Miss Corinne and Jimmy Earl had to come back home and live with Miss Peggy and Miss Peggy's now deceased husband, Mr. Cecil.

A lot of days my whole job revolved around keeping Miss Corinne quiet. Usually that meant listening to her while she sang from the Methodist hymnal. If she got restless, I would just make a song request to calm her down.

"Sing me 'To God Be the Glory,' Miss Corinne," I might say, and she would run off for her hymnal even though she knew nearly every song in there by heart. I'd make her sing song after song until she was worn completely out. Other times, if she wasn't interested in singing, I would take her for a long walk. We'd go from Miss Peggy's house all the way out to mine and Granny's house over in Colored Town and then back again. Sometimes we'd do it more than once in a day's time if she was really riled up, but this heat had made it impossible for me to take her walking.

I was thankful Miss Peggy had convinced her to sleep. I wouldn't have been able to cook and tend to Miss Corinne too.

"Miss Peggy, all I've got left to do is make the biscuits and let these greens cook for another half hour and then everything will be ready," I said.

"What about the deviled eggs? Jimmy Earl loves Birdie's

deviled eggs. Should you make some of them too?" Miss Peggy asked, wiping her forehead with her handkerchief.

"Miss Peggy, we've got so much food here now, it'll take Jimmy Earl and half of the county the rest of the week and part of next to eat everything. I hardly made this much when he came home for Christmas last year," I said, determined not to cook one more thing that we hadn't already agreed upon.

I was beyond tired. Of course, I understood Miss Peggy's excitement. Jimmy Earl hadn't been home since Christmas. He was studying pharmacy at the University of Georgia, and during the breaks and holidays, he worked at a pharmacy up there in Athens, and he did some janitorial work at the local hospital to help pay for his schooling. So his deciding to come home for the summer and help around the farm and work at Mr. Lowen's Drugstore was a big deal. And, I had to admit, I had missed him too.

Jimmy Earl and I had grown up together. He was five years older than me, but he always treated me like a little sister. It never mattered that he was white and I was Colored. Granny said when I was a toddler and she would bring me to work, Jimmy Earl insisted that he was in charge of taking care of me.

"Earl! Earl Ketchums, where you at?" I heard Miss Corinne call from the front room, startling both me and Miss Peggy.

"Blessed Savior," Miss Peggy muttered.

I still needed to mix up my biscuit dough and get the red-eye gravy cooking. The last thing I needed was to have to go deal with Miss Corinne. I looked at Miss Peggy.

She patted my hand. "I'll tend to Corinne. You just go on

and finish up the cooking. And when you get done with them biscuits, you fix two plates . . . one for you and one for Birdie, and then you head on home. Birdie probably ain't ate today."

"Are you sure, Miss Peggy? Soon as I get these biscuits in the oven I can go see about Miss Corinne," I said. I was tired but I knew Miss Corinne did better with me than she did with Miss Peggy or my granny. I hated to see Jimmy Earl's homecoming spoiled because Miss Corinne was acting out.

Miss Peggy smiled, but the sadness was all over her face. "No, honey. You go on home once those biscuits are done. You been cooking and cleaning all week. I'll get Corinne to settle down," she said and walked out the kitchen, almost dragging her left leg behind her.

It wasn't easy seeing Miss Peggy and Granny getting old. It was like one day they were middle-aged, still spry and in complete control of their faculties and their bodies, and the next day, they were old women with brittle bones and labored breaths. It scared me.

I gave the greens one last stir and then turned them down real low. Everything looked good. Then I started making the biscuits and the gravy. I was so good at making Granny's cathead biscuit recipe, she never bothered to make them anymore. She just called on me to make her biscuits. The gravy was easy as well. I just used some of the juice from the ham I had baked, stirred in some flour, and then added the melted butter and half of a cup of this morning's coffee to give it that strong taste everybody loved so much. I turned the gravy down low so it would keep warm until Jimmy Earl got home.

Once those two things were done, I was officially finished cooking, and I was happy for that. I just wanted to get my things and go home, where I could lay out on the porch underneath the stars and catch a breeze if I was lucky. I started fixing plates for mine and Granny's supper. I hoped she would feel up to eating. Then I tidied up the kitchen, making sure Miss Peggy didn't have anything to do but serve the food when Jimmy Earl got home. She and Granny had set the dining room table with the fancy china the day before, so all I needed to do was go find Miss Peggy—but before I could go looking for her, I heard Miss Corinne getting louder and louder in the front room.

"I want to go see Earl Ketchums, Mama," I heard Miss Corinne yell. "And I want to go see him right now."

Clearly Miss Corinne had forgotten that the last time she snuck off to see Earl Ketchums, her daddy had still been alive and had shot Mr. Earl in his rear end, promising to aim higher if he didn't stay away from Miss Corinne. Even after Mr. Muldoon's death, we kept a clear eye on Miss Corinne, making sure she never went off on her own to see him. Jimmy Earl saw his daddy every now and then, but even he would admit that it was best she not be around Mr. Earl because he lived like somebody thrown away. He didn't work, except for selling moonshine, and, as Granny would say, he stayed drunker than Cooter Brown most of the time.

"Corinne, you are getting yourself riled up for nothing. Now go somewhere and be still," I heard Miss Peggy say back to her.

What a Friend we have in Jesus, all our sins and griefs to bear!

What a privilege to carry everything to God in prayer!

"Oh, Lord," I said under my breath. Miss Corinne was about to get wound up and it was going to take an act of God to settle her down. I hurried into the sitting room just in time to see Miss Corinne pull her dress over her head as she continued to sing the words to her favorite song, but she was singing it so fast, all of the words seemed to run together.

Ohwhatpeaceweoftenforfeit,
Ohwhatneedlesspainwebear,

"Corinne Louise Muldoon Ketchums, have you lost your ever-loving mind?" Miss Peggy yelled, her face turning all shades of red.

Allbecausewedonotcarry,
EverythingtoGodinprayer.

I ran over and pulled Miss Corinne's dress back down. "I've got her, Miss Peggy."

Miss Peggy sank into the closest chair, the color steadily draining from her face. I worried that she might just pass out, but I turned my attention back to Miss Corinne, who was trying to pull away from me. I wrapped my arms around her waist and tried to pull her close. She struggled, but then, after a moment or two, she relaxed in my arms.

"I want to go see Earl Ketchums," Miss Corinne said, tears streaming down her face. "You'll take me, Opal? You'll take me now? I need to see him right now. Right now. Right. Now!"

"Let's talk about it tomorrow, Miss Corinne. Jimmy Earl will be home in a few minutes and you don't want to miss him, do you?" I asked. I reached into Miss Corinne's dress pocket and retrieved one of her daddy's handkerchiefs that she's kept with her since he died three years ago. Normally, she would have on a pair of his dungarees. They would nearly swallow her up, but wearing them was the only thing that seemed to keep her calm when she started missing Mr. Cecil, which was all of the time. I had convinced her to wear a dress today in Jimmy Earl's honor. She looked like a fragile white baby doll. I wiped the tears from her face.

"Jimmy Earl's coming home?" she asked, a half smile on her face. "He's coming back? Is Daddy coming back too?"

I decided to ignore her last question. "Yes ma'am, Jimmy Earl will be here any minute and you don't want him to find you all wound up, now, do you?" I smoothed down her brownish-blond hair that looked just like her mama's used to look before it became thinned out and gray colored. I had French braided Miss Corinne's hair earlier during the day, but between her restless sleeping and the heat, it looked like I hadn't even touched it. "Why don't we go upstairs and get you changed and fixed up again?"

"You'll take me to see Earl Ketchums tomorrow?" she asked, not to be thrown off from her original request.

I took her by the hand. "Let's get you cleaned up and we'll talk about that later."

I looked over at Miss Peggy. She was watching us closely, and I could see tears trickling down her face, which was unusual because Miss Peggy wasn't a crying type of woman. She mouthed, "Thank you." I nodded and led Miss Corinne out of the sitting room and up the stairs to her room.

Clearly, I wouldn't be going home anytime soon.

2

ummer nights in Colored Town were always my favorite. I looked around my granny's porch, seeing all of my aunties, uncles, and cousins and a smattering of neighbors and friends. As always, I felt so much love for all of them that it seemed like my heart might just burst wide open. Most of us were domestic workers, field hands, or sharecroppers, so we made our living by the soil or dirt of other folks' houses, but once we got home and washed off the dirt and sweat of the day, we always found a way to come together and congregate underneath those starry Georgia skies.

My Uncle Lem was playing his guitar and singing "Little Black Train." I looked over at Granny. She disapproved of secular songs, but she didn't say anything right then. I knew her, though, and she would let him play one or two songs before she'd tell him to sing something about Jesus. And, of course, Uncle Lem would comply and flow right into "Precious Lord" or "Pearly White City." If Mr. Tote, our next-door neighbor, hadn't already had too much to drink for the night, he would join in and play his harmonica. Once he and Uncle Lem started playing gospel songs, all of Colored Town would join in singing from the various porches. It sounded like a celestial choir singing.

I leaned back, resting my head on my cousin Lucille's leg. The porch was so full of people that by the time I got home from work there were no more seats.

About thirty houses lined the street of Colored Town, and almost all of them were my kin, or folks who'd loved me like I was their relation. The houses were so close that whatever went on inside those thin walls, everybody close by heard it. On any given night you might hear soft quarrels, the sounds of lovemaking, or the giggles and laughter that were just natural sounds to hear among those of us who lived in Colored Town. Not a one of us was rich, but we had all that we ever needed, and that was each other.

All throughout our little community the smells of summer squash, mustard greens, or sweet corn cooking filled the air along with the sweet, mouthwatering smell of peaches almost ripe enough to pick from the trees. And it wouldn't be a summer night if somebody didn't crack open a watermelon, causing all of the young children to line up, impatiently waiting for some of nature's candy. I had already eaten supper, but I was tempted to get in the watermelon line myself. My Uncle Little Bud had a gaggle of youngins lined up to get a slice. Even with the drought, those melons would be refreshing in weather like this.

We all worried how this lack of rain was going to affect our crops and our gardens. So far, things were doing okay, but we were in the early days of this rainless weather. Granny said this morning when we were getting ready to go to work that we all better start talking to God about sending us a few of his teardrops to cover the earth.

"Why you so quiet, Opal?" my cousin Lucille asked. She was braiding my hair for me. Mostly, I kept it braided and pinned up. I worked so hard cleaning and cooking every day, I didn't have time to fool with my hair.

"Girl, I couldn't be you with all this hair. I wouldn't never pin it up," Lucille said, not able to keep the good-natured envy out of her voice. Her mama, Aunt Shimmy, said Lucille would have broken her neck swinging her hair all over the place if God had blessed her with as much hair as mine. I didn't mind Lucille doting on my hair. It made me feel special.

Of all of my girl cousins, I considered myself the dowdiest. I was thin as a reed with not much of a shape, my features were plain, and I was quiet most times unless I was talking to someone I was close to like Lucille or Granny. But even with them, I usually let them do most of the talking and I would listen.

No one ever said I wasn't pretty. Actually, I think Granny and the aunties spent more time telling me how beautiful I was than they did the other girl cousins, but that just was never a word I connected with myself. Folks said I favored my mama, and my mama favored my granddaddy. Since I'd never known either one of them, I just took folks' word for it. Granny didn't believe in pictures, so there wasn't a single photo of Mama or Granddaddy lying around anywhere for me to compare myself to.

Granny had four sons and my mama. From them, she had twelve grandchildren, and she was months away from having her first great-grandchild. So even though I didn't have any brothers or sisters, to my knowledge, I was never alone, and Lucille was the one I felt closest to. She was two years younger than me, but she acted twenty years older. Where I was shy and closemouthed, Lucille was outgoing and quick with a comeback no matter the situation. Her hair might not have been a minute long, but she always kept it styled like the women in the movie picture magazines she liked to read.

"Opal, did you hear me? Why are you so quiet tonight?" Lucille asked again, but she kept right on talking before I could answer. Which was good. I wasn't entirely sure why I was feeling so moody.

It was like my spirit was telling me that something was about to happen. I didn't know if it was good or bad, I just knew something was brewing. I had felt this way most of my life. Somehow, I could just feel when something was about to happen—so much so, folks in the family would ask me if I had a feeling about something before they went off and did it. Granny would fuss if she heard anyone talk that way. "Ain't nothing but hoodoo," she would say, but still folks would ask. Sometimes I had a strong feeling, other times just an inkling. But I kept that away from Granny.

I started having one of my feelings soon after I left Miss Peggy's house. I was able to get Miss Corinne settled pretty quickly, leaving before Jimmy Earl even made it home, but as I walked from Miss Peggy's to Colored Town, I started feeling strange. Sometimes I felt a bit off right before my monthlies, but I'd just finished with that. I tried to shake it off, but it wouldn't go away.

"Opal, you feeling all right?" Granny asked from her seat on the porch. Normally, the grown folks didn't pay us no mind, but Granny had been looking at me peculiar ever since I got home. If nobody else noticed I wasn't myself, two people always did: Granny and Lucille. "This weather's got everybody feeling out of sorts," Granny said. "Maybe you oughta go inside and take you a good dose of castor oil. A good working out might do you a world of good."

Everybody on the porch laughed. I felt my face flush. Whatever Granny thought to say, she said it. Didn't matter to her if you got embarrassed. She used to say getting embarrassed was Satan's revenge on vain men and women.

"Mama, you figure giving folks the runs is the answer to everything," teased Uncle Little Bud, Granny's youngest son, as he came back to the porch. Granny reached over and slapped him playfully on the arm.

"You just too mouthy, Little Bud," Granny scolded, but she did it with a smile. Everybody said Uncle Little Bud was her favorite, at least after Mama ran off. Uncle Little Bud was just shy of thirty and was newly married to his longtime and long-suffering girlfriend, Cheryl Anne. Uncle Little Bud farmed, like all of my other uncles, and Cheryl Anne took in wash. She was quiet like me, but she loved herself some Uncle Little Bud, and in his rascally way, he loved her too. But then, all of Granny's sons were good husbands, uncles, and fathers. The only bad apple in the bunch was my mama. As I let thoughts of her creep into my head, the bitterness rose up in my throat, almost making me choke. You would think somebody as old as me would be over her mama's leaving her, but there were times when the pain was so fresh and so raw, it felt like she had just left.

"I'm fine, Granny," I said. "Just tired."

"Well, you sure worked yourself to death this week. I'm sorry I couldn't be more help to you," Granny said. "Why don't you take tomorrow off? I can take care of things myself."

I shook my head. "No, Granny. I wouldn't do that to you. Tomorrow's wash day. I'll be fine after a good night's rest."

"Neither one of you needs to work like you do," Uncle Myron, Granny's oldest son, scolded. I groaned underneath my breath. I knew where this conversation was going. I could have kicked myself for even bringing up the fact that I was tired.

"Come on, Myron. Don't get started with all that tonight," Uncle Little Bud teased. He knew where the conversation was going too. Everybody did. "You ain't got but one note, and you like to sing it ever chance you get."

Everybody laughed, but Uncle Myron was not to be deterred from saying his piece. He was the leader of our family, second only to Granny, and he was the most prosperous of everybody, so sometimes he acted like that meant his words were the only words that mattered. Uncle Myron had a farm that he leased out while he ran a little country store at the edge of Colored Town. To hear him tell it, me helping Granny keep house at Miss Peggy's was just a step above blaspheming the good Lord.

"I'm going to say what I know is right to say, Little Bud. Mama is too old to be working like she do at them white folks' house, and Opal ought to be somewhere in school. She's too smart to be a domestic worker," Uncle Myron said.

I gently pushed Lucille's hands away and stood up. I wasn't fixing to sit and listen to him preach to me and Granny about how terrible our life choices were. Not on this night. I didn't even care that my hair was only half fixed.

"I'm going for a walk. I won't go far. Just down to the end of the road," I said and took off before anybody could try and stop me. I was safe, and they knew it. Everybody around here looked out for everybody else. It was a rare night when there wasn't some grown folks walking down the street or sitting on their porches keeping an eye on the younger kids and us teenagers. There were always eyes on us.

I heard Lucille ask Aunt Shimmy if she could go with me, and I was thankful that Aunt Shimmy said no. I didn't feel like hearing Lucille's mouth right then. I loved her, but at that moment, I needed the solitude of the dirt road leading to the edge of Colored Town where the peach orchard was. I also heard Aunt Shimmy fussing at Uncle Myron for hurting my feelings. I just kept walking until I got to the orchard, not even wanting to hear his reply.

Because of the drought, the trees weren't doing as good as they normally did. The young boys tried to keep them watered, but the humans, the livestock, and the vegetables were more important than the orchard, so the trees were suffering now. When normally the peaches would have been plump, almost ready to burst, they were smaller and knottier. The peach smell still permeated the air, but not like in previous summers.

I continued to walk, not stopping until I reached the peach orchard. I found a comfortable spot underneath one of the trees and sat. I was determined to get away from the sound of my family's voices discussing me. This was a conversation that happened regularly. Everybody seemed to think they knew what was best for me, but seldom did anybody ever ask me what I wanted.

I wouldn't say my feelings were hurt; I was just tired of the same old conversation. Uncle Myron's three sons and two daughters were all college graduates or attending college. His sons all graduated from Morehouse, and one taught there and the other two taught at Colored high schools in Atlanta. His two youngest children, the twins, Emma and Eveline, were juniors down in Alabama at Tuskegee Institute. They both wanted to be nurses. All of Uncle Myron's children were smart from the time they were little, and it made perfect sense that they went to college.

Uncle Myron and late Aunt Josephine had worked themselves to death to make sure all of their kids went to college, and I was proud of my cousins. I probably screamed as loud as anybody at the boys' graduations, but school just wasn't my thing. I hated it. I always mixed up my letters and I could hardly add two plus two. I was so thankful when Granny let me drop out in eighth grade. As far as I was concerned, I had stayed eight years longer than I needed because I just didn't seem to hold on to much of what I got taught from those schoolbooks. We had some good teachers at the Colored Training School. I just wasn't quick to catch on to book learning.

But where I felt stupid in the classroom, I felt like a shining star in the kitchen and in the house in general. There was something about cooking and cleaning that made me feel good about myself. I liked that I could take little or nearly nothing and turn it into a meal. I liked that I could clean house better than anybody I knew, old or young, and I loved that I could take scraps of material and, before you knew it, I would have a dress or a pair of pants or a quilt made. Those things were my passion . . . my joy, and I hated that Uncle Myron tried to make me feel like something was wrong with me for wanting to be a housekeeper like my granny.

Uncle Myron said he farmed and ran his mercantile so his sons wouldn't have to and so his daughters could be married to professional men, but I wondered if just maybe one of his sons wouldn't have minded being given the chance to till the soil or plant some tobacco or peanuts. Uncle Myron called what most of us all did slave work. He didn't set out to be mean with his words, but he was, and he never paid attention to the hurt on Granny's face every time he brought the subject up.

I also resented that he made it seem like I wasn't taking care of Granny. Most of what Granny did every day was sit and keep Miss Peggy company while I worked. I made sure that Granny only did what she wanted to do. If she was forced to stop working, I just knew she wouldn't be long for this world. She got joy out of cooking and cleaning, and Miss Peggy never made us feel like we were slaves. She paid us good money for what we did, and Granny and I saved nearly every nickel so that when the day came that Granny couldn't work anymore, she would have a little nest egg—although I knew Miss Peggy would probably keep paying Granny until the day she died, work or no work.

I never intended to leave Granny. If anybody ever bothered to marry me, they would have to know Granny and I were a package deal. I always planned on taking care of her and making sure she knew that unlike my mother, I would never leave her. And as was my custom, I felt the tears begin to fall. The thought of Granny dying someday always left me overwhelmed and in tears, but since I was alone, I let the tears fall. Then I heard a voice.

"What you doing out here all by yourself, pretty gal?"

I looked up and saw it was Cedric Perkins, the preacher's son. I hadn't even heard him walk up. I reached up to my hair. One side was hanging down my shoulder and the other side was plaited and pinned. I was mortified, but I tried not to show it. What was I going to do, anyway? Run?

Cedric was still wearing his farming clothes. It was still light enough outside that I could see his face, and definitely those pretty white teeth of his. The sky had become a beautiful mix of purples, oranges, and yellows with a hint of gray. But even with all that beauty, I was still caught up by the handsomeness of Cedric.

He sat down beside me. I could smell the faint scent of cigarettes, sweat, and cow manure on him, and his pants were painted red with dry Georgia clay. But it didn't bother me none. That was a familiar smell if you grew up in the country. Most every man I'd ever known who was worth anything carried the smell of the land on his body. Even Uncle Myron wasn't too stuck on himself to move some dirt around in his garden.

Cedric reached over and brushed the tear from my face. His hands were rough but nice at the same time. No boy had ever touched me in such a tender way before. My instincts said to get up and run home. But something else told me to stay put. I listened to the something else.

"Why you crying out here all by yourself? Somebody hurt you?" he asked. "Do I need to go beat somebody up, pretty gal?"

I shook my head. "I'm fine." I didn't feel comfortable sharing what I was thinking with anyone, let alone Cedric, one of the cutest boys in Henry County, Colored or white. Plus, I figured he would just make fun of me, so I continued to sit still, barely breathing I was so nervous.

Cedric leaned back against the tree we were sitting under. "You know, before my Grandma Apple died, she used to come out here and sit underneath these trees. She said the chinaberry tree was her favorite, but the peach trees did all right too," he said. "You ain't got to talk if you don't want to. Do you mind if I sit here beside you and rest for a spell?"

"I don't mind," I whispered, even though I worried what my granny or uncles might say if they saw me sitting out in public with Cedric like this. Everybody knew that even though Cedric, or Stank, as most everybody called him, was the son of a preacher, he could be a bit of a hot head and a bad boy. One minute Cedric could be heard singing beautiful hymns in church and then a few hours later he was cussing somebody out for something or another on those same church grounds. He was not the kind of boy my granny was praying about for me.

"I bet your kinfolks would mind me sitting out here with you," he laughed. "Miss Birdie shore don't like me, do she?"

"It's just she don't know you that well. That's all," I said. Of course, I didn't know him either. This time, and one time before, were probably the most words he and I had spoken to each other our entire lives. Yes, we went to the same church on Sundays and on Wednesday nights, but the Perkins family lived a few miles outside of Colored Town and they pretty much stayed to themselves. I would see Cedric coming and going through our little segment of the town, but he and I had never really struck up much of a conversation with each other. I thought about the last time we did speak. It wasn't very cordial.

He and my Uncle Michael's son—Michael Jr., whom we called M.J.—were throwing the baseball around the day of the church picnic a few weeks ago, and I couldn't help but watch. I was helping my Aunt Shimmy with the cooking, sweat pouring down my face from the heat of the fire. Cedric had on a short-sleeved shirt, and his muscles bulged each time he threw the ball. He was like something I had never seen before. Cedric caught a glimpse of me looking at him before I could look away.

"Hey, hey, M.J., isn't that your cousin over there with them great big eyes?" Cedric yelled. "She shore has turned out pretty." I turned away and started back flouring the chicken for Aunt Shimmy to fry up in the cast-iron pot that was sitting on the fire Uncle Lem had made. I could hear the crackling of the grease, and I acted like I was so into getting that chicken to Aunt Shimmy that I didn't even have time to give Cedric Perkins a second look. I acted so well, I didn't even notice when he came up to the table.

"Hey there, Opal Pruitt. Ain't you gone speak to me?" he asked. He was good-looking. Couldn't nobody argue with that, but he was also arrogant as any one person I had ever met. Cedric was nearly eighteen like me, and also like me, he chose to work instead of go to school. I'd also heard M.J. say Cedric was hoping to get picked to play with the Atlanta Black Crackers. M.J. said Cedric wasn't no Satchel Paige, but he wasn't no slouch either.

"Hello, Cedric Perkins. There. I spoke. You satisfied?" I said. I kept on flouring the chicken, thankful that none of the grown folks were paying us any mind.

"Well, I'd be more satisfied if you'd give me one of them piping hot chicken legs your auntie just fried up. They looking all golden brown and juicy," he said, flashing a mouthful of white teeth. Against his rich black skin, those teeth almost sparkled. I felt my face grow hot. I had to remind myself to stay focused on what I was doing or I might have stopped flouring chicken and just gazed at him like some lovestruck ninny.

So instead of flirting with him like my cousin Lucille would have done, I flashed him angry eyes. "Well, what with you being the preacher's son, I reckon you can get your chicken from anybody's table. We got just enough for ourselves."

He threw back his head and laughed. I looked down, fearing that my aunts, or worse, my uncles, would see me talking to Cedric.

"Well, since you put it that way, I reckon I'll just mosey over to Hazel Moody's table. I just bet she has a leg or a thigh she can spare," he said and started laughing as he walked away. I coulda just melted into the ground, I was so mortified, and I couldn't believe I didn't have something flirty and girlie to say back to him. I had basically invited him to go off and be with Hazel Moody.

I smiled to myself now, wondering what she would think about me sitting here underneath this peach tree with the boy she all but claimed as her own.

"Humph. Well, I guess the way your granny feels about me is true for how most folks feel about me in this town. They judge me by my loud mouth and flirtatious spirit, as Mama calls it," he said.

"I try not to judge anybody that way. I don't want nobody judging me," I said.

He laughed. "Look at you over there quoting Scripture. 'Judge not, that ye be not judged. For with what judgment ye judge, ye shall be judged: and with what measure ye mete, it shall be measured to you again.'"

"You know that by heart," I said. I was amazed by this side of Cedric.

"Well, they do say even the devil can quote Scriptures, so I reckon you ought not be too surprised that I can rattle off a few here and there," he said with a smile.

"Don't liken yourself to the devil," I said in a quiet voice. "That ain't nobody you should want to compare yourself to."

"Well, ain't that who you thought I was the other week when you wouldn't even offer me a little ol' chicken leg?" he teased.

I turned my back to Cedric. I was feeling way too shy to be having a conversation like this with a boy. I tried to think what Lucille would say, but before I could come up with something sassy, Cedric reached out and touched my arm.

"Hey, I'm sorry. I was just teasing," he said. "And just so you know, I didn't go to nobody else's table. If I couldn't eat at yours, I didn't want to eat at nobody's."

"You could have," I said, trying to sound bold, but my words barely came out above a whisper.

"Not if I wanted to ask permission to keep company with the prettiest girl in Colored Town," he said.

I looked at him in confusion. "Who is that?"

He reached over and pushed a lock of my hair out of my face. "That would be you, pretty girl."

"Oh my," I said. I didn't know how to take this Cedric Perkins at all. To be honest, this side of Cedric scared me a little. I knew how to handle myself with him when he was being flirtatious and teasing. But this? This serious, manly side of him was a bit scary. "I better go," I said, getting up in a hurry.

Cedric jumped up quickly too. He was tall. At least six feet, and even though I was tall for most girls at five foot seven, I still felt small and petite next to him. Cedric brushed his fingers against my face. I shuddered a bit. I couldn't help myself. My body was responding to his closeness in ways I had never felt before.

"I enjoyed talking to you, Opal. I guess I better start cleaning up my ways so your granny will let me come over and sit with you on your front porch sometime," he said. Then he kissed my cheek and hurried off into the peach tree orchard. I just stood there for a moment after he left, touching that spot on my face where he had kissed me. My first kiss. I felt like the sun had just dipped down low and grazed my face with its warmth.

"Opal! Opal, you out here?" a voice called out to me. It was my Uncle Little Bud. I didn't want him to catch me standing around staring off into space.

"I'm here," I said as I walked out of the orchard and onto the dirt road leading back home. "I'm here."

3

*B*efore I left for work at Miss Peggy's, I went out to feed my granny's chickens. I guess you could call them her pets. Other than giving us eggs, Granny's chickens never found their way on a platter. They always died from old age. Everybody teased her that she could knock a pig in the head with no problems during hog killings in the fall, but those chickens, she loved them like they were her babies. Anytime I couldn't find her, I knew to look out at the coop because she was probably out there talking to her feathery youngins, as she called them.

I greeted them as I threw dried corn into their chicken coop. "Morning, Daisy. Morning, Cleo. Morning, Bessie and Claudine. And Mr. Lincoln, how are you doing, you old ornery rooster? Y'all got anything out here for me?" Mr. Tote had built the coop for Granny several years ago, and it looked like a palace fit for royal chickens instead of a bunch of country chickens like ours. After I got them fed and watered, I collected five eggs. That was pretty good. I took them inside and laid them in a bowl on the table, and then I crept out as quiet as I could so I wouldn't wake up Granny.

I loved walking to work, especially when the sky was still dark—right before the sun began to rise majestically above the horizon. I didn't hardly hear a peep from any of the houses as I passed by. Some of the farmers were probably already up and out getting the farm animals fed or watering their crops, but other than a few lamplights in some of the windows, I felt like it was just me and God awake this early on a Saturday. I loved walking late at night, too, when the moon was high above the trees and the stars would sometimes look so alive, it was like they were raining down from the heavens. This morning the moon was still holding on to its place in the sky, so it was in the moonlight that I passed through town.

Parsons didn't have the same sentimental feeling for me that Colored Town did. Even though, really, they were one and the same. Colored Town was my heart and soul. Parsons, on the other hand, was just buildings and businesses that belonged to the white folks whom I only really knew in passing. There was Mr. Monk Davis's gas station where Uncle Myron would stop for gas, but only he would have conversations with Mr. Monk. Me and Granny would sit and stare straight ahead, because even in 1936, it wasn't safe for Colored folks to look a white person in the eye, especially a white man. Somehow, Uncle Myron got away with it. I never understood how, but white folks seemed to respect him and give him a much wider berth than they did the rest of us. Maybe because he was a business owner. Or maybe just because he was Uncle Myron.

Farther down the street was Mr. Lowen's Drugstore where Jimmy Earl was going to work that summer and Miss Betty Powell's Dry Goods. I probably went to Miss Betty's more than any other place to pick up new sewing patterns and thread and cloth for Miss Peggy. Miss Betty didn't allow Colored folks into her store, so you had to tell your order to her helper, Baxter Lee, and then, after Miss Betty rounded it up, she would have him come collect the money and give it to her. You would have to stand there and wait while she counted up the money to make sure you didn't cheat her.

After Miss Betty's store was Doc Henry's house and office. Doc Henry would doctor on you no matter if you were Colored or white, rich or poor. One time my throat got so sore I was crying out in pain, or at least as much crying as I could do with a throat that was on fire. Granny had tried every trick she knew to help me. I gargled with cayenne, honey, and hot water. I sucked on cloves of garlic. I drank licorice root tea. You name it, and Granny gave it to me. But it wasn't until Doc Henry came by with some white powder that he poured into a small glass of whiskey (Granny allowed it because he said it was for medicinal purposes) that I started to feel better. As I passed his house, I noticed his car was gone. Knowing Doc Henry, he was probably out tending to some sick soul or delivering a baby.

Once I went past his house, there wasn't a whole lot to see besides farmland. Some of the farmers were already out lugging water buckets from the stream to their crops, trying desperately to save their bounty from the drought.

It was probably a good three miles to Miss Peggy's house,

but I didn't mind. I enjoyed the journey because it gave me time to think. I always felt safe going from Colored Town to Miss Peggy's. I had been making that walk since I was a little girl.

I walked by the Parsons Plantation where Jimmy Earl's best friend, Courtland, lived, and many of the Black Parsons who never left after slavery. And not too far from their house was Miss Lovenia Manu's place. Miss Lovenia was a root woman, and people went to her for anything as simple as the common cold to requests to get in touch with spirits that had already passed on to the other side. I looked up at her house as I walked by. I saw a single flickering light in the front window, but no sign of anyone being awake. I hurried on by. Miss Lovenia and her twin sons gave me the jitters.

Uncle Myron had started picking us up and driving us to Miss Peggy's because the walk was too hard on Granny now, but I didn't want to be in the car with him this morning. I was feeling too good to get drowned in his negative talk, and I knew without knowing that he would have just picked up the conversation where he had left it the night before.

Uncle Myron's wife, Aunt Josephine, died a few years back, and his bitterness toward the world seemed to get worse after her death. His only joy seemed to be centered around his children's successful lives. So I tried to be understanding, but sometimes I just needed to avoid him. And anyway, I was still feeling the excitement of my time with Cedric. When I got back to the house last night, I didn't tell anybody about meeting up with him, not even Lucille. I knew she wouldn't have told anybody, but I wanted that memory to be just mine—at least for a while.

I made it to Miss Peggy's house and stepped onto her porch but was startled when I saw Jimmy Earl sleeping in the porch swing. Back when we were children, he would sometimes sleep out on the porch with his cousin Skeeter and Courtland, but I hadn't seen him do that in years. Because he was so long and lanky, his legs spilled out over the edge. He had also grown a short beard. I wondered what Miss Peggy thought about that. I went on inside without waking him. He looked tired, so I just let him rest.

I went to the bathroom and collected the basket of dirty clothes and sheets that I had rounded up the day before. Jimmy Earl had come home with a ton of dirty laundry, I saw, because my wash load had doubled since the previous day.

Miss Peggy had a nearly brand-new Maytag washing machine, but Granny and I never used it more than once or twice. In my opinion, it was too rough on the clothes. I wasn't going to argue that it got things clean, but the clothes just didn't seem the same, so I used the washboard and tub that Granny had been using for years. It took a little more time to get the wash done, but some things ought not to be rushed. I was out on the back porch giving one of the towels a final soak when I heard someone clear his throat. I laughed and turned around.

"Good morning, Jimmy Earl Ketchums," I said. "'Bout time you got up. You done turned city boy, getting up at seven in the morning?"

I tended to be shy around most boys, but not Jimmy Earl. He was like a brother or one of my cousins, so I didn't feel awkward around him—even though looking at him then, he didn't look like the same gangly boy who had gone off to college a few years ago. He was still thin as a rail, but his features looked manlier. If the truth be known, he favored his daddy, Mr. Earl Ketchums. Of course, I never would have said that in front of Miss Peggy. She couldn't stand one thing about Jimmy Earl's daddy except that if there hadn't been an Earl Ketchums, there wouldn't be a Jimmy Earl.

"Well, if it ain't Stringbean the Washing Queen," he said, grinning at me like always. After I hit puberty, Jimmy Earl started calling me Stringbean. I got tall but I didn't get very big. "When are you and Birdie going to enter into the 1930s and use the washing machine? Washing by hand has to take three times the energy, not to mention the time. What's wrong, you scared of the Maytag?"

"You let me worry about the washing, Jimmy Earl, and you just worry about that scruffy mess on your face. I'm surprised Miss Peggy hasn't made you shave it off already," I said, flicking some bubbles from the wash at him. He laughed.

"Surprisingly, she didn't say a word about it," he said. Suddenly his face grew serious. "Opal, is Gran okay? She's lost a ton of weight since last Christmas, and she seemed like she was having difficulty breathing last night."

I wrung out the last of the towels and put them in the basket with the other wet sheets, towels, and pillowcases. I wiped my hands on my apron before answering him. "I don't know, Jimmy Earl," I said honestly. "She hasn't said anything to me, and if she told Granny, Granny hasn't shared, but then, you know those two. They are closemouthed when it comes to each other's secrets."

"Well, I'm going to take her in to see Doc Henry on Monday," he said. "A woman her age can't be too careful, and I doubt she's seen Doc Henry in years."

"Actually, Doc Henry stops by to check on her every so often, but it might be wise for you to take her to his office," I said. "Listen, you might want to go check on the livestock, since there ain't no telling when Mr. Tote will come in to work. Mr. Tote is probably feeling"—I cleared my throat and smiled—"a little poorly this morning, I imagine."

Jimmy Earl shook his head. "Poorly my foot. Hungover, you mean. Tote's getting too old to be carrying on like that. Birdie just needs to go on and make an honest man of him. Maybe he'll stop some of that cattin' around and drinking."

I put my hands on my hips. "Don't be wishing Mr. Tote off on my granny. She's doing just fine, thank you very much. And anyway, Mr. Tote don't believe in God. Or at least not how Granny does. That wouldn't work if the Lord himself came and joined them together."

"I'm just teasing," he said, laughing. "I know as good as you that Tote and Birdie wouldn't last ten minutes. Let me get on out there and check on things. Do you know if the other fellows are coming today to water the crops?"

Along with Mr. Tote, there was Mr. Jimbo, Mr. Laz, and Mr. Montgomery Lee, and when things really got hectic in the fall, Mr. Silas Griffin would come and help out. He was this poor white man who lived out near Jimmy Earl's daddy's house. The both of them sold moonshine, but when harvesttime came around, both would go and do some work on the local farms.

I shook my head. "No, I don't know if they're coming. I

handle the indoors and Mr. Tote is in charge of the outdoors. But you might go on out there and see if they're already working. Sometimes they just start doing things without coming up here to the house first. I'll have breakfast ready when you get back," I said.

"Thanks, Bean," he said, returning to his old nickname. He grabbed a hat from the hook by the door. He started to walk away and then stopped. "It's good seeing you. I've missed all of you. Thanks for taking care of Granny and Mama. I couldn't do what I'm doing if I didn't have you here to manage things for me."

"You're welcome," I said, feeling my cheeks get hot. I wasn't used to this grown-up Jimmy Earl who paid me compliments. "Don't forget about breakfast. I'll make poached eggs for you." I knew that was his favorite.

"You are all right, Opal Pruitt. For an ugly, old, skinny stringbean," he teased, sounding like the Jimmy Earl I had grown up with again.

I splashed him good with some of the soapy water as he hurried past me. I was happy to have my childhood friend home for the summer. I could tell Jimmy Earl was more mature, if one could imagine that, because he was already mature before he left. Oh, he was a prankster and a jokester, but he was always making sure the women in the house were happy, and that included me and Granny.

He was still the good-natured boy I used to play hide-and-seek with as a child, but I could tell he was different. We both were. This growing-up thing was not all fun and games. I remember as a little girl always wishing I was older. The day after my birthday, I started throwing in the "half." If someone asked how old I was, I would respond, "I am twelve and a half" or "fifteen and a half." As the childhood days became faint, sweet memories, I found myself longing for them. Afternoons at the pond fishing with Jimmy Earl and his mama, Miss Corinne. Playing house with my cousins, or explorers, where we pretended like we had discovered new lands and new people. But now, everything was changing. Jimmy Earl didn't sound as much like home as he did before. But I guess that's what happens when you leave. You never come back the same again.

"Hey there, Opal," Granny said from the door. "You need help getting the wash out on the line?"

I turned and smiled. I hadn't even heard Uncle Myron drive up. I guess he let her off and kept going, which was fine with me. I was still feeling a tad bit salty about the things he had said the previous night. I didn't want to have an argument with him this early in the morning.

Granny was a big woman who carried herself like royalty, or at least how I imagined a queen might walk and move about. Even with arthritis, she still forced her body to retain its dignity and height, which I got from her. So where others might be stooped, Granny continued to walk proud and tall. I knew how much it took out of her to always keep her body straight and unbent. Not a day went by that I didn't thank God for her and her strength.

"I'm fine, Granny. I just need to wash out these pillowcases and then I'll be done with this load. If you want to get started on breakfast, that would be good. I promised Jimmy Earl poached eggs, though. You mind making them?" I asked.

"No, honey. I don't mind at all," she said and came over and hugged me.

"You're gonna get yourself all wet," I chided, but I melted into her embrace. Granny was a stern woman, but she never short-changed me on hugs and kisses. I always knew I was wanted by her, even if I couldn't say the same about my own mother and father.

"Wouldn't be the first time I got all wet," she said and then backed away and gave me a serious look. "Opal, you listen to me, and you listen to me good. You are just fine the way you are, and there is no shame in the work we do. Don't you never let nobody make you feel less than what you are because of what you do. You hear me?"

I nodded. "Yes ma'am." I knew she was talking about what Uncle Myron had said.

She patted my cheek. "I better get in there and start working on poaching eggs. It's been a good hot minute since I've cooked them that way. You're much better with all that fancy cooking than I am."

I watched as she walked back into the house. I finished wash-ing the pillowcases and then picked up the heavy basket and carried it out to the clothesline. Jimmy Earl's dog, who had become my shadow after Jimmy Earl went off to college, followed behind me.

"Levi, did you get fed this morning?" I asked as he rubbed up next to my leg. I put the basket of wet clothes onto the little bench that I'd gotten Mr. Tote to make for Granny in case she got tired while we were out putting up the laundry. "Poor thing. Your boy is back home and he ain't paying you no never mind, is he?"

Levi looked up at me with that lopsided grin that always

seemed to be on his face. If he was hurt by the slight from Jimmy Earl, he didn't show it.

"Well, don't you worry. I'll see that you get fed soon as I finish hanging up these wet things," I said. Almost like he understood, Levi lay down by the bench and watched me hang up my wash. But before I could get to the towels, I heard the loud roaring of a car engine. I groaned. I knew that sound. Levi raised his head at the sound of the motor, and when Jimmy Earl's cousin Skeeter got out, he started a low growl.

"Shh," I said in a soft voice. "It's okay." I didn't want Skeeter to notice me. Levi got up and stood next to my leg. He was usually playful and loving toward everybody, but now he was standing rigid and at attention. They say dogs recognize evil, and Skeeter was just that.

Skeeter was always being hauled away by the law for fighting or just plain intimidating folks. He was big and muscular and loved to throw his weight around. Skeeter was heavy into making and selling moonshine with Jimmy Earl's daddy, Mr. Earl Ketchums, but more than that, Skeeter was in the Klan and made no secrets about it.

Though the Klan had been on the decline, Skeeter and his daddy, Mr. Rafe, along with a handful of other no-account white men, were determined to keep it alive. As far as I knew, Jimmy Earl's daddy wasn't part of it, but he let them meet out in the woods where he lived from time to time, or at least that's what I heard.

The Klan would sometimes ride around late at night and try to spook folks. So far, other than getting into a few fights here and there with some of the local Colored boys and men, they hadn't done too much more than put on their white robes and hoods and march up and down Main Street in Parsons and yell at any Colored person who might be walking by, until the sheriff would ride through and tell them to go on home. The last time they marched was last year, a few days before Founder's Day.

Some of the Colored boys had wanted to play baseball with the whites on Founder's Day, and the Klan had marched through downtown Parsons over into Colored Town to let us all know that wasn't going to happen. Not on their watch. And Skeeter had led the procession. Needless to say, there was no baseball between the Coloreds and whites.

Everybody, including Jimmy Earl, knew that Skeeter, Skeeter's daddy, and Skeeter's brothers were mean, ornery men, but Jimmy Earl loved Skeeter like a brother, and in his eyes, Skeeter could do no wrong.

"Skeeter's harmless," Jimmy Earl said one day when I mentioned how much Skeeter scared me. "He and them boys are just a bunch of backwards hillbillies trying to flex their muscles. They aren't going to hurt anybody. Not really."

I had just looked at Jimmy Earl. He was blind to anything Skeeter did. When they were younger, Skeeter took up for him when nobody else would. Folks used to tease Jimmy Earl about not having a real daddy, and Skeeter would blacken an eye and bloody the nose of anyone who would dare say such a thing about Jimmy Earl. Jimmy Earl never forgot that, and one thing about Jimmy Earl, he valued family above everything else, even if they were in the wrong.

And I think being close to Skeeter was his way of being connected to his daddy's side of the family. He needed so badly to love and be loved by the Ketchums. Mr. Earl hadn't done right by Jimmy Earl or Miss Corinne. That's why Miss Peggy and Mr. Cecil went and got them shortly after Jimmy Earl was born. Granny said when they got to Mr. Earl's house, Miss Corinne didn't even have shoes to wear, and poor Jimmy Earl was looking yellowish in the face. He didn't have a stitch of clothes on beyond his diaper, even though it was freezing cold outside.

Mr. Rafe and Skeeter tried to make up for how bad Mr. Earl had been as a daddy. Mr. Rafe would come by and pick up Jimmy Earl and take him hunting and fishing with his boys. When Christmas or birthdays would roll around, Mr. Rafe brought gifts, claiming they were from Mr. Earl, but everybody knew Mr. Earl drank and gambled away every nickel he ever made.

I watched as Skeeter walked out toward the fields where Jimmy Earl was. I made sure I stayed out of sight behind the large crape myrtle tree. I didn't want to relive the last time Skeeter and I had been in the same space together.

One day a few months ago, Uncle Myron picked up Granny from Miss Peggy's, but I wanted to get some wild strawberries to make us a strawberry shortcake that night. I was headed out near the Colored cemetery where they grew the best, when Skeeter drove up in his old jalopy. He used to pick on me around Jimmy Earl, but Jimmy Earl always teased him into stopping. But this day, there was nobody in sight to protect me.

Skeeter blocked the road, so I just stopped. Scared to death. I looked left and right, and there was nothing but wide-open fields and not a single person in shouting distance. I was all alone.

"Well, if it ain't Jimmy Earl's Negress," he said, getting out of his car and walking toward me.

"Leave me be, Skeeter," I said, trying not to act afraid. They say an angry dog will attack you if you act scared. Looking at Skeeter and his hateful eyes, in that moment I would have rather faced down a dog with rabies.

"That's Mr. Ketchums to you," he said, walking up on me so close, I felt like I was caged in like Granny's chickens in their coop. I could smell the liquor on his breath and the faint odor of chewing tobacco. I looked all around to see if I could find something to hit him with to give me time to run, but there was nothing. I was trapped.

Skeeter reached out and grabbed my arm. I flinched and then knocked his hand away. He laughed and grabbed my arm again, tighter this time, almost willing me to strike at him once more. My instincts told me not to fight. Not then. I couldn't believe he was doing this to me in the middle of the road in broad daylight.

"Please leave me alone, Skeeter . . . I mean, Mr. Ketchums. Please," I begged.

"I like the sound of that," he said. "From now on, you make sure you call me Mr. Ketchums."

I nodded, feeling tears welling up in my eyes.

"Maybe you and me ought to take a little walk out into the woods," he said, smiling, most of his teeth dark from all the tobacco he chewed. He spat out a big wad of it and then put his arm around my waist. I struggled but he held on tighter. Just when I thought the worst was about to happen, I heard another car coming up the hill behind us. Skeeter quickly let me go, and I turned around to see it was Doc Henry. He was coming from Miss Peggy's house. He stopped his car just behind us and then got out and stood by his car door.

"You having car trouble, Skeeter?" he asked. I could tell by the look on his face that he knew what was happening in the middle of the road that day.

"No sir. Not at all," Skeeter said. "Just making small talk with Opal here."

"Well, I'm going to give Opal a ride home, so we're going to be needing you to move your car," he said and motioned for me to come get in the car with him. I ran and got in the passenger side. I sat there, breathing hard the whole way, tears streaking my face. Doc Henry just acted like nothing was wrong and talked about the weather. Neither one of us ever talked about what had been going on between me and Skeeter, not to each other, and I definitely never told any of my kin. But seeing Skeeter again brought all of those memories flooding back to me. Thoughts of what happened, and what could have happened if Doc Henry hadn't come along.

I finished hanging up the last towel and then took my basket and hurried back to the house. Levi ran behind me. I burst into the kitchen like hellhounds were chasing me.

"Girl, what you running for?" Granny asked, looking surprised and worried all at the same time. She was taking the biscuits out of the oven and putting Jimmy Earl's poached egg on a plate.

"Nothing, Granny. I was just . . . I was just playing with Levi," I said, and almost like he was agreeing, he barked from outside the screen door.

"Well, don't you be running like that in this heat. It's already hot and it's not even nine o'clock yet," she said.

"Yes ma'am," I said. Then I heard Skeeter's car roar off. A few minutes later, Jimmy Earl came in, and he looked worried.

"Birdie, I need to talk to you about something," he said.

Granny smiled. "You came in just in time, Jimmy Earl. 'Course, you always did growing up. You seemed to have an inside clock to let you know when I was done cooking. Come sit down and—"

"Birdie, we need to talk now," he said, his face more serious than I recalled it being in a long while. Normally, that look was reserved for his concern over his mama or something stressful going on with the farm or his schooling.

"What is it?" she asked, her eyes intense and serious.

"I need to talk to you outside," he said. He didn't even look at me but stared straight at Granny.

Granny wiped her hands on her apron. "Okay," she said. She turned to me. "Everything is done. Just go get Miss Peggy and Miss Corinne and let them get started eating. We won't be long."

"Yessum," I said and watched them both go out the screen door. I walked over to it as they walked out toward the barn. Jimmy Earl put his arm around Granny's shoulder and talked quietly in her ear. I tried to see the expression on Granny's face, but Jimmy Earl's arm had her face shielded from my sight.

Levi, who was still standing by the door, looked up at me as if to say, "What's going on with them?"

"I don't know what's going on, Levi," I said. "But whatever it is, it can't be good."

*S*unday morning had always been one of my favorite days of the week. We got to rest from work and we got to fellowship at church with all of our friends and relatives in Colored Town. The white folks had two churches: "Big Bethel" Methodist Episcopal Church South and St. Stephens Baptist Church. But there was only one Colored church, and that was "Little Bethel" AME. Some folks were dressed up in store-bought clothes, and others wore hand-me-downs or hand-stitched clothing, but no matter how anybody dressed or looked, we all came for the same purpose, and that was to praise God and show love to one another.

Granny's people had worshiped at Little Bethel since it first opened its doors in 1873, when Granny was just a toddler. According to church history, the Parsons family had donated the land, the lumber, the pews, and the stained-glass windows for the church. For a time, they even paid the preacher's salary.

Granny said it was a great day when the church was able to

take over all of its finances. "We finally felt like we could serve God exactly the way we wanted to without worrying about them white folks breathing down our necks," she said.

Granny and I walked to church this morning. Uncle Myron was running late, and Granny did not believe in walking into the church after the service had begun, so she and I had set off on foot. We weren't alone. Most folks in Colored Town didn't have cars. There was a chorus of "Good mornings" and "Bless the Lords" as we all walked to church together.

Granny was quiet, but then, that wasn't unusual. For her, Sundays were always a time for reflection and communion with God, but this morning I wondered if some of her quietness was due to her conversation with Jimmy Earl the day before. After he took her off to the barn to talk, the two of them stayed in and out of conversation the rest of the day; whenever I tried to ask either of them what was going on, they both said, "Not now," or they would tell me "later."

I had planned on talking to her about her and Jimmy Earl's secret on the way to church, but when we got to the peach orchard, Cedric was there. I tried not to let my face split open with a smile that he was there waiting. I hoped for me.

"Good morning, Brother Perkins," Granny said, greeting Cedric with a head nod.

Cedric was dressed in a fine-looking tan suit with a matching straw bowler. Cedric tilted his hat at Granny, not even looking at me. That startled me a bit, but I didn't say anything.

"Good morning to you, too, Sister Pruitt," he said. "On your way to church, ma'am?"

Granny smiled a tight smile. "Well, of course, Brother Perkins. Where else would two God-fearing women be heading this time of day on a Sunday? The better question is, where are you headed?"

"Oh, to church, ma'am. Of course," he said. "And if you wouldn't mind, I would love it if I could walk with you and your granddaughter."

"You are welcome to walk with us," Granny said, and she took my arm as we continued walking down the road. Cedric got on the other side of Granny and matched his pace to ours.

Well, I wondered. *Is this courting?* I wasn't sure because Cedric never said anything to me directly. By the time we got to church, he and Granny had talked about the weather, the peach orchard, some verse in Deuteronomy, and whether Cedric felt he might someday become a preacher.

"Ma'am, I can't rightly say," he replied. "But right now, my heart is set on playing baseball. I want to be a pitcher for one of the Negro League teams like Satchel Paige or 'Bullet Joe' Rogan."

"I see. Well, may God bless you," Granny said. Although by the look on her face, her blessing seemed more like a curse. Granny didn't hold much stock in baseball players. "They are a bunch of fast men, and I don't just mean on the baseball field," she had once said. She turned to me. "Let's get inside before service starts."

"Thank you for letting me walk with you and Opal," Cedric said.

I looked at him and smiled and he smiled back, but Granny almost pushed me up the stairs of the church. As soon as we got inside, Granny went straight to Reverend Perkins and to Brother Clark, one of the deacons. I wondered if what they were discussing had to do with Jimmy Earl's secret. I couldn't imagine anything being so important that Granny would have to take it to the church leadership. I tried not to worry, but when Granny came to her seat beside me, she took my hand and held it. I looked at her, trying to will her to tell me what was wrong. She just shook her head, and we both turned our attention to the services that were just beginning.

Church dragged by. Normally, I could throw myself into the worship service and enjoy the singing and the preaching, but all I could think about was Granny's secret and Cedric sitting over in the Amen Corner with the other men. Every so often he glanced at me and smiled, and my heart turned over. The hands on the clock showed it was already eleven thirty in the morning. I couldn't believe it. We were just now repeating the Decalogue, which is a fancy name for the Ten Commandments. The preacher read and then the congregation answered him in unison: "Lord, have mercy upon us, and incline our hearts to keep this law."

And it went on and on.

My cousin Lucille, who was sitting on the other side of me, leaned over and whispered in my ear, "Your boyfriend is shore gazing at you all lovey-dovey today."

I punched her in her ribs. I almost regretted telling her about Cedric and me at the peach orchard. I had planned on keeping it a secret, but Lucille was my favorite cousin and my best friend. So I broke down and told her last night, pulling her to my bedroom from the front porch, where everyone was sitting.

"He said what?" she had asked, sitting on my bed, grinning from ear to ear.

"He said, 'I guess I better start cleaning up my ways so your granny will let me come over and sit with you on your front porch sometime,'" I said down low, careful not to speak too loud just in case Granny happened to walk past my door.

"Oh, Opal," she said, almost swooning with excitement. "That's like something out of a movie." For Lucille, saying something was like a movie was the highest compliment. Nearly every Saturday afternoon I went with Lucille and her mama, Aunt Shimmy, to the matinee. We would sit up in the balcony that was the Coloreds' section, watching some new movie that Lucille was excited to see. Half the time I fell asleep during the movie, so tired from a week of hard work, but Lucille always poked me during the good parts.

"I don't know if it's quite a movie, but it's special, isn't it?" I asked last night. I needed validation that the words I had heard were really as amazing as I believed them to be.

"Girl, Hazel Moody is going to come for you," she said with a laugh.

"She need not worry about me none," I said, trying to be as modest as I could. "I can't compete with somebody like Hazel."

"It don't sound like you are going to have to compete. It sounds like Cedric Perkins has already made his choice," she said.

She and I had continued to talk about me and Cedric until Uncle Lem and Aunt Shimmy were ready to go home. But now, here in church, she was still acting silly. Times like this was when I realized how much older I was than my cousin. I looked over at her and shook my head. She stifled a laugh by putting her hand over her mouth. I tried to keep my eyes focused on Cedric's daddy, who was kneeling in the pulpit, preparing himself to get up and preach. But I couldn't help but sneak a peek at Cedric again, and sure enough, he was still looking at me. I turned my attention back to the choir, who were just standing up to begin song service—my favorite part of church. I prayed I could keep my mind focused and keep my eyes looking forward instead of across the church at Cedric.

> This may be the last time
> This may be the last time, children
> This may be the last time
> May be the last time, I don't know
> May be the last time we stay together
> May be the last time, I don't know

Several of the older ladies in the church, my granny included, stood up and swayed and clapped along as they sang. They were a beautiful sight, donned in their white dresses, with white hand-kerchiefs pinned to their heads. As much as I wanted church to end that day, I couldn't help but notice how they looked like angels.

Brother Clay was playing the piano, and the choir—seeing that the spirit was high that morning—continued to sing, adding their clapping to the now growing clapping of the congregation. I stood and pulled up Lucille with me. We knew better than to stay seated when the Holy Ghost was riding, as Granny would say. Neither one of us had ever felt it for ourselves, but according to Granny, the Holy Ghost never caught somebody who was sitting down daydreaming. So I opened my mouth and started singing and clapping with the rest of the people.

I looked over and saw my Aunt Shimmy waving her hand and singing. My Uncle Little Bud was sitting, but he was clapping and patting his foot. His new wife, Cheryl Anne, sat beside him, her hand lightly touching his shoulder. She was smiling, yet quiet as always. All around the church was my family. My twin cousins, Emma and Eveline, had come home to visit, and they had two nice-looking fellows sitting next to them. Then, of course, there was Brother and Sister Walker, who had been like second grandparents to me. They didn't have any children of their own, so Sister Walker would tease Granny and tell her she had to share me with them. Sitting next to the Walkers was my Sunday school teacher, Sister Mattie Lee Freeman, who had taught me since I was nine or ten. And then all throughout the sanctuary was the rest of our family and friends I'd grown up around since I was in diapers.

As I continued to clap and sing, I caught a glimpse of Cedric still looking at me. He and my cousin M.J. were sitting together. Cedric leaned over and whispered something to M.J., and M.J. grinned but shook his head. I wondered what in the world they were talking about. I got so deep into my thoughts, I stopped singing and clapping. I was just standing there like some silly girl.

"Opal. Opal." A loud whisper pulled me out of my daydreaming. I glanced over and my Aunt Shimmy had reached over Lucille to talk to me. "You better focus yourself."

Lucille giggled, but Aunt Shimmy pointed her finger at Lucille, and she immediately stopped. We both started singing and clapping again.

This may be the last time
This may be the last time, children
This may be the last time
May be the last time, I don't know
May be the last time we ever shout together
May be the last time, I don't know
This may be the last time
This may be the last time, children
This may be the last time
May be the last time, I don't know

The choir sang several more songs, and after what seemed like an eternity, we finally got to the preaching part of the service. Reverend Perkins took his time standing up. Once everybody had settled down, he finally spoke.

"Good morning, saints."

"Good morning, Reverend Perkins," we all said in unison. This was what we did every Sunday: greet one another. Usually after we spoke to Reverend Perkins, we would then walk around and say hello to one another and any visitors who were there that day, but Reverend Perkins held up his hand to stop us.

"Saints, I come to you this morning with a heavy heart," he said, and then he went silent, like he was trying to figure out exactly what to say next.

Reverend Perkins was an older man, nearly my granny's age, but his wife, Sister Perkins, was young, in her thirties. They say Reverend Perkins spoiled her and Cedric so much because he was grateful to even have a family at such an old age. Preachers in the AME church spent a lot of years moving from one congregation to another. He didn't want to get a family until he could come back home to Parsons. The bishop over our area assured Reverend Perkins he would let him stay at Little Bethel until he was ready to retire.

I looked over at Sister Perkins. She didn't have her usual smile. She looked solemn—scared even. I was afraid of what Reverend Perkins was going to say. I knew it had something to do with Granny. She was sitting with her head bowed and her hands folded. I wondered if this moment was why I was feeling funny the other day—before Jimmy Earl even had his talk with Granny. I hoped that whatever it was, it wasn't going to be nearly as bad as what my feeling was telling me.

During the quiet, various ones said, "Bless him, Lord," and "Have mercy, Father." The entire congregation could sense that all was not well.

Finally, Reverend Perkins began to speak. "This morning, the Lord led me to a bit of news that I need to share with you all. The devil is going to be sending his legion of demons into our community this evening. Brothers and sisters, the Klan will be riding the countryside tonight, and from the report I received, they have said they won't stop riding until they have somebody strung up in a tree. We don't know what has set them off, but today, Church, we must pray and prepare."

I looked around at the faces of the people who had just been glowing from the Spirit of God. Now their faces ranged from fear to anger, and when I looked at Cedric, his face looked like a storm cloud about to burst. He and one of the boys sitting next to him began to mutter to each other. I tried to catch his eye, but this time he didn't look my way.

"Saints, I know these are scary times. And in a while, we will dismiss service and talk about what we can do to make sure we all survive this night. But right now, I want to talk to you about faith and trust. I want to talk to you about even if this is the last time we all congregate together here on earth, we don't have to fear."

"Yes, Lord. Preach!" someone called out.

"No, we don't have to fear because we know that as the devil rides the highways and byways tonight, we've got a God that sits high and looks low."

I found myself clapping with everyone else. I reached over and grabbed Lucille's hand. She was shedding tears and shaking.

"It's gonna be all right. Don't be scared," I said, even though I was scared too. In that moment, I truly felt like the older cousin. We reached our arms around each other, holding each other tight like we used to when we were little girls. As I looked around, I saw other folks holding each other too. I also saw M.J. and Cedric looking like they could explode into little pieces from the anger that was nearly consuming them. I finally caught M.J.'s eye and shook my head. He just turned away. Cedric still wouldn't look at me.

"I'm going to read you all something from the Scriptures, but first we're going to have a little talk with the Master," Reverend

Perkins said. "After that, the menfolks and I are going to hold a meeting and talk about what we all need to do tonight to stay safe. This is not the first time the Klan has rode through our part of town, and sadly, it probably won't be the last. But even still, and no matter what, God will be with us tonight. That much I can attest to, saints."

I heard a loud noise and looked over at Cedric, who had pushed a chair out of his way so he could get out of the pew. Several folks gasped. His mama called out to him, but he came and stood in front of the congregation.

"If our plan ain't involving us putting some bullets through those crackers' heads, then we're just wasting breath," Cedric yelled. "All this singing and praying alone ain't gonna change what they plan for us tonight." Several of the boys his age, including M.J., yelled out in agreement.

"Cedric Alowishus Perkins, you are out of line," Reverend Perkins bellowed, the veins in his face looking like they might burst. "Singing and praying is what got us through slavery."

"But this ain't slavery times, Daddy," Cedric said. "And the last time they rode through Colored Town, y'all didn't do nothing to stop them, and here they come again. When we gonna be men? When we gonna fight for our families . . . for our women?" And this time he did look over at me. I turned away. My cheeks were on fire. I didn't like hearing Cedric talk like that. I had never seen him so angry before.

One of the older deacons tried to come up and lead Cedric away, but he snatched his arm from the man.

"I ain't gone hush, Daddy," he yelled. "We all know who them white ghosts is. They the same white trash that's always causing trouble for Colored folks. The Ketchums, the Suttons, the—"

Uncle Lem rushed up to help grab Cedric and lead him out. "Boy, respect the Lord and your daddy," Uncle Lem said.

"Let him speak. Let him speak," somebody yelled out, but by this time, several of the men were dragging Cedric out of the sanctuary.

He kept right on shouting, "Y'all know who they are. Y'all know. Y'all know."

The room was in chaos. People were yelling and crying and fussing. And then, what seemed like out of nowhere, Granny began singing.

> Why should I feel discouraged,
> Why should the shadows come,
> Why should my heart be lonely,
> And long for heaven and home,
> When Jesus is my portion?
> My constant friend is he,
> His eye is on the sparrow,
> And I know he watches me.

At first she was singing by herself, but by the time she got to the chorus, most everybody was singing with her, including me and Lucille.

> I sing because I'm happy,
> I sing because I'm free,

For his eye is on the sparrow,
And I know he watches me.

Granny pulled me into her arms and hugged me tight.

"That was just what we needed," she said, tears falling down her face. I felt my own tears falling as well.

Reverend Perkins's face had tears too. I watched as Sister Perkins left her seat to go outside to see about Cedric, I guessed.

After a minute or two, Reverend Perkins cleared his throat. "Brothers and sisters, I apologize for my son's behavior. I understand where his anger and frustration is coming from, but we cannot fight evil with evil. The Lord teaches us that he will move in his time, not ours. So even if the Klan becomes violent tonight, we must not become like them. I would rather see my Maker tonight with a pure heart and no blood on my hands, than to try and stand before him and explain how I became like the very ones we are speaking against."

Some of the older folks said, "Amen," but I could tell the young folks, in particular the young men, weren't exactly agreeing with him. Reverend Perkins didn't let that stop him. He kept right on talking.

"Saints, I ask you all to come forward to the altar and bow down with me and pray for ourselves and the souls of those who wish harm on us. Let's pray that the good Lord will fix the hearts of these evil men so that the Death Angel will not stop at anyone's doorpost this night."

Granny took me and Lucille by the hand and guided us up to the altar with her. Everyone knelt together, and out of the corner of my eye, I saw Cedric walking slowly toward the altar too. His mama was beside him. They went over to where Reverend Perkins was kneeling and knelt beside him. Reverend Perkins put his arms around both of them.

Everybody prayed in their own way. Some folks called on God in a real loud voice. Others quietly moved their lips, but you could tell their prayers were just as earnest. After a moment, I closed my eyes tight and asked God to just take care of us all. To not let anybody get hurt. To do what Reverend Perkins asked, which was to change the hearts of the men who wanted to do harm to us. As painful as it was, I prayed a special prayer for Skeeter Ketchums. I prayed that somehow his heart would be softened. It felt like a wasted prayer, but I prayed it anyway. I also prayed for Jimmy Earl, because I then knew it was he who gave the warning to Granny. Evidently Skeeter was boasting about it yesterday, and Jimmy Earl chose us over his family. I prayed he would not pay for his actions.

I also prayed for the boys and men who wanted to fight back. I understood their rage. As a woman, I didn't feel like there was much I could do, but I prayed that the men and boys would keep their heads and not retaliate, because that would only make things worse.

Soon after the group prayer, the service ended and the women and children made their way outside, while the men and boys stayed inside the church to talk about what they were going to do tonight.

I went over and sat near Granny, who was sitting underneath her favorite tree. I didn't go stand over with the young folks my age. I needed to feel Granny's strength. She stroked my hair as I leaned against her.

"You a good girl, Opal," she said and continued stroking my hair. "God is going to test us today, but I feel that we all are going to make it through this night, if we keep our heads. But some of these wet-behind-the-ear boys have me worried."

I knew she was talking about Cedric.

"Granny, Cedric is just—"

She put her finger to my lips to stop me. "Listen, I know that boy Cedric is sweet on you, and you're almost grown, so I can't stand in your way when it comes to who you choose. But choose wisely. Choose prayerfully. Don't let your feelings overrule your common sense."

I didn't reply. There was nothing I could say. I had feelings for Cedric and I wasn't sure what to do with those feelings. So I just leaned back against Granny as we waited.

Finally, the men finished with their meeting. All of the uncles came over to where we were sitting, and Uncle Myron said he wanted me and Granny to come over and stay at his house tonight.

"I ain't leaving my home, Myron," Granny said. "I ain't letting them ghosts run me off my property. Your daddy worked too hard to buy that piece of land and build that house. Ain't no sheet-wearing cowards gone make me leave tonight."

"Mama—"

She held up her hand. "Myron, I done spoke. Now, I know every one of them redneck boys, and they know me. They ain't gone do me no harm if'n I'm in my house, minding my own business."

"Mama, then we'll stay with y'all," Uncle Myron said, mopping his face with a handkerchief. "I ain't leaving you alone."

Granny shook her head. "You know they'll take a head count of the menfolks at every house. If'n you ain't where you s'pose to be, them drunk scoundrels will think you out there somewhere plotting and planning against them. No, everybody need to go to they own place and pray till this night is over."

I could tell Uncle Myron was about to say something else, but I sat up. "I'll be there with Granny, Uncle Myron. We'll be all right. Won't no harm come against us," I said, trying to sound brave. Granny looked at me and smiled. I tried to smile back, but in my heart, I was frightened. I knew the danger behind those white sheets and I also knew tonight was not going to be an easy night at all.

*I*n the summer months, it didn't get dark until late. Some-times not until eight or nine, around the time Granny and I would usually be lying down for the night. But when dark did set in, it was sometimes black enough to make your bones shiver—especially on a night when you knew the Klan was heading your way.

Granny and I ate ourselves a quick meal of sausage and left-over biscuits from breakfast after we got home from church. Neither one of us was all that hungry, but we made ourselves eat because we knew we needed to keep up our strength for the long night ahead of us. Now we sat together in the rocking chairs that used to be Granny and Grandpa's and waited. We didn't even have a lamp lit. Granny said we didn't want to give them old white devils a reason to come in on us. Even though I hated being in the dark, I knew Granny was right. So we waited and watched and prayed.

Everybody in Colored Town got home early after church that

day. Didn't nobody want to get caught outside with those crazy white men running around, just daring a Colored person to cross their path. It was hot as all get-out in the house, but we didn't open not one window; we just let the heat wash over us. Both Granny and I were steady wiping sweat, but we didn't complain. Uncle Myron and Uncle Little Bud both came by before it got dark and begged Granny one more time to let one of them stay or us go to one of their houses, but Granny stayed firm.

"Everybody needs to be at their own home. Those trashy white men are looking for reasons to mess with some of us tonight," she said, basically repeating her words from earlier. But this time, she was even firmer. "We will not give them a reason to hurt us. I remember the Klan rode through here, Myron, when you were still in knee britches, and they hung a man for being somewhere other than where they thought he belonged. I am not burying any of my kin over this. I'm just not."

Finally, both uncles agreed to leave, but they said if anything didn't seem right, they would be back. Uncle Little Bud stayed behind when Uncle Myron left. Granny went to her room to lie down some, and when she left the room, Uncle Little Bud pulled out a paper bag from his pocket and handed it to me. It felt heavy. I was about to look inside but he said not to.

"Opal, I want you to keep this bag close to you," he said. When he said that, I knew what was inside: a gun. Probably the same gun he taught me and Lucille to shoot last summer. He said back then he wanted all of his nieces to know how to handle a gun just in case. I guess tonight was a "just in case" situation.

"I don't know how bad things are going to get tonight, Opal, but I don't want you and Mama sitting up here defenseless if me or one of the men in the family can't get to you soon enough. Don't shoot it unless you have to, but if you have to shoot, shoot to kill. Fire right between their eyes, and then, after that, me and the uncles will take care of the rest. You hear me?"

I nodded. Uncle Little Bud was always the laughing and joking one in the family. Seeing him serious like this told me just how bad things might get.

"Me and some of the younger men talked after church, and we are going to be close by. We can't be everywhere at once, but we will be close. Don't tell Mama. It would just worry her," Uncle Little Bud said. "I need you to be strong, Opal. Stronger than you've ever been before. You think you can do that?"

"Yes," I whispered, willing the tears away. "I will take care of Granny and myself."

He and I hugged like it was going to be our last hug.

Before he left, he made me promise not to let Granny know he had left me a gun. I slipped the bag inside my purse, and I made sure to keep my purse close to me at all times, even when I went outside to the outhouse. Once it got later in the evening, Granny said we needed to stop going outside and instead use the slop jar. I hated having to squat and pee on that thing. It was bad enough when I was sick. I sure didn't want to use it when I was feeling just fine, but I understood. Nighttime and the outside were no longer our friends.

This time of the year, right before spring turned into summer, folks would normally be out and about, visiting with one another, enjoying the one day of rest we all had in common. The little ones would be running from one house to the other, trying to find somebody to play jump rope or hide-and-seek with, and those who were older would be roaming around trying to court one another without getting noticed by the adults. The young wives and older ladies would sit on each other's front stoops and sip iced tea and gossip, and the menfolk would be somewhere talking 'bout work and, this time of the year, the Negro baseball league.

On nights like this, I would lie in my bed and drift off to sleep to the sound of Mr. Tote's harmonica. He'd play every kind of music that came to his mind. Sometimes he would play "jooking music," as Granny would call it. Other times he played the kind of gospel wail that almost made you want to shout.

Not this night, though. On this night, there didn't seem to be no sound—not one night owl squalling or dog barking. This night, not even the good Lord himself made a sound. It was like something had come along and spirited all of the people and animals away. Everybody and everything was waiting—wondering when the night sky would turn bright orange from the fire sticks them Klansmen carried. Wondering whose husband, son, or nephew might be the one to get carried off and hung up in some tree. Granny used to say that the trees all over the state of Georgia had stories they could tell, and none of them was good.

"Granny, are you sure we shouldn't go on up to Uncle Myron's house? It probably ain't too late for us to go," I said, my voice shaking. I had felt so confident about us staying at home this morning when I was surrounded by family and friends, but now

I wasn't feeling so sure. I wanted to be where my uncles were, not sitting up here waiting for Skeeter and those other crazy men to come riding through Colored Town. I thought about Cedric and his words. Colored folks seem to always be waiting to see what white folks like Skeeter will do next. We are always the hunted, never the hunter. I didn't want to see anybody die tonight, but I didn't want to feel like we had just given up, and this sort of felt like that was what we had done. Given up.

"Gone be all right. This will be over before you know it," Granny said.

I tried to believe her. Granny had never lied to me to my knowledge, but this night, I wondered if maybe she was lying to us both for the first time. If those Klansmen did ride through like they said they would, I knew there was no way things would be all right. I tried to calm myself by knitting on the little sweater I was making for my cousin Lanetta's baby, and not focus on the time. Cousin Lanetta was due any day, and I tried to always make something for any new babies in our family. I didn't need light to knit. I could nearly do it in my sleep. Granny sat and held her Bible. It was too dark for her to read it, so she just cradled it like it was a baby. Before long, I felt myself dozing off, and what seemed like immediately after closing my eyes, I woke to Granny shaking me.

"They out there, baby," she said in my ear, although I could hear the whooping and yelling, and I could see the flickering flames outside of the window. My heart quickened and I reached down beside my chair and felt around for my purse. Once I felt it, I placed it on my lap. I couldn't imagine shooting anybody, but if it came down to it, I knew I would do what I had to do to protect me and Granny.

Granny reached over and took my hand as we listened to the loud crashing sounds from out in our backyard. Then we heard Granny's chickens squawking in such a loud and frightening way, I didn't even want to think about what was happening.

"Hey in there. Y'all niggers come on out," a loud male voice shouted. "We about to make y'all some fried chicken. We know how much you darkies love yourself some fried chicken."

"No," Granny whimpered. "Not my chickens."

Granny crept over to the window. She made a painful sound, but thankfully she stayed put.

"What's going on, Granny?" I whispered.

She didn't answer. I crept over to the window where Granny knelt, and I was horrified by what I saw. Those bloodthirsty demons were busy dousing Granny's chicken coop with some type of liquid that had to be kerosene or gasoline. I wanted to run out and stop them. Those chickens were like family to Granny.

Granny would sit for hours talking to those chickens and babying them. It almost broke her heart for us to use their eggs. When one of those chickens died, you would think it was a friend of Granny's. She would laugh at herself for being so silly about her baby birds, but they meant the world to her.

I watched in horror as one of the men tossed a fire stick into the coop. The flames leapt into the sky, and they all yelled and cheered like they were witnessing the winning run of a baseball game. The sounds those chickens made as they died in the blaze set by those Klansmen will live in my heart forever. Seemed like their screeching would never stop. I wrapped my arms around Granny. Her entire body shook with grief, but she kept quiet. I prayed they would leave, but they seemed to be getting louder. Then we heard a loud knocking at the door. I wondered where Uncle Little Bud and the other men were. I wondered if they were out there watching this happen. I tried not to think about the fact that in that moment, I didn't believe anybody had the power to protect us, including God, who was painfully silent right then.

"Bless your name, Jesus," Granny whispered, pulling me down to the floor so we couldn't be seen. The light from the burning chicken coop cast an eerie glow outside our window. "Protect your children, Father," she continued to pray. "Let that fire in the yard burn down low so as not to do harm to this house or others. And please, Lord, let the fire to hurt and harm burn down low in the bellies of those evil men."

"Come on outta there," we heard someone yell. "Come on. Ain't nobody gone hurt y'all if you come on out."

I knew that if they wanted to come in, it was just a matter of time before they broke through our front door. I was not planning on Granny and me becoming victims that night. In that moment, I felt what Cedric and the other boys had felt in church today. Rage. Anger. Resolve not to die. If those Klansmen came into our house, they would not be leaving on their own steam. I had never killed another living being in my life, but I was determined that on this night, if it meant dying myself, nobody was going to hurt us without me fighting back. I reached around on the floor until I found my purse. I quickly pulled out Uncle Little Bud's pistol. Satan was not going to have his way with us. And if

God really did care about Colored folks, then I prayed he would give me the strength I needed to do what had to be done.

"What are you doing with that thing?" Granny hissed. "Put that thing away, baby. They'll kill us dead if they think we got something like that in here. Lord Jesus, I know that had to be Little Bud's doing."

Before I could answer, we both looked at the door. Somebody was pushing against it.

"I guess y'all want us to come on inside where you are," the voice called out as he continued to ram against the door. "I don't mind coming in there. I bet that little pickaninny gal will be just as tasty as these chickens."

Granny continued to pray. At first she was soft, but the more they rammed against the door, the louder her prayers became.

"Granny, they gone hear you," I whispered. I stood and aimed the gun toward the door. For the first time that night, I did not shake. My hands were steady, just like Uncle Little Bud had taught me. Whatever or whoever came in, I planned to fill them with bullets and send their soul to hell.

"Don't ever aim a gun at anything or anybody unless you mean to use it," Uncle Little Bud had taught me and Lucille last summer.

"I got a gun in here," I yelled out. "I got a gun and I'll use it."

"Baby, hush," Granny pleaded. "You'll just stir them up worse."

I heard laughter. "Y'all hear that? One of them nigger wenches said they have a gun. Well, shoot it then. Shoot your gun and you'll both be dead before the bullet leaves the chamber good."

There was more laughter. Then I heard what could only be Skeeter's voice.

"Well, I'm coming in, and you better be ready to use that gun, pickaninny, and you better kill me with one shot, because otherwise you and your granny will be swinging from one of these trees," he said. "I guarantee you that."

He rammed the door again and again and again. It just never seemed to stop, and just when I thought the door couldn't possibly stand another second, the knocking and ramming stopped, and I heard a voice that sounded better than any church song we sang on Sundays. The voice belonged to Jimmy Earl.

"Y'all go on. You've had your fun, now go on before the sheriff rides up here," he said.

My hands began shaking again, but I continued to aim the gun toward the door.

"You threatening me, Jimmy Earl Ketchums?" another familiar voice said. That voice was Jimmy Earl's Uncle Rafe. As bad as Skeeter was, Mr. Rafe, his daddy, was ten times worse.

"No sir. Just telling you I don't want to see any of y'all getting hauled off by the sheriff tonight, that's all. You know he don't like Klan riding around this countryside."

The next voice that piped up sounded like it belonged to one of Jimmy Earl's other cousins. "We own this countryside, Jimmy Earl. Not that nigger-loving sheriff, and sure as hell not these niggers. They may call this Colored Town, but this here is white man's territory. We owned this land when they were chained up like yard dogs."

A bunch of the men yelled out their approval.

"Jimmy Earl, this ain't your fight," Mr. Rafe said. "You don't want to be on the wrong side of right, now, do you, boy?"

"Y'all know this is Birdie's house. She's worked with Gran's family since she was a girl. Please, don't do no harm to her or her granddaughter," Jimmy Earl begged. "Y'all done had your fun. You burned down her henhouse. Ain't that enough?"

"Jimmy Earl, that nigger said she was going to shoot us. Ain't no nigger gone get away with threatening a bunch of white men," Skeeter bellowed. "Not even your favorite pickaninny."

"Skeeter, you know as well as me neither Birdie nor Opal got a gun. They scared to death. They just want y'all to leave, so that's why they said they had a gun. Use your noodle," Jimmy Earl chastised.

"Lord Jesus, please open their hearts to Jimmy Earl's words," Granny whispered.

Jimmy Earl continued to try and reason with them. I knew he was hoping that them being his kin would be enough for them to listen to him. I hoped he was right, because I was seconds away from firing that gun.

"Uncle Rafe, my gran begged me to come see about Birdie and Opal. I shore don't want to have to go back and tell her the two of them got hurt tonight," Jimmy Earl said.

"Please go. Let this night end," I whispered. All I could think of was some of my uncles or cousins coming out and getting hurt. I prayed that these awful men would listen to Jimmy Earl and leave.

"All right, Jimmy Earl. If these niggers mean that much to you, then we'll ride on down the road a piece farther. But I'll tell you what, Jimmy Earl Ketchums, you better stay your nose out of Klan business from here on out. Don't make me forget that you're my nephew," he said. Then I heard a lot of whooping and yelling and then . . . quiet. Seconds later, there was frantic knocking at the door.

"Birdie! Opal! It's me. Jimmy Earl," he called.

Granny struggled to get up from the floor, but then she ran to the door and pulled him into the room, hugging him so tight, it was a wonder he could even breathe.

"Oh, Lord Jesus," she cried. "Thank you, son. Thank you for coming to see about us."

I still stood holding the gun. It was like I couldn't move. It was like my entire body was frozen.

"Opal," Jimmy Earl called out to me, his voice soft and even-keeled. I watched as Granny let him go, and they both turned toward me. I still couldn't move. I just stood there with that gun in my hand and I couldn't lower it. I couldn't do anything but stand there with that thing aimed in the direction where Jimmy Earl and my granny stood.

"Opal," Granny called. "It's all right, honey. Put down the gun."

All of a sudden, my whole body started to shake so violently, my teeth were chattering, but I still couldn't put it down. It felt like holding that gun was all that was keeping me from falling apart.

"Opal?" Jimmy Earl called. "Bean? Do you hear me? Bean . . . listen . . . I'm going to come over to you. Okay?"

I tried to answer him, but I couldn't. I just stared at him and tried to focus. Tried to lower the gun because I realized I must have looked crazy still holding it now that the danger was over, but I just. Couldn't. Put. It. Down. Jimmy Earl reached me, took my hands, and lowered the gun.

"You okay?" he asked. I shook my head no. I wasn't okay. I was still feeling like at any moment those awful men would come rushing through the door and do God knows what to me and Granny. I wasn't okay. Jimmy Earl seemed to understand. He didn't keep pressing me for answers; he just took the gun from my hand and pulled me into his arms.

For a moment, I let myself relax into his embrace. I didn't think about the fact that Jimmy Earl and I were hugging, something we hadn't done since we were little children. I didn't think about the fact that he was white and I was Colored or that half of the people who had come to bully us had been his kin. No, I just focused on being safe in his arms where nothing and nobody could get at me. It felt good being held. For the first time that night I felt safe, as if all of the bad that had gone on outside no longer existed. I buried my face against his chest and sobbed.

"Opal. Jimmy Earl," my granny called to us, but I stayed where I was. "We got to go outside and see about that fire. With this drought going on, it could spread in a few minutes flat," she said. I heard her, but I was afraid to leave Jimmy Earl's protective embrace.

"Bean, we need to go tend to the coop," he said in a soft voice, but he didn't move. He just kept right on holding me, stroking my hair that was loose and wild on my shoulders. I could smell the faint scent of cologne. I had never known Jimmy Earl to wear cologne before. I guess this was something else new about him since he left Parsons for college. I tried to keep my mind clear, but I just kept seeing the events of the night playing in my head over and over again, and Jimmy Earl coming to the rescue.

"I know," I managed to choke out, but I didn't move either. I just kept standing there.

Then the door burst open. I screamed and tried to grab the gun from Jimmy Earl, but he kept the gun from my reach.

"It's okay. It's okay," he kept repeating. And it was okay.

Coming into the room was Uncle Little Bud, M.J., and Cedric. I ran to them, and Uncle Little Bud caught me in a fierce embrace. When my face touched his, I could feel sweat and what might have been tears.

"You all right, Mama? Opal?" Uncle Little Bud asked, glancing over at Jimmy Earl. "I saw the coop blazing all the way up to the house. Me and the boys got here as fast as we could. The coop done burnt down to nothing now, though, I'm afraid."

"Yes, son," Granny said, hugging him, and me, and M.J. "Me and Opal is all right. I ain't worried none about that chicken coop. Just happy all y'all is okay. You shouldn't have come out with them crazies riding around the countryside. Jimmy Earl there came over and saved the day. He told them old Kluxers what's what."

"Don't look like he saved the day for them chickens out there, Miss Birdie," Cedric said, eyeing Jimmy Earl with a grim look on his face.

Jimmy Earl walked toward us. "We should go out and put out the fire. I'll get—"

"Thank you mighty kindly, Jimmy Earl, but we can handle it from here. The fire done 'bout gone out on its own anyway," Uncle Little Bud said with a cold look on his face. "God had his hand in things tonight. That fire could have killed my mama and my niece. Had that happened, there would have been bloodshed all over this countryside."

"Little Bud, hush. Don't say such things," Granny reprimanded.

Jimmy Earl coughed. "Yes sir." He turned and looked at Granny and me. "I better be going, Birdie. Bean. I'll come pick you two up in the morning, just in case the boys are still out and about, still ramped up from tonight."

"Ain't no need of you doing that, Jimmy Earl. We Colored menfolk will make sure all our women get safely to their places of employment in the morning," Cedric said, putting emphasis on the word *our*. "I'm sure we can handle 'the boys' if we need to."

Jimmy Earl looked over at us but spoke to Granny. "Is that what you want, Birdie?"

"Her name is Miss Birdie, you—" Cedric started and then stopped. "She older than you. She deserve respect."

Granny went to Jimmy Earl and patted his arm. She didn't even look at Cedric. "Opal and me will be just fine. You might want to peek in on Tote and make sure he's okay, though. I ain't heard from him since them Kluxers left outta here. He's the scared sorts."

Jimmy Earl nodded. He walked over to Uncle Little Bud and handed him the gun I had been holding. He gave Cedric a challenging look and then left. It was quiet for a time, but then Uncle Little Bud spoke.

"Mama, what was that Ketchums boy doing here?" he asked. "And gal, what was you doing all hugged up with him like you was outta your fool mind?"

I didn't know that they had seen that. I was embarrassed, but then I got angry. They weren't here and Jimmy Earl was. I didn't need them lecturing me on a night when we all could have been dead, a night that wasn't over yet, if the truth be known.

I glared at Cedric and Uncle Little Bud. "Y'all mad and you don't even know what it was like for me and Granny having them awful men just right outside the door, trying to get in here on us. Jimmy Earl saved us. I was grateful. That's all."

M.J., always the peacemaker, came over and put his arm around me. "We just happy y'all both is fine. Stank, why don't you go on with Uncle Little Bud. I'm gone stay here with my granny and cousin tonight."

"M.J.," Granny said, "there ain't no need in you doing all of that. Them drunken fools is probably all done gone home by now. Ain't gone be no more trouble tonight."

"We gone make sure there ain't no more trouble tonight," Cedric said, sweat pouring down his face, which was full of rage. "They burnt down Brother Walker's barn and they burnt a cross in Deacon Myron's yard. That's what took us so long to get here. I'm ready to go after them. They need to pay for the harm they've done once and for all."

"Stop talking crazy talk, boy," Granny hissed. "You ain't got the good sense God gave a billy goat. You think them Kluxers is scared of the likes of you? Get somewhere and be still. Be prayerful and be thankful that we all is standing here with breath in our bodies. Could be more burnt up than just a coop full of chickens and a cross. All of us could be burnt to a crisp, and no matter how much that white sheriff promises he gone deal with them Kluxers, at the end of the day, white caters to white."

Cedric had the good manners to duck his head, but I could tell he was still hot about the collar.

"Stank, let's go check on Brother and Sister Walker again. They the last ones on our list," Uncle Little Bud said.

"What list?" Granny said, eyeing Uncle Little Bud with suspicion.

"Mama," Uncle Little Bud started, squeezing Granny's shoulders. "Some of the menfolk all decided at church today we would check on all of our elders after them crackers got done showing their tail tonight. 'Course, I was going to check on you. Now all we have left to do is to circle back by the Walkers', and Stank, M.J., and me will have checked on the ones we said we would check on."

"Be careful, son," she said.

"I will, Mama," Uncle Little Bud said. He looked back at M.J. "You take care of your granny and cousin. Me and Stank will throw some water on them dying embers out there just to make sure we don't end up with a worse fire. The wind was picking up a bit."

M.J. nodded his head. "Yes sir. I'll take care of them."

Cedric looked over at me. He looked like he wanted to say something, but he clamped his lips shut. He was angry at me for hugging Jimmy Earl. I could see that. I wished I could go to him and let him know that my feelings for him were strong, but I couldn't. Not with everybody standing there, so I just stayed quiet. Granny went to Cedric and put her hand on his arm.

"You be safe, too, son. Don't go out there and do nothing fool-hardy," Granny said. "God won't be pleased with that."

Cedric looked like he was going to push against Granny's words, but he just looked at her with empty eyes. "Yes ma'am."

Before he left, Uncle Little Bud came over to me and hugged me tight. "I'm proud of you, little girl. I put the gun back in your purse. Trouble might be over for tonight, but trouble ain't over forever."

I nodded as he walked out the door. I went to the window and watched him and Cedric carry several buckets of water to the chicken coop that was nothing more than burnt memories of what once was there. I thought about Granny's pets. I knew chickens don't have souls, or at least, I didn't think they did, but just in case, I said a little prayer for all of them.

"Be with God, little chickens. I hope heaven has a place for you," I whispered. I imagined a beautiful place with no hate and no heartbreak, where Granny's pets could flap their wings, cluck, and eat to their hearts' content.

"Let's go on and turn in. Morning will be here before you know it," Granny said. I went and got some quilts, a sheet, and a pillow for M.J. to lie on in the front room.

I was about to go back to my room when he stopped me.

"That boy cares about you, Opal," M.J. said. I knew who he was talking about. I didn't say anything. "That Ketchums boy ain't your friend. He's your boss man and that's it."

"He's my friend," I said in a soft voice. "He's been my friend since we were children."

"Ya'll ain't children no more, though," he said. "Don't ruin what's right in front of your face. Stank is good. He's a little rough around the edges, but he's good."

"I know that," I said and then walked toward my room. I could hear Granny in her room praying, right before I closed my door.

"Lord," she said. "Cover us with your blood this night. Watch over every soul who's out there in the highways and byways, including them white devils trying to vex us with their hate."

I knelt down beside my bed. I tried to think of something to say to God. I tried to find the words to show appreciation for him sparing our lives tonight, but all I could think of was the sound of those poor chickens screeching and cawing out their final call to me and Granny to come out and save them, and how sad it was that there was nothing that either one of us could do.

*M*y God, Opal. You are so beautiful," Jimmy Earl whispered, stroking my face. No Bean. Just Opal. I sighed. Hearing him say my name like that, well, it was like no feeling I'd ever had before. It wasn't quite light outside, and he and I were sitting underneath one of the peach trees in the orchard. The smell of ripe, juicy peaches filled the air. I was wearing a new dress. It was purple and yellow—my two favorite colors. For the first time ever, I wore my hair loose in soft curls cascading down my shoulders. Jimmy Earl was wearing the same suit he had worn to his Grandpa Muldoon's funeral, but he had loosened his tie and taken off his jacket. I had never seen him look so relaxed.

"We shouldn't be doing this," I said. I tried looking around, but the fog was so thick, I could hardly see anything. I couldn't even really see any of the houses in Colored Town. It was as if there was nothing and no one but me and Jimmy Earl. "You and I are friends, Jimmy Earl. This isn't right." I was trying to call up whatever reason was left in my mind. I thought about Cedric. I knew it would tear him up to see me carrying on like this, but I wanted Jimmy Earl's kisses and his embrace.

He lowered his head and brushed his lips against mine. "This is completely right. I love you, Opal. I've loved you since we were little kids playing out in Gran's yard together."

"Don't say that," I said. His words were making it harder and harder for me to do the right thing. Part of me wanted to move away, but another part of me liked being right where I was. A gentle breeze tickled the sides of my face. I could smell rain in the air. *Maybe this drought is about to be over*, I thought.

Almost out of nowhere, Jimmy Earl took out a knife and began slicing one of the peaches. I hadn't even seen him pick one. Everything about this moment felt magical. He fed the slice to me. I closed my eyes as the juice began to run down the corners of my mouth. Jimmy Earl began kissing my lips, softly licking away the peach juice, and all I could do was moan.

"Opal! Opal!"

"Oh, God," I whispered. "It's Granny." I tried to open my eyes. I was panicked she was going to find us together, but it was like my eyes were glued shut.

"Opal," I heard again, and this time I felt strong hands shaking me, almost roughly.

I opened my eyes and saw Granny standing over me.

"Girl, what you moaning and groaning about? You having a nightmare?" she asked.

I sat up in my bed, twisting and turning. I couldn't believe what I just experienced was a dream. It felt so real, right down to the scent of Jimmy Earl's cologne. I had never had a dream like that before. I felt ashamed. I couldn't even look Granny in the face.

"I'm fine, Granny," I mumbled.

"Well, you need to be getting up and getting ready for work," she said. "Myron will be here in a minute. M.J. done already left to feed the animals up at his family's farm. Today ain't gone be a day for dragging around. Miss Peggy is having that quilting circle today with her church girls. We got to go on and get ready for them. They ain't but a bunch of girls, but they always bring a big appetite with them."

"Yessum," I said. I watched Granny as she walked out of my room. I knew better than to stay in the bed daydreaming, so I got up and peeled off my sweaty gown. Granny had brought me some warm water in a basin, so I quickly washed myself off. I tried not to think about the dream as I put on my work clothes, but it was hard because it all still felt so real.

In just a few days I was going to turn eighteen, and I had only been kissed by one boy: Cedric Perkins. And up until that crazy dream I had about Jimmy Earl, Cedric was the only somebody I had dreamed about in a romantic way. Those dreams had been tame compared to this. In my dreams with Cedric, he and I had only shared chaste kisses. Nothing remotely like what I just experienced in my dream about Jimmy Earl. That dream took me to a place I wasn't even sure I wanted to visit again. In that dream, Jimmy Earl was a man and I was very much a woman, and it scared me. Terribly. I told myself I never wanted to dream anything like that again. But I couldn't stop myself from touching my lips. It felt like I could still feel the heat from his kisses.

I tied a fresh head scarf onto my head and walked out into the living room. The pallet I had made for M.J. was gone. Granny was still in her room, so I tried to be quiet as I fixed myself a plate of leftover biscuits and cheese. I wondered what my dream meant. Granny wasn't very superstitious . . . She said God wasn't the author of confusion. But she did think dreams were different. "Look at how Joseph interpreted dreams in the Bible. No, dreams are our way of understanding things," she would say. But I knew without knowing that she wouldn't take kindly to this dream. Times like this I wished I had a mama.

Granny was good for so many things, but she wasn't comfortable talking about boys and love. Anytime I would bring up boys, she'd say, "They ain't nothing but trouble. Trust God. He'll send you a husband when the time comes." But that response never satisfied me. I wanted to ask things like "How do you know when you're in love?" or "What is that warm, funny feeling that passes over you when a boy touches or kisses you?"

I wanted to learn about courtship, and all Granny wanted to talk about was marriage, but even then, she remained vague. "A wife's job is tedious at times, and often you feel like the mule out in the fields—but every now and then, a good husband will let you know that you are appreciated." I never said anything, but that always sounded awful to me . . . to the point that I almost decided marriage wasn't for me. I didn't want to feel like an old mule. I wanted to be loved and cherished by the man I married. I wanted to be his partner. Not his workhorse.

I wanted what Uncle Myron had with Aunt Josephine: a love so pure and so enduring that it existed even after Aunt

Josephine's death. I wanted the tenderness I saw between Uncle Little Bud and Cheryl Anne. I wanted the laughter and flirting I saw happen with Uncle Lem and Aunt Shimmy. Those were the qualities I wanted in my eventual marriage someday. I wanted what I had seen in the relationships my uncles had with their wives.

"Gal, get on out here. Your uncle is here to take us to work. Don't make us late," Granny said.

"Coming, Granny." I didn't know she had gone outside to wait for Uncle Myron. I quickly gathered my things and joined Granny and Uncle Myron in his baby, a 1930 Model A he had bought for cash from old man Little Jack Parsons. Mr. Little Jack was the wealthiest white man in Parsons, so much so that the town was named for his family. He had told Uncle Myron to pay him over time, but Uncle Myron hated the thought of being in debt to anybody for anything, especially white people. He had bragged that Mr. Little Jack was so shocked to see a Colored man with that much cash that he had stood there with his mouth open so wide, every fly in Henry County had flown in. Everybody had laughed, of course. Anytime we could get an inch over on white folks, it was cause for celebration.

"Good morning, Uncle Myron," I said.

"Morning, chile," he replied, opening the front door for me to sit beside him. Granny refused to sit in the front of anybody's car. She said cars weren't nothing but death traps, but if she had to ride in one, she wanted to be as far away from the front as she could manage.

When Uncle Myron had tried to make her sit in the front

seat when he first bought his car, Granny had said, "No, give me the back seat. Leastways I'll have a chance if we get hit head-on. And anyway, those rich white ladies always sit in the back. They must know something the rest of us don't know about these contraptions."

There was no arguing with Granny once she made up her mind about something. Every now and then Uncle Myron would try to coax her into riding up front, but Granny was just like what the Bible says; she was "steadfast and unmovable."

"Did y'all rest all right last night, Mama?" Uncle Myron asked once he got back inside the car. He started easing his way out of the driveway. "I don't think I slept a wink."

"I slept just fine," she said. "I prayed and left the night in God's hands. And when you do that, you know that God don't need you up and about wrestling with something you had just asked him to handle. Now, Opal seemed to be a tad bit restless. What had you all riled up in your sleep, baby girl?"

Before I could make up something to say, Mr. Tote came out of his house and asked to ride with us to Miss Peggy's. He climbed in the back with Granny. I was thankful for the interruption. I didn't want any of them to see the shame on my face. There was no way I could have explained what I was going through in my sleep last night. I didn't even know how I was going to face Jimmy Earl, let alone explain to my granny and my uncle that I was having unsavory dreams about a white boy. No, that was a dream I would take to my grave.

I listened as Mr. Tote, Granny, and Uncle Myron talked about last night.

"Sure am sorry about your chickens, Miss Birdie," Mr. Tote said. "I know how you loved them little critters. I can get you some more little chicks if you want me to. I can have you a new coop built by sundown, and new little chickens in there to wake you up by tomorrow morning."

"That is mighty kind of you, Mr. Tote, but I think I'm gonna take a rest from owning chickens for now. Last night . . . well . . ." Her voice trailed off. I could hear the pain. I turned around in my seat and reached for her hand.

"There is a special place in hell for those people," I said. "I pray that in hell they will lift up their eyes one day."

"Opal," she exclaimed, pulling her hand back from mine like it had just burnt hers. "Don't say such a thing. As Christians, we want everybody to find their way to God. We don't wish eternal death on nobody. Them chickens meant a lot to me, but another human's soul will always outrank some critter. Always. Now repent of such wicked thoughts. The hell we pray for somebody else is very well the hell we will have to contend with, and we surely don't want that. Tell the Lord you're sorry."

"Sorry, Lord," I mumbled. I turned back around and stared straight ahead as Uncle Myron continued to drive us through Parsons. I didn't pay attention to anything we passed by. I didn't care what Granny had to say about those awful men who came and terrorized us last night. I hated them. I hated them for thinking that they were so much better than us that they could treat us any kind of way and get away with it. I hated that they made our menfolk feel less than human . . . less than men. They made it clear that our men were useless when it came to protecting us, and for that, I despised all of them and prayed hell truly was where they would lift up their eyes someday; to be honest, I didn't feel bad for thinking that way at all. They were evil, and no matter what Granny had to say, as far as I was concerned, they didn't deserve to go anywhere else but hell.

"Well, us deacons are gonna go have a talk with that new sheriff, Sheriff Ardis," Uncle Myron said. "It's 'bout time he earn his keep around here. He keep telling us he's gonna stop them rednecks from ripping through our town, causing havoc. It's time for him to stand up and do what he promised he would do. He said he was a man of integrity and a man of his word. Now is time for him to prove it."

"Deacon Myron, I mean no disrespect, but you ain't so green that you really think that white man is gonna stand against another group of white men for the likes of us, is you?" Mr. Tote asked.

I nodded my head in agreement but kept quiet. I didn't want Granny or Uncle Myron getting angry with me. Like Mr. Tote, I didn't trust nothing white folks had to say, either, for the most part. Other than Miss Peggy, Jimmy Earl, Miss Corinne, and Doc Henry, I had not witnessed any white men or women doing much standing up for us. This new sheriff seemed nice and all, but I had no faith in his ability to make much of a difference. Them Klansmen who rode through Colored Town would just as soon kill the sheriff as they would Granny's chickens. They didn't care about no human lives but their own, and they especially didn't care none about Colored folks' lives or those of our sympathizers.

"We are taxpayers, Mr. Tote. We live peaceable lives and we don't mess with nobody. We are hardworking, and all we ask is that folks leave us alone to live our lives without fear of violence. If the sheriff can't give us safety in our own community, then we don't need him in the office of sheriff," Uncle Myron said as he made his way past Doc Henry's house. The lights were off, and Doc Henry's car was in the driveway. That was a good sign. If anybody had gotten hurt last night, Doc Henry would have been all over the countryside seeing about folks, Colored or white.

"That sheriff means well, but he ain't no match for these crazy white folks in that Klan," Granny said. "One good white man by hisself can't right all the wrongs in the world."

"If we want safety in our community, we better stock up on some rifles and some bullets and make our communities safe ourselves," Mr. Tote said. "Slavery been done ended, yet most of us still carry ourselves like slaves. Either we men or we ain't. Maybe if some of them peckerwoods would have felt some buckshot in their behinds last night, Miss Birdie's chickens might still be alive."

"Mr. Tote, you are speaking foolishly. The last thing Colored folks need to do is start shooting at white folks. There'll be another civil war in this country before you can count to three," Granny said. "The best thing we can do is stay out of their way and keep ourselves on bended knee every chance we get. God is the only one who can fix this situation. He's the only one that can make this situation right."

"Well, no disrespect to your God, but he ain't done nothing to fix things so far. What makes you think your God is gonna all of a sudden start doing right by Colored folks now?" Mr. Tote asked in his quiet, thoughtful way.

My ears perked up. Mr. Tote didn't make no secret that he wasn't a practicing Christian. He liked sitting on the porch playing the spirituals, but he made it very clear that he thought God was something white folks made up to keep Colored folks in line. And when he got really tipsy, he sometimes got into shouting matches with folks over God and whether or not he was even paying any mind to the plight of Colored people.

"Don't you start with me, Tote Johnson," Granny warned. "I'm not interested in hearing you blaspheme the good Lord this morning."

"Ain't starting with you, Miss Birdie. And I ain't got to say nothing 'gainst your God. He doing a good job of showing us all whose side he's on. That's all I'm saying," Mr. Tote said. "He let us get stolen from our homeland and then become slaves, and now, here we are, running from the Klan when all we trying to do is live. So is you telling me that the God that let all that happen is the God you want us to worship and fall out over at church every Sunday?"

"Too early for all that, Mr. Tote," Uncle Myron interrupted before Granny could get really wound up. I was a little put off. I wanted to hear how Granny was going to answer Mr. Tote because what he said made good sense to me. I was too scared not to believe in Granny's God, but I can't say I never wondered some of the same things Mr. Tote brought up.

Uncle Myron continued talking. "We ain't having that conversation this morning, Mr. Tote, especially so soon after last night. Whether you believe in God or not is up to you. But last night, we were all spared, and that is worth us thanking somebody for it. So as for me and my family, we choose to thank the good Lord for his mercy and his grace last night and all the nights before and after. All of us could be dead this morning, and something bigger than us intervened."

"Amen to that," Granny said down low. I could tell she wanted to say more, but she didn't. Uncle Myron had spoken, and I knew Granny always tried to let her sons be men, so in her mind, talking over them was a no-no, especially in situations like this.

"Didn't mean no disrespect, Myron," Mr. Tote said, as Uncle Myron pulled his car up to the barn. "Y'all have a good day, and thank you kindly for the ride." Mr. Tote got out of the car in a hurry. I watched as he made his way into the barn. I knew he would be avoiding Granny all day today, and she'd be doing the same.

"Well, I'll tell you what . . . ," Granny started.

"Let it go, Mama. Mr. Tote always been how he is. No point in us going down to his level," Uncle Myron said. Granny got quiet, but I knew I would be getting an earful all day long. She wasn't ever gonna talk over her sons and grandsons, but she had no problem giving me and the other women in the family an earful.

Uncle Myron drove me and Granny to the front door of Miss Peggy's house. Miss Peggy insisted we always enter into her house from the front door. She even gave Granny a key so we could come and go as we pleased. Granny said no other white woman in Parsons—or maybe even all of Georgia—did something so kind for their Colored Help.

When I first asked Granny why we were allowed to go inside from the front, she had smiled and patted me on my back. "Miss Peggy has always been a stand-up kind of woman. She never did believe in all that back door mess. She always treated us like we was human beings that mattered."

When we got to the front door that morning, Miss Peggy jerked it open and pulled Granny into a full embrace. Miss Peggy nearly sank to the floor, but Granny held her up, keeping her from falling all the way down.

"What you doing up so early, Miss Peggy?" Granny snapped. "Ain't no need in you being up this time of the morning. You know Doc Henry been saying time and time again that you need to be getting your rest. Who you think he was talking to? Those cows out there in the pasture?"

Granny's tone was sharp, but her eyes were full of love and concern. She talked to Miss Peggy like she talked to me sometimes. Even though the tone sounded harsh, it was always filled with love. I hoped Miss Peggy took it that way too. I saw her smile and pat Granny on her face. I knew by that gesture that she did.

"I was worried about you and Opal," Miss Peggy said, leaning against Granny. "I know Jimmy Earl said he ran them fools off, but for all I knew, they could have hightailed it back out there once Jimmy Earl left, and killed the both of you. Now, since y'all are both okay, help me into my sewing room so I can get it organized for today's quilting bee with the girls."

"Why are y'all meeting again so soon, Miss Peggy?" I asked, taking her other arm and helping Granny lead her to her sewing room. At one time it was her parlor, but since she started teaching some of the young white women from the community how to sew and make quilts, she just decided to start calling it her sewing room.

"We just got a few more meetings to finish this wedding quilt for Cindy Lou Murphy and Dale Thompson," she said. "Do you know Cindy Lou, Opal? She's around your age. Lord, it is hard to believe you gals are old enough to be marrying. Seems like y'all was just in diapers, and now y'all are husband hunting."

"I don't know Miss Cindy Lou, Miss Peggy. I hardly know any of the white young ladies in town other than in passing," I replied.

"Well, you ain't missed much with that one," Miss Peggy said, and both she and Granny laughed.

"Opal, you wasn't here the last time Miss Cindy Lou and the girls came to quilt, but she couldn't pick up on Miss Peggy's stitches to save her soul. Miss Peggy called her dull as dishwater, and Miss Cindy Lou was not happy. You reckon she'll even come?" Granny asked.

"Of course she'll come. For a free quilt, that girl would deal with my tongue and the devil's," Miss Peggy said. "And Birdie, I told you to stop calling those ragtag girls 'Miss.' They are your junior. Neither you nor Opal need to talk to them like they're the Queens of England. You wouldn't dare catch me calling somebody that age 'Miss.' I don't even like you doing it to me." Granny and I guided her to her favorite sewing chair near the window.

She liked sitting there so she could see who was coming to the front door at any given time.

"Miss Peggy, you know the rules that work for you ain't the same for me and Opal," Granny said in a quiet voice. "The world ain't quite caught up to you yet."

Miss Peggy grunted. "Well, it should. Especially when it comes to matters of civility. I guess next y'all will be calling Jimmy Earl '*Mr. Jimmy Earl*.'"

"I don't see a thing wrong with that," Jimmy Earl teased as he walked toward us. We all jumped. None of us had heard him come into the room. "In fact, why don't all of y'all start calling me 'Mr. Jimmy Earl'? You too, Gran. It has a nice ring to it," he said, giving his gran a kiss on her cheek, and then he did the same with my granny, who swatted him lovingly.

I turned away. After my dream about him from the previous night, I didn't even trust myself to make eye contact. I was afraid my face would show that something wasn't right. In fact, I excused myself and went to the kitchen so I could get breakfast started.

I decided to go light. Boiled eggs, toast, and some of the homemade peach preserve I had put up last year. I knew I could have breakfast done long before Jimmy Earl had to go to work at the pharmacy. This was going to be his first day, and I wanted to make sure he went on a full belly. That was the least I could do, I quickly told myself. It wasn't because Jimmy Earl was special to me or anything. Or at least no more special than he always had been.

"He's just a boy," I said out loud.

"Who's just a boy?" Jimmy Earl said, entering the kitchen.

I almost made matters worse by groaning, but instead I came up with a quick fib. "My cousin Lucille wrote a story and she gave it to me to read. I was just thinking out loud."

"Hmm," he said. Like I figured, he quickly lost interest in what I had just said. The last thing Jimmy Earl was interested in was some story, especially one written by a girl. But then Jimmy Earl walked over to me where I was pouring the grits into the boiler. "Bean, are you okay? I mean really okay? After last night and all."

I just nodded, afraid that I might reveal the discomfort I was feeling.

"I'm sorry for what happened. I'm especially sorry half of the troublemakers were my kin," he said, placing his hand on my shoulder. I was prepared for his touch to feel awkward and strange, but it didn't. It just felt like my old friend Jimmy Earl putting his hand on my shoulder. What a relief. The only thing I wanted to feel about Jimmy Earl was friendship. I hoped this also meant no more inappropriate dreams about my friend.

I looked up at him. "It's okay, Jimmy Earl. They ain't you, and you ain't them. If it weren't for you, me and Granny might not have lived through the night. So thank you."

"You ain't gotta thank me," he said. "You and Birdie are family. In some ways, more family to me than my cousins, daddy, and uncles. Y'all take care of my gran and my mama like they was your own. I promise you this, Bean. I will always protect you and Birdie. No matter what." Then he squeezed my shoulder one more time and cleared his throat. "So when is breakfast gonna be ready? A man needs his sustenance."

I laughed. Now this was the Jimmy Earl I knew and loved. This Jimmy Earl was safe . . . like a brother. "Very soon, Mr. Jimmy Earl," I said, and we both laughed.

"I'll go check on Tote and the boys while you finish up. I want to get to work early. I don't want Mr. Lowen getting anxious. Oh, and Bean. I'll probably be late tonight. Getting ready for the big Founder's Day baseball game."

"Y'all are going to have heatstrokes out there trying to play baseball," I mumbled. Sometimes boys did the craziest things.

"Aww, you worried about me," he teased.

I threw a dish towel at him. "I'm not worried, Jimmy Earl Ketchums. Just don't want to have to wait on your silly self if you do have a heatstroke. I have enough to do already."

"Well, I will do my best to not have a heatstroke. Just for you," he said, laughing. "I'll be back in a few minutes." He walked out of the kitchen, and soon I heard the screen door shut.

I smiled. Maybe, just maybe, things were going to get back to normal, or at least something that felt normal. I guess if you live in a world where angry white men can come out of the blue and burn down your property without any fear of payback, there is no normal. There's just getting by from day to day.

I hoped that the worst was over. I hoped that the Klan wasn't going to come back and mess with us anymore. I hoped Jimmy Earl and I would remain friends for the rest of our lives. That was my fervent prayer. That is what I laid at Jesus's feet, hoping against hope that he really was up there listening to the prayers of girls like me.

7

*I*t didn't take long for me to finish making breakfast; once it was done, I went into the sewing room to see if Miss Peggy wanted to eat there or in the kitchen. When I got to her, I found her slumped down in her chair. I shook her and she quickly came back to herself, but I was scared. Granny was out in the garden checking on the vegetables, and Jimmy Earl was still helping Mr. Tote and the other men out on the farm. It was just me and Miss Peggy, and all I could think was that I needed to get her to bed. Bed just seemed safe.

"I don't need to go to bed, Opal. I just got a bit light-headed. I feel better now," she said, sitting up in her chair. But she still looked weak around the eyes to me.

"Please, Miss Peggy," I begged. "Let me get you to your bed. Just until you feel more like yourself. Please." It was all I could do to keep my voice calm. Seeing her slumped over like that had put my heart into my throat. Miss Peggy was like a second granny to me. It was Miss Peggy who taught me how to can things and sew. Granny was an amazing cook, but making jellies, jams, and preserves just wasn't her thing. Miss Peggy had patiently taught me everything from how to prepare the jars to what to do with the fruit to help it maintain its color while in them. Losing her would hurt almost as much as losing Granny.

"Opal, honey, I will be okay," she said in a soft voice.

"Can I at least let them young ladies know there ain't going to be no quilting circle this afternoon?"

Miss Peggy shook her head. "No, don't do no such thing," she said in a breathless voice. "I'll be fine by this afternoon, and if it will make you stop looking so scared to death, I'll go back to bed for a spell. Just don't tell Birdie and Jimmy Earl what happened. They'll worry themselves to death. Just tell them I was tired after getting up so early and decided to sleep a little longer."

"Yes ma'am," I said, thankful she was going to let me help her to her room. She managed to get up from her chair, and with my help, we slowly made our way down the hallway to her bedroom. Once I got Miss Peggy back into bed and settled, she looked up at me with tears in her eyes. Other than when Mr. Cecil died, I had never seen her cry. But these last few days, she had been shedding quite a few tears. I took her hand.

"I'm okay, sweetheart. I don't want you worrying. I'm just getting old, that's all. And it feels like cow dung," she said. We looked at each other and burst out laughing. "Yes, I said 'cow dung,' and you better not tell Birdie. She'll be praying over me all day for using such language."

"I won't tell. It'll be our secret, Miss Peggy," I said, still giggling.

"Opal, you look so much like your mama," she said. "MayBelle was a pretty gal. Just like you."

I stopped laughing and smiling. It was like she had just thrown cold water in my face. I dropped her hand and turned my back to her. "I sure hope I don't get none of her awful ways."

I felt Miss Peggy reaching out for my hand. I started to ignore her. Started to snatch my hand away from her reach because she couldn't have paid me no greater insult than to say I was like my mama, the same mama who left me behind like a stray puppy. The same mama who we never heard from again. But I knew I couldn't do that to Miss Peggy. Not even over her hurting my feelings. I turned back toward her and took her hand.

She squeezed it. "I'm so sorry, Opal. I didn't mean no harm by my words. MayBelle was a real beauty, and you are too. That's all I meant to say."

I smiled, but it wasn't a for-real smile. "That's okay, Miss Peggy. I know you didn't mean no harm. Do you want me to bring your food in here?"

"Yes, honey. If that's no trouble."

This time, my smile was genuine. "Of course it's no trouble, Miss Peggy. I'll be right back with your plate."

Just then, Miss Corinne skipped into the room like an oversize little girl. You wouldn't know by how she acts that she is in her thirties, except for the fine lines around her mouth and eyes. The other giveaway that Miss Corinne was older than twelve was that she seemed to carry this huge weariness. I sometimes wished I could reach out and take that weariness from her and let her have a day or two when she didn't have to carry such a heavy, heavy load.

"Morning, Mama. Morning, Opal," Miss Corinne said, coming over and kissing us both. "I'm having a good day."

"That's good, sweetheart," Miss Peggy said.

I thanked God silently. We all could use a good day, and a lot of times Miss Corinne's good or bad days determined how good or how bad our days were. She didn't mean no harm. It was just her nature, or at least that's what Granny said.

"Miss Corinne was a change of life baby," Granny said one day when I asked her why Miss Corinne was a bit addled in the head. "Them babies struggle sometimes. They weren't meant to be conceived to mamas that old, so sometimes they come here carrying the nature of an old woman going through the change."

"Miss Corinne, do you want me to bring you a plate so you can eat with your mama?" I asked. She nodded, and I left Miss Peggy's room to make both of their plates.

Sometimes Mama and Granny would just do things for Miss Corinne without ever asking her what she thought about it. If they were cooking, they wouldn't ask her if she was hungry; they would just make her a plate and tell her to eat. I tried to treat her as if she were one of my older aunties. I never tried to act like I knew what was best for her unless I absolutely had to. And even then, I tried to be respectful about it.

Although Miss Corinne had some rough days, she also had some days when she was just like everybody else—when she would do the things the rest of us took for granted, like being a good daughter or a good mama. It was Miss Corinne who taught me and Jimmy Earl how to fish and catch crawdads. "Patience," she used to say. "If you want to catch something in nature, you gotta have patience." And it was Miss Corinne who taught me what to do on the day I started my period.

I was thirteen when my "friend" first visited me. Granny and Miss Peggy had gone to town, and it was just me and Miss Corinne at the house. By that time, Jimmy Earl was in his first year of college, and even though it was summertime, he had decided to stay up there in Athens and work. I was mopping the kitchen floor, and I looked down and saw little droplets of blood coming down my leg. I mopped them up as best I could, and then I ran outside crying to where Miss Corinne was pulling the weeds out of Miss Peggy's flower bed. She stood up smiling and then wiped my tears.

"You gonna be okay, Opal. I know your granny told you about your friend visiting you," she said. I nodded, but it was one thing to be told and another to have blood streaming down your legs. "Don't you worry none. I'll take care of you," Miss Corinne said. She took me upstairs to the bathroom and showed me how to put on the sanitary pad and belt. Then she handed me two more pads.

"Wash them out good when you get done with one. That way you'll always have clean ones to change into. Let me know if you need more," she said in her whispery voice. She kissed my forehead. "You're a woman now. It ain't all that bad. Your friend will come see you once a month, and sometimes your belly will hurt, but most times it'll just be blood . . . leastways that's how it's been for me. Just make sure you stay away from the boys, or you'll get yourself a little Jimmy Earl in your belly like I did."

I promised her I would stay away from boys, and I was

thankful I didn't have to have a talk with Miss Peggy or Granny about how to deal with my woman issues. Neither one of them was good with moments like this, so having Miss Corinne guide me through it was a blessing that I never forgot. Ever since then, Miss Corinne has held a soft spot in my heart. There wasn't much I wouldn't do for her, whether it was on one of her good days or bad days.

I quickly fixed plates for Miss Corinne and Miss Peggy. Just as I was putting their plates on a tray, Jimmy Earl walked in the door. He was already sweating.

"That's for Mama and Gran?" he asked.

"Yes. I'll fix yours now."

"Don't bother, Bean. I'm so hot I'm liable to get sick if I tried to eat a hot meal. Here, I'll take this to them. I ain't told them good morning yet, and I need to get ready and get out of here, or I'll be late on my first day," he said.

"You need to eat something, Jimmy Earl," I said. "Maybe a bowl of those cornflakes your mama likes so much?"

Jimmy Earl scrunched up his nose, and I laughed. I didn't like that cereal mess, either, but Miss Corinne could almost eat it straight out the box.

"I'll make it up at lunch," he said.

"I fixed you a couple of ham sandwiches with some of that leftover ham. Make sure you keep it cool once you get to work. It's in the cooling box in a brown paper bag," I said.

Jimmy Earl laughed. "Bean, you are as country as they get. It's not a cooling box. It's a refrigerator."

I snapped at him, ashamed. "Well, whatever you call it,

there's sandwiches in there waiting for you." I turned my back. I felt his hand on my shoulder. I shook it off.

"Bean, I'm sorry. I was just teasing," he said.

I kept my back to him. "I know you done outgrown all of us with all your book learning. I know better than anybody that I'm not as smart as you or all of your new college friends."

Jimmy Earl turned me around so I was facing him. "Bean, I was teasing. You are smarter than any girl I know, and that includes those ninnies at the University of Georgia. I value common sense over book sense any day. Okay?"

"Okay," I said.

"Now let me get this food to Mama and Gran. You gonna be okay?"

"I'm fine. Go see about Miss Peggy and your mama."

He glanced at me once more and then made his way down the hall carrying their plates.

A tear slid down my face, and I swiped at it angrily. "You're the ninny, Opal Pruitt. If you don't stop crying at the drop of a hat, you—"

"Crying about what?" Granny said, coming into the kitchen. "Lord, those poor vegetables are hanging on for dear life. I picked some of those new potatoes, and a few cucumbers I can make into a soup for supper, and sandwiches for Miss Peggy and her girls. I also found a couple of knotty watermelons you can stick in that cooling box."

I smiled. "They call it a refrigerator, Granny."

Granny clicked her teeth. "Well, whatever they call it, you can stick one of these melons in it. Corinne will love it. I think she could eat her collard greens cold if I served them to her that way."

I laughed and started taking my dirty dishes to the sink to wash.

"So what was you crying about, little missy? I didn't forget," Granny said.

"Nothing, Granny. I'm fine," I said. Before she could ask me any more questions, I heard someone calling for Granny at the screen door. I went to see who it was, and it was Sister Mattie Lee Freeman, my Sunday school teacher. I almost didn't recognize her without her church clothes on. She was dressed like most of the Colored women on a Monday morning: a housedress, an apron, a headscarf, and comfortable shoes. Miss Mattie Lee didn't have steady work like me and Granny. She cleaned part time for two white families and for Miss Lovenia Manu, the root woman.

"Mattie Lee, come on in, gal. What you doing out in this heat?" Granny asked as Sister Mattie Lee opened the door. She made her way to the kitchen table, plopping down in one of the chairs as she mopped the sweat from her face. "Chile, go get Mattie Lee some ice water," Granny said. I hurried and plopped some ice cubes in a glass and then poured in some of the water from the pitcher. I took the glass to Sister Mattie Lee, and she smiled.

"Thank you, Opal," she said and then took a big gulp of water. "Lawd have mercy. Birdie, how you reckon we made it without ice water back in the day when we had to go out to the fields and pick cotton and peanuts?"

"Gal, you know I ain't never picked no cotton. You know us high yallers didn't have to go outside the big house," Granny said as she and Sister Mattie Lee both burst into laughter like silly girls.

I knew Granny had picked cotton and peanuts when she was younger. It wasn't until her teen years that she got a job keeping house for Miss Peggy, but she liked to joke that her fair skin color used to get her special favors like doing jobs that didn't put her in the sun.

Granny continued, "Chile, Old Man Little Jack Parsons didn't care if you was high yaller or black as coal; when harvest season came around, everything that could walk or crawl had better be out in them fields."

"Yes, Lawd," said Sister Mattie Lee. "Old Man Little Jack sho didn't play. Birdie, I didn't come to keep you from your work. Miss Lovenia sent me over to talk to you."

"I'll go check on Miss Peggy and Miss Corinne," I said. I had heard Jimmy Earl's pickup that used to be Mr. Cecil's crank up a few minutes ago, so I knew he had left for work and Miss Peggy and Miss Corinne were alone. If nothing else, I could go and collect their tray.

"Don't go, Opal," Miss Mattie Lee said. "This is about you."

I suddenly got nervous. I couldn't imagine what it could be. Then I panicked. What if Sister Mattie Lee had seen Cedric and me kiss the other day, or what if someone else had seen us, or what if Miss Lovenia had used her magic, and . . .

". . . help her," I heard Sister Mattie Lee say. Help her? Help who?

"Ma'am?" I asked, feeling embarrassed that I had missed hearing what Sister Mattie Lee had said the first time.

"Miss Lovenia wanted me to see if you could come help her a few days a week after you get off here," Sister Mattie Lee repeated. "I'm finally gonna retire, or at least be at home. Before I could recommend somebody, she asked me about you."

"Why my Opal?" Granny asked. "Why that hoodoo woman want my chile to work for her? No offense, Mattie Lee. It's one thing for a grown woman like you to be up in that house, but my chile, that's another thang altogether."

"No offense taken, Birdie," Sister Mattie Lee said, putting her handkerchief back into her pocket. "When I first started working for Miss Lovenia two years ago, I told her I was a God-fearing Christian and I wasn't there for no mess. I don't fool with her room where she does her work. She don't talk to me 'bout it, and I pray before I walk in that house and pray when I leave it. She got them twin boys who are about forty or fifty, but they stay to themselves upstairs in their bedroom, and she told me they could clean up their room themselves. She pays good, and I told her she would have to do the same by Opal as she did by me. A couple of hours a day is all she needs. Opal is young. That'll be some good money for her to make and sock away for a rainy day."

"Ain't enough rainy days on God's earth for me to send my chile to some hoodoo woman," Granny said. "You tell Miss Lovenia I said thanks but no thanks. My Opal has plenty to do right here at Miss Peggy's."

I wanted to beg Granny to let me go to work for Miss

Lovenia, but I knew better. Yes, I was a bit afraid of Miss Lovenia's hoodooing, too, but the money would be good. It would allow me to buy a pretty new dress right out of the store like Lucille, or go to Miss Chellie's house and let her wash and straighten my hair. But Granny had spoken. It didn't matter that the extra money would help us both out. Granny's word was law with me. So I said goodbye to Miss Mattie Lee and went to check on Miss Peggy and Miss Corinne.

When I got to Miss Peggy's room, both Miss Peggy and Miss Corinne were asleep in the bed, dozing under the cool breeze of the electric fan. Their plates were empty and sitting on the tray on the floor. Miss Corinne had her head pressed against her mama's shoulder. I smiled at them both. It was nice to see them resting. Neither one of them looked stressed or out of sorts. I imagined it was because the room was so comfortable. I'd been after Granny to let us get electricity, but she kept saying no, and that God sends us all the light and breezes we need. I stood there for a moment and let the cool breeze blow on me.

"Feels good, don't it?" Miss Peggy said.

"I thought you was asleep," I said as I turned around and faced her.

"You was blocking the air," she said and laughed in a soft voice. Neither one of us wanted to wake up Miss Corinne.

I moved over. "I'm sorry," I said.

"I was teasing you, Opal. I wasn't asleep. Just resting my eyes. Now this one," she said, motioning toward Miss Corinne, "is hard asleep. I thought I heard another voice in the kitchen."

I explained that Sister Mattie Lee had come by, and I told

her about Miss Lovenia wanting me to work over there for a few days a week once I was done at her house.

"Well, are you gonna do it?" Miss Peggy asked.

I twisted my lips and laughed as quietly as I could. "Miss Peggy, you know Granny ain't gonna let me work for no hoodoo woman."

Miss Peggy laughed, and Miss Corinne stirred slightly. Miss Peggy patted her back to sleep like you would a little baby.

"You're right. What was I thinking?" she said with a smile. "I can talk to her if you want me to. Once in a blue moon, Birdie will listen to me."

"No ma'am. That's all right," I said. I didn't even want Granny to know I had mentioned Miss Lovenia's words to Miss Peggy. I suppose I should have been as nervous as Granny about me working for Miss Lovenia, but I thought about all that I had learned in church. We were told there was no such thing as hoodoo. But for some reason, we all seemed scared of it. Granny said just like folks can talk to the Lord, folks can talk to the devil, and as far as she was concerned, anybody who did hoodoo was bosom buddies with Satan. Before I could think about it any more, Granny came to Miss Peggy's bedroom door.

"Opal, honey, we need to get ready for Miss Peggy's company. They'll be here before you know it," she said and then looked sternly at Miss Peggy. "You stay on in that bed and rest just as long as you can."

"Yes ma'am," Miss Peggy said, smiling. She snuggled back close with Miss Corinne and closed her eyes. I hoped she would rest, even if she didn't sleep.

Granny and I went back to the kitchen, and because we were so much in step with each other, we already knew how to divide up the cooking for Miss Peggy's quilting party.

"You gonna make your lemon squares?" she asked.

"Yes ma'am," I said. "Everybody seems to like them." I also thought that I would secretly make a few extra for Cedric. I was hoping to see him later. I needed a way to apologize to him for finding me hugged up with Jimmy Earl. I needed him to know it didn't mean nothing.

"I wish Miss Peggy would have canceled with those girls today," Granny said as she cut some cucumbers into thin slices. "She ain't well enough to be worrying with no quilt. Especially on a hot day like this."

I agreed with Granny, but I didn't say it out loud. I just kept measuring out everything I would need for my lemon squares. I didn't want to mess around and say too much. I seldom kept secrets from Granny, but it felt like the older I got, the more secrets I had to carry. Kissing Cedric. Dreaming about Jimmy Earl. Miss Peggy fainting this morning. It was almost more than one body could stand. But, I thought, as I started grating my lemons, I guess that was what it meant to become a woman.

8

I stood quietly in the corner of the room by the table we had set up for the young white girls to get their food. We decided to have them eat here rather than go into the dining room.

"I'm not trying to make more work for you and Birdie," Miss Peggy said. "Putting everything in the sewing room makes sense. That also keeps them from traipsing all over my house."

"If that's what you want, Miss Peggy," Granny said. "Me and Opal got this down pat, so we can put things however you want it. You and Jimmy Earl will even have some leftovers to eat on tonight."

I was happy that Miss Peggy didn't change her mind. I wanted to get out early as possible, so maybe I could see Cedric on my walk home and share the lemon squares I had made.

The girls started arriving around one o'clock. It was seven of them and they were loud and chatty. A few of them spoke to me and Granny, but the others just walked around us without a mumbling word. We might as well have been part of the furniture. I was used to that with white folks. Excusing Miss Peggy and a smattering few others, white folks thought all we was good for was to cook and clean up after them. One thing I did know was, even though I loved cooking and cleaning and could see myself doing it for the rest of my life, I had no intentions of working with people like these girls. People who thought they were better than me and therefore didn't have to show respect. No, if I couldn't keep working for Miss Peggy or some white family like hers, I wouldn't keep doing it.

I didn't like how it made me feel on days like this. I thought about Uncle Myron. He would be saying, "I told you. I told you they don't see you. They just see their cold glass of water or their cleanup woman to empty their slop jars." Unfortunately, in this moment, I would be hard-pressed to argue against him.

Once the girls all got settled, I stood by the food table just in case Miss Peggy or one of her guests needed me to go fetch something or help with their quilting. Miss Peggy had rested most of the morning before her company came, but she still seemed tired to me. Her walking was a little slow, so if I could save her a step or two by going over and showing a girl how to do a stitch properly, well, that was what I planned on doing.

Granny said she would stay in the kitchen and straighten up. I didn't know what she was straightening up. I had cleaned the kitchen before any of the girls got here. I figured she was in there listening to the radio. Granny loved listening to WSB. They was always playing the Carter Family, and Granny loved their song "Keep on the Sunny Side." Sometimes, if she couldn't find it on the radio, she would get Miss Corinne to sing it for her.

I didn't mind if she was resting. All I wanted to do was make sure Granny, Miss Peggy, and Miss Corinne were taken care of to the best of my ability. Sometimes, though, I wondered what it would be like to put myself first. What would it be like to be these carefree white girls who could come calling in the middle of the day and sew and laugh and talk and daydream about their future?

I looked at the other side of the room. Miss Corinne was working hard on her piecework. She was good. She would drop a stitch every now and then, but most times she caught it and I would see her squinch up her face as she worked through making her stitches perfect. The quilting also seemed to relax her. Sometimes, when her singing wouldn't calm her down, I would hand her some embroidery work or some quilt squares to piece together. It was nice that today Miss Corinne seemed to be herself. No demons messing with her mind.

"Miss Peggy. Miss Peggy, did I do this stitch right?" one of the girls asked. I watched as Miss Peggy walked over to the girl and then grimaced slightly. I put my hand over my mouth to hide my smile. I knew what that look meant. When she was first teaching me to sew, I would get that look on a regular basis. One thing Miss Peggy could not abide was someone making a mistake after she had just showed them how to do it the right way.

"Well, honey. Your stitching is . . . well . . . getting better. Yes, your stitching is much improved," she said as she smiled that sideways smile of hers that never reached her eyes. "Now remind me of your name again, honey."

"Lori Beth. Lori Beth Parsons," the girl said, smiling, showing a mouthful of pretty white teeth. She had red hair that she had tied up in a ponytail, and skin so smooth and rich looking you'd never think the light of day had ever touched her face. She reached and touched Miss Peggy's hand. I could tell Miss Peggy wanted to yank her hand back, but she didn't. "I just want to say thank you for offering these lessons, Miss Peggy. Today is just my second time attending your quilting circle. I've been away at boarding school, and I just finished my semester two weeks ago. I'm very eager to learn how to properly make a quilt. I find this all so fascinating."

I frowned, irritated on behalf of Miss Peggy. A Parsons learning how to quilt. Really? What in the world was she doing here pretending to want to learn how to sew scraps of fabric together? Miss Peggy was trying to teach these young white girls of the community how to actually make quilts that their families would use. Parsons could just buy their quilts from stores or get their Colored Help to make them for them. Most of these girls came from poor families, Miss Peggy had said to Granny and me when she first started the quilting circle.

"These girls' mamas and daddies don't have two nickels to rub together. That Depression wiped most of them out except for their land, and some of them lost that," she said. "Thank God Cecil was smart enough to manage our money, elseways we would be in the same shape."

I looked over at that Miss Lori Beth Parsons again. Her family had enough money to purchase every quilt made in Henry County and beyond. Somehow that fact made me resent her presence even more. Here I was, not even eighteen, and I had to work for everything I got. Granny would never take anything from the family to help with my upkeep, so from an early age I learned that nothing in life was free. Leastways not for me. If I wanted something, I had to work for it. But this white girl . . . she had everything handed to her, and in spite of myself, it made me angry. Maybe even a tad bit jealous. I knew Granny would tell me to repent right then, but I didn't. I wasn't ready to let go of what I was feeling, not even to please Granny or God.

"Girls, why don't you take a moment to rest and partake in these nice refreshments Birdie and Opal have prepared for us. And please, tell them thank you," Miss Peggy said as she made her way to her chair, moving like she had bricks in her shoes, weighing her down.

All of the girls said thank you in unison, with Lori Beth Parsons the loudest of them all. I don't know why, but even her politeness grated at me some kind of a way.

Miss Peggy motioned for me to come over to where she sat.

"I need some medicine, Opal. Go tell Birdie. She knows where it is," Miss Peggy whispered. I turned on my heels and went to the kitchen where Granny was dozing by the radio.

"Granny," I said, shaking her as easy as I could. Granny opened her eyes and smiled. "I'm sorry, honey. Didn't mean to go to sleep on you. That Carter Family lulled me right off. Is the quilting circle over?"

"No ma'am," I said. "Miss Peggy said she's hurting and she needs her medicine. Granny, what's wrong?"

Granny jumped up and hurried out of the room without saying a word. I went behind her. I was determined somebody was going to tell me something. I followed Granny into Miss Peggy's bedroom. Granny was on her knees, reaching underneath Miss Peggy's bed. She pulled out one of Mr. Cecil's old cigar boxes.

"Granny, what's going on?" I asked.

Granny got up from the floor with a weariness I had not seen in a long while. Tears were streaming down her face. "Miss Peggy is dying," she said, trying to choke back the tears. "Her heart is bad, and every day it gets a little bit worse. Poor Doc Henry is doing all he knows to do, but her heart just ain't responding. Most times I have to make her take her medicine. If she's asking for it, then I ain't gone have my friend much longer."

I went over and tried to put my arms around Granny, but she shook her head.

"I gotta go give this to Miss Peggy," she said. I could tell by looking at her that she didn't need to go out as upset as she was. I took the medicine from her hands.

"I'll do it," I said. Normally, I would be the one crying, but I knew this time wasn't about me. Granny needed me to be strong, and I meant to do that for her. I looked at the two bottles she handed me. One was a big word I didn't know how to pronounce. Nitroglycerin. The other was just as hard. Laudanum.

"Give her both?"

"She'll not want the laudanum," Granny said, wiping her tears. Granny reached in her pocket and handed me another bottle. "Here's some aspirin. See if she'll take a couple of those if she won't take the laudanum."

I walked back to the kitchen and got some water, and then walked back into the sewing room where the girls were eating and talking and laughing. They didn't notice that Miss Peggy was sitting quietly to herself on the other side of the room. I went over to where she sat.

"Granny gave me the medicine to give you, Miss Peggy," I said in a low voice.

Miss Peggy looked up at me, and I saw so much in her eyes. Questions about how much I knew. Concern about why Granny wasn't bringing her medicine. But mostly . . . mostly I saw sadness in her eyes.

"It's okay, Miss Peggy," I said, handing her the nitroglycerin. When I tried to hand her the laudanum, she shook her head no. I gave her the bottle of aspirin, and she took two. "Should I send the girls home?"

"I'll be okay. Is Birdie all right?"

"Yes ma'am," I answered. I didn't want to say anything else. I didn't want her to know how upset Granny was.

"Would you get the girls started at the quilting frame?" Miss Peggy asked. "I'll just sit here for a few more minutes and then I'll be over."

"I've got it, Miss Peggy. You just rest up," I said.

I looked around the room at the girls. All of them, except for Miss Lori Beth Parsons and another girl, were busy filling their faces with the sandwiches and my lemon squares. Judging by how quickly the sandwiches were disappearing from the platters, I guessed this was probably the first meal some of them had eaten all day. I found myself feeling sorry for them. Although they all probably thought they were better than me, at least I had a roof over my head and food in my belly every single day. Times were hard, but I was blessed.

"All right, ladies," I finally said. "Miss Peggy wants you to go and work some on the quilting frame. I'll help you with anything you don't remember."

Before I could walk away, Miss Peggy reached for my hand and squeezed it.

"Thank you," she said.

"You're welcome," I said, following a few of the girls who were starting to move toward the quilting frame. I imagined a few of them would have liked to eat more.

Miss Peggy didn't sit for long. Before I knew it, she came over to inspect the girls' handiwork. "You've got just a little more quilting to do, girls, and we'll be ready to wrap up this quilt and give it to Cindy Lou and Dale for their upcoming nuptials. I must say, I love how it is looking. You have all done very nice work using a very complicated pattern. What do you think, Cindy Lou?"

Cindy Lou's face was a bright red as the tears began to fall. "This is the most beautiful quilt I have ever seen. And knowing it was made with such love and care from all of you . . . well . . . I just don't know what else to say."

One of the girls standing beside her gave her a hug. Since Miss Peggy seemed to be back to herself, I decided to go over and start cleaning up. Before I could get to the table, Granny came out in her apron and started picking up plates and cups. She looked like herself again. No tears, just her usual stern face, which hid all the heartbreak she was feeling.

"I can do this, Granny."

"I know, baby," she said. "Granny's okay. Thank you for taking care of things out here. I see Miss Peggy barely let the medicine get into her belly before hopping up. Well, if it makes her happy . . ." Granny trailed off.

"It does," I said in a quiet voice. "This is what she wants to do." I tried not to let myself think about Granny's earlier words about Miss Peggy. Miss Peggy was strong. The only stronger person I knew was my granny. I wasn't going to count Miss Peggy out, and even though I wasn't as strong of a Christian as Granny, I said a silent prayer that God would give Miss Peggy a little more time. I thought about Jimmy Earl. First his grandpa and now . . . I wouldn't let my mind go any further.

"Excuse me," I heard a loud voice say. I almost groaned. It was that Miss Lori Beth Parsons girl. I didn't want to talk to her now. Not when my emotions were every which-a-way.

"Yes ma'am?" I said, barely looking up.

"Oh, you don't have to call me ma'am. I'm probably your age or younger," she said, smiling like she wanted every tooth to show. "Just call me Lori Beth."

I wasn't about to fall for that. White folks liked to set Colored folks up with their fake friendship. One minute they were your friend, and the next they was accusing you of something. "Can I help you, ma'am?" I asked.

"Do you want more to eat, ma'am?" Granny asked, with both her hands on her hips, looking Miss Lori Beth Parsons up and down. I could tell Granny didn't trust her either.

"No. I was hoping to speak with Opal for a minute," she said, holding tight to a notebook and pen that she had just been scribbling in.

"What's that you're writing?" Granny asked. Come to think

of it, she had been scribbling in that notebook ever since she'd gotten here. Miss Peggy would say something and she would "scribble scribble." Even when Miss Peggy was just showing the girls things, she was doing the same thing: "scribble scribble."

She kept smiling as she talked. "Well, my father is going to let me do some writing for the *Parsons Gazette* this summer, and I thought I'd write about the quilting circle," she said.

"Did you clear that with Miss Peggy?" Granny asked. "I don't know if she would like to have her business strewed all out there for folks to read."

"Clear what with me?" Miss Peggy asked. I jumped. I didn't even hear her walk up.

Miss Lori Beth Parsons had the good graces to look flustered, but only for a moment. "Well, Miss Peggy, I was able to convince my daddy that he could get more readers—women readers—if he printed more stories that women would like, besides just the occasional sewing or quilting pattern. He's giving me a chance to prove my words by allowing me to write the occasional story, starting with my write-up about the quilting circle you've been hosting. Just look around you, Miss Peggy. So many young women in this community know how to quilt because you taught them. Now that's a story worth telling."

"It would have been nice if you had asked first," Miss Peggy said in a dry voice.

Miss Lori Beth hung her head. "I'm sorry. You're right. I can go."

"Well, for you to be a newspaper girl, you aren't very persistent. You gonna give up that easy?" Miss Peggy asked.

"No ma'am," Miss Lori Beth Parsons said, unhunching her shoulders.

Miss Peggy's face softened. "I guess it's all right for you to do a story. A short story. I don't want a whole lot of brouhaha over what we're doing. Just a small write-up will suffice."

Miss Lori Beth Parsons smiled, nodding her head in agreement. "Yes ma'am. I'll keep it short and to the point."

Miss Peggy nodded her head. "You're mighty young to be taking on something like this. Is this for school?"

Miss Lori Beth chewed on the end of her pencil, as if trying to pull together just the right answer. "No ma'am. I can't take journalism classes at boarding school until I'm a junior, and I'm just a sophomore. I'm just trying to show my father that I truly have what it takes to take over the newspaper someday. When I'm done with high school, I hope to study journalism in college. I want to be more than just a pretty little face. I want to be a journalist like Dorothy Thompson."

"Who?" I asked.

Granny and Miss Peggy looked at me quickly, but I couldn't help myself. I wanted to know more about what Miss Lori Beth was saying. Finally, she had me interested.

"Dorothy Thompson," Miss Lori Beth said. "She interviewed Adolf Hitler in *Harpers Monthly* a couple of years ago. 'Good-by to Germany' was the name of the article she wrote. Her writing was positively brilliant and I want to be just like her."

"Well," Miss Peggy said, starting to look weary again. "I suppose writing little articles every now and then can't hurt. But eventually, you're going to have to give all that up."

"Why is that, Miss Peggy?" Miss Lori Beth asked.

"Mothers and wives don't have time for extra foolishness," Miss Peggy said. "You can't write stories and run a household at the same time. But I guess it's okay for you to play at it for now."

I watched Miss Lori Beth as she winced at Miss Peggy's words, but all she said was, "Yes ma'am." I could tell by the look on her face she didn't agree with Miss Peggy, and maybe she had something else in mind for her future . . . something besides getting married and birthing babies.

I had never met a girl quite like her. Every girl I knew, Colored or white, was waiting for the day she could become a wife or a mother. That was all we knew. That was all we had ever seen. Even my girl cousins who went off to college were still determined to get married someday. I couldn't imagine living Miss Lori Beth Parsons's life, but it was sure interesting and so different from mine.

"Why don't you come sit by me and ask your questions. No need worrying Birdie and Opal anymore," Miss Peggy said.

A part of me wanted to hear the rest of that conversation. A part of me wanted to hear someone talk about a life that wasn't like my own. But I knew better than to march myself over to Miss Lori Beth and Miss Peggy. Granny and I kept cleaning up, and by the time we were done, the girls had packed up all of the materials and had said their goodbyes. All except Miss Lori Beth. She and Miss Peggy were deep in conversation with each other. I wondered if she planned on staying for dinner. Even though Jimmy Earl was practicing baseball for the Founder's Day game between the white Methodists and the white Baptists, I knew he should be getting home any minute. The cucumber soup was ready and chilling in the refrigerator along with the left-over sandwiches. I had wrapped up the lemon squares and put them on the counter. I had already packed up two of them for Cedric and put them into my bag. Normally, Miss Peggy and Miss Corinne would straighten up after their evening meal so Granny and me wouldn't have to stay so late.

"Granny, I think I'll walk on home," I said, taking off my apron and hanging it on the hook by the back door.

"Chile, it is hotter than a hornet's nest outside. Why don't you wait here for your Uncle Myron," Granny said. "He'll be here in a little bit. And to be honest, I don't want you out there by yourself after last night."

"I know, Granny," I said. "I just like walking, especially after being cooped up inside all day. And I promise, I won't take any back roads."

"I just worry about you out there by yourself," she repeated, her eyebrows knitting together.

"I'll stay on the main road," I promised again.

"All right then," she said. I was just about to leave out when Miss Peggy walked into the kitchen.

"Opal, I know it's about time for you to leave, but I wondered if you could wait until Jimmy Earl gets home so you could ride with him to take Lori Beth to her house. I don't want her out this late in the day by herself on some bicycle. And it ain't fitting for her to be riding alone with Jimmy Earl," Miss Peggy said.

Before I could respond, Granny spoke up for me. "Of course she'll wait. Isn't that right, Opal?"

I nodded my head and said, "Yes ma'am. I'll wait."

Somehow, I knew I wouldn't be giving those lemon squares to Cedric.

9

It didn't seem like Jimmy Earl would ever get home. Four o'clock became five, and five o'clock became six, and before you knew it, Uncle Myron had already come to pick up Granny. Before he got there, I had asked Granny if Uncle Myron could take Miss Lori Beth home. Granny had looked at me like I was crazy.

"Your uncle can't be driving around some strange white girl," she had said. "Them Parsons don't know him like that, and even if I was sitting up in there, they'd be liable to have a fit. No, it's best if you do what Miss Peggy asked and wait on Jimmy Earl. He'll be home soon, and once y'all are done taking her home, he can bring you to the house."

I truly wanted to talk back to her and say, "I don't want to be their chaperone." I wanted to go find Cedric and make things right between him and me. But I knew she didn't know that there was anything special between me and Cedric. And then again, who knew if there was? We'd only really had that one time . . . that one kiss.

After Granny left, I tried to make myself busy. First I cleaned up Miss Peggy's sewing room while she and Miss Lori Beth went into the living room and continued talking. Next I went up to Miss Corinne's room and helped her straighten up.

Miss Corinne's bedroom looked like a little girl's room. Her daddy, Mr. Cecil, had painted it this really girlie pink color before he died, and everywhere the eye could see there was a baby doll. For each birthday, Christmas, Mother's Day, Easter, you name it, Miss Corinne got a doll. And she tended to them just like they were her babies.

I started picking up clothes she had tossed to the floor, and the little children's picture books that she liked to read to her doll babies. Her hymnal that she liked to sing from was placed neatly on her side table by her bed.

"Today was a good day, wasn't it, Opal?" she asked, folding some of the doll dresses Miss Peggy and I had made for her babies.

I reached over and smoothed down Miss Corinne's wild curls. "Yes ma'am. You did mighty good today. I'm proud of you."

Her face split into a wide grin. "Aww. You are too sweet, Opal Pruitt. Proud of me," she repeated and giggled like a little girl. "Nobody says that to me."

For some reason, it made me sad to hear her say that. Granny was all the time telling me she was proud of me about one thing or the other. I didn't want to think of anyone not hearing those words. I knew Miss Peggy loved Miss Corinne, but I also knew that she was a bit disappointed about how Miss Corinne turned out. She never said so, but I could tell by the look in her eyes when Miss Corinne was having one of her spells.

"Well, if nobody ever tells you them words again, you just know I will always be proud of you, Miss Corinne," I said.

Miss Corinne reached out and pulled me into a hug. "You're a good girl, Opal. I love you and I am proud of you too."

We stood there and hugged for a moment. I was taller than Miss Corinne, so she laid her head on my shoulder like she was a little girl. Miss Corinne and my mama weren't too far off in age. They pretty much grew up together like me and Jimmy Earl. Granny said they never took to each other like me and Jimmy Earl did. She said Miss Corinne was a bit strange even when she was a girl, so it made it hard for her and my mama to connect with each other.

"You ready to go back downstairs and eat?" I asked Miss Corinne.

"Yes. Maybe Jimmy Earl will get here soon. That girl sure is pretty. You reckon Jimmy Earl will be sweet on her?" Miss Corinne asked as she reached down and picked up a stray shoe that we had missed. I took it from her because I could see she was about to toss it across the room. I took it to her closet and put it next to its match.

"I don't know, Miss Corinne," I said. "Miss Lori Beth Parsons is pretty. I reckon if Jimmy Earl is gonna be sweet on anybody, it'll be a girl like that."

I took Miss Corinne by the hand and we went downstairs. Jimmy Earl had finally made it home. He was filthy from playing baseball, and his face was as red as his hair.

"Hey, Lori Beth," I heard him say. "Your cousin Courtland didn't say you'd be home this week."

"This is my second week home," she said. "I've just been working on a few things, so nobody really knows I'm back. And anyway, I hardly know anybody, what with me being away at school so much."

Miss Corinne and I went closer to them. I cleared my throat and was just about to ask if Jimmy Earl was ready to take Miss Lori Beth home, but Miss Peggy cut me off before I could say a word.

"Everybody, Lori Beth is going to stay and have supper with us. I sent a message by Tote to take to her family so they know she is okay," Miss Peggy said, smiling like Miss Lori Beth was her new best friend. I nearly groaned. This meant it would be really late before I got home. *Oh well*, I thought. *I guess my lemon squares for Cedric will just have to wait.*

"I'm gonna run upstairs and get cleaned up," Jimmy Earl said. "I'll be back down before Bean can get the table set." Then he took off running, taking the stairs two at a time.

Things got quiet, and then Miss Corinne went over and touched Miss Lori Beth's hair. To her credit, Miss Lori Beth did not flinch or anything.

"Corinne, get your hands out of that girl's hair. What are you thinking?" Miss Peggy asked, her face red from embarrassment. Miss Peggy hated when Miss Corinne acted up in front of guests.

"I think it was in *Ladies Home Journal* that I read Joan Crawford washes her hair with beer to make it shiny and soft. You do that?" Miss Corinne asked.

"Corinne," Miss Peggy said, continuing to look scandalized. "You did not read no such thing in *Ladies Home Journal*. They wouldn't print such smut inside those pages. Whoever heard of any kind of upstanding woman like Joan Crawford putting spirits in her hair?"

I looked from Miss Corinne to Miss Peggy, silently praying they weren't about to have one of their famous knock-down, drag-outs right there in front of Miss Lori Beth Parsons.

Miss Lori Beth didn't seem flustered by their squawking in the least. "Mrs. Ketchums, I've heard of women using beer to condition their hair. Not sure where I read it, but I just wash my hair with soap and water. Sometimes I rinse it with vinegar. Or sometimes Omer, our housekeeper, will make something for me to use. I think she uses honey and raw eggs or something like that."

"You should think about washing it in beer too," Miss Corinne continued, her face solemn and thoughtful, speaking as if Miss Peggy hadn't already fussed her out for talking about such things. "Joan Crawford's hair is beautiful and the article said it was the beer that did it. Your hair is pretty, too, but I bet it would be even more beautiful if you used beer. What kind of beer you 'spect she uses?" she asked, but of course she didn't slow down enough to wait for an answer. "Daddy used to drink Pabst beer, but me and Mama didn't wash our hair in it or nothing. Maybe we should have, though, since Joan Crawford uses it. Don't y'all think her hair is beautiful?"

"Miss Peggy, would you like for me to go ahead and serve supper to you, Miss Corinne, and Miss Lori Beth?" I said.

"Yes, Opal," Miss Peggy said with a grateful look on her face. "Jimmy Earl can just catch up with us when he is done. Corinne, go with Opal and help her with whatever she needs help with."

I went over to Miss Corinne and took her by the hand and led her to the kitchen. I handed her the tray that was stacked high with ham and pimento cheese sandwiches.

"Miss Corinne," I said.

"Hmm?" she said.

"Maybe you shouldn't talk about washing hair with beer any more today," I said.

She nodded her head. "Okay, Opal. Is Mama mad at me? Is you mad?"

"It's okay. Nobody is mad at you, but that's not a good conversation for you to have. Maybe talk about your sewing or your doll babies."

A tear slid down Miss Corinne's face. "You're not proud of me anymore, are you, Opal?"

I groaned. Sometimes Miss Corinne could be extra sensitive. "Miss Corinne, I will always be proud of you. No matter what. And so will Granny, Jimmy Earl, and your mama. Okay?"

Her face brightened right back up.

"Now let's go take this food out to the table so y'all can eat. Okay?" I said.

Miss Corinne followed me back out, and just as we were putting the food on the table, Jimmy Earl came running back downstairs. He was dressed in his Sunday pants and shirt, and he reeked of cologne. I guessed Miss Corinne was right. It seemed that Jimmy Earl was sweet on Miss Lori Beth. I excused myself and went back to the kitchen. They could finish serving themselves. I was tired. I was ready to go, but I had to wait until they got through eating. Once again, I found myself not liking Miss

Lori Beth Parsons that overly much. Because of her, the most I was going to be able to do with the rest of my day was go home, get washed up, and go to bed, and then start the day all over again tomorrow.

Around seven, Jimmy Earl came to the kitchen where I was sitting and waiting. I wasn't going to clear a single dish. I was ready to go.

"Bean, you ready?" he asked.

I almost said I had been ready for hours, but I didn't. It wasn't his fault I had to stay late. I went in and said good night to Miss Peggy and Miss Corinne and told them I would straighten up in the morning, and then I went outside and stood by Jimmy Earl's truck. There was still a few more hours in the night. I tried not to think about Cedric. He was probably already at home eating dinner with his family, not even giving me a second thought.

Miss Lori Beth Parsons and Jimmy Earl finally came outside laughing and carrying on about something. My patience was worn. I stood there tapping my foot as they made their way to the truck.

Jimmy Earl helped Miss Lori Beth into the truck, and I slid in beside her. I didn't care that he didn't think to help me up into the truck. I was just ready to go home. He slammed the door shut, and then he ran around to the driver's side and hopped in.

"Lori Beth, I'm gonna apologize ahead of time," he said. "This old truck used to be my Grandpa Muldoon's, and it rides rough as an old bucking horse."

"That's okay. Thank you for agreeing to take me home,"

she said. "Oh wait. My bicycle is outside by your granny's front porch. Would you mind getting it for me?"

"No problem at all," Jimmy Earl said and hopped out of the truck again. I was thankful for the quiet, but it didn't last long.

"Did you have a good day, Opal?" Miss Lori Beth asked, smiling that toothy smile of hers again.

"Yes ma'am," I said, stopping myself from gritting my teeth. *Of course my day was just lovely*, I thought to myself. *There ain't nothing I love better than waiting on a bunch of white girls my age or younger all day long.*

"Oh, Opal, I'm sorry," Miss Lori Beth said. "You've been cooking and cleaning and waiting on all of us today. I must have sounded like an arrogant ninny."

I looked at her, really looked at her, and I could tell she was sorry. I had never experienced that before. Most white folks, especially rich white folks, took us for granted and never really thought about our feelings. They never even considered that maybe, just maybe, we got tired sometimes, too, or maybe we didn't feel well all of the time, or just maybe we didn't want to have to be at their beck and call each and every day. Being a housekeeper is what I liked to do, but some days I just wanted to be like Miss Lori Beth. I wanted to be free to be young and care-free too. But before I could say something back to her, Jimmy Earl put her bicycle into the back of the truck and then climbed in.

"That bike must be hard for a little thing like you to maneuver. It's heavy as lead," he said, laughing.

"I'm stronger than you might think," she said.

"I reckon you are," Jimmy Earl said, looking at Miss Lori

Beth Parsons like she was a vision or something. She looked away like she was embarrassed. I turned my back to both of them. I just wanted to go home.

Jimmy Earl finally cranked up his truck and we were off. Like he warned, it was loud and a rough ride, but that didn't stop him from talking and flirting with Miss Lori Beth. By the time we got to the outskirts of town, not far from Miss Lovenia's house, I was done being their chaperone. The two of them had chatted the whole way without saying a word to me, so I was ready to leave them alone to their flirting.

"Jimmy Earl, why don't you let me off here," I said. "Y'all don't have far to go, and anyway, Miss Lori Beth's folks know you're bringing her home. They won't be angry if it's just the two of you."

"Oh no, Opal. Let us take you home. And please, for heaven's sake, call me Lori Beth," she insisted again. "You make me feel like I'm my mama's age. I'm just a girl. Just like you."

I looked at her like she was plumb out of her mind. Just like me? If this rich white girl thought she was just like me, well, something inside her head wasn't working quite right.

"I don't mind walking," I said as Jimmy Earl slowed the truck to a complete stop in the middle of the road. "I like being outside instead of being cooped up inside of a car or truck."

"But Opal," Miss Lori Beth said in a soft voice. "The Klan. Didn't they—"

"They ain't gonna hurt me. They did all of their damage last night," I said.

"Don't worry about Bean, Lori Beth," Jimmy Earl said. "She

knows these backwoods better than the patterns on her own hands. She'll be fine. The Klan won't be at it again anytime soon. They did all they were going to do last night. Crazy fools."

"See," I said. "Jimmy Earl says I'll be fine." Of course, both he and I knew there was no way to predict what the Klan might do. Anything might set them off, and once again we would have a repeat of last night. But at that moment, I was willing to face the Klan and anyone else if it meant I could get out of that truck and breathe in some fresh air. All day I had been cooped up inside. I just wanted the solitude of walking alone in the last few minutes of light.

I got out of the truck and started walking as fast as I could. I could hear Miss Lori Beth Parsons calling me to come back, but I was done. I was done with her insisting I call her "Lori Beth," and I was done with Jimmy Earl's rudeness. I wanted to be home in Colored Town, where I didn't have to be around the Lori Beths and the Jimmy Earls. Between yesterday and today, I had gotten my fill of white folks.

The sun was beginning to set. The sky had those beautiful colors that no paint could hope to imitate. I looked all around me, making sure no one was coming toward me or behind me. I was still spooked from the night before. I still had about twenty minutes of walking to do. If I was lucky, I would make it to the house just before the first star reached the sky.

I knew Granny was going to fuss at me for walking out in the dark by myself. I probably should have just let Jimmy Earl drive me home after he dropped off Miss Lori Beth, but I was tired and not exactly feeling like myself, so if I couldn't be walking down the road hand in hand with Cedric Perkins, then the next best thing was for me to be outside walking underneath the heavens with just me and God. Night was my favorite time of the day. Nighttime was when I could be alone with my thoughts and my dreams.

At nighttime, I was free to dream about my mama, and no matter what, the dream was always the same. I would be walking home from Miss Peggy's house by myself, sort of like what I was doing now, and all of a sudden, this pretty, dark-skinned woman who looked a lot like me would walk up to me and pull me into her arms. At first I would be startled, and then angry, but then all I would feel was love.

"I'm so sorry, baby," she would say over and over and over. "Mama will never leave you again. Please forgive me." And every time when I got to that part of the dream, I felt loved and safe. The fact that she and my father had left me days after I was born didn't matter anymore. All that mattered was she was back and she was sorry she had left me.

I was thinking so hard about my mama and how much I wished my dream could come true, I didn't hear him walk up. I didn't even know he was there until he grabbed me. I screamed, but he put his hand over my mouth. I couldn't see him, but I could smell him. He smelled like chewing tobacco and sweat.

"You thought it was over, didn't you?" the voice said. I immediately recognized it. I bit down on his hand as hard as I could. He yelped, but then he grabbed me hard and slapped me across my mouth.

"You dirty black . . . ," he said. "I'll kill you for that."

I felt blood begin to form inside my mouth from the hard slap. I tried to pull away, but he held on to me tight. I looked around blindly; there was no one to be seen. It was almost all the way dark.

"Don't. Please don't," I begged as he pulled me off the road into a ditch. "Please just let me go home."

"You'll go. But not until I'm done with you," he said and pushed me to the ground. My head must have hit something because everything began to fade to black.

10

leep, little baby, don't say a word. Mama? Mama, why did you up and leave like that, and why won't you come back for me? *Mama's gonna buy you a mockingbird.* "Wake up, daughter. God's grace done saved you this day. So you gotta open your eyes and give the Creator some thanks." *If that mockingbird don't sing.* "Nigger, I told you I was gonna have a piece of you one way or another." *Mama's gonna buy you a diamond ring . . . ring . . . ring.*

I tried to sit up, but my body was screaming out with pain so bad, I just lay there, moaning as I tried to figure out where I was. I squinted, moving my eyes around the room, and not a single thing looked familiar. Everything was cast in shadows. No real light was coming in because there were shades on the windows. All I could make out was the flickering light of a candle across the room. The smell was thick with eucalyptus and peppermint, and some other deep, earthy smells I didn't recognize.

"Granny," I uttered. My voice felt ragged and raw. "Granny?"

"Shh," a voice said. "Drink this."

A small hand held a cup to my lips. I tried to make out the face, but my eyes were swollen and blurry with tears. I reached up and touched my face and winced. It felt painful. Like it had been skinned up or something. I tried to move, but my stomach and my sides felt bruised and battered. I tried to swallow, but my mouth was raw and sore. My body was a bundle of pain the size of Saturday's wash that I carried from the creek up to Miss Peggy's house. I tried to move my lips away from the cup, but the hand was stubborn.

"Drink," the voice said again, urging the cup toward my lips. "Drink and you will feel better. Don't you want to feel better?"

Thinking that maybe I was dreaming, I decided just to drink. Almost immediately, I felt a warm calm making its way from the tippy-tippy points of my toes all the way to the farthest end of the longest strand of hair on my head.

My body floated. "Am I dreaming?" I managed to ask, although my tongue felt huge.

"Yes. If that thought soothes you, then yes, you are dreaming, daughter."

I think I smiled. I also wondered if the voice calling me daughter was my mother, but I remembered she left me a long time ago. She probably wouldn't even recognize me now. I felt like tearing up over that fact, but the sleepiness overtook me, and I slept.

❋

"Opal, wake up. Wake up," a strong, masculine voice said. A voice I instantly recognized.

"Jimmy Earl," I said, straining to open my eyes. But they refused to budge. I groaned. Things had to be bad. He didn't call me Bean.

"Yeah, it's me. Open your eyes," he said. He sounded so upset. In that moment, I couldn't understand why he wanted me to wake up so bad. I wondered if maybe I'd fallen asleep and burnt something on the stove. I'd done that once before, and Granny nearly tore my butt off.

"Jimmy Earl," I said again, still not able to open my eyes. My eyes flickered. They felt heavy, like somebody had put weights on them.

"What did you give her?" I heard him ask in an even angrier voice. "She can't even focus."

"I made her a tea with some things you wouldn't understand, young man," the woman said. Her voice sounded like music. Even though she was speaking tough words to Jimmy Earl, she still sounded almost like she was singing the words instead of speaking them.

"Try me," he said. "I'm going to medical school to be a pharmacist. There's nothing you could give her that I don't already understand isn't safe. Opal needs real medicine."

I tried to sit up, but the pain in my head was so strong, I just couldn't. I let out a huge groan. I tried to wipe my eyes so at least I could see, but touching them hurt so bad I groaned even louder.

"Hold on, daughter," the woman said. "Let me wipe your eyes with this warm rag, and you'll be able to open them easier."

Before I could say something back to the now familiar female voice, I felt something so soothing and so healing to my eyes that

I let out a sigh. I didn't want her to stop rubbing them in that gentle circular motion. In fact, I wanted her to wipe my entire face, arms, and legs with the wonderfully warm cloth, but she abruptly stopped.

"There. Open your eyes," she said.

In small little steps, I opened my eyes. Halfway at first, just to test whether the pain I'd felt in them was really gone, and it was. I opened them wide . . . well, as wide as I could open swollen eyes. I blinked a few times and then saw Jimmy Earl and a smooth-faced Black woman with long white plaits standing over me. Jimmy Earl's face was red and angry.

"Did I burn the food?" I asked.

"What? What food? What is she talking about?" he asked the lady with the pretty white hair.

"She's confused. Her head took a powerful blow. She's got a knot on it the size of a turkey egg, and whoever she ran into beat her from top to bottom. She fought him, but he was too strong. Bless her."

"What y'all talking about?" I asked, trying again to sit up. I felt stiffness in every joint. Not the pain I'd felt the first time I woke up. Just the kind of achiness you feel after you've worked a long, hard day. The way I sometimes felt when I helped Mr. Tote with the garden out back of Miss Peggy's house.

"Opal, who did this to you?" Jimmy Earl growled.

"Not a question you want answered," the woman said.

Jimmy Earl growled again. "Yes, it is. Do you know?"

"It's not for me to know," she replied.

"Opal, who did this?" he asked again.

"Give her time to breathe. Daughter, this is Miss Lovenia. This young man is going to help you sit. I hurt my arm a few days ago, so I'm not strong enough to do it myself. Do you mind if he helps you sit up?" the woman asked.

"No ma'am," I said. Jimmy Earl seemed to hesitate for a moment, but then he put his arms around my shoulder and back and helped me sit up in the bed, as the old woman adjusted the fluffy pillows underneath my back. I felt dizzy, like I was about to fall off the bed onto the floor. I sank back down into the bed and closed my eyes until I felt the movement stop. Then I opened my eyes again.

"How did she get here?" I heard Jimmy Earl ask.

"My sons that flagged you down when you came back this way brought her here. They was out walking when they saw Opal get outta your truck and figured you would come back this way."

"I don't remember seeing them out walking," Jimmy Earl said, his voice sounding suspicious.

"My boys did not hurt Opal," she said.

"I never said—"

She cut him off. "You didn't have to say the words. The person that hurt her is not Colored. There is not a Colored man in Parsons, Georgia, who would have done this child like this. My boys found her after it was over. I wish they could have been there to stop it from ever happening."

"I never should have let her walk home," he said. "Bean, I'm so sorry. I'm so sorry."

"I'm okay," I said.

"No, you're not," he said and put his hand on mine.

"Best you be getting over to her grandmother's place. Let her know the girl is okay, but with that injured head and those bruised ribs, she is going to need to stay put for a day or two," Miss Lovenia said.

"No," I said, trying to sit up again, but the dizziness was too much. "Granny will worry. I gotta go. Jimmy Earl, help me get up."

"You got a hard head, daughter, but you're hurt. Whoever got at you hurt you in more ways than you could know right now. You stay put till the morrow, or the morrow after that," she said. "Your granny can come here if she likes."

"I need to know who did this to you, Opal. Who did this?" Jimmy Earl asked again.

"This what?" I said. By that time I knew something had happened to me, but I couldn't quite wrap my brain around what. I remembered getting out of Jimmy Earl's truck. I remembered walking down the road past Miss Lovenia's house. I remembered . . . I remembered . . . nothing, really. Fragments of things. White hands grabbing at me, pushing me down into a ditch. The sound of my dress tearing. Loud cursing. A loud thud. Then, darkness until I woke up in Miss Lovenia Manu's house.

"Miss Lovenia," I said, looking at her. Why, she had to be nearly a hundred years old, and she didn't look no older than my granny, who was in her sixties. "Miss Lovenia, what happened to me?"

She patted my hand. "The devil tried to hurt you. My boys, Mars and Ares, saved you. That's all you ever need to know. This world we living in is 'bout ready to explode and send us all into little bitty unrecognizable pieces. The best thing we can all do is to move past moments like this. This ain't the time to get sideways in our thinking."

Jimmy Earl looked like he might burst into flames, he was so angry.

"The best thing Opal can do is tell me who did this so I can find the monster and kill him," he said, clenching and unclench- ing his fists. I tried to smile at him to let him know I was okay, but it hurt too much. I couldn't believe Jimmy Earl was carrying on that much about me when just a little while ago he all but threw me outta his truck.

"Too late for you to fix things now," Miss Lovenia said as she pulled up a chair beside my bed and sat down. "Won't change her hurting if'n you did haul off and kill somebody. And do you really want the answers to your questions, Mr. Jimmy Earl Ketchums? Answers that might make you have to choose to bring the clouds or bring the blue sky? You can't do both."

"What the hell are you talking about? Clouds and blue sky," he spat. "I don't care about all of your hocus-pocus. I just want to know who hurt my friend. That's it."

"Oh, she's your friend," Miss Lovenia said with a smile. "Friend? All right then. You need to go tell your friend's granny that she is with me and she is okay. All right, friend?"

I looked from Miss Lovenia to Jimmy Earl. I tried to make my mind tell me what happened. What could I have done to make somebody hate me like that? I felt the tears pushing at my eyes again. I couldn't stop myself. I started blubbering.

"Jimmy Earl, go get Granny. Please," I begged.

"Bean, we have to figure out who did this. I—"

"No. I just want my granny."

"Okay," he said. "I'll go get Birdie. But then you're talking. She'll make you talk." He stomped his way out of the room, leaving me alone with Miss Lovenia.

"Miss Lovenia, I—"

"Daughter, when I was born, I had a caul around my face. Do you know what that means?" she asked. I watched her as she lit a corncob pipe and pulled on it several times before releasing smoke into the air. I loved the smell of a pipe. Jimmy Earl's granddaddy used to smoke a pipe, and when he did, the whole house smelled sweet and spicy.

"No ma'am," I said.

"It means I was born with the eye to see things in ways others can't. Just like my great-great-grandmother, Ona, who was a slave on the Parsons plantation, and my father, who was also a slave on the very same plantation."

"Who did this to me?"

"That will come to you in time," she said. "I see things, chile. Good things, bad things, in-between things. Sometimes I share what I see. Other times, I let people see in God's own time. I believe that is what you must do."

"But don't I need to know? How do I keep from getting hurt again if I don't know?"

Miss Lovenia reached over and stroked my hair. "Evil will find us if it is our time to fight with it. You can't run from your demons. Either you stand up to them, or they eat you up and spit you out."

"But I . . . I . . ."

"Shh," she said, continuing to stroke my head. "The battle you must fight comes later. So don't worry today about what tomorrow will surely bring."

"But I don't know what that means," I said. She was making my head feel like it was going to blow up into little bitty pieces. Everything about this day was a jumbled-up mess in my mind. I couldn't remember who beat me, and I was worried to death that somehow what happened to me was going to start all sorts of trouble for the people I loved. I wished she would stop talking around in circles and just say what it was she was hinting at but not really saying.

"Daughter, we are living in the last days. Your Jimmy Earl Ketchums is about to have to decide if he is on the side of good or evil. The battle spoken about in Revelation is about to begin. Nothing else will matter," she said. "The blood is about to rain down and cover us all."

I tried to twist my body so I could see her better, but the light in the room left her hidden in shadows. She was like a ghost in her white clothes. I was getting scared. I wanted my granny to come and get me. I tried to sit up again, but she reached out her hand and touched my arm. I felt a heat from her hand that didn't seem natural. I tried to pull away, but she kept her hand right where it was.

"You can't run from the future, daughter. Believe me, I've tried," she said as the heat got warmer and warmer. "All you can do is go where it leads you. Sometimes you can change its direction some. Bend it. But you can't break it. The future is going to happen whether we are there to see it or not. So all we . . . all anyone . . . can ever do is try to stay prepared for the battle. That's it."

She put the cup to my lips again. "Drink, daughter. Drink," she said, and because I was ready to escape from Miss Lovenia and all of her confusing words, I did drink. Almost immediately I started to feel warmth come over my entire body . . . a warmth similar to Miss Lovenia's touch, except this warmth was in my insides. It almost scared me, but Miss Lovenia started rubbing my arm and I felt myself relax. I felt my eyelids flutter, and then, I slept.

*

What felt like seconds later, but I know must have been longer, I heard a voice call out to me. It was Granny. Even in the midst of the drowsiness, I knew my granny was there, because I could smell the rosewater perfume she always wore at night after she got done washing off. I felt so bad to make her have to come back out after she was nearly ready for bed.

"Granny! I'm here. I'm here," I cried out in a raspy voice. Miss Lovenia removed her hand from my arm, and I watched as she rose and lit another candle that was on the table beside the bed. The light made it bright enough for me to make out my granny's face. But she wasn't alone. Jimmy Earl was with her.

"Who hurt you, baby?" Granny asked, sitting in the chair beside the bed, placing my hand into hers.

"I think it be best if she just rests and not worry about all that, Birdie," Miss Lovenia said. "Some questions don't need answering. Some questions be just like the wind. If you just be still and let God be God, everything will reveal itself in time."

"How can we protect her if we don't know who did this?" Jimmy Earl nearly yelled.

"She's not yours to protect, Jimmy Earl," Granny said in a soft voice. "Opal is my child. Me and her uncles will look after her. You should just go home."

"But, Birdie, I—"

"Go home, Jimmy Earl. Let Miss Peggy know me and Opal won't be coming in for a few days. And make sure you tell her exactly what I said. No more, no less. You hear me, Jimmy Earl?"

Jimmy Earl looked angrily from Miss Lovenia to Granny, but then his face softened. He walked over to me and lightly took my other hand.

"The second you remember who did this to you, Colored or white, I don't care. You tell me who hurt you and I will take care of him one way or another."

"That's enough," Granny said. "That's enough. Right now, I need to see about Opal. Go home, Jimmy Earl."

"I'll stop by after work tomorrow," he said and looked from Granny to Miss Lovenia as if to dare them to say no to that. Neither one of them said anything.

Jimmy Earl placed my hand back on the bed and walked out of the room.

"I want to go home, Granny," I said, the tears spilling out of my eyes causing them to burn.

Granny took my hand and shook her head. "No. We gone

listen to Miss Lovenia. She said you need to stay put, so stay put is what we both gonna do until you can be took home."

"Doc Henry—" I started, but she interrupted.

"No. We gone stay put, and there ain't no need pulling Doc Henry into this mess," Granny said, and then she looked up at Miss Lovenia. "If that's okay with you, Miss Lovenia."

I was shocked. Where was all of Granny's hoodoo talk? Where was her "We Christians don't fool around with hoodoo people"?

"Y'all just make yourselves at home. Y'all might hear some bumping around during the night. Don't be scared," she said, moving toward the door. "My boys get restless during the night and they sometimes go out walking."

"They might shouldn't do that," Granny said. "It ain't safe for Colored men to go walking out here with them evil men still around and about."

"My boys are covered. Won't no harm come to them," Miss Lovenia said with such certainty that I believed her words. She walked out before Granny could say something back to her.

"Does anyone in the family know what happened?" I asked. I was scared to death that the uncles might get themselves in trouble because of me. I still didn't remember who hurt me, but I didn't put it past them to go out and just start hunting down white folks.

"No. Nobody knows. It's best that way till we get you home," Granny said. "Jimmy Earl knows to keep his mouth closed."

"What we gonna tell folks happened to me, Granny?" I asked as Granny climbed in the bed beside me.

"We ain't gone worry none about that tonight," she said. "You just close your eyes, say your prayers, and rest. You'll feel better in the morning, and by then we'll know exactly what to say."

"Granny," I whispered, the tears starting to fall again.

"Yes, baby?"

"Why do some white folks hate us so bad?" I asked. I couldn't remember who did this to me . . . no face was coming to my mind . . . but I remembered white hands pushing me down, and then . . . nothing.

Granny didn't answer me; instead, she put her arms around me and began to whisper her prayers.

11

*A*re you okay, baby?" Granny asked from the door of my bedroom. This was probably the hundredth time she'd asked me. It was early Thursday morning, and she and I hadn't long got home from Miss Lovenia's house. Miss Lovenia had gotten one of her sons to bring us home in their Model T car. Granny still wasn't ready to explain our absence to the family. I didn't mind. I wasn't looking forward to that conversation, either, especially since I couldn't remember anything yet. Miss Lovenia said it was because I hit my head so hard on the rock, it caused my memories to get thrown out of whack. She also said God sometimes protects us from the truth until we are well enough to handle it.

"Baby, did you hear me?" Granny called out again. "Are you feeling okay?"

"Yessum, I'm fine," I said, sitting up some to show her I was feeling better.

She smiled. "All right then. Make sure you finish drinking that tea I put by your bedside earlier. Miss Lovenia said it would help that knot at the back of your head to go away and help out with the pain. I'll check back with you later." She crept back out the room.

I let myself slump back down on my pillow. I hoped she went somewhere to sit down and rest, but knowing Granny, she was probably just pacing the floor till she could come back to check on me again.

Of course, I wasn't fine. I was still pretty banged up, and I still couldn't figure out who had hurt me. I knew somebody roughed me up, and I could remember the hands being white, but that's about all I remembered. Miss Lovenia said my not remembering was a blessing from God. I didn't know about all of that, but I had to admit, in some way, I was happy I couldn't put a face to all of this. I didn't really want to know that somebody I had to see on a regular basis had done something awful like beat me up. Granny said I was blessed that the man didn't have his way with me. I was thankful for that too. I'd heard stories of Colored girls getting raped by white men. I said several thank-yous to God for sparing me from that. When I mentioned it to Miss Lovenia, she said her boys might have scared him off, or maybe he got scared when he saw me black out from hitting my head on the rock.

"Whatever the reason, we shall give thanks," she finally said, and that was good enough for me.

For the last few days, Granny and Miss Lovenia had hardly left my side, making sure I didn't overdo it. Miss Lovenia kept giving me different teas to drink. One tea she made out of pennyroyal. It didn't taste bad like some of the other things she had me drinking. It had a minty taste to it. She said it would help my headache. And, to my surprise, it did.

"Everything we ever need to heal ourselves grows out of God's good earth," Miss Lovenia said. She'd also made a poultice out of burdock leaves for the swelling and bruising on my face, arms, and legs. "After a few days, won't nobody even be able to tell you got them bruises."

But I'll be able to tell, I thought. *Even when those bruises have faded away to nothing, I'll remember them. Every one of them. And I'll remember that somebody hated me enough to beat me for no reason other than my skin was a dark shade of brown.* Or at least that was all I could come up with to explain the treatment I had received.

I heard a knock at the door.

"Come in," I said, knowing it was Granny. Sure enough, it was her, but her face looked worried.

"Opal, that Parsons gal is outside. Jimmy Earl must have told her what happened," Granny said. "You want me to tell her you don't want no company?"

I paused for a moment. A part of me wanted to see her just to have someone to see, but the other part of me didn't want to be bothered, especially with me being bruised in the face still. Finally, I decided maybe it would be best for me to talk to her and see what she wanted and to make sure she didn't tell anybody what had happened to me.

"Tell her to come in. At least for a little bit."

"I'll go get that gal, but don't let her tire you out," she said, and then she bent down and kissed my forehead. "I'll give you a minute or two to get yourself pulled together."

I watched as Granny walked out, and I looked around my little room. It wasn't fancy. Miss Peggy had made me some lacy yellow curtains for my windows, but other than that, it was pretty plain. This was my uncles' bedroom when they were growing up (I had refused to sleep in the room that had been my mama's), and I hadn't changed too much about it. Lucille had asked me several times if I wanted to redo the room so it was more fitting to my personality, but to be honest, I didn't know what that even meant. So I just always said no. And because I spent so much of my time at Miss Peggy's house, it just didn't seem like a good use of my time trying to make this bedroom feel "more like me," as Lucille put it. But now, with Miss Lori Beth Parsons about to enter my room, I wished I had listened to Lucille and at least tried to make it a little less like my uncles'.

I reached up and touched my hair. It was all over my head. I smoothed it down as best I could and fluffed up my bed coverings some. All that motion made my headache come back full strength. I reached on the table for one of the BC Powders Granny had left for me. I opened the packet, leaned my head back, and let the fine white powder slide into my mouth. I swallowed the bitter powder and washed it down with the rest of the tea that was on my nightstand. I was trying to wipe the powder from my mouth when Miss Lori Beth walked in. She was wearing a pair of yellow trousers and a crisp white shirt. I wondered what Granny thought about Miss Lori Beth's outfit. She didn't have anything good to say about girls and women wearing pants. I watched as Miss Lori Beth Parsons hurried over and sat down in the chair beside my bed.

"Oh, Opal, I am so . . . I am so . . . ," she uttered, and then she started crying. I was shocked. I didn't even know Miss Lori Beth Parsons that well. I didn't understand why she was taking on so. I didn't know what to say, so I just sat there in the bed real quiet while she sniffled and took long breaths. "Oh, I'm a mess," she said, reaching into her purse and pulling out this dainty-looking handkerchief. She dabbed at her face and then put the handkerchief back inside her purse. "Opal, I didn't mean to take on so. Just, seeing you there all bruised and bandaged up, well, I can't believe someone would do this to you."

She just kept going on and on. I tried to peer at her face to see if she was being serious or if she was making fun of me, but the more I stared and the more she talked, the clearer it became that she was serious.

"Hearing you had been hurt, Opal, was, well, it was scary to hear because it could have happened to me as well, considering all the times I'm out riding alone," she said.

I almost said, "No, it wouldn't have happened to you because you're Lori Beth Parsons, not some nobody from Colored Town," but I didn't. I just made myself listen to the rest of what she had to say.

"I took Jimmy Earl's grandmother some fabric this morning," she said. "My mother wasn't going to use it, so I told her it might help with the quilting circle. I was shocked when Jimmy Earl told me what happened to you on the day you and he were taking me home. He said not to tell anyone, and I haven't, but I just had to come and see you for myself. Opal, I feel totally responsible. Had you not been trying to help get me home, this might not have ever happened," she said. She looked like she might start crying again.

In the words of my granny, I was fit to be tied over Jimmy Earl telling this girl what had happened to me. He had no right. Here we were trying to keep this a secret from my family, and he just hauled off and told this silly young white girl all of my business. Right then, even as bad as I was feeling, I could have marched downtown to Mr. Lowen's Drugstore and given Jimmy Earl Ketchums a piece of my mind.

"It's not your fault, Miss Lori Beth," I finally said, trying to keep the anger out of my voice. "Whoever did this to me didn't do it because of you." It's funny how I was the one hurt, but she was carrying on like the wrong had been done to her. I didn't doubt that she felt bad for me. It just rankled me a little that I had to comfort her instead of it being the other way around.

"You're being nice. So very nice, Opal. Thank you. But please, please call me Lori Beth," she said. "I'm no different from you. Just a girl."

I couldn't believe she said that. Again. Sitting there in all of her white glory. Smart as a whip. Me and Miss Lori Beth were nothing alike. The only things I knew about for sure was cooking and cleaning up behind white folks. I didn't know a thing about the places she had talked about the other day when Jimmy Earl and I were taking her home. I didn't even know what direction someone would head if they wanted to go to New York or Chicago or "merry ole England," as she had called it. Being around her just made me feel awkward and clumsy and stupid. Suddenly, the only thing I wanted her to do was to leave.

"Opal, are you going to tell the police what happened to you? Jimmy Earl said he didn't think so, but I just wanted to urge you to report this. Whoever did this to you needs to be caught and punished." She spoke with such righteous passion, I almost laughed out loud, but I knew it would just make my head hurt. I couldn't believe how simpleminded she and Jimmy Earl were acting. Didn't no law care about what happened to us Colored folks. And even if they did, telling on the folks who burnt down Granny's chicken coop or who beat me up real bad would only make things worse. Them KKKers would come after us for sure then. So I tried to explain things to her like I was talking to a child.

"Miss Lori Beth, I'm all right. Didn't nobody get killed or nothing. My aches and pains are getting better. We just gone have to watch ourselves more careful now. That's all," I said. "And anyway, don't none of my kin, besides Granny, know what happened to me. It's best if we just let this go."

"You're just going to pretend like nothing happened?" she asked, her eyes stretched wide. "What about other girls? What if the man who did this to you hurts somebody else like me or some other girl? How would you live with yourself? Please . . . think about what you're saying, Opal."

"Miss Lori Beth, I ain't pretending nothing happened, but I ain't pretending the law or anybody else will side with me, a Colored girl, who don't even remember who did this to her," I said. "I just want my head to stop hurting so me and my granny can get back to work at Miss Peggy's. That's all I want."

"Please call me Lori Beth," she said, then her face changed.

She looked so excited, almost like a sunburst about to pop. You'd think she didn't even hear a word I said. "Opal, why don't I take your picture and run an article in the newspaper? Father said I could write about anything I wanted. Why not write about this atrocity that happened to you? Why, any young girl could have gotten assaulted that day, white or Colored. Let me at least do that." Her face was all lit up with excitement, but all I felt was panic as she started rummaging in her bag.

"Miss Lori Beth, your daddy's paper ain't never gonna run no stories 'bout Colored folks. It ain't that kind of paper," I said, trying to reason with her. "And what happened to me wouldn't have happened to a white girl. It just wouldn't have."

She pulled out the camera from her bag. "You can't know that, Opal. Danger isn't out there for just the Colored folks of Parsons. And as far as the paper goes, it should be about everybody who lives in our town, white and Colored. And it definitely should tell the citizens of this town when one of its fellow citizens has been wrongly injured like you have been. Oh, Opal, I don't want to write about quilting circles and Founder's Day celebrations. I want to write about things that matter. And this matters."

I didn't hardly know what to say. I knew I had to stop her. All I could see was my badly bruised face sitting up on the front page of that paper of her daddy's, and the Klan burning down all of Colored Town because of it. "No, Miss Lori Beth. That wouldn't be a good idea for you to do a story about what happened to me," I said. "I can't let you do that."

"But, Opal, this is the least I can do. Please let me tell your story." She reasoned with the innocence of someone who didn't know a thing about the world we both lived in. Her version of the world was all black and white, right and wrong. Mine was every shade of gray you could imagine, where right and wrong only existed for the whitest members of the world. Before I could say anything else, she had the camera pointed at me. She was ready to take my picture when my granny came bursting into the room. She stepped in between me and Miss Lori Beth, blocking her line of sight to take the picture.

"No ma'am. There will be no pictures, and there will be no stories written in white folks' newspapers about what happened to my Opal," Granny said. Granny had complained of her arthritis earlier that day, but right then she was standing tall and firm and unbending.

"But ma'am, I just want to let folks know what happened. I—"

Granny interrupted. "You think folks around here don't know about such as this, Miss Lori Beth? Negroes have known from the second they took their first breath that white folks can't be trusted. You think writing about my Opal in some newspaper is going to make things better? The only thing you will do is get my grandbaby killed. Like I said, there will be no pictures and no stories." She turned and looked at me and then back to Miss Lori Beth. "Judging from the looks of my Opal, she is tired. So I think you should go now." She stepped aside so I could see Miss Lori Beth again. She had put her camera back into her bag, and the sadness had returned to her face again. I felt sorry for her. I knew her heart was in the right place. She just didn't understand how things were.

"I'm sorry. I just wanted to help," she said, tears falling down her face.

I watched Miss Lori Beth walk out the room. Her shoulders were slack and stooped. Like somebody who'd just been beaten in a terrible battle of wills. For a time, neither my granny nor I said anything. We both just kept staring at the door Miss Lori Beth had just left from. Finally, Granny turned back toward me.

"Granny, do you ever think there will be a time when Colored and white folks can just be friends?" I asked. "Like you and Miss Peggy?"

"Me and Miss Peggy are as close to friends as any Colored and white person can be, but even that has its limit," Granny said. "I love Miss Peggy, but I also know that she is my boss before she is my friend."

"It shouldn't be that way," I said.

Granny came and sat beside me on the bed. "There are a lot of things in life that shouldn't be," she said.

I nodded. All of this was way too much, so I closed my eyes, feeling safe just having my granny sitting beside me as I drifted off to sleep.

12

The sound of voices woke me up from a deep sleep. I sat up, looking around the room, a bit confused about where I was. Last night was the first night all week that my head had not hurt to the point where my sleep was fitful. Restless. Nonexistent. I didn't even need any of Miss Lovenia's magic teas last night. Maybe because my body was just plain worn out. Maybe because my mind was so full that sleep was the only reprieve it could find.

The voices in the other room were getting louder, and I wondered what was going on. I could hear my uncles talking to Granny in a tone I had never heard them use with her before.

"You had no right to keep from us that Opal was hurt," Uncle Myron said.

"I had every right not to tell anyone anything about this mess. Opal is mine. I make the decisions for her well-being," Granny said. "Y'all might be my grown-up sons, but I still run this house. Ain't neither one of you my ma or my pa. Let's not forget that."

"Mama, what happened to Opal could have happened to any Colored girl or woman. In fact, it still could," Uncle Myron argued. "Keeping that situation to yourself could have put this entire community in harm's way. It could have put you and Opal in harm's way. How do we know that animal won't come at Opal again? Or you? Or some other Colored woman?"

"Watch your mouth, Myron. What happened didn't happen to just any Colored girl or woman. It happened to my Opal, and I had to protect her *and* I had to protect you boys from rushing out to try and find that white devil who did this to her. I did what was best," Granny said.

"I know that's what you think, Mama, but you was wrong," Uncle Myron said.

"And what about that newspaper article, Mama? Did you agree to that? Did you agree to tell them Parsons what happened to Opal before telling it to her uncles?" That voice was my Uncle Little Bud. His words got me up. What newspaper article?

I slowly tested my feet on the floor. This was the first time in days I had felt steady enough to walk without Granny holding me up. I put my robe over my gown, and I went out into the living room where Uncle Myron, Uncle Little Bud, and Granny were all sitting. No one noticed me. I cleared my throat.

"What newspaper article?" I asked. They all turned and looked at me, but no one spoke at first. "What newspaper article?" I asked again, trying to ignore the horrible looks on their faces when they saw me.

"Father God, what did they do to you, baby?" Uncle Myron said as he stood and walked over to me. He cupped my chin with his hand and raised it slightly so he could see my face better, and I was shocked to see tears in his eyes. I had not seen Uncle Myron cry since Aunt Josephine died. I knew he loved me, even though we were constantly at odds over my being a housekeeper like Granny, but I didn't know, until that moment, just how much he loved me.

"I'm okay, Uncle Myron," I said in a soft voice. He gently hugged me. In that moment, I felt closer to Uncle Myron than I had ever felt before. Uncle Little Bud came over and hugged the both of us. He had the newspaper in his hand, and I took it.

"Baby, don't. You don't need to see that mess," Granny said.

"If it has to do with me, I have a right to see it," I said. I turned the pages in almost slow motion. I didn't really want to see what was to come, but when I did, the headline almost jumped off the page. "Young Colored Girl Assaulted," it said. "My God," I muttered under my breath. I read out loud. "'Parsons, Georgia, was once a place young women could feel safe to walk the backcountry roads with or without the accompaniment of an older brother, cousin, uncle, or father. Not anymore. On Monday, June 15, 1936, a young Colored girl was attacked as she walked back home after working all day in a local home as a housekeeper. She doesn't remember who hurt her, which makes this all even more terrifying. This attack was not just an attack on this young Colored girl but an attack on all women and girls.'"

I stopped reading and looked up at Granny. "She said she wouldn't print it," I whispered. Uncle Myron led me over to Grandpa's rocker. I gratefully sat down. I was feeling wobbly from my head injury and this conversation. He and Uncle Little Bud went back to the couch and sat on either side of Granny.

"No. She never said those words. She never promised us," Granny spat out. "I shoulda never let that gal inside this house."

Before we could say anything else, there was a loud knocking at the door. Uncle Myron got up to answer it. Before he could reach the door, Cedric came inside, his face filled with rage. He was wearing his work clothes, and his face was dripping with sweat. I couldn't tell if it was from the heat or from his anger. Maybe both.

"It was you," he said, his voice sounding all gruff. "You the one the paper was talking about, ain't you?" I couldn't say anything. My face was still bruised. There was a bandage around my head. There was no way I could deny the obvious.

"Stank, what you mean bursting in here like somebody outta their fool mind?" Uncle Myron asked. "You need to go. We got family business to tend to."

Cedric walked over to me like Uncle Myron hadn't said a word. He stopped in front of the rocking chair I was sitting in and knelt down on one knee.

"This ain't the time for you to come calling. My brother done told you we busy, son," Uncle Little Bud said. "Go on about your day. We've got this under control."

Cedric reached up and gingerly touched my face. "You okay?" he asked. Still ignoring my uncles.

I nodded. It was like I couldn't find my words with his fingers brushing against my cheek. It was like there was no one in the room but me and Cedric. Finally, I found my words again. "I'm okay."

"Boy, get your hands off my niece," Uncle Myron said, coming over to where Cedric knelt. I thought he was going to yank Cedric away, but Uncle Myron just stood clenching and unclenching his fist. Cedric still didn't pay him no attention. He took my hand and held it.

"Who did this to you?" Cedric asked in a soft voice. "Who hurt you like this, Opal?"

"I don't know. I don't remember," I said. I felt a tear slide down my face. Before I could wipe it away, Cedric took his thumb and blotted it, and every tear that fell behind it. It was the sweetest, kindest thing I had ever experienced. Just that one thing, wiping away my tears, made me feel like the luckiest girl ever. In that one gesture, it was like he was trying to wipe away every tear I had ever shed. I wasn't thankful I got hurt, but I was glad that getting hurt brought Cedric to our house this morning.

"Cedric Perkins, you best go on home now. My sons are riled up enough," Granny said.

I looked around and saw everyone's faces and realized as much as I wanted Cedric to stay, I had to convince him to go because my uncles were spoiling for a fight and I didn't want it to be with Cedric.

"I'm okay, Cedric," I said. "I appreciate you coming over to see about me, but you didn't have to do that. I'm okay."

"Yes, I did have to come see about you," he said as he got up from the floor. He stood looking straight in the eyes of Uncle Myron. "Sir, I mean you no disrespect. I mean none of you no disrespect, and I understand I'm not who y'all would probably want for Opal, but I care about her. Miss Birdie, Mr. Myron, and Mr. Little Bud, I hope you will let me and her start keeping company."

"Keep company," I heard Granny snort. "Opal is too young to be keeping company." Before I could say something, Cedric spoke again.

"She'll be eighteen in a few days, ma'am," he said in a quiet voice. I was shocked he would know such a thing. I guessed my cousin M.J. and he had been talking about more than baseball. "I haven't been the best person I can be. I'll own up to that. But the thought of having Opal by my side someday makes me want to be a better man. I know I will need to prove myself to all of you, but I am willing to do what it takes to win y'all over."

"God is the only somebody you will need to prove yourself to. And son, if the Father, the Son, and the Holy Ghost don't make you want to be a better man, there ain't nothing my Opal can do for you," Granny said. "Now, Cedric, don't make us have to tell you again. This is family business. You need to be on your way."

"I—" he started, but was interrupted by a knock at the door.

"Lord have mercy. Is all of Parsons gonna knock at my door this morning?" Granny asked, slowly raising herself off the couch to go to the door.

Uncle Little Bud motioned for her and the rest of us to be still as he took a gun out of his pocket.

Granny gasped. "Boy, put that thing away."

Uncle Little Bud ignored Granny and went to the door. "Who is it?"

"It's me, Jimmy Earl Ketchums and Sheriff Ardis," Jimmy Earl called out. Uncle Little Bud slipped his pistol back inside his pocket. He opened the door and let Jimmy Earl and the sheriff into the room. Uncle Myron motioned for me to go to the bedroom. Grateful, I got up to leave, pulling my robe tight, but before I could make it to my bedroom door, the sheriff spoke.

"Young lady, I need to speak to you, please," he said. His voice was so loud I jumped, and Granny jumped up with a quickness I couldn't remember seeing for some years. She came over to stand in front of me, shielding me from the view of the sheriff.

"What do you need to speak to my niece about?" Uncle Myron asked, walking over to the door and standing by Uncle Little Bud, keeping Jimmy Earl and the sheriff from getting any closer to me. "She ain't got nothing to say about nothing."

I looked over at Cedric. His face was blank, but I could see the anger in his eyes. He finally looked at me, but I couldn't take his stare. I turned my eyes to the floor.

"I believe your niece has got something to do with that article in the newspaper," Sheriff Ardis said. "And judging by the bruises and the bandage, I 'spect I'm right. Ain't that so, gal?"

Before I could say something, Uncle Myron spoke again. "We don't know nothing about that newspaper story."

"Then what happened to your niece's face?" he asked. He pulled out a bag of Red Man chewing tobacco and packed his jaw full of the sickly smelling stuff. No one said anything. It was like we was all frozen and couldn't speak. "Well, I see now. Nobody wants to answer me that. Well, why don't we talk about something else? Let's talk about that burnt-down chicken coop. What happened to that?"

Uncle Little Bud finally spoke up. "An accident. We was burning trash for my mama, and it got out of hand."

The sheriff pushed his way around Uncle Myron and Uncle

Little Bud. "I ain't here for no games. I know the Klan rode through Colored Town this past Sunday. I know the next day a Colored girl from Colored Town got beat up by somebody, and lo and behold, this young girl looks like she's gone a few rounds with Jack Dempsey. So I need y'all to cut the crap and tell me once and for all what happened to this girl."

"She fell," Uncle Little Bud said.

"She fell," the sheriff repeated with a harsh laugh. "She fell. Well, I imagine she did after somebody knocked the mess out of her. So if y'all are ready to speak the truth, I'm ready to listen. And right now, I want the girl to speak for herself. I don't have all day. Jimmy Earl over there can't seem to tell me the truth, either, so I need this gal to tell me who or what bashed her face in like that."

"Officer, we don't want no more trouble," Granny said. "We don't know nothing about what you're talking about."

"Gal, I said for you to speak," the sheriff said, ignoring Granny and focusing his eyes on me. "You people say you want the law to protect you, and when we try to, y'all lie and give us half-truths. So, gal, I'm gonna ask you one more time, who did this to you?"

"I don't know, sir," I mumbled. "All I remember is waking up with my granny looking after me." I didn't want to bring Miss Lovenia into this conversation. I didn't know what she might say. I felt bad enough that my kinfolks were lying on my behalf.

"You heard my niece. She don't know nothing," Uncle Myron said. "Now, Sheriff, if you know all the things you say you know, why are you over here asking my niece questions? Why aren't you somewhere talking to them white boys who like to dress up in white sheets? Everybody knows who they are. They ain't trying to keep no secrets about it."

"Then you name some names. If you know who the Klan is, name them and I'll gladly go find them and question them," the sheriff said.

The room got quiet again. The sheriff let out a loud sigh. "I don't have time for this. When you people are ready to talk, y'all come find me; otherwise, I guess y'all are on your own." The sheriff turned on his heels and left out of the house with a loud slamming of the door. For a good few seconds, didn't nobody say nothing.

"I'm sorry," Jimmy Earl finally said, looking around the room at everyone. "I didn't know what to do. The sheriff had already spoken to Lori Beth, so he knew the girl in the newspaper story worked for Gran. I'm—"

"Sorry," Cedric said, his voice full of anger. "You're sorry. You—"

"Not your battle, Stank. It's time for you to head on out," Uncle Myron said.

This time, Cedric took Uncle Myron seriously. "I'll be back this afternoon when I'm done working, if that is okay with you, Miss Birdie?"

"We'll be here, Cedric," Granny said.

Cedric looked at me hard until I turned away. His stare was so intense, it made it almost impossible to look him in the eye. I heard the door shut, and then the room got quiet again.

"Bean, I'm sorry. I never meant for you to get hurt. I swear I didn't," Jimmy Earl said. I turned and looked at him, but I had no words of comfort to offer him. So I hurried out of the room to my bedroom. I lay down on my bed and closed my eyes, praying sleep would find me again, but all I could do was stare up at the ceiling. After a while, I started hearing doors close. I figured my uncles and Jimmy Earl all went on to work. I didn't get up, though, and finally Granny came into the room and sat in the chair by my bed.

"Opal, are you—" Granny said.

I raised myself up in the bed. "I want to keep company with Cedric Perkins. I will be eighteen next week. That's old enough for me to have a beau. And I want to start helping Miss Lovenia a couple afternoons a week. I won't get behind on my work at Miss Peggy's. I promise," I said.

I didn't look Granny in the eyes. I couldn't. This was the first time in my life that I had ever challenged a decision Granny had made about me, and in this one breath, I was challenging two of them. But I wasn't going to back down. Considering what I had endured this week, I had earned the right to make some decisions for myself.

Granny sat for a few more seconds without saying a word, but then she cleared her throat and said the words I never thought I would hear her say. "You got a right to keep company if you like, and Cedric Perkins seems to want to do right by you. I won't argue with you. And if you are bound and determined to work for Miss Lovenia, you just make sure you keep your Bible with you at all times, and you don't let her practice any of that hoodoo magic on you."

"Thank you, Granny," I said.

I watched Granny as she left out of my room. This seemed like a victory, especially the part about seeing Cedric. And going to help Miss Lovenia only seemed right, considering her sons may have saved me from something unspeakable. And even though she had to know what Granny thought about her and her hoo-doo, she still took care of me. We owed her, and I meant to repay her kindness, even if it did scare me just a little bit.

Ordinarily, I would have said a prayer asking God to give me courage, but I wasn't ready to say too much to God yet. I was still wondering where he had been while that evil person was beating me up by the side of the road.

13

When Cedric knocked on the door about thirty minutes after Granny and I got through eating supper, Granny pulled me close and whispered in my ear. "You might be old enough to keep company, but I ain't gonna have you sitting out there with some boy without me keeping my eyes and ears open. I don't care if he is the preacher's son. I'll be just inside the door sitting and reading my Bible."

"That's fine, Granny," I said. I wasn't gonna complain about Granny staying close by while I visited with Cedric. If the truth be known, I was a bit nervous about being alone with him, or any boy for that matter. Other than my boy cousins and my uncles and Jimmy Earl, I hadn't spent a lot of time around boys. Granny didn't allow it, and I wasn't comfortable with it. The first time Cedric and I had been alone together was the other day, and it was by accident. This was for real. This was a boy coming courting, and I felt unsure about everything.

I wished I had had time to talk to Lucille about it. Even

though I was a tad bit older than her, she was far more knowl-edgeable about everything concerning boys. She wasn't a fast girl, but she watched and she experimented with flirting. I, on the other hand, didn't know the first thing about being a flirt with a boy. I hoped I didn't make a fool out of myself.

I started toward the door, but Granny stopped me.

"Don't ever let a boy think you is too eager. Be patient when it comes to showing your feelings. Boys will respect you for that," Granny said down low. I thought about Hazel Moody. She seemed pretty fast to me with her makeup and quick words, and the boys seemed to love her. But I didn't say that out loud. I knew Granny would have had something to say about that. Every time she saw Hazel Moody, her lips turned down in disapproval.

I watched as she went to the door. I stood behind her, just out of eyeshot.

"How you doing, Cedric?" she asked. Her voice was not as warm as it normally was when company would come calling. I guess considering this was the first boy to ever come calling for me, her dryness was understandable.

"Good evening, Miss Birdie," he said. I waited for a moment, and then I walked up to the door. Cedric immediately began to smile. "Hi, Opal."

I still couldn't get over how pretty his smile was. It almost didn't feel right for a boy to have such a pretty smile. I could hardly speak, I was so busy staring. Granny poked me gently in my rib.

"Hi, Cedric," I said, my voice sounding hoarse. I was ashamed I had been caught gazing at him like that. It didn't seem to bother

Cedric because he smiled even bigger. I couldn't resist his smile, so I smiled back. I realized then that I was completely and totally smitten with Cedric Perkins. I knew me and Lucille were going to have hours of talking to do after this.

I noticed that he had gone home and cleaned up after work. He looked so handsome in his clean pair of jeans and white shirt. I was happy I had put on a fresh dress and fixed my hair. I had started off putting on one of my church dresses, but then finally decided on a dress Miss Corinne had made for me with her mama's help for my birthday last year. It was beige colored with yellow flowers. It had a V-neck, short, puffy sleeves, and a mid-calf flared skirt. I felt so adultlike in that dress. Until today, I hadn't found a good reason to wear it. I was glad I had saved it.

I still had bruises on my face, but they weren't as bad as they had been. My dark skin didn't allow for the bruises to stand out as much as if my skin were light like Granny's or Lucille's, so that was another reason for me to love my dark complexion.

Granny finally cleared her throat, pulling me out of my daydreaming. "Y'all children can go sit out on the porch for a while. It's cooler out there than it is inside. Have you eaten supper yet, Cedric?"

"Yes ma'am. Mama had supper cooked when I got done in the fields, so I ate before I left," he said. I had never heard Cedric sound so proper. He sounded exactly like the type of boy Granny said she wanted for me.

"Well, that's good," Granny said. "You tell Brother and Sister Perkins I said hello when you get home. I'll leave you children to visit for a while. I'll be right in here reading my Bible." And true to her word, Granny sat down in a chair she had pulled close to the door.

"Thank you, Granny," I said. I allowed myself to be guided outside by Cedric, his hand barely touching the small of my back. We went over to the porch swing, and Cedric started to gently swing us. For a moment, we didn't say anything. He just took my hand in his, and we enjoyed each other's company. The swinging created a slight breeze. It was still powerfully hot outside, but I barely felt it.

Finally, I couldn't take the silence anymore. "Did you have a good day?"

He shrugged. "It was okay. I spent most of my time making sure the farm animals didn't get too thirsty. I don't think we gonna have much of a crop this year if this drought don't let up soon."

I nodded and then added, "I was listening to Lou Zoller earlier today on the radio. He said he didn't think things would get better anytime soon," I said. I felt silly talking about the weather, but I didn't know what else to talk about. I had never talked to a boy like this before. I had known Cedric my entire life, but he and I had never really talked to each other. I worried that my inability to act flirty like Lucille and womanly like Hazel Moody would cause Cedric to get bored with me.

"He's probably right. There ain't been a hint of rain for weeks. Something's got to give soon, or we'll be in a mess of hurt with the crops and the animals," he said. Then he paused and caressed my hand.

Somehow, Cedric sure knew what to do to nearly 'bout make

my heart stop. All of this kissing and caressing felt good, but it also felt scary. I looked over toward the door to make sure Granny wasn't staring at us, but her eyes were in her Bible. I was grateful for that. I should have pulled my hand away, but I liked how it felt when he touched me. I looked at him, and he was gazing at me with what looked like concern. "You look like you feel a bit better than you did this morning. Do you?" he asked me.

I ducked my head. "Yes. I know I was looking a mess." I felt embarrassed that I had sat there in front of Cedric this morning with my robe on and my hair going every which way. Hazel Moody never would have let herself be seen in such an unkempt state.

He tilted my chin up so I was looking at him. "That's not what I meant. You always look amazing to me, Opal. I love everything about how you look. Your eyes, your skin, your hair, everything. I'm so glad you aren't one of those girls who packs on the makeup. You don't need anything extra to make you look beautiful."

I smiled at him. His words almost left me speechless. Finally, I found my manners and spoke. "Thank you. You are quite handsome yourself." I felt strange saying it, but it was true. Cedric Perkins was the handsomest boy I had ever seen. Period.

Before I knew what was happening, Cedric leaned in and kissed me. Do you know when folks say they saw stars when someone kissed them, and it always sounds silly or downright crazy? Well, I promise you, when Cedric kissed me, it was like the heavens opened up and all the stars rained down to the earth.

I heard Granny clear her throat from the door. I didn't care.

This was my second kiss, and I wasn't going to let Granny's hovering ruin it for me. The first kiss caught me off guard. This kiss was like magic. Cedric pulled away and stared at me with an emotion that I wasn't accustomed to seeing. Was it desire? Was it attraction? Surely it wasn't love. I know in the books and movies Lucille likes, love happens so fast, but I didn't really think that was real. Surely people don't do that in real life?

"I am not the man I plan to be, Opal. I know I got a lot of work to do to become who you deserve, but eventually I will be, and I hope you will wait for me," Cedric said, stroking my cheek with the knuckles of his hand. Before I could answer, Granny stepped out on the porch.

"Would you children like some lemonade?" she asked.

Cedric looked up and had the good graces to look embarrassed. "Thank you, ma'am. That would be nice," he said.

"Opal, come help me with the lemonade," she said. I didn't really want to get up, but I did. I followed Granny to the kitchen and went and got some glasses out of the cabinet.

"Don't you go moving too fast with this boy," Granny said. "Boys and men don't have the sense to know when their nature is leading them in the wrong way. It's up to the girl to be the voice of reason and say stop when stop needs to be said."

"Yes ma'am," I said. I prayed Cedric couldn't hear us talking.

"I should have said this to your mama. It was my fault for thinking she knew better when clearly she didn't," Granny said.

"I ain't my mama," I said, taking the pitcher from Granny and pouring the lemonade in the two glasses. We didn't have a fancy refrigerator like Miss Peggy, just a cooling box with no ice;

there was an ice shortage due to the drought and the extreme heat. I hoped the lukewarm lemonade would taste all right. "Can I go back out?"

"Yes," Granny said. "Opal, I know you ain't MayBelle. But you young and I don't want you to do anything you'll regret later."

"Cedric is a good person. I like him and he likes me. But I got good sense, Granny. I would never do anything to embarrass you or the family." I picked up the glasses of lemonade and walked back out to the porch, only to find my cousin M.J. sitting on one of the porch steps.

"Hey, M.J.," I said. I gave Cedric his glass of lemonade and gave M.J. the one I had poured for myself.

"Thanks, cousin," M.J. said, grinning. He knew I wasn't happy to see him. "I thought I would come by and keep y'all company."

"You shouldn't have," Cedric said, but he had a huge smile on his face.

"How you feelin', cousin?" M.J. asked, suddenly getting very serious. "I heard—"

"I'm fine," I said quickly.

M.J. nodded. He seemed to understand. "Well, glad you okay. Go tell your granny I'll make sure you kids don't get out of hand," M.J. said.

I went inside to get myself a glass of lemonade, and Granny was back sitting in her rocker with her Bible on her lap.

"M.J. is outside," I said.

"I heard him," she said. I looked to see if she was smiling, but she kept flipping the pages of her Bible. I guessed my courting was over for the night and went over to the cooling box and took out the lemonade and poured myself a glass. When I got back outside, I knew for certain it was over. M.J. and Cedric were deep in conversation about baseball, their favorite topic.

"They say ole Satch is gonna pitch for the McDonough Brown Thrashers this Saturday," M.J. said, the excitement clear in his voice. As I sat beside Cedric, it was clear he was excited too. Lucille had mentioned it to me a week ago. Seemed like a week was so long ago, with all that had happened between then and now. The Klan riding through Colored Town. Me getting beaten up. Cedric wanting to be my boyfriend. My mind was almost spinning.

"You lyin'," Cedric said. "I didn't know that was for certain."

"Watch y'all's tongues," Granny called out.

"Yes ma'am," Cedric said, but even Granny's rebuke couldn't take away his excitement.

"Aww, man. Nothing is ever certain with Satchel Paige, but that's what everybody is saying," M.J. said. "I heard the owner of the Brown Thrashers paid Satch a pretty penny to come and pitch a few innings. You know ole Satch ain't gonna pitch more than a few innings."

"He old as dirt," Cedric said, laughing. "It's amazing a man his age can still throw a ball."

"He ain't that old. Just in his thirties. But I did hear his arm ain't always consistent," M.J. said. "Some folks say he ain't got much left."

Cedric turned toward me and whispered, "You think your granny will let me take you to the game?"

I shook my head. "Not likely. Granny doesn't like ballgames, and she doesn't think it's fitting for young girls to attend. It's a miracle she's letting you come over here to see me."

M.J. got up from his seat on the steps. "Leave it to me. We all know I'm Granny's favorite. I'll get her to let you go."

Before I could say something, M.J. got up and went to the screen door. "Granny?" he called.

"What is it, baby?" she called back. He looked at me and winked. I covered my mouth to keep from laughing, and so did Cedric.

"Granny, a bunch of us cousins are going to Atlanta this Saturday to see Satchel Paige play. Lucille, me, and all the rest plus the uncles are going. I think some of the aunties might be going as well. My mama said she would probably go. Do you 'spect Opal can go too? I'll look after her myself."

Granny came to the door. "All of y'all are going to this baseball game?"

"Yes ma'am," he said. "Satchel Paige is going to pitch for the McDonough Brown Thrashers. You ought to come, Granny. You would enjoy yourself."

Granny laughed. "You know I ain't interested in no ball playing. I don't mind watching you kids play, but I don't know nothing 'bout these Thrashers or whatever you called them." Granny turned to me. "So, you interested in watching baseball?"

"I would like to go, Granny. If you don't mind," I said, trying not to sound too eager.

"Where's it at again?" she asked.

"It's in Atlanta, but Uncle Myron will take his car and Uncle Little Bud will take a slew of folks in the back of his truck. Plus, some other folks with cars are going, so there will be plenty of rides, and we will all meet at the church Saturday morning and follow together so we can all look after each other."

Granny clicked her teeth. "I don't want Opal in the back of no truck. I don't know about all of this, Michael Jr. Opal ain't really healed yet from all she been through this week."

"I'll make sure she rides inside a car, and I promise you I won't take my eyes off her the entire time we at the game," M.J. said.

She snorted with laughter. "Boy, if that Satchel Paige is playing ball, you won't be taking your eyes off him. Opal could walk to the end of the moon and back and you wouldn't notice one little bit," Granny said and walked out on the porch and stood before me and Cedric.

"I reckon you going to this ballgame too," she said, putting her hands on her hips. She didn't even try to make it a question.

"I hope to go, Miss Birdie," he said. "I'm hoping I might get the attention of the managers of the Black Crackers or the team they're playing, the McDonough Brown Thrashers."

"Is that right?" Granny said in a dry voice. "How you plan on doing that?"

"Well, I'm hoping to show them my pitching arm. Maybe ole M.J. here will play catcher for me," Cedric said.

"So you just gonna haul off and start throwing the ball in the ballgame?" she asked, looking at him sideways.

Cedric laughed. "No ma'am. Sometimes right before the game or after the game they'll let folks show them what they can do. Almost like a tryout."

"Granny, Ole Stank's arm has got some heat on it," M.J. said. "Any Negro team would be happy to get him."

"So you ain't interested in being a man of God like your daddy?" Granny asked, a serious frown on her face.

"Miss Birdie, I don't know what I'll be doing for the rest of my life, but I love baseball, and I would like to try my hand at it, while I'm still young enough to do it," he said. "And I don't think playing baseball means I can't still love the Lord. One don't cancel out the other, I don't think."

"I see," she said. "Well, Opal can go with her uncles, and if she sees you there, then that's all right, I guess," she said. She turned to go back inside, but then she stopped and looked at M.J. "I'm depending on you to be my ears and my eyes. If anything seems wrong with your cousin, you make sure she is okay. Is that clear?"

"Yes ma'am. You know I won't let nothing bad happen to Opal. Not on my watch," M.J. said. I smiled at him.

"Well, all right then, I guess. I guess y'all better be going home. Tomorrow is a workday for all of us," Granny said as she walked back in the house and stopped at the door.

"Yes ma'am," M.J. said. "We 'bout to leave out. You need anything 'fore I leave? I can bring you in some water. Or at least what there is in the well."

"No, honey," she said. "We fine for tonight. Y'all be careful going home. Cedric, you be extra careful going home. Tell the Reverend and Sister Perkins I said good night and be blessed. God willing, I'll see them on Sunday. Is they going to the ballgame too?"

"Papa might go. I doubt Mama will go. She ain't that big about baseball. She'd rather go shopping in Atlanta than go sit and watch a game," he said, laughing.

Granny laughed too. "I guess that's true for most settled women. These games and such is for you young folks. Not us elders."

"Yes ma'am," he said. "Thank you for letting me come visit tonight. I am grateful for your kindness."

This time Granny smiled. "You welcome, son. You been right nice company for Opal tonight. You can come visit again."

"Thank you, ma'am," he said as Granny went inside.

M.J. got up. "I'll wait for you down the way," he said to Cedric. "Opal, you going to work with Granny tomorrow, or you gonna take the rest of the week off?"

"If I feel as good as I did today, I'll go help her at least in the morning. Miss Lovenia said I shouldn't work for a week or two, but I can't keep staying around here."

"I'll check on y'all before I go help Daddy in the fields. I don't want y'all walking alone," M.J. said, and then he walked down the stairs but stopped. "And Opal, when you do remember who did this to you, you tell me first."

"Thank you, cousin," I said. M.J. had always been my protector. It didn't surprise me that he was still trying to do the same. But one thing I knew . . . when or if I did remember who hurt me, I would not tell M.J. first. Not by a long shot.

"I'm here to serve," he teased, then made his way out the yard, making sure he gave us plenty of privacy.

"I don't mind coming by here in the morning and walking

you and your granny to work," Cedric said. He reached out and briefly touched the last of the bruises on my face. The pain of it had finally gone away. I watched as Mr. Tote came outside his house and sat on his stoop and started playing his harmonica.

"Hey, Mr. Tote," I called out.

He stopped playing and waved. "Hey, baby. You doing all right?"

"Yes sir," I said. "Thanks for asking."

He waved again and went back to playing his harmonica. I couldn't quite make out the tune, but it didn't sound like a gospel song. I wondered how long before Granny came outside and started their nightly fussing about Mr. Tote's musical choices.

I turned my attention back to Cedric. "Thank you. I imagine Uncle Myron will come by and take us. He usually does," I said. I felt shy all of a sudden.

"I wish I could have been there with you when that dirty dog attacked you," he said. "It kills me to think whoever did this to you is walking around free and clear. If you ever remember who did this to you, all you have to do is tell me."

I shook my head. "I don't want to remember. Miss Lovenia said my not remembering was a blessing in disguise. I believe that too. I don't want you or any of my kin getting into it with some no-'count white man or boy. I just want this behind us all."

"As long as he is still out there, it ain't behind us, Opal," he said. He brushed my face gently. "If somebody tried to hurt you again, well, I would kill them. With my bare hands. I care about you, Opal."

"Please don't say such things," I said, feeling the panic rise inside my chest. "Don't ever say such things as that. I don't want anybody killing somebody for me. I wouldn't be able to live with myself."

"You deserve to be protected, Opal. You have the right to walk these streets between work and home without worrying about somebody coming out of the bushes to hurt you," he said. He pulled me into an embrace. I felt his lips graze my hair. This moment should have been filled with excitement and joy, but instead, I was terrified that my memories might come back and leave vulnerable the people I cared about the most. For the first time in days, I prayed. I asked God to keep my memories. To put a wall between me and them.

Granny called out to us. "Time to come inside. It's 'bout to get late and these boys don't need to be walking home in the dark."

"Yes ma'am," I called back. "I'll see you Saturday," I said to Cedric in a soft voice.

"All right then," he said, lightly kissing my cheek. "I had a good time visiting with you tonight, Opal. I'll be counting the seconds till Saturday." He stroked my cheek once more and ran off the porch and caught up with M.J., who was waiting just down the road.

"Opal," Granny called.

"I'm coming, Granny," I said, my face about to burst with all the emotions I was feeling.

14

I'll take care of the wash today," I said to Granny once we got settled at Miss Peggy's. I usually did the wash on Saturday mornings, but since I was going to be gone this Saturday, I wanted to get my wash done early. The last thing I wanted to do on Saturday was spend it feeling guilty that I had left Granny with my share of the workload to finish. I just wanted to enjoy the day and be all carefree like all of the other young folks.

"Just make sure you don't overdo it," Granny said. "I don't want you down in the bed again."

I promised her I wouldn't, and I got busy with the wash. All in all, I was feeling pretty good physically. My bruises had nearly completely healed, and the knot at the back of my head was gone. But my mental pain was something else altogether. I dreamed bad dreams all last night. I should have been dreaming about Cedric and me, but instead I was back on that road, getting pushed into the bushes by a faceless white man. I didn't want to alarm Granny, though, so I just told her what I knew she wanted to hear.

"Granny, I'm fine," I said before she went back inside for

what seemed like the hundredth time. "I ain't gonna make myself sick. I promise." Finally, she believed me.

I was going to work until two o'clock at Miss Peggy's, and then I was going to go over to Miss Lovenia's and find out exactly what she wanted me to do and maybe get started working some before it got late. I promised Granny I would finish up at Miss Lovenia's in time to get home by six. Uncle Myron said he would drop me off and pick me up. I didn't dare tell him I could walk. I knew my walking alone days were over and done with as far as my family was concerned. As far as Cedric was concerned too. That detail should have made me feel good, but I was already missing the solitude of my walks.

I always felt closest to God when I was out walking alone. When I was a little girl, I would sometimes walk for hours, having imaginary conversations with my mama or God. I wouldn't go far; I would just go from one end of Colored Town to the other. Always staying in eyeshot of an adult, but still feeling like I was alone with my thoughts. Other times I would walk out to the peach orchard and curl up underneath a tree and daydream about what being a grown-up might feel like. But now, thanks to this unknown attacker, I wasn't going to have that same freedom anymore, and it made me both sad and angry.

I started hanging up the last of the sheets from Miss Peggy's bed when I turned around and found Jimmy Earl standing behind me. I let out a startled sound as I backed up, almost falling, but he reached out and steadied me. I pulled away.

"Lord God, Jimmy Earl," I said. "You trying to give me a heart attack?"

"I'm sorry, Bean," he said, his face genuinely concerned. "I thought you heard me calling out to you."

"Well, you thought wrong," I snapped, reaching into my apron pocket and taking out my handkerchief. I mopped the sweat from my forehead. My hair was tied up in a scarf, but the scarf was soaking wet. I would need to replace it when I got through with the wash. Realizing how harsh I must have sounded, I took a deep breath. "It's okay, Jimmy Earl, and please, stop saying you're sorry. I'm truly okay. I'm just a bit nervous still, I guess."

"I'm sor . . . shoot. I am sorry, Bean. You know—"

"I know," I said and lightly touched his arm. I knew he didn't mean for any of this mess to happen. Jimmy Earl had been one of my closest friends through the years, and I wasn't ready for that to end over some evil folks that had nothing to do with him.

"How are you feeling today?" he asked, lifting his baseball cap from his head and fanning himself with it.

I smiled a little. "Like somebody who's been beat up." I reached down and got one of the wet towels out of the basket. When I looked back up, I caught the look on his face.

"I was just joking, Jimmy Earl. I'm better. I feel pretty much back to normal," I said. "This heat is awful, but it was awful before . . . well, before all that happened."

"You're right about that," he said. "I ain't never remembered it being this hot before. You sure you need to be out here doing this alone? I could go wake up Mama and get her to come help."

I shook my head. "Don't go bothering Miss Corinne. Your gran said Miss Corinne was restless last night. I don't want you disturbing her rest over no wash. I can take care of it."

"I guess you're right about waking Mama. I wish Mama . . . well . . . you know. It ain't like we ain't talked about Mama and her ways before."

"She's been doing better, Jimmy Earl," I lied. From the time we were little children, Jimmy Earl and I had compared notes on our mothers. My notes didn't consist of much. No one ever talked to me about MayBelle when I was young, and by the time I got older, I didn't want to talk about her. Jimmy Earl had his mama around, but sometimes his situation seemed worse than mine; Miss Corinne was here, but then she wasn't here.

"I'm almost done," I said. "Granny is getting breakfast ready. You should go up and eat before you have to go to work at Mr. Lowen's."

"I'll go. I can see you're trying to get rid of me," he said, but with a smile.

I thought he was going to head back to the house, but he kept standing and I stopped what I was doing and waited for him to speak again.

"Bean, do you remember anything yet?" he asked, taking the towel from my hand and hanging it on the clothesline. Jimmy Earl hadn't helped me with the wash since before he went away to college.

"No. I don't remember nothing. Sometimes I think I can call up the memory, but then everything gets murky. It's a terrible feeling to know that something so awful happened to me and I can't remember who did it."

"Bean, I talked to Skeeter. I had to see if he knew anything about what happened to you the other day."

I got quiet for a moment. "What did he say?" I would be lying if I didn't admit that Skeeter had crossed my mind. I just chose to ignore the thought.

"He said he would never do that to you. He said he was angry at me for even thinking such a thing."

"And you're satisfied with his answer?" I asked. I thought back to Sunday when Skeeter threatened to break into my house after he got finished burning down Granny's chicken coop.

"Bean, I can't imagine how scared you must have been the other day. And I know my cousin can be a son-of-a-gun, but I would like to believe that even he has his limits," Jimmy Earl said.

"Jimmy Earl, I don't want to talk about this anymore. It just makes me anxious."

Before Jimmy Earl could reply, his dog, Levi, ran over. Instead of going to Jimmy Earl, he came to me and started licking my hand and brushing himself against my leg.

"Levi, stop all of that," I said, but I laughed. "He's acting like it's been years since he seen me."

Levi started jumping up and wagging his tail. "That ole mutt loves you a heck of a lot more than he does me," Jimmy Earl said, laughing too.

"He loves attention, and with you being away at school, I've been the only one paying him any mind. Sometimes your mama will play with him, but Granny and Miss Peggy can't stand him jumping and slobbering," I said, still smiling. "Lay down, Levi," I ordered in my stern voice. He slowly sank to the ground.

"Well, will you look at that," Jimmy Earl said. "He ain't that quick to obey me."

"I got the magic touch," I said and laughed again. I watched as Jimmy Earl's face got serious again. "What is it, Jimmy Earl? Is there something you want to tell me?" I worried that it was Miss Peggy.

"Bean, Lori Beth came by here yesterday to apologize to you for the article," he said as he picked up another towel from the basket. "She wanted to go over to your house, but I told her not to. She didn't mean to hurt you. She was just trying to help. She cried so hard I thought she was going to make herself sick. Her daddy has forbidden her from writing for the newspaper indefinitely. She is truly upset that she hurt you."

I couldn't say anything at first. Mainly because I was furious that he would come telling me some mess like that. First he was trying to plead the case for his cousin not being the one who hurt me, and then here he was making excuses for that nosy white girl, Lori Beth Parsons. I didn't care none about how Lori Beth Parsons was feeling, and I was angry that he cared.

Finally, I reached over and snatched the towel from his hands. "White folks always thinking they know what's best for Colored folks," I muttered as I hung the towel on the clothesline. "Then when they mess up, they try to act all sorry. She did this to herself and to me, not to mention my family. She can take her 'I'm sorries' somewhere else."

"Bean," Jimmy Earl said, his face looking hurt. "Why would you say that? All white folks aren't bad. I'm not bad and Lori Beth isn't either. You know this. You and I have been friends since you were in diapers. Lori Beth thought she was doing the right thing. She was just trying to help."

Once again, I was the one who was hurt, but suddenly Lori Beth Parsons was the victim. I had to work hard to measure my words. I didn't want to hurt Jimmy Earl's feelings, but he was hurting me now and he didn't even seem to notice.

"Well, Jimmy Earl, she thought wrong and she shore nuff didn't help me none. She could have gotten me or all of Colored Town killed. It wasn't but just a few days ago that the Klan rode through and burnt down my granny's chicken coop. It could be one of the same ones who hurt me, including your cousin Skeeter. This ain't about bad or good. It's about respecting folks' wishes," I said. "It's about respecting Black folks' wishes. It's about trusting that we know what we're talking about."

"But—"

"But nothing, Jimmy Earl Ketchums," I yelled. "I told her to leave it alone. I told her this wasn't none of her affair."

Jimmy Earl folded his arms across his chest. "Dang it, Bean. I don't understand why this has to be about Black or white. This isn't like you. Yes, the South is still a racist place, but don't you think things are getting better? Don't you think we are heading toward better days between the races?"

I looked at him with the shock of all my ancestors on my face. I couldn't believe the words coming out of his mouth. He was smart as a whip when it came to book sense, but clearly Jimmy Earl didn't have a lick of common sense when it came to issues related to race relationships right here in Parsons, Georgia.

I turned toward him, feeling like fire was coming out of my ears, nose, and throat. "What else is it about if it ain't about Black or white, Jimmy Earl Ketchums? Them Klan folks didn't march out here to your land and burn crosses and kill your live-stock. It wasn't your precious Lori Beth Parsons who got beat like a dog the other day, left for dead in a ditch. So if it ain't about Black or white, what is it about?" All that book learning and Jimmy Earl Ketchums didn't know a cotton-pickin' thing. "You just tell your precious girlfriend to not try and help me anymore. Her type of help will get a body killed."

I tried to make my way around him, but I stumbled a bit. Jimmy Earl grabbed me to keep me from falling.

"Bean, you okay?" he asked. "Dang it. I didn't mean to upset you. Are you okay?"

I couldn't speak at first. I felt light-headed all of a sudden, and I felt my knees begin to give way.

"Opal. Opal!" I could hear him calling out to me as he continued to hold me up. I tried to answer, but it was taking everything I could do to keep from passing out completely. "Take slow breaths." He guided me to the bench Mr. Tote had made for Granny to sit on when she was out helping me with the wash. "You okay?" he asked, kneeling in front of me once he got me sitting.

I nodded and gradually I did start to feel better. "I'm okay," I managed to say. "I must have moved a bit too quick. Don't tell Granny, Jimmy Earl. If she hears I had an episode, she won't let me go to the ballgame tomorrow."

"Bean, you don't need to go to no ballgame. That heat is gonna be brutal. You probably need to go home now and rest, or go up to the house and lie down," he said.

I shook my head. "I'm fine. Please, just let it go. I'm fine."

"Bean, you could have died the other day," Jimmy Earl whispered, taking my hands in his. "We could have lost you. I'm a numbskull. A complete and total numbskull. I shouldn't have said any of those things. You're right. You're absolutely right. Lori Beth could have gotten you killed, and that's that. I wasn't trying to take her side over yours. You're family to me. You mean more to me than any silly old girl like Lori Beth."

I pulled my hands away. I didn't want to think the thoughts I was thinking or feel the emotions I was feeling. What kind of person was I? I shouldn't be having thoughts about any boy but Cedric. Not more than a few hours ago, I was sitting on the porch kissing Cedric, and now here I was feeling warm inside over Jimmy Earl's kind words. I looked around but I didn't see anybody. I was grateful for that. I was determined to get back to the safety of the kitchen, where Granny was. I would get her to pray over me or something. Clearly, I was as awful as my mother. Nothing but a Jezebel like it says in the Bible. There was no doubt that I needed my granny's prayers before I did something both Jimmy Earl and I regretted.

"I should go inside," I said. I tried to speak in a strong and forceful voice, but my words came out in a hoarse whisper. I tried to stand, but the dizziness continued and I felt myself about to fall again. Jimmy Earl caught me, and this time he held me tight against him.

"Opal," he said in a tight voice. He brushed his lips against my cheek and I shuddered . . . not from revulsion but from something else. "Opal, I—"

"We can't do this. I need to go inside," I said, but I didn't move. I didn't want to move, and I felt awful about myself. His lips brushed my cheek again, and just as he was about to drag his lips from my cheek to my mouth that was already ready to receive his, someone began coughing behind us. Loudly. We both pulled away like the awful sinners we were.

"Mr. Jimmy Earl," the voice called out. Jimmy Earl and I both turned. It was Mr. Tote. He had his face turned away from us like we were Adam and Eve naked in the garden. I dropped my head, staring at the ground, wishing the ground would swallow me up. "Mr. Jimmy Earl," he said. "That ole mule done fell out dead. Too hot out here. I'm gone need some help getting him buried."

"Ah, yes, Tote. I . . . I . . ." He stopped and looked at me, and his voice went tender again. "Do you need me to take you back up to the house?"

I shook my head. I could barely speak, but I managed to find my voice, desperate for him and Mr. Tote to leave. "I'm fine. I'll sit here a spell and then I'll head up to the house. Breakfast will be ready soon." I kept my eyes looking down. I didn't want to see Jimmy Earl's eyes, and I surely didn't want to see Mr. Tote looking at me like I was the criminal on the cross.

"All right then," he finally said. "Let's go, Tote."

I sat there and breathed in and out until I was sure they were gone. After a moment I made my way back to the back porch leading into the kitchen. When I got in the kitchen Granny was making some hominy. She was dripping with sweat just like me. She looked up and smiled, but then her smile went away when she saw the look on my face.

"What's wrong?" she asked.

I opened my mouth, but no words would come out. I went to her and she wrapped her arms around me.

"What's wrong?" she asked again. "You feeling bad? We need to call Doc Henry?"

I finally shook my head. "I'm awful. I'm awful, Granny." The tears poured down my face.

"What you mean, chile?" she asked, pushing me away so she could look in my eyes, but by then I was almost overcome with the emotions I was feeling. I buried my head in her chest.

"Pray for me, Granny," I finally choked out. "Please."

Granny reached around me and turned off everything on the stove, then guided me to the pantry.

"What's done happened?" she whispered. "What happened to you out there?"

I shook my head. I didn't want to put it into words that twice in one week, I had feelings for two different boys. The MayBelle spirit was on me. The spirit of my mother. The fallen angel of our family. I was becoming her, and I hated myself in that moment . . . I hated her and her awful genes. I wanted to be like my granny. Not like MayBelle.

"Did somebody do something to—"

I shook my head even harder. "No, Granny. This is about me. I need you to just . . . to just pray for me. I'm confused and I don't know what to do."

Granny pulled off my wet head scarf. "You done got yourself all worked up. You burning up. Probably even got a fever. I knowed I shouldn't have let you leave that house today."

"Granny, I'm evil," I said in a quiet voice. "I'm just like my mother."

"Have you been with a boy?" Granny asked in a gruff voice.

"No ma'am," I nearly wailed. "I didn't mean that. I just mean I have feelings. Evil feelings."

Granny shook my shoulders. "Don't you say that no more. You ain't evil. You ain't even close to being evil. You listen to me, Opal Pruitt. You is a normal young girl. Girls have a nature about them, just like boys. I know I ain't talked to you about things the way I should have, but I can't have you going around here thinking you evil just 'cause you have feelings. Feelings ain't evil. Actions is evil. You just growing up, and your nature has got you twisted all sorts of ways. You is just how you is supposed to be."

Granny reached out and wiped the tears from my face. "Now, I'll pray for you, but not because you evil. I'll pray because you is so full of goodness that I don't want anything in this world to change that. Do you hear me?" she asked, pulling me tight. "Jimmy Earl has been in your life since you was a baby. Granny ain't been walking with her eyes closed. I've seen the looks y'all have shared since he's been back from school. Innocent looks, but dangerous all the same. What you both have to realize is y'all can't step over the line. When Colored and white step over the line, bad things happen. Do you understand what I'm saying?"

"I won't forget," I said to Granny, and for a while, she and I stood holding each other. She said soft prayers underneath her breath until finally I felt the peace I had been seeking for the entire week.

15

I was still shaken over the Jimmy Earl situation when Uncle Myron came to get me to take me to Miss Lovenia's house. I felt like a fallen angel . . . like I had committed a horrible sin against God, myself, the family, and Cedric. Every time I went past a mirror, I looked the other way because I couldn't bear to look at myself. I didn't want to see my eyes looking back at me knowing I had almost kissed Jimmy Earl . . . that I wanted him to kiss me and, had Mr. Tote not walked up on us, there was no telling what might have happened.

When Jimmy Earl came back to the house after he and Tote buried the mule, he went upstairs, got dressed, and left with barely a word to anyone. I had no words for him and, thankfully, he had no words for me. He did look at me long and hard before walking out, but I hurried away when the stare became too much.

"What's wrong with that boy?" I heard Miss Peggy ask Granny as I headed back to the kitchen. I didn't wait to hear what Granny said. By the time I came back out, Miss Peggy had moved on to talking to Granny about other things. For the rest of my time at Miss Peggy's that day, I stayed focused on my chores, not saying much to either Miss Peggy or Granny, and they didn't seem to pay me too much mind either.

When Uncle Myron pulled up, I kissed Granny and rushed out to the car and hopped in, barely getting out more than a "hello." I couldn't get out of my own mind. Uncle Myron must have figured out I wasn't up for talking, so he turned the radio on to WSB, where the Carter Family was singing "Keep on the Sunny Side." We rode in silence until we got to Miss Lovenia's house.

"Thank you, Uncle Myron," I said as I gathered my things, ready to jump out of his car just like I had jumped into it. But he reached over and grabbed my hand.

"This has been a difficult week for you. For all of us. Let me say a quick prayer," he said. I nodded and bowed my head. "Lord, take care of my niece as she undertakes this new job. Surround her with ten thousand angels of protection, and keep her sound in mind and body until I can come back for her. In your Son's name we pray. Amen."

"Amen," I whispered, trying to hold back my tears.

Uncle Myron continued to hold my hand. "Even though I fuss at you and push you to be all that I know you can be, you know I love you, baby girl, don't you?"

I nodded, a single tear sliding down my face. "I know, Uncle Myron. I love you too."

Uncle Myron pulled me close, and I laid my head on his shoulder. "You are a wonderful young woman, Opal Pruitt. I am so sorry you've had such a hard life, what with my sister leaving and all, but you need to know you have made the sorrow of losing her bearable. I look at you and I see the best of my sister. You gave this entire family hope after she left. You are a gift to us all."

"Oh, Uncle Myron," I managed to say before bursting into tears for real.

If only he knew just how unworthy I was for such kind words. He continued to hold me and rock me as if I were a little girl all over again. Finally, I raised my head. "I better go inside."

Uncle Myron swiped at the tears on his own face. "Yes. I'll be back for you about five. Don't tire yourself out."

"I won't," I said and got out of the car. I looked up at Miss Lovenia's door, and she was standing there like a statue dressed in white. She had her hair tied up in a white head wrap, and I could see that she had on gold necklaces and earrings.

Granny said the Bible spoke against women wearing jewelry. First Peter something, I think. The only jewelry Granny owned were some pearls my grandfather had given her, and I never saw her wear them, although she said she wore them once at Grandpa's funeral. Sometimes she would take them out and look at them, but then put them back inside their case. I knew she would not have been pleased with how Miss Lovenia was looking. She probably would have told me to run the other way, but something told me not to. There was something in what Miss Lovenia was offering that made me at least want to hear her out.

I started walking toward the door, turning to wave at Uncle Myron as he drove away. When I reached the door, Miss Lovenia pointed at my feet.

"Please take them off," she said, not smiling. But her voice seemed to hint that there was kindness there.

"Yes ma'am," I said, hurriedly reaching down and untying the laces to my shoes, slipping them off, and picking them up. I didn't have on any stockings, so I was standing there in my bare feet. Miss Lovenia moved to the side and motioned me to come in.

"Put them over there," she said, pointing to a shoe rack by the door that had several pairs of shoes on it already. "We do not bring the outside in. Unclean spirits dwell in all things, but especially on the bottoms of our shoes and feet. Sit here," she said, nodding her head toward a little footstool by the shoe rack.

"Yes ma'am," I said and sat. I watched as Miss Lovenia pushed toward my feet a basin that had water in it and what looked like some type of dried flower petals floating on top of the water. I caught a flowery, musky odor coming from the water, but I could not identify all of the smells.

Miss Lovenia knelt down in front of me and dipped a rag inside the water basin, wrung it out, and then picked up my left foot and began washing it.

I tried to reach for the rag. I felt embarrassed. "I can do that, Miss Lovenia. I didn't mean to bring dirty feet into your home." I didn't want her to think I didn't bathe and take care of myself. Before I left Miss Peggy's, I had washed up and changed to a fresh work dress and head scarf.

She kept wiping in gentle motions as if I had not spoken. Finally, she answered me. "I know you can wash your own feet,

Miss Opal Pruitt, but that ain't the point. Washing another person's feet is biblical. Surely you Methodists have studied the Scriptures about Jesus washing his disciples' feet?"

"Yes ma'am," I said. "I remember studying that before. But I'm no—"

"Disciple?" she said, cutting me off with a tinkle of a laugh. "We are all disciples. *Disciple* simply means 'a follower.' Aren't you a follower of Jesus?"

"Yes ma'am," I said. "I am."

"Then hush, chile, and close your eyes and think about the beauty of this moment," she said. "Whenever someone comes into my home, I always ask them to wash their feet and remove the impurities they have picked up through the passing of the day. If I feel a special kinship to them, I will do the washing myself. Many African cultures were practicing this ritual long before the Bible as we know it was written."

She began washing my other foot. I wanted to keep protesting, but I didn't. To keep questioning her felt rude, so I tried to close my eyes and think on Jesus, but all I could think about was the turmoil I was feeling over my almost kiss with Jimmy Earl.

"Release your thoughts, chile," she said. "There is no room in this moment for you and them."

I opened my eyes in surprise. Them? How did she know there was a "them" floating around in my head? For a moment, I wondered if I had spoken their names by accident. I was too afraid to ask, so I closed my eyes once more.

After she was done, she dried my feet on a towel she had on her lap. "Okay then," she said, getting up like she was my age instead of a woman in her nineties. "You look much better than when I saw you last. How are you feeling?"

"I feel better. Thank you for taking care of me," I said, feeling shy. Miss Lovenia was so different from any of the elders I knew from Colored Town or the church. She just felt like she was of a different time and place. She wasn't scary, but she did make me feel a bit uncomfortable.

"You are welcome, daughter. I am thankful you were not hurt any more than you were," she said. "God truly smiled on you that day."

I have to say, I was surprised by her continued references to God and Jesus. I didn't know hoodoo people believed in God. I guess my surprise showed on my face, because she responded to me as if I had spoken.

"Yes, I believe in the Trinity. I guess you would call me a non-practicing practicing Catholic. I know people call what I do hoodoo. But everything, I believe, is of God. So whatever name a person gives it, it still comes from the Creator when all is said and done."

"Yes ma'am," I said, unsure what else to say in the moment.

"Follow me and I will show you what I need you to do," Miss Lovenia said.

She began walking down the long hallway without even looking to see if I followed. I thought it interesting that her house was closed up with no light coming in or going out, but it felt cool inside. Comfortable. There were candles lit everywhere, and they gave off a soothing kind of glow. The walls had different types of colorful paintings of men and women dressed similar to Miss

Lovenia. Masks on the walls and statues on the little tables that lined the wall were a tad bit frightening, but I didn't have time to gaze at them for long, because she walked without pause. I clutched my bag to me that held the Bible Granny had made sure I was carrying before I got in the car with Uncle Myron that morning.

"Tell your granny I have plenty of Bibles here," she said, stopping in front of a closed door without even looking back. This time I gasped. I couldn't stop myself. How did she know all of these things? "And don't you go getting scared, chile. The Father, the Son, and the Holy Ghost dwell here as well as at your home and your church. Yahweh is everywhere."

"Who?" I asked, looking around her darkened hallway, almost scared that this Yahweh might jump out at me at any moment. Suddenly, I didn't feel quite so brave being back at Miss Lovenia's.

"God, chile," she said, laughing. "God is also called Yahweh. Did you think the Almighty was only mighty enough to bear one name? The Creator answers by many names. Allah, Yahweh, Elohim, Abba, El Elyon, El Roi, El Shaddai, Yahweh Yireh, Yahweh Nissi, Jehovah Rapha, Jehovah Jireh. So many names. Those are only a few. Then, of course, there are the other deities. Those who ruled the heavens and earth long before Jesus was even a glimmer in the Creator's eye."

"I've never heard all of those names for God. Where did you find them?" I asked. If she had said God told her personally, it wouldn't have surprised me at all.

"The Bible," she said. "Everything is right there. You just have to look for it. Now, that is my Bible lesson for the day."

Before I could respond, she walked into a room. "Come," she called back to me. Reluctantly, I followed. Well, if nothing else, she was taking my mind off of everything else that had happened these last few days. At this point, I was just trying to make sure my soul wasn't lost here at Miss Lovenia's house. I knew Granny would have wanted me to leave already, but something continued to draw me to this woman and this house. I wanted both to stay and to go, so for the time being, I decided to stay to see what she would say next.

Miss Lovenia went to the window and pushed back the curtains, revealing a room with bookshelves filled with more books than I had ever seen before.

"Once a week I will want you to come in here and dust. My sons enjoy reading in that section of the room over there, but the other side of the room is primarily mine," she said. In the opposite corner of the room there was a little table with photos, candles, a clear pitcher filled with something that looked like water, a wine bottle, and other things I couldn't see from here. In front of the table was a stack of colorful-looking pillows in bright greens, oranges, and purples. "You are not to touch that table. It is where I honor my ancestors. When I walk into this room, I want to smell cleanliness so that when I burn my incense, it will have a pure burn."

She turned on her heels and walked back toward the door. She motioned for me to follow, and I ran behind her even though I wanted to stay and see more. She stopped in front of another door, but she didn't open it. "That room is where I work with my customers. If any of them come and I can't get to the door, make sure you have them take off their shoes and wash their feet. Then walk them to this door and have them sit on this bench," she said. "You are not required to go inside. I doubt your granny would want you in that space. But you are welcome." She started walking again, and as I followed, I began to hear a loud thumping sound.

"What is that, Miss Lovenia?" I asked, nervous that I had asked too much. I didn't want to be nosy, but at the same time, I didn't want to run into some strange spirits.

She turned to me and smiled. "It's the boys talking to the spirits in the spirit realm."

She must have seen the look on my face because she laughed. "They are playing their djembes, which are drums that come from West Africa. Their father, Kwaku Manu, was an African from Nigeria. He taught them to play before he died. When they play, I know they are feeling the distance between their spirits and his. The drumming brings them closer to their da."

I didn't say anything at first. I wasn't entirely sure what to say. The world Miss Lovenia lived in was so different from that of other Colored folks in Parsons. We honored our dead, too, but not in the same way. Our belief was that dead people's souls went either to heaven or hell, and once they crossed over, there was no way to talk to them again until hopefully, upon our death, we would all meet up in heaven. In some ways, we were just Black extensions of the white folks in Parsons. There wasn't a whole lot of difference in the white folks' ways and customs and our own, but Miss Lovenia and her sons, well, they seemed like they were from somewhere else. Somewhere far away that no American Colored person had ever been.

"Opal, if you ever have questions, ask them. One thing I do not allow in this house is lies and half-truths. I don't have the answers to everything, but what I do know I share, and what I don't know I ask. I hope you will follow that same principle while you help me. And by the by, thank you. I am ninety-seven years old, and for the first time in my life, I am beginning to feel my age, which means I have to share my journey with others now so that they can help me to transition. So I appreciate you entering this journey with me. Getting old is a messy process, but for those of us who are blessed enough to grow old, it is a part of the process of moving on to the spirit realm."

"I don't exactly know what you mean, Miss Lovenia, but I will do my best to try and help out," I said. "Miss Lovenia, I do have a question."

"And what is that, daughter?" she asked with a smile. A knowing smile. Almost like she already knew what I was going to ask.

"Why did you ask for me to work here for you?" I asked.

"I asked for you because when I asked around, it was said that you were the best at what you do, and that is who I wanted to help me," she said. "Does that make sense?"

"Yes ma'am," I said. It was nice to know my name was associated with my work being good. I tried. Whether I was cleaning house or making a dress for myself or someone else, I really made an effort to do my very best.

Miss Lovenia touched my arm. "So let me continue to show you around the house and explain to you the things that will help me." She led me to the kitchen. "Do you cook, Opal?"

I nodded. "Yes ma'am. I do most of the cooking at Miss Peggy's house and at home."

"That's good," she said, and she started showing me where everything was in the kitchen. "One thing, though. We don't eat chicken, pork, or beef. Every now and then we'll eat some fish from the creek down the way, but mainly we eat vegetables. I can show you some of the meals we like. My boys and I are pretty simple eaters."

"Yes ma'am," I said. Once again, I was amazed by how different Miss Lovenia was from every other Colored person I knew. No meat? I couldn't imagine not having ham in the fall or fried chicken at summer picnics. And how in the world did she season her vegetables if not with some dried fatback? But I wasn't going to argue. If she wanted me to fix her sons and her food without meat, then I would do exactly that.

"Now, let me take you upstairs where the bedrooms are," she said. She showed me her room, which was all in white, and her sons shared a bedroom that had two twin beds in it. "Just make sure you keep the bedrooms clean. I change my bedsheets every other day, so you will be doing quite a bit of washing. I wash my own clothes, but I would like for you to wash my sons' clothing. That will be a big help."

"Yes ma'am," I said.

"Now, let me take you down to the cellar where I make my teas and poultices and, well, other things," she said.

She took me down the stairs until they led to a powerfully hot and dank room. It housed all sorts of jars and containers filled with some things that looked familiar and other things that I didn't recognize. Granny made teas out of ginger root and peppermint for my periods and for colds, but other than that, I hadn't seen most of what Miss Lovenia was showing me.

"At some point, if you are ever interested, I can teach you a few things, like how to make those teas I gave you the other day," she said. "Our people are not used to this white man's medicine. That's why we stay sick in this country. Their medicine was not meant for our African bodies. That white doctor is all the time coming to me to help him when he runs into cases his medicine won't handle."

I was surprised to hear Doc Henry came to Miss Lovenia for help, but I didn't say the words, even though I imagined she already knew I was surprised.

"Thank you, Miss Lovenia," I said. "I would like to learn." And I did want to. I didn't have such good luck learning in school. I was never a good student when it came to learning poems or stories in books, or even math problems, but when it came to sewing or cooking, I was always quick to learn. Learning more about medicines from Miss Lovenia sounded interesting to me.

"Well, good then," she said. "Let's head back upstairs. I reckon your uncle will be back for you soon. I am grateful that you are willing to split up some of your time to help me. I promise you that I won't expose you to anything you don't want to know."

"Yes ma'am," I said as we walked back to her sitting room to wait for Uncle Myron. But before we could say anything else to each other, there was a knock at the door, and for some reason, I didn't think it was Uncle Myron. Miss Lovenia was about to get up, but I stopped her. "I'll get it. That's what you have me here for, Miss Lovenia."

She smiled and motioned for me to go to the door. When I got there, there was an older lady and a little boy I didn't recognize.

"Hello," I said, smiling at them, but neither one of them returned my smile. "May I help you?"

The lady gripped the boy's arm so tight, I wondered if his arm was hurting. "I need to see Miss Lovenia Manu. Is she busy?"

Before I knew it, Miss Lovenia was standing beside me. "I'm Lovenia Manu. How may I help you?"

The older lady looked from me to Miss Lovenia. I could tell she wasn't sure if she should talk in front of me, but Miss Lovenia reached out and took the lady's hand. "Come in, my dear. This is my assistant, Opal. Anything you say to me you can say in front of her. We do not discuss what happens underneath this roof. Now, you and your boy need to remove your shoes. What are your names?"

The woman and the boy removed their shoes and put them on the rack.

"Patrice Olden is my name. I come here from McDonough, Georgia. My friend, Elvira Miller, said she came to you before and you helped her with some things," Miss Patrice said.

Miss Lovenia smiled. "Of course. You must give my best to Mrs. Miller. Opal, please go to the kitchen and heat up some water for some tea. I'm going to take Miss Olden and—"

"My grandson, Theophalus," she said, still gripping hard to his arm. "Tell the ladies hello, Theophalus."

"Hello, ma'ams," he said in a soft voice, not making eye contact with either Miss Lovenia or me. I wondered if he was the reason why the old lady was here. I looked at her face and she looked years older than Miss Lovenia, whose face looked soft as butter.

"I am going to take Miss Olden and her grandson to my special room after they wash their feet. Please bring the hot water to us when it is ready. I'll decide what tea we want when you get back," Miss Lovenia said, sounding all businesslike.

I took my leave and went to the kitchen to boil the water. She had a nice teakettle that I filled with water from her sink. It wasn't long before it was whistling loudly. I poured the water into a fancy-looking teapot. I placed it and three teacups on a tray that was on the counter and carried it to the room where the door was closed. I didn't think I needed to just rush in, so I knocked.

"Come in, Opal," Miss Lovenia said. I walked inside and the woman was sitting at the table facing Miss Lovenia while the grandson sat on the other side of the room rubbing a cat that I hadn't seen until just then. "Theophalus has discovered Possum. That cat belongs to my boys. Sometimes he comes out to visit if he likes the company." Miss Lovenia motioned for me to take a seat on the chair next to the window, after I put the tray with the hot water and teacups on her table. Miss Lovenia turned over two of the cups. "Miss Patrice was telling me that she is having some difficulties at home."

Miss Patrice looked over at me and then at her grandson, as if she wasn't sure she should talk about herself in front of us. Miss Lovenia reached over and patted her hand. That seemed to give her the power to speak.

"I shouldn't never have married that young man," she said.

"He knew I was lonely after my old man died, and he came to me carrying some dark magic, I 'spect, 'cause even though I know he got me with magic, I don't want to let him go. He has spent my money unwisely, and he doesn't treat me fair, so I had no hope other than you to help me figure this out."

Miss Lovenia reached into her desk and took out an old snuff tin. She opened it and put a pinch of whatever was inside into one of the teacups I had brought. "Pour the water into the cup and drink all of it before we speak again."

Miss Patrice picked up the teapot to pour the water into her cup, but her hands shook so much that I jumped up and went to her to help her. But Miss Lovenia raised her hand to stop me.

"She must do it herself. She will be fine," Miss Lovenia said and locked eyes with Miss Patrice. "If you waste any, Opal will clean it up, but you must pour this for yourself. Although the Christian Bible does not say, 'God helps those who help themselves,' it should, because if we want something so bad that we are willing to go to extreme measures to get it, we must guide the process ourselves. Do you understand?"

The old lady nodded and poured the steaming hot water into her teacup, not even spilling a drop. Miss Lovenia nodded in approval.

"Drink," Miss Lovenia said. "Drink it all."

The old lady did what she was told, and after a few minutes of total quiet, Miss Lovenia spoke. "Do you feel calm?"

"Yes," the woman said, her voice sounding surprised. "Calmer than I have felt in days, maybe weeks or months. What is inside that tea?"

Miss Lovenia nodded. "Calmness. Calmness was inside that tea. So let us begin. We should always be calm before we ask the spirits to intercede on our behalf. They will listen to us if we ask for their help in the right way. *But* we must always make sure we are truly asking them for what it is we want. For what we really want. Now, do you believe in the Father, the Son, and the Holy Ghost?"

Miss Patrice nodded her head, tears rolling down her cheeks. "I do. Yes ma'am, I do very much."

"Then we will talk to them first," Miss Lovenia said. "What is it you want me to ask? And think carefully before you respond."

Miss Patrice looked down at the teacup and then she raised her head. "I want my husband, my young husband, to be satisfied with me and me alone. I want him to stay put and love me."

"Does that mean you want him to have relations with you or simply stay at home?" Miss Lovenia asked. "Remember, what we ask for is what the godheads will give us. We must always say what we mean, and mean what we say."

"I want him in my bed making love to me at night. I want him to look at me with fresh eyes, and to love what he sees. I want him to stop running the streets and stay at home when he is not at work," she said in a careful voice. "I want my man underfoot, and I know what that means. I am sixty. I won't be here for another sixty years. Maybe not even for another ten or twenty years. I don't mind spending whatever years I have left having a man nearly half my age looking at me as if I were a young girl again."

"Do you still have the stamina for a young man's love?" Miss

Lovenia asked in a slow voice. By this point, I was feeling very embarrassed by the conversation, but I dared not get up. So I stared down at the floor while they continued to talk. I glanced over and noticed the grandson was still playing with the cat as if nothing strange was happening.

"I would like your help with that too," Miss Patrice said. "I would like to be able to please my man whenever he wants me to."

Miss Lovenia slowly nodded her head. "Okay then. If you are sure that is all you want, then we will approach God and see if that is acceptable to him."

There were three candles on Miss Lovenia's desk, and she lit all three. "Take my hand," she said to Miss Patrice. "Thank you, God, for your blessings. Today we ask you to bless this request. You were here the entire time, so you know what she asks for. Honor her request if you feel it is within your will to do. Amen." Then she turned to Miss Patrice. "Do you have something for me?"

Miss Patrice reached into her purse and took out a wad of crumpled-up bills and gave them to Miss Lovenia. Miss Lovenia smoothed them out and then put the money inside her desk.

"For the next year, day after day with no interruption, you are to wash your armpits and your private lady parts, and you are to make a tea or a broth from that water and give it to your husband to drink. I will give you a bag of herbs to add to the tea or broth. Just make sure he gets a belly full each and every day. If you do that, he will not stray again. Then you should take hair from your head and hair from his—you can get that from combs and brushes—and put each other's hair in the other's sock. Tie those socks together and pin them to the bottom of the mattress of your marital bed. Do this, and you will be able to satisfy your man, and your man will be able to satisfy you. Understood?"

"Yes ma'am," she said as relief came across her face. "Bless you, Miss Lovenia. Bless you," she said. She got up and motioned for her grandson, who hopped up and came over to his grandmother. She placed her hand on his arm to steady herself. "If this doesn't—"

"No 'if.' *When* it works," Miss Lovenia said. "Do exactly what I said, how I said it, and it will work for you. Along with the things I said, dress yourself up. Every day. When your man comes home, be clean and fresh. Listen and ask questions about his day. Touch him every chance you get, whether it be a gentle rubbing of his brow or a hug around his waist as you lean into him. Just make sure when he is around you that he knows you have eyes and interest only for him. Does that make sense to you?"

"Yes ma'am. Thank you," Miss Patrice said. "Me and this boy won't take up any more of your time."

Miss Lovenia reached into her drawer again, and this time she pulled out a brown bag. "Inside are tea leaves that you should make into a tea for yourself every day. It will help you live longer and in far less pain than you are in right now. Avoid meat as much as you can. Chicken and fish is okay, but no meat is even better. Feed your body the correct things, and it will serve you longer."

"Oh my, Miss Lovenia. This is more than I even asked for. Praise Jesus," Miss Patrice exclaimed. She opened her purse, but Miss Lovenia was already standing, pressing the bag into her hand.

"You do not owe me anything else. Be happy, sister," Miss Lovenia said, and I watched as she walked Miss Patrice and the grandson out of the room. I began the process of straightening up. When Miss Lovenia returned, she went and sat in the chair I had been sitting in.

"So, Miss Opal Pruitt, what are your thoughts from all of that? Did old Miss Lovenia Manu scare you with her magic?" she asked, with a look on her face that I could not quite figure out. It was almost a smile. Almost. But she also looked as if she was studying me in some way.

I tried to choose my words wisely. "What you did was not scary. And what you said wasn't scary either. It sounded a lot like common sense."

"Oh, did it now," Miss Lovenia said, and this time she did smile. A full-on smile. "Please explain."

"Well," I said, wondering if I had overstepped my boundaries. "All the things you said for her to do at the end sound like how a person should treat their husband or wife. If she does all of that, you would expect him to show her more attention. Not to take away from the other things."

This time, Miss Lovenia laughed a loud belly laugh. "I chose well with you, Opal Pruitt. I definitely chose well."

There was a loud knock at the door. Judging from the time, I knew it had to be Uncle Myron.

Miss Lovenia took the tray from me. "I will take those things to the kitchen," she said. "Opal, thank you for coming to an old woman's rescue. I think we will be good for each other."

"I appreciate that," I said, and I truly meant it. I went into the hallway where my things were. Miss Lovenia stood down the hallway watching. "See you on Monday, Miss Lovenia."

"If God says the same and delays his coming, I will see you Monday, Miss Opal Pruitt," she said. I was about to open the door when, like lightning, she was beside me. I hadn't even seen her move. I jumped. "Little sister, do not be afraid. I need to tell you this. Those two boys love you. They both care about you in different ways, but neither of them will ever be whole. The boys that they are now will be lost to you. Be careful what you ask God for."

All I could do was nod my head and hurry to the door. I opened it, and Uncle Myron was there. He looked over my shoulder and spoke to Miss Lovenia, but she only nodded her head and went back toward the room where she did her work.

"Hey, baby girl," he said. "Are you ready?"

"Yes sir," I said. "Very much so."

As he guided me to his car, all I could think of was her words. *Lost to you. Lost to you. Lost to you.*

16

"Are you almost ready, Opal? Papa and Mama are gonna be here any minute to pick us up," Lucille said as she jumped on my bed. Lucille had spent the night with me so we could help each other get ready. We had laid out our clothes last night, but by this morning I was torn all over again on what I should wear. I wanted Cedric to be pleased to have me on his arm, especially since it would be a first for many of our friends and family to see us as a couple.

"Girl, you done tried them four dresses on over and over," she said, laughing. "Make up your mind already. You look gorgeous in all of them."

"Thank you. But I just don't want to pick the wrong dress," I said. Unlike Lucille's outfits, most of my clothes were handmade. Yes, they were pretty, and no, most folks couldn't tell they didn't come from some Atlanta store, but I could tell, and it made me a tad bit self-conscious. Lucille always wore clothes from the stores she and Aunt Shimmy went to when they took trips to Atlanta.

Today, Lucille was wearing a brand-new, orange silk, drop-waist dress with delicate pintucks across her hips. She looked like she was from some big city instead of a little ole town like Parsons.

Lucille had done my hair earlier, pinning it in a chignon at the base of my neck. She'd asked if I'd wanted makeup.

"You still have just a little bruising on the left side of your face. A little foundation and face powder could cover that right up," she said.

I quickly told her no. Granny would have been fit to be tied. Every time Granny saw women painting their lips red or putting on rouge, she shook her head and mumbled under her breath that they looked like bawdy women with all that makeup on.

"You better not let Granny see you with makeup. How did you get it anyway?" I asked. I hoped she hadn't bought it without permission.

"Girl, I got it when we went to Atlanta the other week," she said. "Mama said as long as I looked natural in it, she was okay with me wearing a little."

I shook my head. Lucille was so spoiled. Luckily, she didn't act like it. Well, at least most times she didn't. And, really, if the truth be known, Aunt Shimmy was pretty spoiled herself. My Uncle Lem treated them both like they were queens. If they wanted it and he could get it, it was as good as theirs. One time, Lucille had caught a glimpse of this baby doll inside the Sears, Roebuck catalog. Well, before she could finish saying, "I want," Uncle Lem had ordered it for her. He would spoil me, too, but Granny won't let any of the uncles do extra for me very often. She would always tell them that I was her responsibility, not theirs.

Lucille got up and went to her bag. "What you're wearing now is pretty. Purple suits you. It's the color of royalty. Did you know that?" she asked. "Miss Tolson told us that in school."

I smoothed down my dress as I stared at myself critically in the mirror, wanting to catch any loose thread or stain. But everything looked good, and Lucille was right. The purple dress did look the best on me. I had made it myself, copying one of Miss Peggy's McCall's patterns, right down to the yellow embroidered flowers around the rounded neck that Miss Peggy had helped me with. It was a little dressy, made out of this paper-thin crepe material, but from what Lucille had said about these ballgames, the girls all came dressed like they was going to a fancy party or something.

"It's all about catching the eye of one of them Negro ball-players," she had said last night when we were talking about what to wear. Uncle Lem was going to drive me, Lucille, and Aunt Shimmy to Atlanta, where the game was going to be played. Aunt Shimmy had promised she would let me sit with Cedric, as long as I stayed in her eyesight.

"You be good, though. You're not going to make me have to explain to Birdie Pruitt that her grandbaby got spirited away by one of them handsome ballplayers," she'd teased. Now, as I examined myself in the mirror, I didn't know if anyone would find me attractive. I looked country. Homely. My dark skin seemed extra dark, especially in comparison to Lucille and Hazel Moody. My saving grace was my long hair, but it was pulled back so I wouldn't get too hot. All of a sudden, my self-confidence was waning.

"I wonder about that pink dress, though," I said, about to change again, but we heard the car honking outside. I was both excited and nervous at the same time. Lucille came over and put her arms around me.

"You just be yourself, Cousin Opal. Cedric Perkins is going to love you. Oh, and I have something for you," she said and hurried back to her purse. When she came back, she handed me a box. I opened it, and there were some little clip-on earrings with purple stones that matched the color of my purple dress perfectly.

"I got these for you when we was up in Atlanta the other week," she said, her smile so broad.

I laughed and hugged her tight. "You knew I would wear the purple dress."

She laughed too. "I figured you would. It is the prettiest dress in your closet. So I took the chance and got you earrings that will match. Don't put them on until we get past Granny, and for the Lord's sake, take them off before you come back inside the house tonight. Granny will have my hide for getting you jewelry."

"Thank you, Lucille," I said. "You are too good to me." I slipped the earrings inside my purse to put on when we got in the car.

She kissed my cheek. "You are the closest I have to a sister. Anything for you, Cousin Opal."

Uncle Lem blew his horn again.

"Girls, Lem is blowing that horn. Y'all get on out of there and stop all that primping and carrying on," Granny said from the door.

We grabbed our purses and ran out to the front room.

Granny wasn't a crier, but she gave us a watery smile. "Y'all girls have become young ladies right before my eyes. How did that happen?"

We both hugged Granny, and I noticed she seemed to hang on a little longer than normal.

"Y'all be good girls. Don't go up there to Atlanta and forget your home training," she cautioned.

We promised her we would be good. Lucille and I walked out of the house arm in arm. It was actually a little cooler than it had been in months. This was especially strange since it was noon, usually the hottest time of the day. The sky was cloudy, but not really cloudy with rain clouds. They were just the kind of clouds where you like to lie back under a tree and watch and name all the different shapes.

"Hey, Uncle Lem and Aunt Shimmy," I said, getting ready to open my door. But he told me and Lucille to wait. He hopped out of the car and opened the door for us both, and we giggled. It felt nice getting treated like young ladies.

Aunt Shimmy twisted around from the front seat and smiled at us both. "Girls, you look like somebody out of the movies," she said. "Should I call you both the Colored Myrna Loy?"

We laughed. Ever since we got to go to McDonough last year and sit up in the Colored section of the movie theater and see *The Thin Man*, Lucille had been Myrna Loy crazy. I secretly thought Claudette Colbert was a better actress, and much prettier, but I never would have formed my lips to say such a thing. It was sweet of Aunt Shimmy to remember how much a Myrna Loy compliment would mean to Lucille.

"Well, I don't know about nobody else, but I'm gonna be the envy of Atlanta, what with me having the three prettiest gals traveling in my car," Uncle Lem said.

"Well, we are going to be busy dealing with those old cats being jealous that we are in the company of the finest man in Atlanta," Aunt Shimmy said in a flirty voice. Both Lucille and I laughed. Those two were always flirting with each other. Out of all of my relatives, they always seemed like they loved each other as much now as they did when they first became a couple.

"Gonna go to the church so we can follow everybody. With that Klan mess just the other week, and with what happened to you, Opal, we all need to make sure we travel in packs," Uncle Lem said.

"You feeling better, baby?" Aunt Shimmy asked, twisting around again in her seat.

"Yes ma'am," I said. "I'm fine. I barely feel any pain now."

She nodded, and a tear slid down her cheek. She reached for my hand. "We wouldn't have been able to stand it if . . . well . . . if . . ."

"I know, Auntie," I said and squeezed her hand. "But I'm just fine."

She squeezed my hand again and turned around.

Lucille and I settled down in the back and started talking. Well, Lucille did most of the talking. She was determined to catch me up on everything Myrna Loy, as well as all of the local young people news. That was fine with me because all I wanted was to forget about Klan marching, blows to my head, Jimmy Earl Ketchums, and anything that didn't amount to my feeling young and carefree. So I turned all of my attention toward my cousin and her chatter.

"I heard—" she started, and from there she was a whirlwind

of information. I just settled back in my seat and halfway listened to her chatter on about everything from Myrna Loy's next movie to Satchel Paige to what she thought everyone was going to wear today. I just said, "Mm-hmm," when there was a lull in her prattling on and on. It was nice to have a Saturday off work. Especially a Saturday when I was going to be able to meet up with Cedric. I was determined to let go of the memory of my almost kiss with Jimmy Earl. It didn't happen, so there was no reason for me to worry about it. Or at least that's what I told myself.

The road to Atlanta was bumpy and loud because the windows in the car were all down, but Lucille raised her voice and talked and teased me just like we were sitting in her bedroom—something we didn't get to do very much because I was always working.

"And girl, your old enemy, Hazel Moody, says she's going to be at the game today and claim her prize," Lucille said, looking at me with knowing eyes, waiting to see how I would react.

"I'm not engaged or married to Cedric Perkins. If he asked me to the game and then turns around and chooses Hazel Moody, well, then he wasn't mine to start with, I guess," I said. And it wasn't that I didn't care if Cedric liked me or not—it was just I didn't want nobody, not even Lucille, to know just how much.

"Well, you go on, Miss Opal Pruitt," Lucille said, a huge grin filling her face.

I decided to change the subject and get her talking about whatever she was reading. I knew she could talk us all the way to Atlanta if she was talking about a book, and sure enough, she started jabbering about some book called *Wuthering Heights* and how she was in love with some character called Heathcliff. I think she said he was a tortured soul, whatever that meant. So, while she went on and on about that book, I sat back in the seat and daydreamed about Cedric and me.

I dreamed about our wedding. Of course Lucille would be my maid of honor, and I would get her to do my hair, because nobody could make hair look just like the women in the magazines better than Lucille.

I would have on a long, white, silk organza dress and a veil that filled the whole length of the church aisle. Cedric would wear a tuxedo like those men wear in the movies, and his daddy would marry us, and afterward we'd take a honeymoon trip to someplace far off like California, and while I was there, I would get an autograph from Myrna Loy for Lucille. I was so deep in my dreaming, I missed the fact that Lucille had been quiet for a minute or two. She finally cleared her throat, and immediately I felt myself blush.

"I'm sorry, girl," I said, ducking my head. "What did you say?"

She smiled. "Nothing important. Looks like you was having a pretty good daydream. Let me guess. Cedric Perkins?"

I looked away. "No. Not really."

She laughed. "Opal Pruitt, you can keep a secret from a lot of people, but you can't keep one from me. We're sisters, remember? And sisters know everything about each other."

I couldn't tell her what I was thinking. I just couldn't. It seemed stupid, and I knew it would feel even more stupid if I said it out loud. Dreaming about a wedding was not what I did. I might have thought in passing what it might be like to be a wife, but all of the girlish dreaming had never been what I did. So I told her I was thinking about the dresses all the women were going to be wearing, and from there she took out a stack of her magazines and showed me dresses she thought we might see.

Before we knew it, we were driving into Atlanta. I had been to Atlanta before, but every time it felt like I was landing inside of a different world. The streets were full of fancy cars, and the buildings seemed to stretch up to the heavens.

"Oh my," I said. That's all I could come up with. Just like the last time I had come to Atlanta, I was shocked by the many stores and restaurants and people. Everybody seemed to be moving around like they had someplace really important to go. In Parsons, you were subject to see folks just hanging around, drinking a soda, not really going anywhere or doing anything. But here, in this place, it felt like it was a city with a purpose. The streets were filled with white and Colored alike, moving with a quickness, not even slowing down enough to say howdy. That part I wasn't sure if I liked too much. I liked the fact that everybody in Parsons and Colored Town at least said "Good morning" and "Good evening." Nobody ever got too busy to not do that.

"What you think about Atlanta?" Uncle Lem asked. He slowed with the traffic, almost coming to a stop in places because there were so many cars and trucks out and about, not to mention people crossing the streets, hardly paying any attention to the cars. I'd be a nervous wreck walking out there. "Is it just like you remembered?"

"Yes sir, Uncle Lem," I said. "This place is so big, though. I don't see how folks can find their way around here."

"It can be a challenge, for sure. We might have to park here and walk to Ponce de Leon Park," Uncle Lem said. We hadn't moved in a while, what with traffic being so heavy.

"That's all right with me," Lucille said, bouncing in her seat. "I just want to go, go, go."

Uncle Lem laughed. "You mighty excited for a ballgame."

"Oh, Daddy," she said, laughing right back.

I turned away. I wondered if Lucille knew just how blessed she was to have a mama and a papa like Uncle Lem and Aunt Shimmy. I never begrudged my cousins for the love they received from my aunts and uncles, but sometimes I wished I had a little bit of it for me. Sometimes I wanted my own papa and mama to smile at me and love on me. But I didn't have long to dwell on that because we had a ballgame to go to, and I was determined to have a good time.

Just ahead, a Colored man was directing traffic, pointing cars toward places they could park. We turned off about a block from the baseball field and parked in a grassy area underneath some trees, where an elderly Colored man sat in a lawn chair. Uncle Lem gave the man a quarter to watch his car. Then we joined the crowd of walkers, all headed toward the baseball field. Me and Lucille linked arms, giggling like little girls. I couldn't believe all of the people. Uncle Lem said the last time the Black Crackers played there was over five thousand people there to see them. It sure looked like it was that many or more on this day. And not just Colored folks, which surprised me. There was white folks too. When I asked Uncle Lem about it, he said, "These peckerwoods always come to see us play. How else is they gonna learn the game?" he boasted. "There ain't a white player who can outpitch Satchel Paige or outhit Josh Gibson, or any of our local boys for that matter. Naw, they come here to see what real baseball looks like."

Today, the Atlanta Black Crackers would be playing in an exhibition game against the newly formed McDonough Brown Thrashers, whose owner, a local white man, it was said, paid a fortune for Satchel Paige to come out and pitch three innings with them. Everybody and his mama was at this game.

"Where you think Stank is?" Lucille asked. I didn't answer her right away 'cause I was scanning the crowd looking for him myself. How in the world was I gone find him among all these people, I wondered. But I shouldn't have worried because when we got close to the entrance, we all saw Cedric and my cousin M.J. standing there waiting for us. Cedric looked good. He was dressed in a Sunday suit, and he had on a purple shirt and a purple tie, with a purple handkerchief in his pocket.

"Look at y'all. Y'all match," Lucille said, grinning.

"You told," I hissed in her ear.

"Maybe," she said, laughing out loud. "A little birdie may have told him I would get you to wear purple. Now let's see if Hazel Moody can beat this."

"We gone look silly," I whispered, my cheeks feeling warm, but not from the heat.

"No, you all are going to look like a couple. Like somebody who belongs together," Lucille said in a firm voice. "And he was happy that I told him to match up with you. He wanted to look like you two were an item."

I couldn't hardly pay attention to what she was saying because

Cedric was now walking toward us. I noticed M.J. stayed back. Seemed like everybody was trying to help me and Cedric become a real couple. When Cedric got to us, he walked up to Uncle Lem and offered his hand.

"Good afternoon, Deacon Pruitt. It's good to see you," he said in his best church voice.

"Good afternoon to you, too, Stank," Uncle Lem said. "You looking like a big shot, as they say."

"Oh, Daddy," Lucille said, laughing. "That's not what anybody says anymore."

"Well, excuse me, Miss Lady," Uncle Lem said, laughing right along with her.

Cedric made his way down the line and spoke to my Aunt Shimmy and then Lucille, and finally, he was standing in front of me.

"Hey there, Opal. You look good," he said, looking at me like no boy had ever looked at me before. I was so flustered I almost turned away, but I made myself not blink and not duck my head or anything silly like that. I was almost eighteen. I should know how to conduct myself in front of a boy. And anyway, I chided myself, it was just Cedric. He and I had sat and talked on my very own porch. I didn't need to be nervous. I just needed to be myself, like Lucille kept telling me.

I took a deep breath, and then I said in a calm voice, "Hello, Cedric. Thank you. You look right handsome yourself." I was proud of myself for not stuttering or misspeaking.

He offered me his arm, and I looked at Aunt Shimmy. She nodded her head in approval. I placed my arm through his.

"Y'all hold on. Let me give you your ticket money, Opal," Uncle Lem said.

"That's okay, Deacon Pruitt. I've got enough to cover her. Her cousin too," he added.

Uncle Lem looked pleased. "Well, all right. You children go on. Just make sure you all stay together," he said, putting an emphasis on the word *all*. "We gone wait here for everybody else to get parked."

"We'll all stay together, sir," Cedric said and escorted me toward the ticket gate. Lucille made sure she walked a few steps behind us.

"I can't believe we gone see Satchel Paige pitch today. You excited?" I asked, tightening my grip on his arm just a bit. The crowd was thick, and I didn't want to get separated from him. "Lucille, you take Cedric's other arm. I don't want us getting lost from each other."

She laughed. "Don't worry about me none. I'm gone run ahead and stand beside M.J. Y'all just take your own sweet time. Satchel Paige won't be coming out to pitch for a good long while."

Before I could stop her, she ran off toward our cousin, who waved when he saw her coming toward him. Cedric turned me around so I was looking up at him.

"You look good, Opal," he repeated, looking at me like I was the most beautiful girl in the world. "And yes, I'm excited to see Satchel Paige pitch. But seeing you show up in this pretty purple getup, well, that's better than seeing Satchel Paige pitch a no-hitter."

I didn't know what to say. But before I could come up with

the words, M.J. waved at us to come on. Cedric took me by my hand and led me to where they were standing.

"They say Satchel ain't gone come out until the seventh inning, maybe the eighth," M.J. said. It was clear he was not pleased with the news.

Cedric laughed. "That sounds about right. The old man's not gone wear himself out for some little ole exhibition game. And anyway, if he started the game, everybody would want him to finish it. He'll come out all fresh as a daisy and entertain the folks for three innings. Must be nice being Satchel Paige."

We all laughed, and I walked up to the ticket booth real proud being on Cedric's arm. I could tell he felt pretty good about himself when he bought my ticket and Lucille's.

"And you can get all the peanuts and popcorn y'all want," he said. "I hauled water buckets all this week to make sure I had enough money to treat you right today."

"Thank you. I'm already having the best time ever, and I haven't seen a lick of baseball yet," I told him.

He laughed a deep, throaty laugh. "Come on, y'all. Let's go get to our seats," he said.

We all followed the crowd of Colored folks to our section. The whites sat in the best seats, but we still had a good view of everything. And anyway, me and Lucille were so busy admiring all the fancy-dressed Colored women and girls that we didn't pay attention to where we were sitting. We were glad we'd dressed in our best clothes. We looked just as good as the other girls, even though the majority of them were from the city. My dress may have been homemade, but I was proud of every stitch of it.

When the McDonough team entered the field, we all stood

and clapped and cheered. We weren't from McDonough, but it was like they were our team, too, since we all were just a few miles from each other.

"That's Pooch Williams pitching today," Cedric said, pointing toward the pitcher's mound. "And that's his cousin Milton over on first base. I met them last year at a revival meeting at their church."

"I bet he can't throw as good as you," I said in a bold voice.

"Aw, I do all right. But Pooch, he's gone show Satchel a thing or two today. He's got a fastball that's wicked. But I'd say my curveball is right up there," he said, smiling broadly. "Y'all want something to eat or drink?" He turned around to where M.J. and Lucille were sitting. "I'll treat."

M.J. laughed. "Well, if that's the case, I'll take a soda pop and some popcorn. Me and Lucille can share."

Like he'd been doing it all his life, Cedric whistled loudly for the guy who was selling the snacks to come our way. Before long, we were eating and laughing and having the best time ever. I should have known things were going too good. Something should have told me not to let myself get so happy.

"Well, well, well. If it ain't Stinky and his nigger gal friend," a voice said from the end of the bleachers. We all looked at the same time. I couldn't believe my eyes. Standing in the distance was Jimmy Earl, his cousin Skeeter, who was doing the loud talking, and Jimmy Earl's friend Courtland.

"Don't," I whispered to Cedric, tightening my grip on his sleeve, but it was too late. He was already on his feet. Instantly, I knew things were about to get ugly.

17

The veins were popping out of Cedric's neck and face, and he was pouring sweat as he clenched and unclenched his fists. M.J. stood with his arm blocking Cedric from lurching at Skeeter. I had my hand on his arm. All we were supposed to be doing was having a good time while we waited on Satchel Paige to come and pitch. It wasn't supposed to turn into a battle between Colored and white. Again.

"Come on, Stinky coon. You want to go a few innings with me?" Skeeter said, as M.J. moved in between Cedric and Skeeter.

"I'm right here, peckerwood. Come for me," Cedric yelled, his voice thick with emotion.

Before Cedric and Skeeter could tie up, two big Colored men grabbed Cedric, and Jimmy Earl pulled a laughing and spitting Skeeter away.

"All right, Stank. He's just funning," Jimmy Earl said. "Don't mind him at all. We all just want to see the ballgame. Ain't no reason getting in no row with each other."

"You better be glad they holding me back," Cedric yelled. He tried to break free, but the Colored men holding him were bigger than he was, and they just kept trying to talk him down.

"That cracker ain't worth it, son," I heard one of them say.

"Let him go. Let him go and let's see how much fight the nigger has in him," Skeeter taunted.

"Shut up, Skeeter," Jimmy Earl said as Skeeter laughed like someone who was out of his mind. "Courtland, get him out of here, for God's sake."

"Come on, Skeeter," Courtland yelled, grabbing Skeeter by the arm and nearly dragging him away.

"Settle down, young buck. Today ain't the day. Go on back and sit with your girl," one of the Colored men said to Cedric.

"Cedric, please," I said. "They ain't worth it."

"Sorry for the trouble," I heard Jimmy Earl say. None of us said anything to him, and finally he left. I could tell by his slumped-down shoulders that my words must have stung, but in that moment, the only person I cared about was Cedric.

It wasn't easy getting Cedric to settle down. I had never seen anybody so angry before in my life. It was like his insides were swollen up with years' worth of anger against white folks. There was no calming him down. I was afraid we were going to get thrown out of the ballpark if he didn't let it go.

"Stupid peckerwoods," Cedric roared, even though Skeeter, Jimmy Earl, and Courtland had long since left the ballpark. He was sitting next to me, but he was still furious. The veins were still popping out on his face, and he was sweating so much I was afraid he was going to have a heart attack. M.J. had gone to find

Reverend Perkins, who came over and told Cedric to take a walk with him.

"I don't want to take a walk. I want to go pound them fools in the ground, is what I want to do."

"And what will that fix?" his daddy asked. He folded his arms in front of himself like he would do when he was preaching about something he really wanted the congregation to get.

One of the men who'd helped keep Cedric from beating up Skeeter chimed in. "Go with your father, son."

Cedric looked at me, and I nodded my head and mouthed the word "Go." He sighed and allowed his father to lead him away. I watched as they walked toward the entrance to the ballpark. The same direction Skeeter, Jimmy Earl, and Courtland had gone. I prayed silently that they had truly left. I didn't want to see Cedric get involved in any fights today. I hardly noticed when Lucille came and sat beside me.

"I can't stand them white boys. They always stirring up trouble. Why did they even have to come here in the first place? This should be our time to not have to deal with white folks," she said, her face angrier than I'd ever seen her before.

"It was just that Skeeter who was causing trouble," I said. "Jimmy Earl was trying to calm things down."

"Stop defending those white people," I heard a sharp voice behind me say. It was Aunt Shimmy. "Don't you know if Cedric would have fought that white trash that all of them would have joined in on the fight? They always stick together."

"Not Jimmy Earl. He—"

"Yes," Aunt Shimmy interrupted. "Even the Jimmy Earls of

the world will stick with their own kind when it comes right down to it. Mark my word, Opal. The day will come when sides will have to be taken in this battle between the races, and you have to learn to see them for what they truly are."

"But Miss Peggy and Jimmy Earl have never been anything but nice to me and Granny," I said, still feeling the need to take up for them.

"Yes, of course they are nice to you both, Opal," Aunt Shimmy said. Her voice sounded patient even though I knew she was not feeling particularly patient with me at that moment. "You and Mama are good Negroes. You work hard, you don't talk back, and you mind your own business. Just what white folks want us to do. But try telling your Miss Peggy you want the right to vote someday. Tell her you want to be able to live next door to her and have your children and Jimmy Earl's children all go to the same schools. Then come back and tell me how good they are."

I didn't know what to say. I had never heard Aunt Shimmy talk that way before.

"Settle down, Mama," Uncle Lem said, putting his arm around Aunt Shimmy. Tears were rolling down her face. Lucille got up and sat beside her mother and put her arm around her too.

Maybe Aunt Shimmy was right, but I didn't want to believe her words. I wanted to believe that at the end of the day, Miss Peggy thought highly of me, and Jimmy Earl thought of me as a friend. Maybe that wasn't possible. But I didn't want to think that everything Aunt Shimmy said was true. Because if it was, it hurt. It hurt a lot. I had grown up in Miss Peggy's house. I had slept in her guest room when Granny had to work late, and

Miss Peggy had read bedtime stories to me and Jimmy Earl when we were little, him sitting on one side of her lap and me sitting on the other. And Jimmy Earl had always teased me like I was a friend and not just some Colored girl who helped keep his house clean. *Surely*, I thought, *those special moments that I remember couldn't all be a lie.* Aunt Shimmy must have seen I was all twisted up inside, because she reached out and touched my face lightly with the back of her hand. A gentle touch, like a mama touching her child.

"Honey, no one is arguing that there aren't good white folks in the world. I truly believe that there are. But there are limitations to their goodness and their kindness. No matter how much they may care for us, they will always see us as inferior. They will never see us as their equals," she said.

For a time, we just sat in silence, each one of us deep in our thoughts. But then Cedric came hurrying back with his father, looking different. He looked happy. Cedric was smiling ear to ear, and I couldn't imagine what his father could have said to make him look so different from the angry boy who had only minutes ago walked away.

He rushed over and squatted in front of me, taking both of my hands. "Opal, you ain't gone believe what just happened. You just ain't gone believe it, girl."

I found myself laughing just from seeing him so happy. "What? What happened?"

"I just met Satchel Paige. Me and *the* Satchel Paige just had a conversation. We talked just like two old friends," he said, and his daddy laughed behind him.

"Well, I don't know if I'd go that far," his daddy said.

Cedric didn't let his daddy stop him. "Opal, Daddy and me were walking, just walking, and who do you think we ran into?"

"Satchel Paige," I said, laughing. He laughed right along with me, and so did everyone who was in earshot of our conversation.

"Right. I just said that, didn't I? Well, me and Daddy were walking and all of a sudden there he was, *the* Satchel Paige just leaning against the finest car you ever did see, and before I knew it, Daddy took me by the arm and walked us up to him, and said I was the best pitcher he'd ever seen short of Mr. Paige himself."

Reverend Perkins cut in. "I sure did tell him that. I told him my boy has one of the best arms I've ever seen."

Cedric looked at his daddy and grinned, and then he turned back to me. "Well, Mr. Paige looked over at me and said, 'Prove it, son,' and before I knew it, he had the McDonough team's catcher all gloved up, waiting on me to throw him some balls," Cedric said, his eyes glowing.

By this time, everybody around us was listening.

"What happened next?" I asked, so excited I couldn't contain myself. It was like all the bad that had happened earlier just disappeared.

"Well, I warmed up with a pitch or two, and I could tell he was liking what he was seeing," Cedric said, squeezing my hands. I almost bounced in my seat.

M.J. chimed in. "Y'all shoulda come and got me."

Cedric looked at him with an apology on his face. "I would have, M.J., but everything was happening so fast. First, Mr. Paige said, 'Let me see your fastball,' and then he just started rattling off the pitches left and right. 'Show me your slider. Curveball. Screwball.' Opal, everything he called out, I did it. And now he said he's gone talk to the manager of the McDonough team and see if he can't get me on as a regular. Do you hear that, girl?"

"Oh, Cedric. That's wonderful news. I'm so happy for you," I said, and I was. This was Cedric's dream. I couldn't think of a single person I wanted more to find what it was they was looking for in life than him.

"Opal, Mr. Paige said along with playing here for McDonough, he might be able to add me to his all-star team. I might be making two hundred to three hundred dollars per month. Can you believe that?"

I shook my head. I couldn't. That was more money than I'd ever seen in my life.

"Man, you'll be rich," M.J. said, a look of envy on his face. "You think you can get me on?"

"I don't see why not. You hit better than anybody I know," he answered. And then he looked back at me. "Think your granny will approve of me now?"

Before any of us could say any more, the announcer asked everybody to stand for the prayer and the singing of the national anthem. Cedric moved real close to me. So close we was almost touching each other. His hand was dangling near mine. I tried to steady my breathing as a rather fat-looking boy with a saxophone came out to where the players were all lined up and played a somewhat off-key rendition of "The Star-Spangled Banner." It took all I could do to remember the words as we all sang. After that, we all joined in and sang the Negro national anthem, "Lift

Every Voice and Sing." I stood proudly beside Cedric and joined my voice with his and every other Colored person there.

Lift every voice and sing
Till earth and heaven ring
Ring with the harmonies
Of Liberty

It was a magical moment to hear that many voices all singing those powerful words together. Once we were done, we all took our seats, and then the ballgame started. And not long after that, the smell of popcorn, peanuts, and hot dogs began to really fill the air, even more than before. The ballgames I'd gone to in the past had all been at the church or at the little baseball field downtown, and there had never been anybody selling food like this. Oh, there would be folks who would bring food with them picnic style, but this was like nothing I'd seen before.

"Get your peanuts. Peanuts. Get your peanuts," men cried as they walked up and down the rows of bleachers. Others yelled, "Cracker Jack. Get your Cracker Jack with a present in the box."

Cedric looked at me. "What you want?"

"I'll get the Cracker Jack," I said. "If that's okay."

He smiled. "Anything you want." He raised his hand and signaled for the guy selling them to come over. "A Cracker Jack for my girl, please," he said, and I almost couldn't contain my joy.

I was somebody's girl.

While Cedric was paying for the Cracker Jack, I watched as

a beautiful Colored lady made her way into the stands. She was dressed finer than any Hollywood movie star I'd seen, and she carried herself like she was a queen or something.

"That's Satchel Paige's wife," Cedric whispered in my ear. "She's the head wife. For now," he said, winking at me.

"She's beautiful," I said, trying to ignore his words, because I wasn't sure if he meant them. I mean, yes, I had been daydreaming about being his wife, but those were silly, girlie dreams. For all I knew, I was some phase Cedric was going through, and before long, especially if he started traveling and playing ball, he might just forget about a country girl like me. I looked over at Satchel Paige's wife. Now, she was the type of woman I imagined Cedric would want one day want. She was fair-complected and her hair hung in gentle waves on her shoulder. She wore a little flowery hat that perfectly matched her yellow dress with pink chrysanthemums on it. She even had on a pair of yellow gloves that she took off and folded inside of her little clutch bag.

"She ain't nearly as beautiful as you," Cedric said down low near my ear. "Soon as I get myself settled in with a team, you'll be sitting right down there with them. Dressed just as pretty as you are today."

I felt my cheeks get warm. I couldn't believe how exciting it was to have a boy flirt with me the way Cedric was. Now I understood why the girls all wanted boyfriends so bad. If I'd known this was how it would make me feel, I would have paid attention to Cedric's flirting a long time ago.

"You gone look and see what your prize is?" he asked after he gave me the box of Cracker Jack. I rifled through it and finally found the prize. It was a little plastic ring. I tucked it into my purse. I wanted to save it to remember the day by.

I looked up at him and was about to tell him how good of a time I was having, but then M.J. cut in.

"Hey, Stank. Look who's up to bat. Leonard Natchez," M.J. said. "If that fool can get on with the McDonough team, I know we won't have no trouble."

Cedric laughed, and before long he and M.J. were talking baseball. I almost wanted to kick M.J. in the kneecaps for interrupting me and Cedric's conversation. I looked around and saw everybody had coupled up. Even Lucille was sitting close to Ray Carver, a boy from church. I decided to go to the bathroom and stretch my legs a bit. And to be honest, I really couldn't care less about baseball.

"I'll be back," I said to Cedric.

"You want me to go with you?" he asked.

I shook my head. "I'm just going over there," I said, pointing toward the direction of the restroom. He nodded, and I could feel his eyes on me as I walked away. I walked toward where I thought the Colored bathrooms might be. I had to go out of sight of where we were sitting. I almost turned back around to see if Lucille or Aunt Shimmy would come with me, but by that time I really had to go, so I kept looking for the bathroom. Finally, I saw it and hurried into the one marked Colored. To my surprise, Mrs. Paige walked in behind me. She was so beautiful and so poised, I didn't know what to say, but she smiled at me.

"That's a pretty dress you're wearing," she said. "Purple is definitely your color."

"Thank you, ma'am," I said. "I like what you're wearing too. Yellow suits you."

"No, yellow suits Satchel Paige," she said and laughed.

I laughed, too, trying not to start dancing in place because I really needed to go.

She waved me on. "Go on before you have an accident in that pretty dress of yours."

I laughed, embarrassed but grateful to go. I hurried into one of the stalls. While I was putting paper on the toilet seat, something Granny had always preached about doing when going in public places, I heard the sound of giggling girls entering the bathroom.

"Did y'all see her hanging all over Stank like she was his girlfriend or something?" one of the girls said. They were talking about me. I couldn't believe it, but by this time, I couldn't hold my pee any longer, so I squatted and listened.

"Oh, girl, and that sad little homemade purple dress is a mess," the other girl said, and I realized I knew her voice. It was Hazel Moody.

She's just jealous, I told myself, but I would be lying if I didn't admit that her words hurt. Hazel Moody's family wasn't rich, but she never wore homemade anything. She always bought her clothes in Atlanta, just like Lucille, or at least that was the story she told. I felt like rushing outside and telling them both off, but I didn't. I wasn't bold like that. Lucille would have been all over them. But that just wasn't me. So I kept listening.

"Girl, you can tell that dress came straight from some out-of-date pattern. That dress went out of style back during slavery," the first girl said. "But even with all that, she's got your man, girl. What you gone do about that?"

Hazel responded, "What am I gone do? I'm gone sit back and let Stank have his little fun with his little servant girl. After a while, he'll get tired of messing around with the Help, and he'll come back to me . . . a girl with pure class who doesn't have to empty slop jars for a living."

I felt tears start to flow down my face. Suddenly, I was doubting everything about myself. Why would Cedric want a girl like me when he could have Hazel Moody, or practically any Colored girl of his dreams? Then I heard Mrs. Paige speak.

"You girls should be ashamed of yourselves."

"What? We . . . It's none of your business," Hazel said in a huffy voice.

"Well, sweet pea, you made it my business when you started talking against another girl right here in a public space. So I have something to say to you both."

"We don't have to—"

"Oh, yes ma'am. You do have to," Mrs. Paige said, cutting off Hazel. "If you can't get a man without down-talking another woman, well, that just means you ain't worth much to start with yourself. I, for one, hope this young lady you've been talking about not only keeps the boy y'all are all hot and bothered over, but I hope she ends up calling him her husband. Y'all are sad. Now leave."

"You—"

"I am Mrs. Satchel Paige. In the twinkling of an eye, I could have you young kittens thrown out of this ballpark and run out of Atlanta if I wanted to. Don't test me. Now, leave."

I heard the rapid footsteps of the girls leaving. I didn't know what to do. I wiped myself and flushed the toilet. I was so ashamed. I was embarrassed by the hurtful words, and I was humiliated that I didn't stand up for my own self, that I allowed Mrs. Paige to fight my battles for me. I just wanted to dissolve into the floor at that moment.

"Come on out, honey," Mrs. Paige said. "Those old jealous girls are gone. Come on now. I don't have all day. Satchel Paige will be pitching soon, and he'll get the attitude if he looks up in those stands and doesn't see me."

I slowly opened my door and walked out. I know I must have looked a mess with my face stained with tears.

"Wash your hands and then wash that pretty face," she said, sounding like a mama.

I did as I was told, the whole time thanking her for taking up for me.

She clicked her teeth. "Girl, that wasn't nothing. Now, you be still. I need to do something," she said and then reached into her purse and took out a tube of lipstick and lightly dotted my lips. When she was done, she turned me around to the mirror.

"Look at yourself, darling," she said. I looked, and I liked how the brownish-red lipstick looked on me. I turned to her and smiled.

"Thank you, Mrs. Paige," I said.

"You're welcome. Now you march back out there and you slide in beside your boyfriend, and you don't let them kittens bother you," she said, linking her arm with mine. "They wouldn't be talking if you didn't have them running scared. Women are all the time throwing themselves at Satchel Paige. But look who's wearing his ring." She held out her hand for me to see the huge diamond ring and wedding band. "So let's go let them know who's really running things in this ballpark."

And much to my surprise, she walked out with me like we were longtime girlfriends and walked me back to my seat. Everybody had stopped talking when they saw me with Mrs. Paige. Hazel and her friend were sitting a few seats back from Cedric. They had been laughing and giggling, but when they saw Mrs. Paige's arm linked with mine, they went silent. I felt happy enough to burst.

"All right, my dear. I've delivered you back to your beau, safe and sound. Y'all enjoy the game," she said, throwing up her hand to wave at everyone. Then she sashayed back to her seat with the other ballplayers' wives.

"What was that all about?" Cedric asked.

I smiled. "Oh, nothing. I just made a new friend. That's all."

I could tell he wanted to ask more questions, but I pointed toward the baseball field where Satchel Paige was warming up on the pitcher's mound. "You don't want to miss this," I said, lightly placing my hand on Cedric's arm. I could feel the stares of Hazel Moody and her friend on the back of my head, but I didn't worry about them at all. I just sat there, imagining myself sitting a few rows down with the other ballplayers' wives, as my man, Cedric, walked up to the pitcher's mound.

18

"ranny. Granny," I mumbled, tossing in my bed from side to side. "Granny, stop him. Stop him," I yelled. I could feel his hands all over me. First, there was the grabbing around my waist from behind, wild hands pulling me off the road into the ditch. Then there was his hot breath on my neck, smelling like a mixture of tobacco and sweat. Then there was his hands grabbing at my breast. Mixed in with all of this were my screams as I twisted and fought him, trying to get away.

"Shut up," he growled. The voice felt familiar. My mind almost allowed me to see his face. In my dream world I tried to focus my eyes to see my attacker, but he was still a blur. It was almost like he was standing in fog. I could make out the form, but I couldn't make out the exact details of his face. But I was remembering his words, clear as day. "Thought you was gonna get away from me," he said, his hand pressing against my mouth so hard, I was having a difficult time getting air. So I went off my instincts. I bit down hard on his hand. I remembered that. I could almost feel the weight of my teeth bearing down into his flesh.

Then he slapped me hard across my face. Over and over again until my eyes swelled and blood trickled from the corners of my mouth. I remembered my eyes crowding with tears, but as the dream became more and more in focus, I could finally make out that face. That awful face. Skeeter. Skeeter Ketchums. All this time, his face had been like a ghost to me. I could see the outline, but not the details. But now I saw him as clear as if it were actually happening all over again.

I felt arms pulling at me and I tried to fight. "Stop. Stop," I screamed.

"It's Granny, baby. It's Granny. You all right," the voice said, holding me tighter, keeping me from fighting her or hurting myself. "Open your eyes. Open your eyes and look at me."

It took me a moment or two, but I was finally able to open my eyes and see that it was, indeed, Granny holding me, and not Skeeter. I relaxed in her arms, but my body was racked with sobs—sobs of thankfulness that Granny was the one holding me and horror that it was Skeeter, Jimmy Earl's cousin, who attacked me. Skeeter was the one person I knew without a doubt my uncles and new boyfriend would want to kill after the truth came out. Skeeter was always the one taunting folks and saying ugly things. He was always the one leading the parade when the Klan marched through downtown Parsons. And he was the one who had nearly gotten into a fight with Cedric at the ballgame. I wished my attacker were anyone but Skeeter. I didn't see any way for things to turn out all right once everyone knew who had hurt me.

"What's going on?" another voice said. I jumped, startled by the sleepy voice across the room. I had completely forgotten that Lucille had spent the night again.

"It's all right, Lucille. Opal just had a bad dream. I got her. Go on to my room and go back to sleep," Granny said.

Lucille mumbled something, walked over to my bed, and kissed me on my forehead. Then she went stumbling out the door toward Granny's room. I looked over at the little clock by my side of the bed. It was 2:00 a.m.

We had gotten back home about seven last night, and it had taken hours after that for me and Lucille to settle down, as we both talked and laughed and giggled over every single thing that happened, from my encounter with Mrs. Paige to Lucille being allowed to sit next to a boy.

Thinking back now, yesterday seemed years and years ago. Now all I could see was Skeeter's terrible face and smell his awful breath like he was standing right over me again.

"Granny. I remembered," I whispered, shaking so hard the bed made loud creaking sounds. "It was Skeeter. Skeeter was the one who jumped on me the other day."

"Skeeter Ketchums," Granny whispered back at me. Neither one of us wanted Lucille to hear, because just as sure as she heard me say it was Skeeter, she would run and tell her daddy or mama. "Are you sure, chile? Maybe you just dreamed up his face. Maybe it was some strange white man like we first thought. Somebody you didn't know."

"No ma'am," I said in a low voice. "It was Skeeter who got at me the other day. I'm sure. What are we gone do, Granny?" I asked after I was done telling her every detail I could remember.

All I could think of was how Cedric was ready to beat Skeeter down at the baseball game yesterday for just talking at us sideways. I didn't even want to think what he and the uncles would do if they found out Skeeter was the one to jump me. I sure didn't want to tell them the truth of what happened, but I knew how angry the uncles got when we didn't tell them the truth about me getting hurt in the first place. They would be even angrier if they found out that I got my memory back and we didn't tell them.

Granny was quiet for a long time. So long, I wondered if she had dozed off. But finally she said what she always said. "Pray, chile. That's all I know for us to do. Pray."

"Granny, but what if—"

"Let me talk to Jesus about it. He always knows what to do," she said.

I tried not to be frustrated. I wanted to yell, "Where was Jesus when all of this happened? Why didn't he stop it before it started? Why? Why? Why?" But I didn't say any of those things. I knew Granny would have either gotten angry at me or said, "God's ways aren't our ways," or "We'll understand it better by and by." So I said nothing, except my usual "Yes ma'am."

I pulled the thin sheet over both of us. It was still hot from the lack of rain and June in Georgia, but I needed something between us and the outside world, even if it was just an old cotton sheet. It wasn't long until Granny's soft prayers to God gave way to her gentle sleeping noises. I tried to go back to sleep, but every time I closed my eyes, that day just kept coming back to me, new details being revealed with such a quickness, I almost lost my breath.

"Let me go. Let me go," I had yelled as Skeeter held me down to the ground.

"Keep fighting me. I'm gone give you something to fight over in just a minute," he had said, trying to put his mouth on mine. But I kept twisting and turning, determined not to let him defile me with his nasty mouth.

Somehow I managed to twist around enough to knee him real good in his privates, and he doubled over in pain but recovered so quickly I didn't have time to move out of his way when he hit me hard in the face with his fist. Then he lifted me up and smashed my head back down. By itself it probably would have hurt me bad, but the back of my head hit a rock, and the next thing I remembered was waking up in Miss Lovenia's house.

Those memories were crashing back into my mind so hard, I wrapped my arms tighter around Granny's waist and pressed my head against her back. Before I knew it, I was waking up to Granny telling me it was time to get ready for church.

Granny had let me sleep a little later than normal, so there wasn't much time to talk about anything. Lucille kept asking me if I was okay, and I told her the truth. Well, sort of the truth. I told her that I had a nightmare about the other day. She came up and hugged me hard.

"You don't have to say another word," she said. "We'll just think about yesterday and how good of a day we both had, and the fact that your boyfriend is going to come walk you to church again. I wish Mama and Daddy would let Ray Carver walk me to church, but Mama said no. Can you believe that they are being so stuffy?"

I could, actually. I knew Lucille acted my age or older, but she was just fifteen. I didn't want to hurt her feelings, but I agreed with my aunt and uncle that she needed more time before getting serious about a boy. So I just sort of nodded. But in true Lucille fashion, she moved right along. Her feelings would get hurt sometimes, but she didn't stay hurt for long.

"So what are you going to wear?" she asked, her excitement renewed.

I groaned. The last thing I wanted to stress out over was my clothes again. Between keeping secrets and all around feeling nervous about me and Cedric, I decided to just go to my closet and wear whatever my hands touched first. I pulled out a light-blue dress I hadn't worn in a few Sundays. My hair was still neat from yesterday, so once I was done dressing and checking myself one more time in the mirror, I went outside and sat on the porch swing. I was glad I did because I got to catch a glimpse of Cedric walking up the road and crossing over into our yard. Mr. Tote, who only went to church once in a blue moon, was sitting on his stoop. I had called out to him when I came out, but he was busy whittling something, so he'd not said much more than a howdy. I was fine with that. My mind was still full.

"Hey there, Brother Perkins," he called out to Cedric. "You been mighty regular over here at Miss Birdie's house, I see."

I felt my cheeks blush when he said that, but Cedric just laughed.

"Ain't no secret, Brother Tote," he said. "Sister Birdie got a beautiful granddaughter, and I'm hoping she'll let me walk her to church. You ought to join us."

"Well, Brother Perkins," Mr. Tote laughed back, "if Miss Birdie would let me walk her to church, I might be heading down that road with y'all."

I was so glad Granny wasn't outside to hear Mr. Tote say that. She would have said he was being too fresh. Granny didn't like Mr. Tote's flirting. She said she didn't even want God to send her a godly man, let alone a rascal like Mr. Tote. She just wanted to spend the rest of her days with her family and friends.

Cedric laughed at Mr. Tote's words and kept walking toward our house, singing to himself as he made his way to the porch steps. When he caught a glimpse of me, he smiled a wide smile.

"Hey, pretty gal," he said, and then I noticed. Cedric was wearing a pinstriped, powder-blue suit that nearly matched the dress I was wearing.

"They're gonna think we planned this," I groaned. "Yesterday was bad enough, but now . . ."

He sat down beside me. "Planned what?"

"Our outfits," I said, as a tear slid down my face. I felt stupid. With all that I was carrying inside, here I was shedding tears over us both wearing the color blue. I just didn't want to deal with the snide looks from Hazel Moody and her friends, and I didn't want to deal with the teasing from M.J. and my other cousins. And I didn't want to deal with the sideways looks from Granny and my uncles. "I'm going to go inside and change," I said, about to get up, but Cedric reached over and took both of my hands in his.

"What's wrong, Opal?" he asked. "I know you ain't carrying on over some matching outfits. They just clothes, and who cares if somebody thinks we a couple. We is, ain't we? So what's really wrong?"

"I—" I started, but before I could finish my thoughts, I heard Granny clear her throat at the door.

"Time to go, children," she said, walking out with Lucille behind her. "Good morning, Cedric."

"Good morning, Sister Birdie. Good to see you again this morning," he said. "Morning, Lucille."

"Good morning, Stank," Lucille said as she took Granny by the arm and guided her down the stairs. Lucille was wearing a yellow dress with blue roses on it. As usual, she looked like a dream.

"Morning, Miss Birdie Pruitt," Mr. Tote called out from his porch. "You looking mighty nice today." And she did. Granny had on a green dress that she wore with a matching green straw hat. She had her walking stick this morning. I felt bad for keeping her up so late last night. Whenever she didn't get her rest, her hips and knees tended to hurt her.

"Praise the Lord," Granny said. "You'd look nice sitting in a pew at the church house."

"You gone let me sit in the pew beside you?" he asked.

"If that was what it took to get you in the house of the Lord, I reckon so," she said, but she didn't slow down walking down the road. We took off behind her as Mr. Tote laughed and waved. Lucille caught up with Granny and walked with her, and Cedric and I walked a few paces behind them.

"What's wrong, Opal? You not acting like yourself today," Cedric said down low.

I looked at him and I wanted to tell him. I didn't want to start off having a relationship with a boy based on lies and half-truths, but at the same time, I didn't want to start a war here in Colored Town and Parsons. I didn't want folks fighting over me, and I sure didn't want somebody I loved to get hurt over something that was over and done with, so I just smiled.

"I think I'm just tired," I said, and I was telling the truth. I was tired. So maybe that was enough for me to say for now.

"Ain't nobody gonna say nothing sideways in front of me when it comes to us, Opal Pruitt," Cedric said. "It took me a while to come to my senses and see that I wasn't living the kind of life I needed to be living, and in just a few days with you as my girl, I finally seem to see where I want to go in life. I see my purpose."

I didn't really know what to say. Hearing Cedric say these things meant the world to me. I had never really pined too hard over not having a boyfriend. I figured the day would come. I figured some boy or man would one day take a shine to me, but I never thought it would be Cedric Perkins. He and I didn't seem to have anything in common at first glance. But these last few days of being his girl made me see different. I always figured I didn't have much to offer anybody besides my cooking and cleaning skills. But Cedric made me feel beautiful and worthy to be loved by someone like him. I couldn't believe I was going into my birthday week and Founder's Day Week with a boyfriend and a new outlook on life.

It didn't take long for us to get to church. This Sunday was way different from last Sunday. Sister Perkins was waiting outside, and we all spoke, but she stopped me as everyone else continued to go inside, including Cedric. Once it was just the two of us, she pulled me into a hug.

"Thank you, Opal Pruitt," she said.

"What are you thanking me for, Sister Perkins? I didn't do anything," I said, feeling shy. I had always liked Sister Perkins, but she was never someone I felt close to like some of the older ladies at church. She was kind to everyone, but she had always been a bit standoffish. I didn't have a clue what she was talking about.

"Chile, you have done more than you can even know," she said, still holding me around my shoulders. "My son is not the same person he was just a week ago. You have changed that boy for the good. God and you, that is. As a mother, we pray that our sons will fall for good girls. Christian girls. Girls with the potential to be good wives and mothers. I know you two are just now starting to talk to each other, but I just wanted you to know, you've got my approval. Sister Birdie is the best there is, and for my son to like a granddaughter raised by her, well, I could not ask God for more than that."

And before I had a chance to say anything else, she squeezed my arm once more and went inside. I was stunned. I didn't know what to do, so I just sort of stood there not moving.

"You okay?" a voice asked. I looked up and it was Cedric. "Mama didn't say anything out of the way, did she?"

I shook my head. "No. She was very nice. She said some very nice things."

He nodded. "I figured. She told me last night when me and

Daddy got home that she thought you was good for me, and she hoped I would be good for you."

"You are," I said. "We better get inside before Granny comes looking for me."

Cedric opened the door, and although we didn't do anything forward like hold hands, we walked together down the aisle of the church. We were early, so there weren't a lot of people at church yet, but as Cedric and I walked down to the front of the church where I normally sat, and he slid in beside me, I could feel the eyes of people watching us. But the only eyes I focused on were Sister Perkins's. She looked over at us and smiled and nodded. As some of the older folks walked in, they all stopped at our pew and spoke.

"You young folks looking mighty nice today," Sister Walker said as she bent down and kissed my cheek. "I meant to come look in after you last week, but my arthritis had me down in the bed. You doing okay?"

I nodded. "Yes ma'am. I'm okay."

"Don't you worry none about that Klan and that awful person who put hands on you," she said. "The Lord sent me a word for you, baby. He said for you to remember Hebrews 13:6. 'So that we may boldly say, The Lord is my helper, and I will not fear what man shall do unto me.'"

"Thank you, Sister Walker," I said, trying not to embarrass myself by crying. It seemed like anytime I was feeling low or bad about anything, one of the elders at church would come to me with a Scripture that they said God had placed on their heart for me. I didn't always understand everything about God or church or the Scriptures, but I did understand these God-loving people. These saints. These amazing people who stood in the gap when I was motherless and fatherless. They always made sure I felt loved, no matter what.

"You okay?" Cedric asked again.

I nodded. "I'm good." And I was. I didn't know what Granny and I were going to do, but I knew this . . . I knew I was going to listen to the words Sister Walker shared with me, and I was going to trust that Granny's prayers made it all the way to heaven to God's ears. I didn't want to be afraid anymore. I didn't want to worry about Skeeter. I just wanted to enjoy my day sitting with the boy of my dreams in the church that I hoped would one day be the place where I would stand before God and everyone I loved and look into Cedric's eyes, and him in mine, as we both said the words, "I do."

19

$\mathcal{F}$inally, the weather was changing for the better. I got up early Monday morning so I could get back on my schedule at Miss Peggy's, especially now that I would be working in the afternoons at Miss Lovenia's house. Lo and behold, just as soon as I walked out the front door to see if Uncle Myron was on his way, it started raining. Not a hard rain, but enough of a rain to make some of the sizzling heat go away. It was so nice, smelling that fresh rain and feeling a gentle breeze behind it, that I just went on out and sat on the porch swing. Maybe this meant the drought was over. Maybe this meant we had all turned a corner and the worst was over. Maybe, I thought as I gently began to swing, thankful for this little rainstorm. Thankful that even when things got bad, God always seemed to send us a sign. I didn't even hear Cedric walk up until he was already standing there looking at me. It wasn't light out yet, but I could feel his eyes taking me in.

"Hey, pretty girl," I heard his familiar voice say.

"What you doing here this morning?" I asked.

"I came to walk the prettiest girl in Colored Town to work," he said. "Unless this rain is too much for you."

"I love walking in the rain. It's like getting baptized by God's tears," I said.

"Why tears? You think God's sad or something?" he asked.

"Not sad tears," I said, getting up and walking over to him. "Happy tears. God is happy when he can bathe the earth with the tears seeping from his eyes."

"I like that. You have a way with words, pretty girl," he said. "And don't worry. I didn't just show up. I asked your granny yesterday after church if I could start walking you to work in the mornings. I know we both like to get up and out early, so I figured you wouldn't mind some company," he said.

I smiled at him. "She said yes?"

"'Course she said yes," he laughed. "I've done grown on your granny."

I laughed back at him. "I don't know about all that, but I do believe she sees something in you now."

"Well, that's good. I ain't no saint or nothing, and I doubt I ever will be, but I'm going to try and do right. You'll help me?" he asked, brushing my cheek with his hand.

"We'll help each other," I said in a soft voice. "I better go tell Granny we're heading out."

"I'm right here at the door," she said, startling us both. "God done sent us a little bit of cooling water, ain't he?"

"Yes ma'am, Miss Birdie," Cedric said. "It's gone make my job mighty easy today. If it'll keep on like this, I won't be having to carry much water out to the crops or to the animals. God willing, it'll keep on raining for a few days."

"That would be a blessing," she said. "Now you children be careful walking out there. Cedric, you make sure my granddaughter don't meet no harm or danger. You hear me?"

"I'll guard her with my life, Miss Birdie," he said.

"Thank you, Cedric," Granny said. "Baby girl, you come inside and get this raincoat. I know you like walking in the rain, but this is a different kind of rain coming right after this drought. I want your head covered."

I walked past Cedric and went inside. Granny pulled me by the arm and led me to her room.

"Don't be talking about anything concerning that Skeeter Ketchums to Cedric," Granny said. "I'm gone get your uncles together tonight after we all get off work and talk about it as a family. We'll figure out what to tell Cedric later. After what I heard nearly happened at that baseball game, he don't need to know that white boy was the one."

I didn't know what to say. I had planned on telling Cedric what happened while he walked me to work. I didn't want there to be secrets and lies between us. And I wanted him to know I trusted him with everything that had to do with me, but now Granny was telling me to do just the opposite of what I was feeling. I wanted to tell her no, that he was my beau and I meant to tell him what happened, but then I thought about Saturday and how close he and Skeeter came to blows. Maybe telling him wasn't the right thing. I just didn't know what was right anymore.

"I won't say anything," I said. "Thank you for letting me keep company with Cedric. I know he ain't exactly the boy you thought I would end up with, Granny, but he's a good person."

Granny nodded as she took the raincoat and put it around my shoulders. "I believe he is trying. He's still a hot head. You gone always have to deal with that if y'all stay a couple."

"He'll be fine," I said. "I'll see you in a little while."

"Y'all be good," she said. I kissed her cheek and went back outside where Cedric was waiting for me.

"You ready?" he asked.

I put the raincoat over my head. "I'm ready."

Normally when I made this walk by myself, I paid attention to everything. I looked at the trees, the farmland, the cows and the horses in the pasture, and the chickens cackling at one another. But this morning I didn't think about any of those things. Light was peeking over the trees, and the rain was continuing to fall at a steady pace, but all I could think about was walking with Cedric Perkins. He and I talked about everything. He told me how he was hoping to try out for the McDonough Brown Thrashers this week, and I told him how I was looking forward to turning eighteen and then going to Founder's Day.

"What do you want for your birthday?" he asked, taking my hand in his as we walked on the back streets of Parsons. None of the stores were lit up yet, but there were a few Colored and white people in their cars and horse and buggies moving around Main Street.

"I don't know. Nothing, really. I have everything I could ever want," I said. And I meant it. I had my family. I had my health and strength. And I had a wonderful boy who liked me. I didn't feel like I needed a single other thing.

Cedric stopped me from walking. "I don't have a lot, Opal. My family does okay, but my daddy is getting old and he's gonna have to stop preaching sometime soon. He used to help me with the farming, but I'm on my own now. I don't want to ever get them in a financial bind, so that is why I work so hard. But I want to treat you like a queen. I want you to feel like you're special."

"I know," I said. "I do feel special. And it ain't about what you can give me. It's how nice you are to me that matters. And I do the same for Granny as you do for your mama and daddy. My uncles try to help us, but Granny is so stubborn. She always tells them to take care of their families and the Lord will take care of us. That's why I always try to put away as much money as I can, just in case Granny has to stop working. Miss Peggy said she'll always look after Granny, but Granny is my responsibility. She took care of me when I didn't have nobody, and now it's my time to take care of her."

Cedric squeezed my hand. "You're a good person, Opal Pruitt. And you don't ever have to worry about your granny. Wherever we are, she'll be there too. Okay?"

"Okay," I said, trying not to feel shy with such intense words from a boy I was just getting to know good. "Do you think we're moving too fast, Cedric?"

"What do you think? I'll do whatever you want, Opal," he said. "I don't want to do anything to scare you or make you feel like I'm being too strong. I just like you and I don't know how to do this any different. In spite of what folks might think about me, I ain't as wild as they say."

That made me smile. But I was serious. "I just don't want anything to mess this up. I haven't never talked to a boy before, Cedric. Not really. This is all new to me, and I'm just a little bit scared," I said.

The rain was slowing down some, but it was still trickling down Cedric's face. It was getting light outside, and I could see all of his features. His chiseled jawline. His light-brown eyes. A slight scar on the side of his face from a knife fight he had gotten into with some white boys from McDonough a few years back. He had told me about that just yesterday. I wanted to reach out and wipe the rain from his face, but I didn't. It felt too forward, even though I had become closer to Cedric than I was to any other person, besides Granny and Lucille.

"I'm not going to hurt you. And I've still got a lot of things I've got to do before I'm ready to be marriage material. But Opal, there ain't another girl I want to spend time with besides you," Cedric said, placing his hands on my shoulders as we stood out in the road, unaware of anything or anyone besides each other. "You are all that I want in a girl. I just need you to be patient. I know I can be a good ballplayer. But it's gonna take time. Will you wait for me? Even if it means waiting a little longer than you might would have to wait for another boy?"

"I don't have no other boy that I'm interested in, Cedric," I said. "I'll wait."

Cedric laughed a loud and happy laugh. "You just give me time, gal. You give me time, and you'll be sitting right there beside Mrs. Satchel Paige and all those other baseball wives. I promise you that."

"That sounds good," I said. "Mrs. Paige is a nice lady. I really liked meeting her."

"So what do you want for your birthday?" he asked me again.

"A whistle," I said.

He laughed. "A what?"

"A whistle," I said, laughing. "When I was a little girl, I used to run behind my older cousins, trying to be just like them. Well, I was pretty good with everything but whistling. I can't whistle."

"Girl, everybody can whistle," Cedric said, still laughing. "Try."

I pursed my lips together and furrowed my brow and tried to whistle, but nothing came out but air. Cedric nearly fell to the ground with laughter.

"That was the most pitiful attempt to whistle I have ever heard," he said.

I laughed right along with him. "I know. I know. I have tried my whole life to whistle, and nothing. But anyway, Uncle Little Bud bought me a box of Cracker Jack, and I found a whistle inside. For the longest time, I marched around here and blew that whistle until finally I lost it. I cried and cried and cried so hard. I tried to find another whistle inside of the Cracker Jack box, but I couldn't. So find me a whistle and that will be the best gift."

"You got it," he said. "As God is my witness, I will find you a whistle."

We kept talking, and before we knew it, we had made it to

Miss Lovenia's house. And almost as if she knew we were passing by, she walked out of her house and down the hill to the road where we were standing. She looked like she was skipping in the rain.

"Good morning, young people. How are y'all doing on this beautiful day?" she asked, smiling. She was dressed in a long, flowing green dress, and her hair was wrapped in a green scarf. She was barefoot, and she looked like she didn't have a care in the world. "There is nothing better than walking barefoot in the rain. Why are you all wrapped up in that raincoat, Opal? Girl, let the rain pour down on you like it's meant to do. God is sending us a washing. A purification for our spirits. It can't get at you if you got that covering on."

"Granny would have a fit if I showed up to Miss Peggy's all wet," I said. "But I love walking in the rain. If it was up to me, I wouldn't have on a raincoat."

"Well, I'm 'bout to get them boys up and take them down to the creek and see if we can catch us some fish. You reckon you would be up to frying me some fish for supper tonight?" she asked.

"Yes ma'am," I said. "I'll make you anything you want."

She clapped her hands like a little girl. "I'm gonna get them boys up right now, then." She looked at Cedric. "You are a handsome young man. Your daddy's the preacher, ain't he?"

"Yes ma'am," he said.

"Good," she said, smiling. "If you take a mind to, you are welcome to come by and have some fish with us tonight. Opal, do you think your granny will let you eat with me, my boys, and your feller?"

I smiled and was about to say I would ask, but then I remembered the conversation we were going to have to have with my uncles tonight concerning Skeeter.

Before I could speak, she reached out and took my hand. "Another day. Y'all run on. Opal, I'll see you later today. And you, young man, take care of this fine girl. She's quite the catch."

Before we could say anything else, Miss Lovenia took off up the hill, moving better than some folks half her age.

"She is ninety-seven years old," I said, shaking my head with wonder.

"My Grandma Apple was the same way," Cedric said as we both watched Miss Lovenia disappear into her house. "Just as spry as she could be, until she took her last breath. We better go. I don't want to get you to work late and have your granny mad at me."

"You don't have to worry about that. She won't be heading out until later," I said. But I started walking with him. I was so distracted that I didn't remember we were coming up on the spot where Skeeter had hurt me. I stumbled and then I almost fell when we were standing just inches away from the spot in the road where Skeeter had grabbed me. If it weren't for Cedric putting a steadying arm around me, I would have hit the ground.

"Are you okay?" he asked. "Did you get dizzy? Should I take you up to Miss Lovenia's house?"

I shook my head no. "I'm okay. It's just . . . this is where it happened."

Cedric said a bad word underneath his breath. I was still too shaken to scold him about it. "I should have known better than to bring you out this way walking. I could have borrowed Daddy's car. I'm so sorry."

"It's okay," I said. "Let's just go."

Cedric kept his arm around me until we had safely made it away from the spot in the road where I had gotten dragged off.

"Do you remember anything?" he asked, breaking the silence.

"Things are still pretty fuzzy," I said, not wanting to lie to him, but not wanting to break my promise to Granny either. "Do you mind if we talk about something else?"

"What you think about working for Miss Lovenia?" he asked as we got closer to Miss Peggy's. I was grateful that he was willing to talk about something else. Anything else but that.

"I like it fine. She's a good person. I know folks think she's into hoodoo and all sorts of evil, but she's been real nice to me," I said. "I think she just talks to God in a different way. I don't think she means no harm."

"I 'spect you're right," he said. "She seemed pretty harmless to me. My Grandma Apple used to like her. She'd go sit for hours and talk to Miss Lovenia when I was a boy. But my grandpa Preacher, Daddy, and Mama wouldn't let me get nowhere around her."

"I understand. Granny only agreed to let me go help her because Miss Lovenia and her boys were so kind to me," I said, realizing I had opened the door back up to discuss the incident.

"Pretty girl, I know you don't want to talk about what happened, and I don't want to make you, but is there anything you remember? Anything that could help us find who did this to you?" he asked.

I shook my head. "Like I said, everything is pretty fuzzy in my mind," I said, trying not to say too much. Leastways not until Granny and the uncles decided what I should say. But I knew as sure as I had breath in my body that if I told him what I remembered, he wouldn't stop until he found Skeeter and did God knows what to him.

We were just walking into Miss Peggy's yard when Miss Corinne came running outside barefoot in a pair of bib overalls and one of her daddy's flannel shirts. "It's raining, Opal. It's raining." She danced and jumped, and then she ran over to me and grabbed my hands and twirled me around.

I laughed as she spun me. She was having another good day, I could tell. "What you doing up so early, Miss Corinne? Does your mama know you're up? What about Jimmy Earl?"

She giggled. "Nope. I snook out as soon as I heard the rain, and guess what, I caught us a mess of fish. We're gonna have some fish for breakfast."

It seemed like everybody had their mind on fresh fish today.

"Who is this young man?" she asked. "Who are you?"

"I'm Cedric Perkins, ma'am," he said. "I'm Opal's friend. I walked her to work."

"Well, ain't that nice," she said. "Well, I'm going inside. The fish is out back, Opal. I'll come help you skin 'em. I got a good mess of fish. Maybe Birdie will make us some cathead biscuits. And I bet we got a jar of sorghum up in the pantry. Mr. Cedric Perkins, are you staying for breakfast?"

He and I both said no real quick. She looked at us and started giggling. "Y'all is courting, ain't you? My Opal is a big girl now. She done got herself a beau."

Before we could say anything, she took off running back inside the house.

"Well," Cedric said, and before we knew it, we were both laughing. "You better get out there and get that fish ready. She don't seem like the kind to wait."

I shook my head. "No, she is not the type to wait at all. Thank you for walking me to work. I had a real good time talking and walking with you."

He bowed low, grinning as he rose back up to face me. "I aim to please, Miss Pruitt. I'll see you later."

"Okay," I said.

Cedric took my hand and kissed it. "You are a wonderful person. Thank you for being my girl." Before I could answer, he took off down the road, running in the rain. I didn't know what God had put in those raindrops today, but they seemed to have everybody laughing and feeling good. I prayed the day would stay just like that.

I went into the house and found Jimmy Earl putting on a pot of coffee.

"You walked here?" he asked as I entered the kitchen.

"I had company," I said. I was still angry with him. He and Skeeter and that friend of his shouldn't have come to our ballgame. Things could have gotten ugly, and Jimmy Earl was too blind to see just how evil his cousin was. I wanted to tell him that it was Skeeter who hurt me, but knowing Jimmy Earl, he probably wouldn't even believe me. "Your mama went fishing this morning. I better get out back and help her skin them fish. She wants fried fish and biscuits for breakfast."

"You need any help?" he asked.

"No thanks," I said. I just wanted him to go. I was having a good day. I didn't want a difficult conversation about Saturday or his cousin to ruin it.

Jimmy Earl walked over to me and reached for my raincoat, which I was still wearing. I pulled away.

"I said I didn't need any help," I snapped. I didn't mean to be ugly to him. But in just a couple of weeks, things between Jimmy Earl and me had changed so much.

"I'm sorry, Opal. I'm sorry Skeeter carried on like he did the other day. If I'd known he was going to act that way, I never would have allowed Courtland to convince me to go," he said. "It was a last-minute decision. We didn't plan for any of that to happen. You have to know that. And you have to know how sorry I am for everything."

"Are you sorry that he came and helped burn down Granny's chicken coop too?" I asked. I could feel the heat burning in my eyes. "Are you angry that him and all of your kin on your daddy's side are always plotting and planning to hurt some Colored person that ain't done nothing to them? Are you sorry I got beat up and—"

"Yes," Jimmy Earl snapped back. "Yes, yes, yes. I'm sorry for it all, Opal. But you acting like I did something to you. Every time I've seen them do something to you or any other Colored person, I try to stop them. But I'm one person, Opal. What else can I possibly do that I'm not already doing?"

"You can . . . you can, I don't know, Jimmy Earl. I don't know what you can do. I just know I'm tired. I'm tired of feeling like trouble is always just minutes away. I'm tired of white folks thinking they can do whatever they want and nothing will happen to them for it. You don't know nothing about what I'm talking about, and there ain't no way I can explain it to you," I said. "I gotta go outside and skin them fish."

Before he could say another word, I pushed past him and went outside, where Miss Corinne was sitting on the steps, already cleaning and gutting the fish.

"The rain stopped," she said, looking up at me with a sad face.

I sat on the ground beside her and took the knife from her hand. I reached up and patted her cheek. "Don't worry. It'll be back."

I prayed that the rain would return. I prayed that God's happy tears would continue to fall on us all.

20

*G*ranny didn't feel like coming to work, so I worked alone. I was fine with that. I liked the quiet. Once I got done cleaning the bream and the catfish that Miss Corinne caught, it was time to make breakfast. Jimmy Earl left early, so it was just Miss Corinne and Miss Peggy who ate. They asked me to join them, but I didn't want anything to eat. My mind was full again, and no amount of fish or biscuits was going to fix that.

I fried the fish, just like Miss Corinne wanted, and I even made her some cathead biscuits. And with a bit of looking, I found the last jar of sorghum. Once I got done with their breakfast, it was time to get ready for Miss Peggy's sewing group. I prayed that Miss Lori Beth Parsons wouldn't show up, but of course, she did. She was the first girl to arrive, and when I opened the door, she nearly fell into my arms.

"Oh, Opal," she said. "I am so sorry. I've been wanting to come see you for the longest time, but Jimmy Earl said no and my parents have had me on punishment, so I couldn't even leave the house until today. They said I caused too much of a ruckus with my newspaper article. You know I didn't mean any harm? Please say you know that."

"Miss Peggy is waiting in the sewing room," I said. "You know how to get there."

I turned to leave, but she reached out and took my hand. "Please don't be angry with me, Opal. I'm just a stupid girl who didn't think."

"My granny and I begged you not to write that article," I said.

She nodded as the tears began to run down her face. I felt myself feeling bad, but I steeled myself against her over-the-top grief. She wasn't the one hurt; I was. And I refused to let her guilty tears persuade me to forgive her right yet.

"You have every right to be mad at me. You do, Opal, but I beg you not to be," she said, wiping the tears with the back of her hand. "I thought that I could do some good with my stupid, shortsighted article. I thought somehow I could say the right words so that everyone would see that there wasn't a whole lot of difference between a Colored girl like you and a white girl like me."

I sighed and then reached into my pocket and gave her my clean handkerchief. She took it and dabbed at her eyes. I felt myself getting more and more angry with each dab she took. "But there is a whole lot of difference between a Colored girl like me and a white girl like you. And if you don't see that, even now, then I don't have anything else to say to you," I said, and this time, I did get away from her.

I served Miss Peggy and her white girls their food once they had all arrived, and I picked up their mess when they dropped needles and thread and fabric on the floor. But when it was time for me to leave, I did not give them more than a "See you later," and I left. I could tell Miss Peggy had her eyes on me all day, but I never gave her a chance to ask me what was wrong. I didn't want to hear another voice of another white person try to tell me my feelings weren't mine to feel. Miss Lori Beth Parsons didn't stay long. She made up an excuse to Miss Peggy and she left, but before she did, she came up behind me and apologized again, slipping my handkerchief back inside my hand. I didn't say anything. I just watched her leave. Between her and Jimmy Earl, my day was ruined, or at least that was how it felt.

I had always liked working at Miss Peggy's house. She had always made me feel like family, but today I just wanted to get away from her and her friends and go to Miss Lovenia's house. I wanted to see the weathered skin of Miss Lovenia. I wanted to hear the voice of a Colored woman who reminded me in some ways of my granny. I wanted the comfort of Blackness, not the choking sensation that whiteness was making me feel.

When Uncle Myron came to pick me up, I was already almost halfway up the road walking. I tried to wait, but the sounds of those white girls giggling inside Miss Peggy's house made my head and my stomach hurt. So I walked. The rain had long since stopped, and the heat was bearing down on me, but I didn't care. I just wanted to get away. Uncle Myron stopped his car when he saw it was me, and before he could get out and open the door, I hopped inside.

"Now you know we don't want you out in this road by your-self walking," he scolded.

"I'm sorry, Uncle Myron," I said. "How's Granny?"

"Oh, she's fine. I think last week just caught up with her," he said as he began driving me down the road. I thought back to this morning and how much I had enjoyed walking to work with Cedric, even when I had the bad moment just up the road from Miss Lovenia's house. What a difference a few hours made.

When we got to Miss Lovenia's, Uncle Myron reached out and took my hand. "Anytime you want to stop cleaning house and cooking for folks, you can. I know Mama doesn't want me and the uncles to get involved, but we will if it means you being happy."

I squeezed Uncle Myron's hand. "I'm happy. I'm just having a hard day right now. That's all. It'll get better." I thought about Cedric and seeing him later today or maybe tomorrow. That would be my better. Somehow, Cedric had become my happy.

Uncle Myron nodded. "Okay then. I'll see you later this evening when I pick you up."

I quickly got out of the car and went up the hill to Miss Lovenia's house. I started taking my shoes off just as she opened the door. She was no longer wearing her green dress and head scarf. She was back wearing all white again.

She took one look at me and then pulled me gently inside, motioning for me to wash my feet in the basin she already had drawn. I quickly washed as she stood and watched me in silence. Finally, she spoke.

"Your spirit is not at peace, chile," she said. "I can feel it all over you, and before it gets all over me and this house, I need you to come into my room and trust that I would never call anything that isn't of God."

Before I could say anything, Miss Lovenia took me by my hand and led me into her room where she met with her clients. I could smell the musky scent of incense, and already the room was bathed in warm candlelight.

"Miss Lovenia, I don't know about—"

"Shh . . . It's all right, my dear," she said. She guided me to the desk, where she sat me down in one chair while she sat in the other. She reached into her desk and took out a black cloth and placed it on the top of the desk. Then she took a white candle and placed it by a bowl of water and lit the candle. Once she did that, she looked at me and smiled. "Now, did you remember to bring that Bible your granny sent with you the last time?"

I nodded. Granny had reminded me last night to make sure I packed it.

"Good. Take it out and put it in front of you," Miss Lovenia ordered. She had her eyes closed, and she was swaying slightly. I was nervous, but I couldn't imagine any bad coming from me having my Bible in front of me.

I reached into my bag and took it out, placing it on the desk.

"Now turn to Isaiah 41:10," Miss Lovenia demanded, still swaying, eyes still closed.

I looked at her for a moment, but then I turned the pages to the book, chapter, and verse she instructed me to find, and read it out loud. "Do not fear, for I am with you; do not be dismayed, for I am your God. I will strengthen you and help you; I will uphold you with my righteous right hand."

"How do you feel?" she asked, swaying, eyes closed.

"I . . . I . . ."

"Turn to John 14:27 and read," she mumbled. Still swaying. Eyes still closed.

Just like before, I turned to the page she instructed and I read. "Peace is what I leave with you; it is my own peace that I give you. I do not give it as the world does. Do not be worried and upset; do not be afraid."

"How do you feel?" she asked again. She had slowed her swaying, and her eyes were half open.

"Better," I said, and I really meant it. It was as if something cool and comforting had washed over me.

"Good," she said and smiled, closing her eyes again. "One more. Go to 1 Peter 5:6–7."

This time, I didn't open my Bible. I knew the verses by heart. I'd had to memorize them for Sunday school. I looked at her and said it from memory. "Humble yourselves, then, under God's mighty hand, so that he will lift you up in his own good time. Leave all your worries with him, because he cares for you."

"Feeling like Opal again?" she asked. Her eyes looked so wise and caring. Her eyes reminded me of Granny's eyes, and getting me to read the Bible to calm myself was definitely something Granny would do.

"Yes ma'am," I said. She reached out and took my hand.

"I never ask people to go places they don't want to go. If your Scriptures are what normally bring you comfort, then that is where we will always start. But," she continued, this time her face getting stern, "you must know to do this yourself. Never knowingly bring your pain or your suffering or your sadness or your anger into another's home. Always take off your burdens at the door and leave them with your Lord. Understand?"

I nodded. "Yes ma'am. I'm sorry. I—"

"Shh . . . ," she said. "You never have to say I'm sorry within these walls. So we did things your way. Now I am going to ask you to trust me. I sense something, and it frightens me, and I never get frightened," she said. Her voice was calm, so I found myself remaining calm too. Miss Lovenia reached into the drawer of her desk and pulled out a white bag. "I have one bag. That is all. Just one. You can keep it for yourself, or you can give it to someone you care deeply about. This bag is not evil. Everything inside of it comes from the earth. White mustard seeds. Angelica root. Cinnamon. And a virgin olive oil that has been blessed with strong prayers. It does not contain anything that will hurt the person carrying the bag, but it will be an added bit of protection for that person and that person alone. Do you understand?"

I shook my head. "No ma'am. I don't understand. This feels different than the Scripture reading."

She nodded in agreement as she pushed the bag toward me, but I wouldn't touch it. "This is different. You might not remember me telling you about my being born with a caul over my eyes. Well, the caul only covers the faces of those who will grow to have the extra sight. Every woman in my family was born with this caul . . . this extra sight. It ends with me. I am the last one to have it. No girls flowed through me, and none will flow from the loins of my sons. So I have to use what God gave me before the gift becomes lost."

"Granny wouldn't want me to take this," I said, trying to sound brave, but I was afraid. This felt dark and different and scary. I would not touch that bag. I just stared at it, afraid to look at it but afraid to take my eyes off of it too.

"I understand that you are frightened, Opal," she said. "But danger is coming this week. Choose wisely. Keep the bag or give it to someone you love. Just make sure, if you do give it to someone, that the person understands they must have it with them at all times. You can't sneak it into someone's possession. They must know they have it. This is all I can do. This is all I have to offer, according to the will of God. Please, take the bag. It will not hurt you or the person you give it to. Nor will it bring harm to anyone else. I vow this to you."

"Miss Lovenia, I can't take that," I said. "My granny would not want me to take that bag."

"Opal, do you ever get feelings? Feelings that something bad is going to happen before it happens?" Miss Lovenia asked. "Or feelings that something good is going to happen?"

I looked at her with surprise. I nodded my head slowly. "Yes ma'am. Sometimes."

"Opal, there was a reason I picked you to come work with me, and it had nothing to do with your cooking or cleaning. Spirit, or God, or whatever you call it, showed me in a dream that you might have the Sight. Not like me and my kin, but—"

"I don't want to hear this, Miss Lovenia," I said, clutching my Bible to my chest. I didn't know what to do. I didn't know if I should run out of that house and go home to Granny, or if I should stay and do the job Miss Lovenia hired me to do. I just didn't know.

"I scared you," Miss Lovenia said in a hushed tone. She closed her eyes again. This time, she looked like someone tortured.

"Yes ma'am," I said. "I am a bit frightened." I realized there was no point in lying to her. The fear was all over me, and I felt bad because I didn't want to bring fear into her house, especially after she told me that was what I had done earlier.

"I didn't mean to scare you, Opal. I said too much too fast. I apologize," Miss Lovenia said, opening her eyes again. "And it was not your fault. You did not bring this fear into my home. I had helped you release your negative energy and then I piled more on top of you. I owe you the apology."

I stood. The fact that she knew my thoughts made things even worse. Still clutching my Bible for dear life, in that moment I was thankful that Granny had sent it with me. It felt like that Bible was the only protection I had right then. "I should get busy. Did you catch any fish today?"

"Not a one," Miss Lovenia said, standing up behind her desk. "I guess it wasn't meant to be."

"No ma'am," I said as she blew out the candle. I didn't know what else to say to that. "I guess not. Well, I'll start cleaning then, and if there is anything you want me to cook, just leave it where I can get to it in the kitchen."

"I think we'll be on a fast this week," Miss Lovenia said as she made her way around her desk. She looked old. For the first time since I had been around her up close, I saw Miss Lovenia's age in her movement, in her face, in her whole being. It was a bit unsettling, especially since I knew it had something to do with me and what she saw. "I have some juices that the boys and I will drink, so don't worry about cooking. Thank you, Opal. And honey, please try not to let an old lady's fears scare you. Sometimes even I, with the Sight, see things wrong. Perhaps that is what is happening now. So please don't fear. Remember those Scriptures. Those are your guide. Not me."

"Yes ma'am," I said, and then I left the room and went about the task of cleaning. I found the items that she had asked me to use to "purify" her home the other day. They were in a closet just outside of her bathroom. I took the one bottle that said "floor solution," and I went to every room besides her bedroom and swept and mopped. I tried not to think about what had happened earlier, and I just focused on cleaning and dusting and making her house smell fresh and pure, as she called it the other day.

The more I cleaned, the better everything smelled, and the more relaxed I felt. The smell of lavender filled the house. For a moment, I wondered if Miss Lovenia was doing something to me to put me at ease, but I realized the relaxed feeling was coming from the cleansers. Miss Lovenia and her boys stayed out of my way. In fact, I didn't see any of them while I was there. I heard some music playing in her boys' room right before I was getting ready to leave, but other than that, I didn't hear anything. Once I was done, I went looking for Miss Lovenia, but she was still sitting in her workroom, slumped over on her desk like she was asleep. But when I called out her name softly, she answered, raising her head.

"Are you done?" she asked.

I didn't walk into the room. It was the only room I didn't clean that day because I just couldn't make myself walk inside of it again. Even now, I just stood by the door . . . afraid to go in. Afraid of the heaviness I felt just from standing outside of it. "Yes ma'am, I'm done. I'm gone sit outside and wait on Uncle Myron."

It had started raining again, but this time, there was some thunder and lightning too. Normally, I was too afraid to be outside during a storm, but it beat the storm that was going on inside of Miss Lovenia's house. Her house felt like a hurricane or a tornado was brewing. It felt unsettled and unsure of itself, and I just wanted to get outside where I could breathe again. The lavender smell was still strong, but it was doing nothing to settle my nerves. I knew then that I wouldn't be coming back to Miss Lovenia's house to work. I didn't like what happened today. Miss Lovenia walked slowly to where I was standing.

"I'm going to miss having you around, Opal Pruitt," she said.

"I . . . I . . ." I didn't know what to say. So I stopped.

She smiled, but there was a weariness to her smile. I looked at her hand and saw she was holding the little bag she had tried to give me earlier.

"Opal, I know I sounded like a crazy old woman earlier. And I know that is what people say. But I'm not crazy. I don't know why God chose me and my family to see things, but he did. We didn't ask for it, it just happened. Normally, I charge people large amounts of money for the work I do. Especially if they are white. I am charging you nothing for this little bag. The bag is innocent. It contains everything God intended for us to use until he comes back to collect us. That's all, honey," she said. "Please, take this bag. It won't hurt anyone, but it will help. I wouldn't lie to you. Will you take it?"

I knew every emotion I was feeling had to have played out across my face. One part of me wanted to say no. The other part of me wanted to say yes, because what if what she had said to me was true? I just didn't know what to do. Finally, I just decided to take it. I figured, if worse came to worst, I would just throw it away or hide it. At the end of the day, I didn't want to hurt Miss Lovenia's feelings by refusing her gift.

"Yes ma'am. I'll take it," I said.

I saw her release some of what she had been carrying. Her smile became real. She took my hand and placed the bag inside of it. "Be blessed, young one. Remember, no matter what happens, you are watched by someone who reigns high and controls all of this madness we call life. God is always there. No matter what. Now, may an old woman give you a hug before you go?"

"Yes ma'am," I said, and Miss Lovenia put her hands around my waist and laid her head against my shoulder. She was much smaller than me, but she felt big and sturdy. I hugged her back. I wished I could continue working with her, but this was too much. Even with my Bible, this was way too much. I heard Uncle Myron blow his car horn outside. "I better go, Miss Lovenia. Thank you for the opportunity to work with you."

"You are welcome, my dear," she said. "You can always return. Anytime."

"Yes ma'am," I finally said. I pushed the white bag Miss Lovenia had given me down inside my purse. I put my Bible on top of it. I figured it would be a wall between me and that bag. I slipped on my shoes and hurried out the door, not looking back. The rain was coming down hard, but I threw the raincoat over my head and ran to Uncle Myron's car, where he had the door already open for me to jump in. A hard clap of lightning struck out in the field just across the road. I jumped quickly inside of Uncle Myron's car, closing the door behind me.

"Hey, little girl," he said. "You ready to go?"

"Yes sir," I said. I leaned back in the seat and closed my eyes.

"Mama said she wanted to talk to me and the uncles tonight. You know what that's all about?" he asked.

"Yes sir," I said. I had forgotten about the talk we were going to have with the uncles about Skeeter Ketchums. I was dreading it. I didn't want to think what they might say or what they might do. But I knew we had to have the talk. There was no way around it.

"Well, I reckon we better go and get it over with," he said, and we drove off, though the rain fell with such force, we had to slow down to a creeping pace. This time, I knew God's tears weren't tears of joy. God was now crying tears of sadness or maybe even anger. I didn't know, but I did know that I felt like crying too.

21

*E*veryone was there when Uncle Myron and I finally got home. We hurried out of the rain that was still falling with a fierceness I hadn't seen in a while. The wind had picked up, and dead tree limbs were falling and flying across the yard. I yelped as I had to step around a flying tree branch. Uncle Myron grabbed me by the arm and rushed me up the stairs.

"Y'all come on in. Lord, that rain has been making up for lost time this afternoon," Granny said, meeting us at the door. She gave us both towels to dry off with. Uncle Michael, Uncle Lem, and Uncle Little Bud were already sitting at the kitchen table. They stood when we entered the room.

"Come on and have a seat," Granny said. "We was waiting on y'all."

I quietly went and sat by Uncle Little Bud. He reached over and hugged me.

"You all right?" he asked.

I shook my head as the tears started falling in earnest down my face. "No sir. I'm not all right," I managed to choke out. These last few days had been emotionally overwhelming. It was like I was feeling everything all at once, but mostly I feared my uncles' reaction to what me and Granny were going to tell them.

Uncle Little Bud pulled me into a hug, and Uncle Lem reached over and patted me on my back. "Gonna be all right, baby girl," Uncle Little Bud said in a soothing voice. None of his usual joking could be found in his voice, only his concern for me. "All of us will make things right. Mama, tell us what's going on."

Granny looked at me, and I guess she realized I wasn't going to be able to do much talking, so she told them about my dream Saturday night. Uncle Little Bud went from being a comforter to being a raging ball of fire.

"That dog. That dirty, filthy dog," he yelled, getting up from the table. He balled up his fists like he wanted to strike something.

"Calm down, Bud," Uncle Myron ordered. "And watch your mouth. There's ladies in this room."

"How can we calm down?" Uncle Michael yelled. "He could have killed Opal. Are we just supposed to do nothing?"

"I'll kill him," Uncle Little Bud roared, as if Uncle Myron and Uncle Michael hadn't said a word. "I'll find his narrow white behind and I'll kill him dead just as sure as I'm standing here. I got a gun in my pocket waiting to fire."

"I'm with you, brother," said Uncle Michael, who was usually as calm as Uncle Myron. He jumped up from the table looking like he was ready to run out the house, find Skeeter Ketchums, and tear him in two.

"Not if I get at him first," Uncle Lem said, pounding his fist on the table. "You should have told us this yesterday, Mama. You should have come woke us up the second this chile remembered what happened to her."

"For what?" Granny yelled, and Granny seldom raised her voice at anyone. "So y'all could act the fool? Now what we ain't gonna do is make this situation worse. I'm telling y'all now because y'all is her uncles and she needs y'all to watch out for her, but what she don't need is for y'all to run off all half-cocked and get yourselves killed along with the rest of us. Them Ketchums have been spoiling for a race war for as long as I can remember. Jimmy Earl is the only good thing that came out of that bunch, and sometimes, on a good day, his daddy, Earl Sr. But for the most part, them Ketchums is crazy fools, and all they want is for y'all to run out there with your threats and your guns."

"If they want a race war, then that's what we'll give them," Uncle Little Bud growled. "I'm tired of us grown men walking around here letting these fools do anything they want to us and our womenfolk. No more, Mama. It ain't slavery days no more. They can't get away with this. Not this time. Not ever again."

"Please," I cried out. "Please don't do this. I didn't want to tell y'all at all. I didn't want this. Please don't do nothing bad on my account. I'm all right. I'm healing. I'm fine. Don't do nothing. Please."

"Little Bud," Uncle Myron said in a quiet but firm voice. When nobody else could settle down Uncle Little Bud, Uncle Myron usually could. "We are not going to make widows out of your wives, and we are not going to leave Mama and this chile with no protection. That, we ain't gonna do. Now, we are going to put a web of protection around our women and our children until we can meet with the other men of Colored Town and figure out the right way to handle this. Am I understood?"

I looked at my uncles. All of their faces looked like the worst kind of storm clouds. It was like what was going on outside with the rain and the wind had entered into our little house. I felt drenched with the emotions we were all feeling.

"So you saying we do nothing?" Uncle Little Bud asked, still pacing, still looking like a raging bull.

"Naw, Bud," Uncle Myron said. "I'm not saying we do nothing, but I am saying whatever we do, we better make sure it doesn't make things worse. Now, that white sheriff says he wants to work with us. Well, let's have a talk with him. All of us. Every man in Colored Town who will meet up at the church can go and let him know our concerns, and then we let that man explain to us what he thinks he can do to keep a battle from happening."

"That peckerwood ain't gonna do nothing," Uncle Little Bud said.

"Then if he doesn't do nothing, we do what we have to do, but we ain't gonna run off like some gang of thieves. We ain't like them white folks. We ain't forming no Klan, and we ain't gonna cause blood to shed unless we have no other choice," Uncle Myron said. "I'm still the head of this house. Daddy left me in charge before he died. His final words to me was to look after this family, and that is what I mean to do. You boys understand me?"

I had never seen my uncles so strong. So protective. Even though their passion scared me, I was proud for them to be my kin. I knew they would lay down their lives for me, and it meant a lot. It actually meant everything. I had never felt so loved before. I watched as all of my uncles slowly made their way back to the table.

"Okay, Myron. You in charge. But let me say this," Uncle Lem said in a quiet voice. "We bring this meeting together soon. In the next day or two, and definitely before Founder's Day on Saturday. To be honest, I don't even know if any of us should take part in it. It might be too dangerous."

"Founder's Day is when we make the most money for the church," Uncle Little Bud said. "We sell them plates of goat meat and pork, and them white folks spend their last quarters to get some of that food, not to mention Shimmy's fried chicken and greens. We wouldn't have been able to fix the church's roof last year if we hadn't sold all that food at Founder's Day. Naw, we ain't letting them white folks run us off. Don't y'all worry, though. I'll have my peacemaker with me. Ain't gonna be no mess. I can promise you that."

"Stop being such a hot head, Bud," Uncle Myron ordered. "I'll get with Reverend Perkins later tonight, and we'll set up a time to meet with the menfolk and the sheriff down at the church. Hopefully tomorrow when we all get done working." Uncle Myron looked over at me. "That boy of yours is going to lose his mind over this. You reckon he can be talked down? At least until we all figure out what to do?"

I honestly didn't know. Cedric had been spoiling for a fight with Skeeter long before he came here and burnt down Granny's chicken coop, and long before Skeeter acted the fool at the ballgame on Saturday. I knew when Cedric learned that it was Skeeter who hurt me, well, he might do anything. I know I should have felt good that Cedric would be willing to fight for me, but all it did was make me feel bad. I didn't want to be responsible for any bullets flying or any punches getting thrown. I just wanted peace. That's all. Just peace.

I thought about the white bag Miss Lovenia gave me. That bag seemed to go against everything I had ever been taught, but it was all I had, and what if it did have some special magic or blessing on it? What if it could keep Cedric from doing harm to someone else? What if, like Reverend Perkins said, God was everything and everything was God? Wouldn't that mean this little pouch had a little bit of God inside of it? I didn't know for sure what to think or believe, but I knew I had to try something. Somehow, I knew I had to make him take Miss Lovenia's bag and keep it with him at all times, just like she said. I was getting one of those feelings again, and although it wasn't clear, somehow I just knew giving him the bag from her was what I was supposed to do.

"I'll tell him. He might take it better if it comes from me. I'm sorry. I'm so sorry."

Uncle Myron came and pulled me up into an embrace. "Ain't none of this your doing, Opal. None of it. And I don't want you worrying none. We been through rough times with white folks before. This ain't no different. God will look after us. He always has."

"You telling the truth now," Granny said. "So, for now, I want you boys to go home to your families. Myron, you go talk to the reverend and send that boy over here so Opal can talk to him. She might be right. If he's gonna listen to anybody, maybe he'll listen to her. You know you tough old birds sometimes need the gentle clucking of a hen to calm you down," she said.

For the first time this evening, everyone laughed a bit, although I didn't laugh much. I felt like so much was riding on my shoulders. If I couldn't get Cedric to calm down, then that meant my cousins like M.J. would get involved, too, because there was no way M.J. was going to let Cedric fight for me if he wasn't in the middle of it. I couldn't let that happen.

I went over to the door and looked outside. The rain was calming down a bit, and the lightning was far off. It was getting close to seven o'clock. None of us had eaten anything.

All of the uncles left except Uncle Myron. He came over to where I was standing, still looking outside the door, watching the rain as it sat in little puddles throughout the yard. I could smell the fresh smell of the peaches from the orchard again. It's funny how just a little bit of rain seemed to bring everything right back to the way it was supposed to be. I closed my eyes and remembered the night the other week when Cedric had come out into the orchard and first showed me that he liked me. It all seemed so long ago.

"You'll tell him to come?" I said to Uncle Myron. I tried to keep the fear out of my voice.

"I'll tell him," Uncle Myron said, putting his arm around my shoulders. "Have some faith, little girl. That boy cares about you, and God knows that. He'll send you the right words to say to help Stank keep a calm head. You just pray. Pray for the words and God will send them."

"He's just so angry, Uncle Myron. So angry against white folks. He don't see the good in them. Not none of them. I mean, I find myself wondering if I've been looking at them with rose-colored glasses on myself. But the rage Cedric has, it is more than I've ever seen before," I said. "Even more than the rage Uncle Little Bud feels."

Uncle Myron turned me around so that I was facing him. "Look, little girl. God gave us women to help us, and he gave us men to women to help you all. You women weren't put here to parent us, but to help us see things in a way that we as men can't always see," he said. "I'll send Cedric over here. You just talk to him from your heart. That's all you have to do."

"Thank you," I said. He hugged me once more and then went over and had final words with Granny. I sat out on the porch as he drove off. There was a nice, gentle breeze blowing. I leaned back against the swing and silently prayed Cedric would be able to come over tonight. It was getting late, but I knew Granny would let us talk. She wouldn't want to see Cedric get in any trouble on my account. Almost as if she knew I was thinking about her, Granny came outside and sat beside me in the swing. She put her arm through my arm and pressed her head against mine.

"Don't you worry none, baby girl. You'll come up with the right words to say to Cedric," she said.

"Thank you, Granny. I pray you're right," I said. She and I sat there without talking any more, just holding on to each other until we saw Cedric walking up the road toward the house.

"There he comes," she said and got up. "Just let the Lord guide you. That's what I always did when I would talk to your grandpa. I'd ask the Lord to tell me what he wanted me to say, and then I let his words come through me. You do the same with your young man."

Cedric walked up onto the porch and smiled big at both of us. "Good afternoon, Miss Birdie. Opal. How y'all doing?"

"We blessed, son. Blessed and loved by the Lord," Granny said and walked toward the door. "Y'all be good. I'm going on in and lay my body down, I think." I was shocked. I couldn't believe Granny was going to leave us up by ourselves, but I guessed with all that had gone on, she trusted me and Cedric. Any other time I would have been pleased, but a part of me felt scared and alone. What if I couldn't find the right words to say? What if I couldn't stop Cedric from running out and doing something crazy? I almost didn't feel when Cedric sat down beside me.

"You okay, pretty girl?" he asked. "I was shocked when your Uncle Myron said you needed to talk to me."

"Cedric, I remembered," I said in a soft voice. "I remembered everything."

"What did you remember?" he asked in a tight voice. I could feel him tense up beside me.

"Cedric, would you do something for me?" I asked.

"Tell me what you remembered, Opal," he said. He didn't raise his voice, but I could tell he was impatient.

"Cedric, please," I said.

"What do you want me to do?" he asked, his voice like steel. Gone was the lighthearted tone he used with me when he was flirting or saying sweet things. I tried not to let his demeanor scare me or dissuade me from saying what I knew I needed to say.

"Pray with me. Let me talk to God before we have this conversation. Please," I said.

"Opal, I . . . Okay. Pray," he said, but he didn't sound like he was happy about it. I didn't care. I took his hand.

"Dear God, I won't beat around the bush. I won't sit here and say all sorts of big words and fancy thoughts 'cause, to be honest, I don't know none to say. But I do want to say this. I care about this boy you sent to me. I didn't pray for no boyfriend, but you sent me one all the same. Thank you. And Lord, I care about his life and I care about his soul, and I ask you to send me the right words. The words that will help us both know what to do. Both of us want to do what is right. Please help us figure that out. Amen," I said. And then I told him. Everything. I told him everything I remembered from that night on the road.

"What do your uncles want to do?" he asked, barely moving, barely blinking.

"They want to meet with all the Colored men and boys at the church. Hopefully tomorrow," I said. Cedric didn't say anything else right away, so I just sat beside him.

"I'm struggling over here, Opal. I know you want me to keep calm and I am trying to do that for you. I thank you for your prayer. I needed it. You did something my mama would have done," he said.

I didn't say anything. I knew he was working through his thoughts, so I didn't interrupt him. I just sat beside him. Cedric reached over and took my hand in his. He turned toward me and touched my face real soft.

"Opal, I love you," he said. I took a deep breath, but before I could say anything in return, he continued talking. "And I know me saying that is awful soon, but I need you to understand that my feelings for you are real. So you gotta know that if I run into that peckerwood, I will kill him. I don't know how to calm my rage like you need me to, so I don't know what to do with all of this."

"Can you promise me not to do anything until after the meeting? Can you stay calm tomorrow and meet with the men at the church tomorrow night?" I begged.

"Yes," he finally said. "I will stay at home and hide underneath the bed if I have to, but I will not kill anyone tonight or tomorrow. That's all I can promise."

I nodded my head and then I reached over and kissed him. A real kiss. A kiss from my heart and soul. "I love you, too, Cedric Perkins. I love you and I believe God will keep us through this time. And . . ." I paused. I didn't know if I should give him the little bag, but it was all I had, so I reached into my pocket and took out the little white bag Miss Lovenia had given me. I pressed the bag into his hand. "Will you keep this with you? Will you keep this in your pocket and not take it out no matter what?"

Cedric looked down at the bag. "What is this? Is this some of Miss Lovenia's hoodoo?"

"I know it seems crazy, Cedric, and I don't believe in nothing but God, but I feel right about this for some strange reason. Please put it in your pocket and carry it for me. It can't hurt nothing 'cause if it ain't of God he'll stop it before it can do any harm. Just, carry it for me. Please," I begged. This time I could feel the tears begin to fall down my face.

He wiped my tears away with his finger. "I would carry anything for you, Opal, and if you want me to walk around with this little white pouch in my pocket, then I will. We gone grow old together, girl. I promise you that."

"I believe you," I said, but a part of me was still worried. Cedric put his arm around me and we sat for the longest time. Not talking, just sitting. This was nicer to me than the talking because it was like our spirits got to speak to each other. My head was against his chest and I could feel his heart beating. I imagined that my heart joined in with his and they became one heart. I knew that even if Cedric and I didn't remain a couple, this moment would live inside of my mind for the rest of my life. When it started to get dark, as much as I wanted him to stay, I told him he should probably go.

"Don't worry," he said, getting up from the swing. I got up, too, and went into his arms. He held me tight like we might not hug again, or at least that was how it felt.

"I love you, Cedric. I love you with all of my heart."

"And I love you too. Always," Cedric said and walked toward the edge of the porch. He stopped just before he stepped down. "Don't worry. Between your prayers and this little white bag, I'll be just fine. Okay?" he said, and I watched as he went walking down the road toward his house.

I went back and sat on the swing and started praying like I had never prayed before. I prayed like every Black woman who had ever loved a Black man had prayed from the beginning of time. I prayed the prayer of a woman who knew she and her man had nothing but prayers and little white bags to cover them in a

world full of Skeeter Ketchumses. Finally, I couldn't sit anymore and I went inside. But before I closed the door, I asked God
one more time to look after my boyfriend and all my male kin.
"Don't let no harm come to them," I prayed as I gently closed the
door.

22

The menfolks from the church all met together on Tuesday night, and they met again on Wednesday night with the sheriff. The uncles, Reverend Perkins, and Cedric all came over to the house Wednesday after the meeting was over to tell us how it went.

"What did y'all think?" Granny asked. "Did that sheriff talk good sense?"

"Yes ma'am," Uncle Myron said. "He listened to us, and he said he was as tired as we was of the Klan running roughshod throughout this county. He said he would have some boys of his own at Founder's Day, and he would keep his eye on Skeeter Ketchums. He said if Skeeter even came near Opal or any of our women, he would kill him himself."

"He said that?" Granny asked, her face looking more unbelieving than mine. "He just said that to make y'all calm down."

"I don't know, Mama," Uncle Lem said. "He seemed earnest with his words. We told him we wouldn't accept no different, and if he didn't stand with us, all of us Colored men would go and form our own militia to fight against these white folks. We told him we wasn't gone live in fear for our wives, daughters, sisters, mothers, and aunties no more. I think he understood where we were coming from."

"He didn't say nothing about arresting Skeeter?" I asked. The thought of him still walking around terrified me. I knew my uncles, and I was beginning to know Cedric; it would be just a matter of time before one or more of them ran up on Skeeter and did God knows what.

"No, sweetheart," Uncle Myron said. "The sheriff said because you suffered from a head injury, he couldn't go by your word alone. He's going to do some digging around and see if Skeeter had an alibi for that day. Meanwhile, we ain't gonna let you out of our sight. Promise."

It wasn't me that I was worried about. But I didn't say any more.

"Well, we'll see how things turn out," Granny said. "At the end of the day, he still white like them. But it's nice to hear he talked like he was gone try and work with us."

I looked over at Cedric, who was being extra quiet. I mouthed at him, "Are you all right?" He smiled at me and nodded.

"Sister Pruitt, I believed the sheriff," Reverend Perkins said. "I think he's gone stand with us on this, and like your sons said, we menfolks ain't gone take this lying down. What happened to Opal could have happened to any of our women or girls. As y'all's pastor, it's my responsibility to preach peace, but when peace can't be had, sometimes we have to do like the children of Israel fighting in the Battle of Jericho. We will not have you women-folks scared to walk outside or go to and from your jobs or to the stores downtown. We wouldn't be men if we left y'all to fend for yourselves. Perhaps if I would have allowed the men to handle things a little more forcefully when the Klan rode through here, maybe what happened to Opal wouldn't have happened. I will carry the blood she shed and the bruises she bore on my heart for the rest of my life. I apologize to you, Opal, and to all of you."

We all looked at Reverend Perkins with shock. Reverend Perkins never talked like that. He was always saying that to turn the other cheek was God's way. This Reverend Perkins shocked me, especially considering just the other Sunday his advice for us to deal with the Klan was to just stay in our homes and be quiet. I wondered what changed his mind. I saw him and Cedric share a look. I think Cedric's passion must have rubbed off on his daddy. Or maybe Reverend Perkins was just tired of the racism and the hate like the rest of us.

After everyone left, Cedric hung around long enough to talk to me.

"You okay?" I asked.

He nodded. "I am. I was proud of how all the elders acted tonight. They made me feel proud to be a Colored man. We gonna all be all right, Opal. And . . ." Smiling, he patted his pocket. "I still got my little white bag. I won't lie. These last two days I have gone out of my way to run into that peckerwood so I could stomp his face into the ground, but between you praying and my mama praying and this little white hoodoo bag, I guess God done put a protection around that white boy's behind. I even went up to his house, and weren't nobody there. It was like a ghost town. Strangest thing I ever did see. You'll have to thank Miss Lovenia."

"Shh . . . ," I whispered, putting my hand over his mouth, but I laughed in spite of myself. "Don't let my granny know I gave you that bag."

"Well, I can just throw it away," he said in a teasing voice, reaching for his pocket like he was going to take it out.

I punched his arm gently. "You better not throw that thing away. We need all the help we can get."

He laughed again. "Guess what?"

"What?"

"The coach from the McDonough Black Thrashers came by the house this afternoon. He said Satchel Paige talked to him Saturday night and said he'd be crazy if he didn't come check me out."

I laughed. "For real? He came all the way over to your house today and you just now telling me?" I punched his arm for real this time, and he laughed right along with me.

"It's happening, pretty girl. I told you it would," he said.

"Of course it's happening. So what did the coach say next?" I asked, and he told me. He told me about the pitching, and he told me how the coach from the Black Thrashers was impressed, and he told me the best news of all.

"He wants me, Opal. He wants me to start playing with the team a week from this Saturday. Well, he wanted me to start playing with them this Saturday, but I told him I couldn't because it was my girl's birthday," he said.

"Oh, Cedric," I said as the tears rolled down my cheeks. "You are amazing. Absolutely amazing. I knew you could do it. I just knew it."

"Oh, and I got even better news. My daddy said I could borrow his car. I will be at your house early Saturday morning to take you to Founder's Day and celebrate you and your birthday all day long. Tell your grandma I'm a safe driver and I would like to escort her to Founder's Day too," he said.

"I love you, Cedric Perkins," I whispered.

"I love you, too, Opal Pruitt," he whispered back and kissed me on my cheek. We sat outside and watched the stars until Granny came out and told us to call it a night, but she didn't sound mad or anything. She just stood there and smiled at us, and when Cedric walked past her, she patted him on his arm.

"You be safe out there, son," she said.

"Yes ma'am," he said and hurried on down the road.

"My little girl has grown up," Granny said, but she didn't sound sad. I went over and wrapped my arms around her waist, and we both stood there and watched Cedric head down the road toward his home, asking God to be with him and all the Colored men we loved.

The rest of the week flew by. Every day Cedric came and walked me to work, and every afternoon he came over to visit when we were all done working. When I told Granny I didn't want to go back to Miss Lovenia's to work, she just hugged me and said that was for the best. That was all she said. She didn't ask me what happened, and I was glad about that.

M.J. joined us most afternoons when he got done with his

chores, so he could play ball with Cedric and some of the other Colored boys in the front yard. I didn't mind. I loved sitting on the porch giggling with Lucille while the boys showed off their throwing and hitting skills. Even her little friend from church, Ray Carver, came over one afternoon, and I thought Lucille was going to jump out of her skin every time he touched the baseball. But it was all in good fun. We clapped and cheered like we was at a real Negro League baseball game. Sometimes Granny and some of the other neighbors would come out to watch the boys play, and everybody would whoop and holler and have a good ole time.

But, of course, I was waiting for Saturday, and finally Saturday morning came. I was nervous as a cat. I struggled to figure out what to wear, and I ultimately decided to wear my purple dress again. I didn't care if I had worn it just the other Saturday. It looked good on me, and today was my day. For once, I wasn't going to worry what anybody but Cedric had to say about me. I decided to wear my hair down. I had spent half the night rolling it up in some old rags, and when I took it down, the curls hung like gentle waves down my shoulders. When I walked out of my room, Granny was wearing a pretty blue dress, and she had on a matching blue hat.

"Lord, chile," Granny said. "You look like somebody in one of the magazines your cousin likes looking at so much."

"Aww, Granny." I laughed. "Thank you. You think it's okay for me to wear this dress again this Saturday too?"

"I don't see why not," she said. "You look good in it, and I know that boy of yours is gonna think you look good. Happy birthday. I got something for you on the table."

I looked at Granny with surprise. I couldn't remember the last time she gave me a present for my birthday. She always remembered me for Christmas, but birthdays was never anything she ever seemed to pay too much attention to since my aunties always made such a special to-do about it.

I went over to the kitchen table and there was a little box wrapped in some pretty pink paper. Once I took the paper off the box, I instantly recognized it and gasped. I knew that inside were the pearls my grandpa gave Granny for their wedding. I just stared at it. I knew she hadn't put something else in the box. I knew her precious pearls were inside.

"Oh no, Granny," I said. Those pearls were everything to Granny. If the house would have been coming apart, I think she would have come for me first and those pearls second. She loved that necklace more than anything. I knew without a doubt I couldn't take them. "I can't take these. These are your special pearls. I can't take these."

Granny came over and took the pearls out of the box. "My special pearls? Those are my only pearls, and I can do with them what I want, and I want my grandbaby to have them. I'd rather you have them now, while I can see you wear them, than you getting them after my passing. So take them and wear them today and any other day that feels special to you. Don't do like me and keep them closed up in a box somewhere. Wear them on a day when you feel extra good about yourself, and on a day when you need to be picked up. I wish I had done that."

"But Granny, I'm not even the oldest granddaughter. I shouldn't get these pearls. One of the twins should get these," I insisted.

"And which twin should that be?" she asked, laughing. She put the pearls around my neck and then stood back to admire them. "No, these pearls are yours, and I dare anybody to say different. Those other grandchildren have everything their little hearts desire. Won't none of them begrudge you this necklace, and if they do, they can come talk to me about it."

"Oh, Granny," I said. I hugged her tighter than I had ever hugged her before, and this time she let me. We stood there hugging until I heard Cedric knocking at the door. "Oh my. My face must look a mess." I wiped away the tears, but Granny squeezed me once more and pushed me toward the door.

"I ain't never seen you look more beautiful. Go open the door while I go get my purse," she said.

I went to the door and opened it, and Cedric was standing there dressed in the same suit he wore last week. Once again, we were matching, but instead of me getting all nervous, I just laughed.

"We gone keep doing this?" I asked, pulling him inside the door.

He laughed too. "Yep. For as long as we got breath in our bodies." He let out a low whistle. "Girl, you shore is looking good. I don't know if I want to let you out looking this good. And that hair. Why ain't you ever worn your hair loose like this before?"

"Stop," I said, but I was pleased he was so pleased with how I looked.

"Happy birthday," he said and reached inside his pocket and pulled out a box.

"I told you I had everything I needed," I said, but I was curious about what was inside the box. I opened it, and then I laughed until I started coughing. It was a whistle. "How?" was all I could get out.

"You said you wanted a whistle, so I think I bought every box of Cracker Jack in Henry County. I finally found a whistle in one of the boxes the other day," he said proudly.

"You are too much," I said.

Granny came out of her room, and when I showed her the whistle and told her the story, she laughed right along with us. "You children do my heart good. You remind me of my husband, Cedric. He was always doing silly things to try and make me laugh. He said I was the most serious little person he knew, so if he could get a smile on my face, he knew I would always keep him around."

"If I can do the same for Opal, I'll consider myself a blessed man," he said, looking at me with such love and devotion I felt a little bit embarrassed. But Granny was already walking toward the door.

"You reckon we need to check on Tote and see if he needs a ride?" she asked.

"No ma'am. He is over at the grounds helping with the cooking of the goat and the hog," Cedric said. "He was there all night. Daddy came home to change a little while ago, and he said Mr. Tote didn't take nary a drink all night."

"Well, praise the Lord," Granny said and we all laughed.

"You ladies ready to go?" Cedric asked.

"I think so," Granny said.

"Well, let's go then," Cedric said and took both of us by our arms and led us to his daddy's car. He tried to put Granny in the front seat, but she insisted on sitting in the back.

"I don't fool with the front seat, Cedric. I still don't quite trust these cars," she said.

Cedric helped her into the back, and then he helped me into the front.

"You are so pretty, Opal Pruitt," he whispered. Then he ran around to the driver's side, jumped in, and pulled us slowly out of Granny's yard. I could tell he was trying to drive his best for Granny. I was happy he was being so thoughtful.

I was so proud sitting beside Cedric as we rode toward the fairgrounds where Founder's Day happened each year. Once we got closer to town, we saw a gaggle of young girls from church waving at us as they hurried across Main Street onto Doster Road, where we were about to turn.

They were wearing their best summer dresses, and the young men who were fast on their heels were wearing either summer trousers and short-sleeved shirts or a suit like Cedric. Founder's Day was a big day for everybody in Parsons and Colored Town. It was the one time each year that everybody came together and acted like we were all one. It was the strangest thing. Granny said she remembered them starting Founder's Day right after the white boys came back home after the Great War, and somehow we all got included in it too.

Once we turned onto Doster Road, it was easy to see the fairgrounds just ahead. And Lordy have mercy, the air was filled with the thick scent of barbecue. I could smell that goat and hog meat even before we pulled into the space where Cedric carefully parked the car underneath a huge shade tree.

"It looks like we'll be able to see everything from here," Cedric said. He hopped out of the car and helped Granny out first and then me. Women from all of the various churches, Colored and white, had already set up tables where they sold everything from their sewing to their cakes, cookies, and pies. Some of the men were selling farm equipment and firearms. There were also games for the children to play, and there was going to be Sacred Harp singing by the white Methodists and Baptists. Miss Corinne had been practicing all week to sing with her church group and, as usual, she sounded wonderful. Several times during the week, Granny, Miss Peggy, and I sat in Miss Peggy's sewing room and listened while Miss Corinne sang songs like "The Lord Is Risen Indeed" or "There Is a House Not Made with Hands." So we had all been looking forward to today when we got to hear her sing with her church group.

After the white groups got through singing, choirs from our church and a few other churches around the county would sing. Then everybody would eat, and after that, the baseball would start. Jimmy Earl was playing on the white Methodist team, and they were going to play the white Baptist team. By then most of the Black folks would start to leave and head over to our church, where our boys would play their own ballgame and the girls would make ice cream for a social after the game ended.

"This is close enough for me," Granny said. "I don't need to be so close to all the goings-on, and I sure don't want to be smelling like goat and pig meat all day," she said. Cedric and I laughed and began setting up some chairs for us that he'd put in the back of the car.

We looked out into the other side of the field where the Colored men from our church were still roasting the goat and the hog real slow over a spit. They would cook that goat and hog meat until the meat was so tender it would fall off the bones, and then folks would line up, sometimes standing for an hour or more to get a plate. This was the one time Colored folks and white folks ate in close proximity to each other, though the white folks always got to line up first, and everybody knew to go their separate ways to eat. The white folks would sit at the nice picnic tables, and the Colored folks would go off and sit on the other side of the field. Sometimes some of the white kids and Colored kids who had grown up near each other would talk to each other, but for the most part, everybody pretty much stayed off to themselves.

The menu for the Founder's Day picnic was always the same: juicy goat and hog meat, potato salad, green beans, and a roll. And along with the goat and pork, Aunt Shimmy and some of the other ladies from our church would always fry up some chicken and make a huge pot of collard greens that they would cook over an open fire. The servers would keep selling plates until the last scrapings were passed out.

"Do you see Miss Peggy or Miss Corinne anywhere?" Granny asked. I turned around and shaded my eyes with my hand.

"That looks like Jimmy Earl standing in the line for food," I said. "I think . . ." I stopped. I couldn't breathe. I saw someone else beside Jimmy Earl. His cousin Skeeter. "We should leave," I said.

"Leave," Cedric said. "We just got here. Why would we . . ." He stopped too. He saw the same thing I saw. Skeeter Ketchums.

"Well, Lord have mercy, what do y'all see?" Granny said, twisting to see around Cedric. After a second or two, she recognized Skeeter also. "Oh, Lord. Let's go, y'all. Ain't no need in there being no trouble today. We need to go find your uncles, Opal. And your cousins. Quick. Before something bad happens."

I squeezed Cedric's arm. "Please don't go over there, Cedric. Please."

He patted my arm. "I'm fine. Ain't gone be no trouble today. Sheriff beat me to it. See. He just walked over there to talk to Jimmy Earl and that cousin of his. Ain't gone be no trouble."

I didn't believe him. Everything suddenly felt wrong about this day. We stood there and watched as the sheriff and Skeeter yelled at each other. Skeeter was talking fast and furious in the sheriff's face, and Jimmy Earl was trying to pull Skeeter away. Then I saw my Uncle Little Bud walking toward the sheriff, Jimmy Earl, and Skeeter, and I guess other men from the church saw him, too, because they took off running after Uncle Little Bud. Uncle Myron, Uncle Michael, and Uncle Lem took off running too.

"Oh, Jesus," I screamed. "Stop. Y'all stop." But before I could take off running, Cedric took off. He looked back at me as he ran. "Stay here. Don't come out there. Stay."

Granny got up quicker than I had ever seen her move before. "Stay here," she yelled and hurried out into the field where everyone was gathering. I tried to go behind her, but she turned and pointed. "Stay there."

I could hear the yelling get louder. I couldn't make out who was who because they were all wadded up together. All I could see were arms flying and menfolks fighting like they had lost their minds. I couldn't make out Cedric or my uncles anymore because they had blended into the crowd that was getting larger and larger. Usually a few hundred folks showed up for Founder's Day, and today was no different. It seemed like every one of them was in that group fighting or trying to see what was happening. I couldn't make out anything but screams and yells and lots of cursing. Granny was still making her way to where all of the madness was happening, and I could just make out her calls to my uncles and cousins. Women and children were running and screaming in every direction, and finally I saw Aunt Shimmy and Lucille running toward the crowd. I started running after them.

"Daddy," I heard Lucille yell at the top of her lungs. "Daddy."

"Oh, Lord. What's happening?" I heard someone beside me yell, but I kept running. And then I heard gunshots. And then. Nothing.

23

*L*et me through," I yelled. "Let me through." But people were running every which-a-way, and they all seemed to be going in the opposite direction that I was trying to run. I kept getting pushed back, and I couldn't see any of my family or Cedric. "Granny. Granny," I called at the top of my lungs, but it was a madhouse. The screams and the yells and the moans filled the air almost as thick as the scent of that barbecue.

I heard another gunshot, and I fell to the ground, trying to get out of the way of any flying bullets. I felt strong arms pick me up. It was M.J.

"Run, Opal. They shooting," M.J. yelled. "Run. I gotta go see about everybody."

"Granny's over there," I yelled, but he was running at top speed.

Then I saw Jimmy Earl taking off like he was running for his life.

"Doc Henry. Somebody get Doc Henry. They shot . . ." But

then his voice trailed off and I couldn't hear who he said was shot.

"Granny," I screamed. "Granny!" Somehow I made my legs run me to the crowd of pushing, shoving people.

"Stand back," I heard someone yell. "Stand back before I start shooting."

"Mama," I heard Uncle Myron yell. "Mama."

I felt arms grab me. It was Sister Perkins. "Come on, chile. We need to get out of here."

"I can't see anything, Sister Perkins. Where's Granny? Where's my granny, Sister Perkins? Where's Cedric?" I yelled, but she shook her head and held me tight, not letting me get any closer.

The next thing I knew, I heard a voice say, "Get out the way," and then Sister Perkins and I got pushed to the ground as someone hurried around us. Then I heard another gunshot. Then two more.

"Run, Opal," Sister Perkins yelled. She grabbed my hand and we ran until we were hiding behind a tree on the other side of the fairground.

"Where's Cedric? Where's my granny?" I whispered. "What's happening?"

But out of the corner of my eye, I saw something that horrified me more than anything I'd ever seen before. The crowd had moved a bit, and I could see the body of my granny on the ground with someone else who I couldn't make out lying beside her. Even from a distance I could see by her crumpled-up body that she was hurt. Bad hurt. I had to get to her.

My screams filled the air. "Granny! Granny! Granny! Granny!" I pushed Sister Perkins's arms away, and I took off running again. My Uncle Myron ran toward me and caught me around my waist.

"She's been hurt, baby," he cried. "I don't know how bad, but Mama's been hurt bad. I got to find Doc Henry."

"Noooo. Noooooooooo," I wailed. "Granny! Granny!" I tried to pull away from Uncle Myron, but he held me tight and wouldn't let me go. "It ain't safe. Run the other way, baby. Run."

"Put down that gun, Rafe Ketchums," a voice yelled back, where Granny was lying on the ground hurt. "Put it down now or you'll die today just like your son. Now put down the gun."

"Any of you niggers move, you gone be just as dead as these niggers on the ground," Rafe Ketchums yelled. "Y'all killed my boy. Somebody is going to pay for killing my boy."

"Stay here," Uncle Myron yelled at me and took off running back toward the crowd.

"Uncle Myron," I screamed, but he didn't even look back. I watched as Rafe Ketchums turned the gun on Uncle Myron and shot him twice. Uncle Myron spun around and then hit the ground hard. He didn't move. Not even a little bit.

"Uncle Myron!" I screamed.

The sheriff aimed his gun at Rafe Ketchums and shot him through his head. He fell like a dead tree, and then everything got quiet. It was like the life was sucked out of the crowd, and then, chaos. People started running and yelling and I could hardly see anything. I tried to put my eyes on Granny again, but the crowd was too thick.

I got up from the ground and saw my Uncle Lem run to where Uncle Myron lay on the ground.

"Doc Henry," he yelled. "Somebody get Doc Henry. My brother is alive. He's alive."

"Thank you, Jesus," I screamed. I took off running back toward the crowd again. I was determined to get to Granny. I didn't fear no stray bullet. I just had to see if she was all right, and I had to find Cedric. I still didn't see him nowhere.

Once I got to the crowd, it was like they knew to let me in this time because a space opened up for me to squeeze through. What I saw was the worst thing I had ever seen before. People were injured and lying on the ground. I couldn't tell who had been shot or who had gotten run over by people trying to get out of the way. Once again I tried to get to my granny, but this time, Earl Ketchums, Jimmy Earl's daddy, stood between me and my granny as he brandished his gun. He pointed it wildly from one Colored person to the next.

"She got in the way. Didn't mean to shoot her, but she got in the way," Earl Ketchums yelled. I hadn't even seen him in the crowd, but he still had a gun in his hand, and he was waving it around at everyone like he was out of his mind. Folks started screaming and yelling again. "Any of the rest of y'all get in the way, the same will happen to you. I don't hate y'all niggers, but you don't mess with my kin. You just don't do that."

Before I had time to drop back down to the ground, two white men tackled Earl Ketchums from behind and took the gun from him. I watched as they led him away, but then I turned my attention back to Granny, who still wasn't moving.

"Granny," I yelled. I didn't care about nothing but getting to my granny. I tried to get up, but all I could do was crawl toward where she lay. It felt like there was a great gulf between where she was and where I was, but I was determined to make it to her somehow. "Get my granny off the ground. Get her up."

Once again I felt arms and hands reaching for me and folks calling out my name, but all I wanted was my granny, and nothing, not even the Lord God himself, could have stopped me. I felt arms grab me around my waist, and I pulled away from the arms and hands like I was some wild animal.

"She's gone, baby. Mama's gone," I heard a voice say to me, but I wouldn't listen to him or nobody. I just wanted to get to Granny. The owner of the voice wouldn't stop pulling, and I turned around and saw the anguished face was Uncle Michael. He was crying, and his face had been badly beaten.

"They shot Cedric too. He's alive, but baby, it's bad. And Mama," he said, but his voice broke.

"Nooooo," I wailed. "Granny! Granny!" I knew Granny could fix this. I didn't know how, but I knew if I could just get to her, this would all go away. She would shake me hard and tell me to wake up. I just had to get to her. When I did, I saw she was lying on her stomach and her dress was wet with blood. Cedric was lying beside her. I could tell he was still alive, but his arm looked like it had been ripped apart. Someone had wrapped it with a cloth, but he was being held down by his daddy and two more men as Doc Henry tried to work on him.

"Take off your shirt and wrap it where the blood is coming out," Doc Henry ordered, and without a second thought Reverend

Perkins ripped off his shirt and gave it to Doc Henry. Doc Henry wrapped Cedric's arm several times with the shirt, which instantly became a bloody mess. "We need to get this boy to my office where I can work on him. Somebody get a truck and get up here with it fast."

Cedric moaned loudly.

I yanked myself out of Uncle Michael's arms.

"Cedric, I'm here. Cedric, I'm here," I cried out. Reverend Perkins twisted around when he heard my voice, and then he motioned for me just as Sister Perkins ran up to Cedric and knelt on the ground too. I tried not to look at my granny's body that was now covered. Somebody had just put a cloth over her body.

I knelt beside Sister Perkins. "I love you, Cedric. I love you, Cedric Perkins, and you are going to be okay. Do you hear me?"

"Pretty girl," I heard him say in a raspy voice. "Pretty girl."

"It's me. It's me," I said, crying so hard I wondered if he could understand a word I was saying.

Sister Perkins took my hand in hers, and we continued to kneel there until someone finally drove their truck over to where we were. Uncle Myron was in the back of the truck, and carefully, Reverend Perkins and a few more men carried Cedric to the truck. Before I knew it, they were driving away.

"Opal, we should go," Sister Perkins said.

I shook my head. "Not without my granny." And I knelt on the ground where she lay all covered up. I sat down beside her and reached under the sheet and took out one of her hands. It was covered in blood. I didn't know if it was her blood or Cedric's blood or both, but I held it tight. "Don't you worry, Granny. It's just me. It's Opal. I'm not leaving you out here. I'm going to stay right here until we can get you home. You hear me? You hear me?" I called out.

"Opal," a voice called. "Opal," the voice called again. I recognized the voice. It was Aunt Shimmy.

I felt her arms around me. "It's okay, baby. It's okay. Mama Birdie's with Grandpa and the Lord now. She's all right. She's all right, baby."

I shook my head and kept rubbing Granny's hand. I didn't want to hear all of that. I wanted my granny's voice to speak to me. That was the only voice I wanted to hear. Lucille finally got away from someone who had been keeping her back, and when she saw Granny on the ground all covered up, she lay on the ground and put her head on Granny and cried. We all cried there together until finally M.J. drove over with Uncle Myron's car. He got out and came to us.

"Y'all get up. We gonna take Granny home," he said, his voice choked. Three Colored men that I didn't know came over and helped us put Granny in the back seat. I climbed in with her and put her head on my lap. It was the first time I got to see her face. She looked at peace. Her face wasn't scared or hurting. She just looked like she was taking a nap.

"I love you," I whispered. "I'm so sorry. I'm so sorry."

This was all my fault. The guilt started to come over me, and I got to the place where I could barely breathe, the pain hit me so bad. All of this started because Skeeter Ketchums hurt me. I shouldn't have told.

"I shouldn't have told," I muttered as the tears streamed down my face. "I shouldn't have told."

"What did you say?" M.J. asked as he drove slowly through the crowd.

"This is my fault," I wailed, barely getting the words out. "I caused this. I got our granny killed."

M.J. turned around, stretching his neck so he could look at me. "It ain't your fault. Listen to me, Opal, and listen to me good. This ain't your doing. Them Ketchums did this, and they got what they deserved. Granny wouldn't want you thinking that way."

I looked back down at my forever sleeping granny, and I cried. I cried harder than I had ever cried before. M.J. tried to comfort me from the driver's seat and drive without hitting anyone. Once we got out of the crowd, we started the slow drive back to Colored Town. Back to home. When we pulled up, Uncle Michael and Uncle Little Bud were at the house. So were Aunt Shimmy and Uncle Little Bud's wife, Cheryl Anne, who was now about six months pregnant and waddling like a duck. Lucille was standing beside Aunt Shimmy, who had her arms tightly wrapped around my cousin's waist. Uncle Lem was back at Doc Henry's office looking after Uncle Myron.

Uncle Little Bud opened my door and helped me out. I was a bloody mess, and my dress was torn. I looked down at Granny's pearls around my neck. They were covered in blood too. All I wanted to do was go soak in the tub and climb into Granny's bed, but instead I stood and watched as they carried my granny's dead body into the house. The aunts all went to work. They heated up some water on the stove, and they made a bath for Granny and began washing her body. I watched. I wanted to help, but I felt so overwhelmed that I was rooted to my spot. Finally, Cheryl Anne came over to me.

"Let's get you out of these clothes. We almost got Mama cleaned up. We need to clean you up, too, baby," she said. I nodded. I let Cheryl Anne take me to my bedroom, and she brought a basin of warm water into the room so I could wash the blood from my body. I felt lost. It was as if I didn't know how to do anything. Cheryl Anne seemed to understand, because she quietly helped me out of my dress, and she carefully put Granny's pearls on my nightstand. Then she started washing the blood from my body. Before long she had me clean, my hair neatly plaited into two braids, and me redressed in one of my good church dresses, Granny's pearls back around my neck, the blood carefully washed away.

"Folks will start to come," she said in a soft voice. "It ain't your fault, Opal. You hear me? It ain't your fault."

I nodded and sat on my bed. She sat beside me, rubbing her belly.

"You remember how my little brother got the way he did?" she asked.

I looked at her and for a moment was confused, but then finally I remembered. "He had an accident in the bathtub."

She nodded. "Yes. I was twelve and he was about eight or nine months old. Mama asked me to give him his bath. He was sitting up already, and I darted out of the room for what seemed like was just a second. When I got back, he was lying in the water facedown. He nearly drowned, but Doc Henry brought him back. Randy ain't never been right since, though. He can hardly walk, and his talking ain't much better than a toddler and he's a teenager now. That happened on my watch, but both Mama and Daddy told me it wasn't my fault, and anytime I get sad, one or both of them will remind me not to look back and to thank God that Randy is still with us. We don't control nothing, Opal. Not life and not death. You didn't do this. It just happened and now we got to pick up the pieces. That is what Mother Birdie would have wanted."

I looked at Cheryl Anne. I had never heard her say so much at one time. I leaned my head against her shoulder, and she held me. We stayed there together for a long while until finally Lucille came in. Someone must have gotten her clean clothes, too, because she was dressed and her hair was freshly combed. She stood at the door.

"Y'all can come sit with Granny now," she said, the tears streaming down her face. I got up and went to her, pulling her into my arms as we both cried together. I reached up and touched my pearls that Granny had just given me that morning. They were all that I had of hers that was special, and I didn't mean to ever take them off again.

"Let's go," I said, and we walked out of my room and across the hall to Granny's. Someone had drawn the curtains so just a little bit of light was creeping into the room. Granny's kerosene lamp had been lit, and it was casting a strange glow throughout the room. The big clock that hung on her wall had been stopped, and the one mirror that was on her dresser had been covered.

That was how we prepared our dead and the space they occupied until we buried them. The clock would be restarted and the mirror uncovered after the funeral.

I didn't know where this custom came from; it was just what we always did. The other custom was that we would sit with Granny's body until the funeral. She would never be left alone. We called it "sitting with the dead." One thing we did do different from a lot of Colored families: we buried our dead quickly. I knew that by Monday evening, Granny would be laid to rest beside Grandpa and the twins, who died during childbirth when she was a new bride. They would have been older than Uncle Myron.

I went over to the bed where my granny lay. Uncle Little Bud was sitting beside the bed with his head on Granny's shoulder. Aunt Shimmy was kneeling by the bed, praying softly, her hand lightly touching Granny's feet. Uncle Michael stood over to the side with his arms wrapped around his daughter, Lanetta; her baby girl, Gloria; and Uncle Michael's wife, Aunt Pearl. Uncle Michael was crying short, hiccupping cries. Almost like a child. I went to Granny and sat on the bed with her.

Granny looked so beautiful. I stroked her face. The warmth was gone, but her skin still felt soft and wrinkle free. She just looked like she was in a deep sleep and if I shook her or called out her name, she would wake up and look at me and smile. I fought the urge to start screaming her name. Instead I stroked her hair. Someone had combed her hair and shaped it just like she liked it, and I could smell the herbs and spices someone had rubbed her body with to prepare her for burial. Granny looked ready to go. She looked like she was prepared to meet God looking her very best. I laid my head on her chest. My head touched Uncle Little Bud's.

"You didn't have to leave me," I whispered. "You didn't have to leave me like this."

Uncle Little Bud lifted his head, his face covered in sweat and tears. He reached for my hand. "You ain't alone, baby girl. You won't never be alone."

I squeezed his hand. That was all I could do. I had run out of words. All I could think about was Granny and then Cedric and Uncle Myron. I prayed they were doing okay. I wanted to go to both of them, but I didn't want to leave Granny either. I was so torn. As if on cue, my Uncle Lem came into the room. I hadn't heard his car drive up. Everybody looked up.

"Myron's gonna be all right," he said. Everyone erupted into cries of thanks. "The twins are with him, and he was resting good when I left."

I got up and went to him. "Cedric. How is Cedric?"

Uncle Lem put his arm around me. "He lost his arm, baby girl. Doc Henry did everything he could to save it, but it was too messed up. The doctor made him comfortable, and his mama and daddy are with him. He's still at Doc Henry's."

"I need to go to him," I said. I looked back at Granny. There was nothing more I could do for her. Right now, I needed to be with Cedric. I needed to see him for myself.

Uncle Little Bud got up. "Take my seat, Lem. I'll take Opal to see about Cedric."

Aunt Shimmy got up from her knees and came over to me

and hugged me tight. "We'll take care of Mama Birdie. You go see about your beau. He's gonna be needing you."

I nodded and followed Uncle Little Bud to Uncle Myron's car. Someone had cleaned the back seat. Then I got angry.

Miss Lovenia had given me just one of those little bags. She hadn't told me that my choosing to give the bag to Cedric meant Granny would be left without a covering. I was so angry, I didn't even know what to do with all the feelings. I wanted to go to Miss Lovenia and scream and yell at her, but I knew it would do no good. None of that would bring Granny back. So instead, I tried to concentrate all that I had left in me on Uncle Myron and Cedric. That was all I could do.

When we pulled into the driveway of Doc Henry's office and house, Jimmy Earl was coming out of the office. I turned my head away from him.

"We'll sit here until he leaves," Uncle Little Bud said in a quiet voice. He reached out and took my hand in his, and finally, we heard the sound of Jimmy Earl's truck firing up. When we heard it leave, we went inside. It smelled like bleach and some other cleansing scent I didn't recognize. Doc Henry was standing at the door and he looked tired, but he smiled a weary smile. He reached out and touched my arm.

"They're both going to be fine," he said. "Your Uncle Myron was shot in his arm and his neck. Thank God neither bullet pierced an artery, so I was able to remove them fairly easy."

"And Cedric," I said in a hesitant voice. "You had to take off his arm? His pitching arm?"

Doc Henry nodded his head, his face pained. "I tried to save it, Opal. God knows I did. He's got a stump. That was the best I could do. But he won't have no use of that arm again. I'm so sorry."

I nodded. I felt numb. Uncle Little Bud put his arm around me.

"I need to go see Cedric," I said.

Doc Henry showed us in and took us to a room in the back of the house. When we walked into the room, Doc Henry went over and gave Cedric a shot of medicine in his good arm. Cedric groaned a bit, but he soon relaxed again. Reverend Perkins and Sister Perkins were sitting by Cedric's bed. Sister Perkins got up and came to me. She pulled me into an embrace, and I cried in her arms.

"It's all right, baby," she said. "It's all right."

"I'm so sorry," I whispered. "I didn't mean for this to happen. I didn't mean for any of this to happen."

She pushed me away slightly so we were facing each other, and her face was stern. "You didn't make any of this happen, Opal. None of this was your fault. Those evil men and boys did this all by themselves, guided by the hands of the devil himself. And I am so sorry about Sister Birdie. Your grandmother was a stalwart for the Kingdom of God, and she is already sitting with our King as we speak. No one blames you for this. Please, don't blame yourself."

"Opal," I heard Cedric call out in a frail-sounding voice.

She smiled. "He's been calling out for you all afternoon. My son loves himself some Opal Pruitt. Go to him, baby. Take my seat. I'm going to step out and get a bit of air."

Reverend Perkins got up from his seat and came over and

hugged me too. "I'll go out and let you and Cedric be alone for a minute or two."

All of them left, and I went over to the bed where Cedric was lying. He had a pained look on his face, and giant tears flowed down his face when he looked up and saw me.

I sat down beside him and took his hand and held it and stroked it. His other arm was wrapped up so tight. I could tell there wasn't much of it left. Doc Henry cut his arm off from the elbow down.

"I'm sorry it took me so long to get to you," I said in a soft voice. "I haven't stopped worrying and thinking about you all afternoon."

"They took my arm, Opal," he said in a hoarse voice. "I tried to help Miss Birdie, but I couldn't stop them. I couldn't stop them and they took my arm."

"Shh . . . ," I said, putting my finger on his lips, which were dry and parched. I reached over to the stand by the bed he was lying in and got the little glass of water. I dipped my finger into the glass and dabbed his mouth. He licked the liquid gratefully. "Granny isn't in pain anymore. Don't worry about her."

"She was your world," he groaned in a hoarse voice. "I wish it had been me instead of Miss Birdie." He coughed, and I dabbed more water on his dry lips. I was afraid to give him too much, so I just kept dabbing. Finally, I spoke again.

I put my finger on his lips. "Don't say that again, Cedric. I am grateful to God that he didn't take you from me too. I love you, Cedric Perkins. I wish my granny was still here, but I wouldn't want to sacrifice your life for nothing. Not for nothing."

ANGELA JACKSON-BROWN

"I ain't gonna be able to play ball. You won't be able to be the head wife like Satchel Paige's wife," he said, his voice starting to sound distant and sleepy. The medicine Doc Henry gave him must have been working.

"Shh . . . ," I said again. "Just sleep. I'll be here. I ain't going nowhere. I'll be here when you wake up."

I watched as Cedric drifted off to sleep.

I looked upwards, barely able to focus because my eyes were so filled with tears. "You done us wrong today, God. Today, you done us wrong," I whispered, and then I laid my head against Cedric's good arm and cried. I cried for my granny. I cried for my Uncle Myron, and I cried for Cedric. But mostly, I cried for myself.

24

I couldn't go to church. When I woke up, I had every inten-
tion to go, but then as I thought about everything that had
happened the day before, I just couldn't go and sing hymns, and
pray, and listen to preaching. I was still mad at God. I didn't feel
like praising him after all that he had allowed to happen. Granny
was the most faithful Christian I knew, and the fact that he let
her get shot down like some wild animal was more than I could
forgive. So I just couldn't go to church and receive the hugs and
kisses and prayerful meditations from the saints.

As soon as it was light outside, I went into Granny's room
and kissed her cheek. Aunt Shimmy had stayed with Granny
throughout the night, but she was dozing in the corner. I scribbled
a note saying I was going to go see about Cedric, and then I took
off walking to Doc Henry's place.

I didn't feel like I had anything to fear right then. Skeeter
was dead, and so was his awful daddy, Mr. Rafe. Mr. Earl
Ketchums was locked up in the sheriff's office. But in case there

was trouble, I still had the gun Uncle Little Bud had given to me on the night the Klan had ridden through Colored Town. I clutched the purse tightly to my side. The state of mind I was in, at that point, I would have shot someone. Thankfully, no one challenged me as I walked past the peach orchard down the dusty dirt road that finally led to the paved road that went through Parsons. It was early, and when I got to Doc Henry's house, I had not encountered a single person. Before I could get to his door, I saw him sitting on his porch, smoking his pipe.

He looked up at me and smiled. "You barely left. I figured you would rest up a bit today."

I shook my head. "No sir. I didn't rest very well last night. And I just wanted to be with Cedric. How did he do after I left?"

Doc Henry rose from the chair he was sitting in. "He did pretty well. I just gave him a small dose of laudanum to take the edge off. He's awake but drowsy. The only thing concerning me is his fever. I can't seem to get it to break. His mama stayed with him, and if you plan on staying today, I'm going to see if she will let me drive her home so she can rest."

I barely heard a word he said. I just nodded and said, "Yes sir," following him into the house to the back where Cedric was. Uncle Little Bud had taken Uncle Myron home yesterday, since his injuries hadn't been that bad. Before Uncle Myron left, he came to me. I was sitting beside a sleeping Cedric at the time. I silently got up and gently hugged him. His arm was in a sling.

"You okay, baby?" he asked.

I shook my head no as the tears fell again. He just hugged me and kissed me on my forehead. "We are gonna make it through this. Your grandmother was so proud of you. You made her last years the best years of her life. Don't ever forget that."

I thought about his words as I went and sat down beside Cedric. Sister Perkins was still sleeping on the cot beside his bed. I didn't try to wake her. I knew she was tired. I took Cedric's good hand in mine and gently kissed it. He looked up at me with feverish eyes.

"Pretty girl," he said in a raspy voice. "Pretty girl ain't gonna want no one-armed man like me."

"Hush now," I said in a soft voice. "Don't say such things. If you think I love you because of your arm, you don't know me very well, Cedric Perkins. You tried to save my granny. How could I not love a man who nearly died trying to save my granny?"

"You should have given her the little white bag," he said as his face contorted with grief and pain. I bent down and kissed his parched lips.

"I did the right thing," I said, and that was all I was going to say to him about that little white bag. I had been up half the night, trying to replay in my mind how things could have been different. Maybe I could have given the bag to Granny and then tried to keep both of them out of the line of fire. *But then*, I thought, *what if the bullet would have hit one of my uncles or cousins instead?*

Granny would have taken a bullet for all of her children, grandchildren, nieces, and nephews. There was no scenario in which she would not have wanted to be the one to die rather than any of us. I could just hear her: "I'm already right with the Lord. You young ones need more time to get your houses in order." I imagined that if she had any moment to talk to God before dying, she would have said to him, "Take me. Don't take any of them. Take me." It reminded me of one of Granny's favorite hymns: "Lord, I'm Coming Home."

> Coming home, coming home,
> Nevermore to roam.
> Open wide Thine arms of love,
> Lord, I'm coming home.

I hoped that was what Granny's death was like. I hoped she got to tell the Lord that she was ready to come home, and somewhere, in the great beyond, Jesus himself ushered her on in through the pearly gates. That's what I hoped had happened. But my fear was that everything happened so fast that Granny never knew what happened to her. I hoped that there was a welcoming committee for Granny in heaven where she saw faces she hadn't seen since she was young. Her mama, her pa, her siblings, her aunts and uncles. Grandpa Pruitt. And depending on if my mama was dead or alive, maybe her too.

I looked down at Cedric. He was sleeping again. I was thankful for that. I looked over at Sister Pruitt. She was sitting up and stretching.

"Oh, sweetie, you should have roused me," she said, smoothing down her hair and yawning. "Have you been here long?"

"No ma'am. I just got here. I figured you needed the rest," I said, still holding Cedric's hand. I no longer felt embarrassed or guilty showing my love and affection for him. I wanted the entire world to know I was this man's girl.

"Did he wake up when you got here?" she asked.

"Yes ma'am. Just for a little," I said. I didn't tell her what he said to me. I didn't want her to worry about his state of mind any more than she already was. "I'm going to stay here today if you want to go home or go to church."

She nodded. "All I really want to do is go home and sleep, but the reverend will need me there today. Lot of folks are going to need comfort. Are you sure you don't want to go to church? It might help."

I shook my head. "No ma'am. I would rather be here with Cedric, if you don't mind."

She smiled. "I wouldn't want anyone else besides you to be here with my son. I'm going to call the reverend and have him pick me up so I can get ready for church. We'll be back by here afterward. Have you eaten anything?"

I thought about it for a moment, and I realized I hadn't eaten since day before yesterday. I was so excited about Founder's Day that I hadn't even eaten the breakfast Granny had cooked. The last breakfast, and I didn't even eat any of it. I willed the tears not to fall. I wasn't hungry. I just felt empty inside, but I didn't think food would fill the hollow spaces.

"I'm not hungry, Sister Perkins."

"You must keep up your strength. We'll bring you food on our way to church," she said and then walked over and kissed the top of my head. "My son is going to need your strength. I know you are struggling right now, but God is still with us. Even during the worst times, God is still in control. You understand?"

I said I did. But I didn't. I didn't understand any of this.

I didn't understand a God who would take the one person who loved me best, in such a brutal way. I didn't understand a God who would allow those evil men to do those horrible things to us Colored folks. I didn't understand how, out of all of the things he could have taken from Cedric, God either took or allowed the devil to take Cedric's pitching arm. So no, I didn't understand what God was doing. I was angry with him, and no amount of pretty words was going to change that right then. Right then, I needed to blame someone or something for all of this, and God seemed as good as anyone to put the blame on.

"Excuse me, sweetheart. I'm going to go use Doc Henry's telephone," she said and walked out of the room. I looked back down at Cedric, who was moaning in his sleep.

"It's okay," I said in what I hoped was a soothing voice, but he kept moaning. I thought about Granny and how she always said she felt better when she heard the Carter Family sing "Keep on the Sunny Side." I didn't much feel like singing, but I thought it was worth a try to help Cedric calm down and rest. So I sang.

Keep on the sunny side, always on the sunny side,
Keep on the sunny side of life.
It will help us every day, it will brighten all the way,
If we keep on the sunny side of life.

I couldn't stop the tears from falling, but the more I sang, the more I felt Granny's presence, and Cedric seemed to relax some. So I just kept singing those words, until finally he went back to sleep. I laid my head on the corner of his pillow and finally I slept too.

"Opal," a voice called out. "Opal."

I snapped to attention. "Granny?" For a moment I didn't know where I was, but when I focused my eyes, I saw it was Sister Perkins.

"The reverend is outside. I'm going to leave now, but we'll stop back by on our way to church and bring you breakfast. Okay, sweetheart?" she asked. Her kindness almost got me crying again.

"Yes ma'am," I said, swallowing back the fresh tears in my eyes.

I watched as Sister Perkins laid her hand on Cedric's head, and then she gently pressed her forehead to his. She stayed there for a moment, and then I heard her say, "Amen."

She wiped a tear from her face. "Take care of my boy," she said.

"I will," I said. "I won't leave until you all return."

I knew I needed to go back home once church was over to help plan Granny's funeral. There were certain things I knew that the others wouldn't, like what dress Granny would want to be buried in or what Scriptures she would want read at her funeral. She and I had had those conversations long before Founder's Day. She said if you get ready for your funeral before it happens, you can save your family a lot of heartache and harsh words. So she had told me things, like she wanted to wear her peach-colored dress, and she wanted daisies, lots of daisies, surrounding her casket. She even told me that she wanted a white casket. I knew we had saved enough money between the two of us for her to be put away nicely. I dreaded the planning, but I knew it had to be done.

After Sister Perkins left, Doc Henry came into the room and started examining Cedric. Cedric moaned, but he didn't wake up fully.

"This fever just won't break," Doc Henry mumbled, taking Cedric's pulse.

"He needs bone broth and elderberry tea," a voice said from the door. I looked up. It was Miss Lovenia.

"Why is she here?" I hissed at Doc Henry. "I don't want her here."

Doc Henry looked from me to Miss Lovenia and back to me again.

"Miss Lovenia helps me out sometimes. This is one of those times I need her. I've tried everything I know to break his fever. Miss Lovenia can help," he said, walking to her and taking the bag she was carrying.

"Heat up the bone broth and pour it inside of a cup so he can drink it. Boil some water and then put one of the tea bags into it that I left on your counter, and let it steep."

"Thank you, Miss Lovenia," Doc Henry said and hurried out of the room. I turned my back to her, hoping she would follow him out, but I should have known.

"I did not know God would take your grandmother, Opal," she said from across the room.

"You knew something. You gave me that white bag. You knew something," I repeated, still not looking at her. I was shaking from the anger and grief that I was feeling. God wasn't close by for me to turn my rage on him. Miss Lovenia was a good stand-in.

I felt a hand on my shoulder. I turned around quickly. As always, I hadn't heard her walk across the room. I tried to pull away, but she kept her hand firmly on my shoulder. Finally, I relaxed and waited for her to finish talking.

"Sometimes my gift of Sight is very clear, Opal," she said. "Other times I get shimmers. Glimpses but no clear images. I didn't see Birdie's death; I only saw death. I wasn't sure whose it would be, but I knew it was someone close to you who needed protection. The spirit only allowed me to make one bag. Even if I had disobeyed and made a dozen more, they would not have saved your granny," she said, her voice sounding weary. "I did all that I knew to do."

"It's my own fault," I said, getting up from my seat next to Cedric. "Granny said not to mess with hoodoo and that's exactly what I did, and now my granny is gone and my boyfriend is missing his pitching arm."

"Honey, I wish I did have power over life and death. If I did, my dear mother and father and siblings would still be here," Miss Lovenia said, looking at me with such kind eyes that I had to look away. "Opal, I know what people think about me. I know people believe that I have a pact with the devil, but that is the farthest from the truth."

"I don't believe that," I said in a low voice, but I wasn't sure what I believed about Miss Lovenia. She had somehow known she needed to give me one of those bags. That was all I knew for sure. "Why didn't you try? Why didn't you give me more than one bag? Why did you leave the rest of the people I loved without protection?"

"Opal, would your granny have taken the bag?" she asked. "Be honest with yourself."

I began pacing. I knew she was right. Granny never would have taken one of those hoodoo bags, even if she knew it would have saved her life, but that didn't stop me from being angry.

"Would she have taken it, daughter?" she asked again.

I turned on her with all the fury I was feeling. "I don't know. Maybe I could have convinced her to take it. Maybe I—"

"Maybe, daughter?" she said, shaking her head sadly. "Maybe is just our way as humans of not facing the truth. You know as well as I do that your granny would not have accepted my blessed bag of protection. None of your kin would have. This boy was the only one who would have taken it, and you and I both know that. He loves you. He might not have believed in the power of that bag, but he believed in the power of your love for him and his love for you."

I ran out of steam. I couldn't argue with the words she was saying. "But we could have tried," was all I could choke out. My eyes were overrunning with tears.

"Opal, I listen to the spirits and I listen to God, and, to be honest, they are one and the same. When our ancestors were kidnapped and brought to this country, we lost our connection to God. But thankfully, God did not lose his connection to us. All that I do is of God. No more, no less. And sometimes God doesn't give me a complete vision. If he had, I surely would have spared you and everyone the effects of this tragedy," she said, just as Doc Henry reentered the room carrying a steaming coffee cup. She looked at me one last time and then she turned to Doc Henry. "Wrap him up tightly in blankets and let him drink the tea until the fever breaks. Make sure he drinks all of the broth. It will help him get his strength."

She then walked toward the door and walked out without turning.

"Opal, she's just an old woman who knows a lot about primitive medicines that work. She's no one to be afraid of," he said. "And she's no one to be angry with over what happened yesterday."

I could tell he overheard part of our conversation. I didn't want to argue about it. Especially with Doc Henry, considering how good he had been to my family and to me.

"See if you can get Cedric to drink some of this tea," he said. "I'll go get the blankets."

"Cedric," I called out. He groaned but didn't answer. "Cedric, I need you to drink this tea. Okay?"

He continued to groan. I lifted his head, which caused him to groan more, but when I put the cup to his mouth, he started taking small sips. I let him take little breaks, but I kept coaxing him to keep drinking, which he did. His head was on fire with fever. When Doc Henry returned with the blankets, we piled them on top of Cedric.

"Is he going to be okay, Doc Henry?" I asked. I couldn't bear the thought of losing Cedric too. It was too much for me to even think about. I had to believe that out of all of my loss, God would surely not take Cedric too.

"We just have to get this fever down," Doc Henry said, the worry clear in his voice. "If this tea doesn't break the fever, I'm going to have to pack him in ice. I already called Luther Barnes to come by with some ice just in case," he said. All of a sudden, Cedric started shaking uncontrollably. Doc Henry moved me aside. "It's not a seizure. Maybe this is a sign that the fever is breaking. He's still burning up, though. Got to get him to finish this tea."

In spite of how angry I was with God, I found myself praying to him. "Please. Please take care of Cedric. Let this fever break. Let him be all right."

"Opal?" I heard Cedric call out to me. "Opal?"

"I'm here," I said, rushing to his side. "I'm right here, Cedric."

Doc Henry motioned for me to give him the rest of the tea. "I'm going to go heat up the bone broth," he said and left the room.

"Drink this, Cedric," I said as he looked at me with blood-shot eyes. "Please drink it, baby."

"I don't have no arm no more. Let me die, Opal. Just let me die," he said, the tears rolling down his face. I bent down and kissed him.

"I don't care about that arm, Cedric Perkins, and I'm not going to let you die," I said, my tears mingling with his. "I just need you to drink this tea. That's all we need to think about right now."

"I shoulda been the one to die," he groaned. "It shoulda been me. I ain't no good for you no more. I'm a cripple. That's all I am. A cripple."

"You are not, Cedric Perkins, and don't say that," I said. "You are whole. You are sound of mind, and once we get you better, you will be sound of body again. Do you hear me? You are not a cripple. I won't listen to such talk."

"Why are you still here?" he said, pushing the cup away with his left hand. "You deserve better. You deserve better. You deserve—"

I cut him off midsentence. "You don't get to tell me what I deserve, Cedric Perkins. I love you. I love you. Do you hear me? I love you. Now drink this tea."

I tilted his head up again and held the cup to his mouth. He looked at me with eyes full of emotion, and although I thought he was going to argue with me, he drank the tea. Then he began shivering again.

"I'm c-c-cold," he stuttered.

"I know," I said. "Just drink this last swallow."

He drank, and then I let his head rest on his pillow.

"When Doc Henry comes back, we'll get you out of these wet clothes," I said to him. "That'll make you feel better."

Seconds later, Doc Henry reentered the room and placed the cup of broth on the table beside Cedric's bed.

"How are you feeling, son?" he asked, touching Cedric's forehead with the back of his hand.

"My arm hurts," Cedric said, coughing and shaking. "And I'm cold."

"I know, son," Doc Henry replied. "I wish I could do more. I want to start weaning you off the laudanum in the next day or two. I don't want you to become reliant on it. So that means you are going to be in a lot of pain at first. Miss Lovenia left some tea for you to drink if the pain becomes too much. I don't know what all is in it, but I know it comes from the earth, which I suppose is better for you anyway."

I didn't want Cedric taking anything that woman left, but I knew firsthand how good her teas and herbs were.

"Doc Henry, Cedric is soaking wet," I said. "Can you help him get into dry clothes?"

"Let's wait until this fever is completely broken before I try to put new clothes on him," Doc Henry said. "I'm going to need to check his bandages as well. I don't want him to get an infection."

"Thank you, Doc Henry," I said. I picked up the cup of broth. "Drink some, Cedric."

He looked up at me and tried to smile. "Have you always been this bossy?"

I smiled back at him. "Yes, I'm afraid so."

He started sipping the broth, and after he was done, he looked more like himself. Doc Henry gave him a dose of laudanum, and Cedric drifted off to sleep, his fever completely broken.

"I'm going to let him sleep for now, and when his father gets here, we'll help him get changed. You've done a good job with him today, Opal," Doc Henry said. "It's clear that you two kids truly care about each other."

"Thank you," I said as Doc Henry left the room. I looked down at Cedric sleeping soundly. I reached for his left hand and began stroking it. "We will be all right, Cedric. Somehow, through all of this, we are going to be all right."

And then I laid my head on the pillow next to him and did my best to go to sleep too. I could feel the weight of the last couple of days weighing me down, and all I wanted to do was to escape my memories and find a sweet place within my dream world to land.

25

T he choir was singing as all of Granny's kin entered the church. The sanctuary was packed with people. The ushers had already brought out extra chairs for people to sit in. I looked around at everyone who had come to celebrate Granny's life. Granny would have liked the turnout. She always used to say you knew how loved a person was by how many people attended their funeral. If Granny's turnout was any indication of how much people loved her, she was well loved.

All of the men in our family wore tan suits, and the women and girls wore white dresses. We wore these clothes last year for Easter Sunday. None of us thought we would be in these clothes again to bury our Birdie Pruitt. Granny told us years ago that she never wanted her family wearing somber clothes at her funeral. She said, "My funeral is going to be a celebration because, finally, I will have gotten to see my Savior face-to-face. Who could feel sad about that?"

I tried not to be sad. For her. I tried to hold back the tears, but as we continued to make our way down the long aisle leading to Granny's pearlescent white casket, I couldn't help but let them fall. I felt myself stumble, but strong arms pulled me up. It was Uncle Little Bud.

"You're okay, baby," he said. "We're almost there."

His wife, Cheryl Anne, got on the other side of me and helped guide me up the aisle, even though her belly was full of baby. Once again, Cheryl Anne came to my rescue. I tried not to think about the fact that Granny would never get to hold and love on their baby. This moment was too much. I wished desperately that Cedric could have been here with me. I would have loved to lean on him and let him guide me through this day. But I was grateful he was alive. That was enough.

I felt my emotions getting stronger as we got closer to Granny's open casket. This would be our last time looking upon her face on this side of heaven. I knew she was long gone, and the body in the casket was just the shell of my granny, but somehow just being able to see her brought me some comfort. I had sat with her until late last night, and I got up early to spend my last morning with her. I couldn't believe that this was about to be the end. I couldn't even sing the words the choir was singing, even though this was one of my favorites: "Blessed Assurance." I just tried to focus on walking toward Granny, allowing the words of the song to wash over me.

This is my story, this is my song,
Praising my Savior, all the day long.
This is my story, this is my song,
Praising my Savior, all the day long.

Reverend Perkins stood up in the pulpit and asked everyone to stand as we continued to march into the church. There were a lot of us. We took up nearly five rows of pews. Kinfolk from all over Georgia came today to pay their respects. I looked over to the right side of the church, and I was shocked to see Satchel Paige and his wife, Janet, the woman who had taken up for me at the ballgame the other week. She did prayer hands toward me when we walked by. I nodded to let her know I saw her. I wondered why they came. They didn't even know Granny.

I didn't wonder long, because we were just a few feet away from Granny's casket, and the feeling of being overwhelmed hit me again. I watched as Uncle Myron touched Granny's face. I knew this was hitting him extra hard. We had just buried Aunt Josephine a few years ago, and now he was having to bury his mama. His heart. Finally, he let himself be led away by my cousins, Hiram and Myron Jr.

Next, Uncle Lem, Aunt Shimmy, and Lucille went up to the casket. Uncle Lem was nearly carrying Lucille, she was crying so hard. I wanted to go to her, but my legs were wobbly again. I clutched Uncle Little Bud's arm for dear life, and Cheryl Anne tightened her grip around my waist. Uncle Michael, Aunt Pearl, and M.J. went next. Both Uncle Michael and M.J. bent down and kissed Granny's cheek. Finally, it was time. There was no way I could avoid this moment. I wanted to be alone with my granny. I wanted everybody in that church to go away, so I could lay my head on her chest and stay there until Jesus came and got me too.

"Come on, baby," Uncle Little Bud whispered. "It's okay. We got you. Come on."

I shook my head but I went to the casket where Granny lay. She looked like an angel. I had done her hair the night before, just like she liked it. I left out some hair to curl all around her face, while plaiting and pinning up the rest. I had even managed to get her little peach-colored handkerchief pinned to her head to disguise the place where one of the bullets had entered her skull. She looked beautiful. And I couldn't believe that they were about to close her inside that awful casket. That place of no return. I watched as Uncle Little Bud kissed her check, and I watched as Cheryl Anne touched Granny's cheek with her hand. I went to Granny. Straightened the collar to her dress. Then I bent down and whispered, "You were always my mama. You were always there for me. I will never love anyone as much as I love you. I will see you in the by and by."

Uncle Little Bud was crying, but he put his arms around me. "Let's sit, baby."

And then I saw the funeral home men getting up to close the casket for the last time, and I couldn't move. A sound came out of my throat that didn't even sound like me. I didn't recognize myself as I moaned, "Noooooo, noooooo, nooooo," feeling myself sink to the floor. I felt arms helping me up, and then I felt someone leading me to the pew, and then I didn't remember much else of the funeral. I kept my face buried in Uncle Little Bud's chest.

I know people said speeches and sang hymns. I know at one point Sister Perkins came and slid in between me and Cheryl Anne, and she pulled me close and rocked me for the rest of the service. I could hear her softly praying, "Give her strength, Lord. Give her strength."

I tried to pull myself together. I knew Granny would have teased me and said, "Opal Pruitt, you carrying on like my soul was lost, and in hell I lifted up my eyes. Don't take on like that for me. I am with the Savior and my soul has been set free." I knew she would have said that, but I couldn't stop the pain I was feeling. I wanted my granny. I *needed* my granny. She was my world. Everything I knew about love, I first learned it from her.

I did remember Reverend Perkins delivering the eulogy. I remember him laughing and crying.

"Saints," he said. "When I first came back to Parsons to preach here at Little Bethel, Sister Birdie came to me and said, 'We need a truth speaker. If that ain't you, then the bishop needs to send us somebody else. There ain't nothing worse than a scared man of God.'"

I remember everyone laughing because that was exactly how Granny was. She didn't mince her words when it came to her church or her family. She was our family's truth speaker, and I couldn't imagine anyone taking her place.

Just like Granny had said she wanted, the service wasn't long, and before I knew it, we were all walking out of the church behind Granny's casket. Sister Perkins walked with me, her arm tightly around my waist. I appreciated her attentiveness. I felt shored up. Supported. Loved.

Then I saw Miss Peggy, Miss Corinne, and Jimmy Earl. I wanted to run the other way, but Miss Corinne broke free of her mama and Jimmy Earl and came to me and pulled me into her arms.

"I'm so sorry," she said, the tears rolling down her face. "I'm having a bad day, but you're having a worse day, and I'm sorry. I'm sorry, Opal. Birdie is where Daddy is now. She ain't coming back to us."

Miss Corinne's words almost caused me to lose it again. Miss Peggy must have seen me trembling because she called for Miss Corinne as she walked toward me.

"Go stand by your son," Miss Peggy told her. Miss Peggy sounded so tired, and her face looked tortured. I wanted to comfort her, but I didn't have any comfort left for myself, let alone for her. Miss Corinne kissed my cheek and then went back to stand with Jimmy Earl, whose eyes never met mine. He stared at the ground the entire time, looking like he wished it would swallow him up into it.

Miss Peggy reached up and touched my tearstained face. Her face was pouring tears too.

"She was my best friend," Miss Peggy said. She tried to smile, but instead she choked back a sob. "I will always be here for you as long as I have breath, Opal. I won't be far behind Birdie, but until the Savior calls for me, I will be your stand-in gran. I am so sorry that her end had to be like that. I'm so sorry."

Before I could say anything, Jimmy Earl walked over to me. I looked at him like I was looking at a stranger. I didn't see the boy I had loved all my life. I just saw Earl Ketchums's son.

"Opal . . . ," he started and then stopped. He swallowed and then opened his mouth. "I am so—"

"We need to get to the cemetery," Sister Perkins said in a strained voice. "Thank you all for coming today."

I was thankful that Sister Perkins took charge. I didn't have any words to offer them. I had told Uncle Myron the day before that I would not be going back to Miss Peggy's house. I knew Miss Peggy needed help, but I couldn't be the one to give it to her. I prayed Jimmy Earl got to have his granny for many more years to come, but I couldn't be in that house watching her live while my granny lay dead in the Colored cemetery. Uncle Myron told me not to worry about it and he would send word to them himself. I wasn't expecting to see them at Granny's funeral, although I should have. I knew they loved Granny, but my spirit was full and I couldn't hold a single other emotion, especially not theirs.

Sister Perkins and I walked around Miss Peggy and past Jimmy Earl and Miss Corinne to the cemetery, where the family was already sitting. Others were standing, waiting for us all to get settled so that Reverend Perkins could finish the service. I sat down by Lucille, who put her head on my shoulder. I wrapped my arms around her. Sister Perkins stood behind us with her hands on both of our backs.

"'I am the resurrection and the life,'" Mr. Perkins recited. "'The one who believes in me will live, even though they die, and whoever lives by believing in me will never die.' Saints, Sister Rachel Elizabeth Banks Pruitt, whom we know as Sister Birdie, gave her entire life to serving God. Today, we stand here and rejoice with her and for her, that she is already reunited with her King. For as much as it has pleased our heavenly Father in his wise providence to take unto himself our beloved Sister Birdie, we therefore commit her body to the ground, earth to earth, ashes to ashes, dust to dust. Sleep well, Sister Birdie, until we meet again. Please, everyone recite after me the Lord's Prayer." Then he wiped tears from his eyes.

We all bowed our heads and said the prayer together. Afterward, everyone took a daisy and threw it on top of Granny's casket. I watched as Lucille got up and dropped her daisy.

"You ready to go, Opal?" she asked. I shook my head no. "Do you want me to stay with you?" I shook my head again. She came to me and kissed my cheek and then joined her parents as they headed back toward the church.

Everyone started to walk away, but I couldn't. I was rooted to my seat.

"We need to go, sweetheart," I heard Sister Perkins say, rubbing my back. "You need to go eat something. There is repast in the dining hall."

I still couldn't move. Reverend Perkins came and sat beside me. "She'll be all right," he said to Sister Perkins. "This one was always Sister Birdie's shadow. She just needs to see this thing through. Am I right, chile?"

I nodded. I couldn't speak. The tears lapped underneath my chin. I felt myself begin to rock. I tried to stop because I knew I must have looked silly, but that was all I could do to keep myself from completely losing it. I felt like I was hanging on by a very loose thread. I needed Granny so bad right then. She was the only one who would know what to say, and she was gone. In that moment, heaven seemed so very far away.

"I'll stay with her, love," Reverend Perkins said to Sister Perkins as he put his arm around my shoulders. "You go make sure everything is in order in the dining room. Tell her family she is fine and is with me. And tell one of the deacons to say the blessing. We'll be in soon."

Sister Perkins kissed my cheek and then went toward the church. Reverend Perkins and I didn't say anything at first. We just sat. Every so often, he would dab at my tears, but other than that, we sat in silence. Finally, one of the men from the funeral home looked at us both and then at Reverend Perkins.

"Reverend, do you want us to begin?" he asked. I didn't recognize him. I wanted to tell him to leave Granny alone and to go away, but I knew that would have sounded crazy, so I just kept rocking.

"Yes," Reverend Perkins said to the man. "You do what you need to do. We just want to stay here until Sister Birdie is in the ground. This is her grandbaby, and wherever one was, the other wasn't far behind. She just needs to see this through to the end. Is that right, chile?"

I nodded and rocked. And nodded and rocked.

"Opal, I want you to listen to me," he said. "Sister Birdie would want you to go on with your life. She wouldn't want your life to stop here at her graveside. She would want you to live and love and be happy. Ain't that right?"

I nodded. "Yes sir," I croaked.

He patted my shoulder. "That's good. And I know there is a young man over at Doc Henry's office who needs your strength. My son has changed in just the brief time the two of you have been keeping company. He wants to be a better man because of you. So you can't let yourself fall to pieces. You've got to pull from that strength inside of you that comes from Sister Birdie. Ain't that right?"

I took my eyes off of them lowering Granny's casket into the ground and looked at Reverend Perkins. His eyes were shining with tears too. I knew he was telling me the right thing. I knew I had so much to look forward to in life. I owed it to Granny to keep going. To not give up. To not become bitter. It was so hard, though.

"I just can't imagine my life without her in it," I said.

"That's the beauty of living, chile," Reverend Perkins said. "We have to say some painful goodbyes if we manage to stay here long enough. When my papa, Preacher, died, I thought I would never recover. And then, when Mama Apple passed away, I truly felt like the world was going to come to an end. But thank God for Sister Perkins and that hardheaded boy of mine. They gave me reason to live. And you have a church full of folks who love you and want you to live a full and abundant life. Sister Pruitt don't need us no more, chile," he said, standing and reaching for my hand. I let him help me up. "She made the trip to heaven on Saturday, and she is already rejoicing with her King. That's not her in that casket. She has flown away, so we can go inside and be with your family. Is that all right with you?"

"Yes sir," I said. He pulled me into a hug.

"You are not alone, chile," he said. "You've got a whole community of folks who love you. You will never be alone."

I cried and cried, and Reverend Perkins let me. And then, once I composed myself, he led me into the church dining hall, where my family was waiting for me. Lucille came to me and hugged me tight. Reverend Perkins made his way over to where Sister Perkins was helping serve plates.

"She was the best granny ever. We were blessed to have her, weren't we?" Lucille asked, smiling through her tears.

"We were very blessed," I choked out.

"Come sit with us," she said, taking my hand. "Mama said she wants you to come live with us."

I shook my head. "I have a home. I don't want to leave mine and Granny's house." The very idea of not being in that house that I had shared with Granny my entire life was almost causing me to have heart palpitations. I prayed they wouldn't try and make me leave my home. That was all I had left of Granny. I couldn't leave. I wouldn't leave.

"But you don't want to be there alone, do you?" Lucille asked, pulling me toward the table where my uncles and aunts and cousins were all sitting.

Everyone looked up at me, and I felt self-conscious.

I sat down beside Aunt Shimmy, and Lucille sat on the other side of me.

"Mama, tell Opal she needs to come stay with us," Lucille said. "She says she wants to stay at Granny's house, but she don't need to be there alone. Tell her."

"Sweetie, Mama Birdie wouldn't want you in that house all by yourself," Aunt Shimmy said. "Come stay with us. At least for a little while."

I shook my head. "I just want to go home."

"Baby, home is where your family is, and Mama is gone," Uncle Lem said. "We don't want you rattling around that house by yourself."

"I can stay with her," M.J. said. "If she don't want to live anywhere else, then let me stay there." We all looked at Uncle Michael, and he nodded his consent. I was so relieved. If I wouldn't have been afraid of falling from the sheer weight of this day, I would have gotten up and hugged his neck.

I looked gratefully at M.J. "Thank you."

He smiled. "You know I'll always have your back, cousin. Always. And as long as you want to stay there at the house, I'll stay there with you."

Sister Perkins came over and put a plate in front of me. "Eat," she said, patting my shoulders.

I looked up at her and tried to smile. "Is Cedric by himself?" Right then, I just wanted to be where he was, and I didn't want to think of him being there suffering alone.

She shook her head. "Mr. Tote is with him. He said he couldn't bear to come to this funeral, so he said he would stay with Cedric." She patted my shoulder again and then went back over to the food table. I couldn't believe that at one time I thought Sister Perkins was standoffish. She had been so sweet to me and our family. I was thankful for her and for Reverend Perkins.

I started picking at my food. I wasn't hungry at all. I just wanted to go where Cedric was and hear his voice.

"Did Miss Peggy and them leave?" I asked Aunt Shimmy. I looked around, but I didn't see them.

"Yes," Aunt Shimmy said in a dry voice. "They stood around for a minute and then they left."

I was happy to hear it. I didn't feel up to talking to them any-more. I wasn't sure when I would be ready, but I knew it wouldn't be today. At some point, I knew I would go back and check on Miss Peggy. She wasn't going to live forever, and I didn't want her to die thinking I hated her or didn't love her. It was just too much for me to think about today.

"Be nice, Shimmy," Uncle Lem said, patting Aunt Shimmy's hand. "They cared about Mama in their own way. Especially Miss Peggy. She and Mama practically grew up together."

Aunt Shimmy made a clicking sound with her teeth, but she didn't say anything.

I was worn out with all of the funeral stuff. I looked over at M.J., and he must have known what my look meant, because he jumped up with a quickness.

"Daddy, you mind if me and Opal take the car and go see about Cedric?" he asked. Uncle Michael looked at us both.

"You children go on. I know you're both worried about Cedric," he said. "Drive careful."

"Can I go?" Lucille asked.

I bent down and kissed her on her head. "Not this time. He's in a bad way. But in a day or two, he'll be happy for more company. Okay?"

She smiled. "Okay. I might be young, but I understand you want some time with your boyfriend."

Just a few days ago, I would have been embarrassed about such talk, but after all that we had been through, I was thankful to have a boyfriend, and I wasn't going to be ashamed of it.

I mussed her hair as I walked away with M.J. It took us nearly a half hour or more to get out of the dining hall. Everybody wanted to hug us and tell us they loved us. Finally, I was able to get to the food table where Sister Perkins was still passing out plates. "We're going to go see Cedric," I said.

She smiled. "He'll like that. Tell him we'll be over there shortly. I would send some food for him, but I doubt he's up to eating anything solid yet. Did you two eat?"

"Yes ma'am," M.J. said. "Not a whole lot, but we ate."

She handed M.J. four plates. "This is for if y'all get hungry later. And please, give one to Mr. Tote and Doc Henry. Tell my boy I love him and we'll see him soon."

Finally we got to the car. M.J. put the plates in the back seat, and then he opened the passenger side for me. Just as he was about to slide into the driver's side, Mr. and Mrs. Paige came over to the car. We both got out, and Mrs. Paige hugged me tightly and Mr. Paige shook M.J.'s hand.

"Oh, sweetheart, we were so sorry to hear about what happened to your grandmother," Mrs. Paige said, reaching her hand out to M.J., who took it. "I told Satch we had to come and pay our respects. And then we heard the terrible news about your beau."

"Thank you," I said, my voice nearly gone from the crying and the emotion of the day. "It was mighty kind of y'all to come to Granny's funeral. I know Cedric is going to hate that he missed seeing you both."

"Well, you tell him when we are back this way, we'll come see the two of you," Mrs. Paige said, standing back and smiling. Mr. Paige stepped closer and handed me a piece of folded-up paper.

"Young lady, you tell that young man of yours that it ain't

over and he is to call me when he's up and about," Mr. Paige said. "I'm all over the place, but Janet will know how to find me."

I was confused. I wasn't sure if I was hearing Mr. Paige correctly. "Sir, Cedric's throwing arm is gone. He can't play baseball no more."

"He still knows the game of baseball, don't he?" Mr. Paige asked, looking at me with a smile.

M.J. cut in. "Oh, yes sir. Cedric knows everything there is about the game. He studies it like some folks study the Scriptures."

I cut my eyes at M.J. I didn't want Mr. and Mrs. Paige to think Cedric was some kind of heathen. Whoever heard of studying baseball like the Scriptures? I would have kicked my cousin on his leg, but before I could, Mr. Paige threw back his head and laughed.

"Good. That's just the kind of pitching coach he needs to be," Mr. Paige said. "You just tell him to call me when he's feeling better, and we'll see if we can't get him on with a team. It won't be the same as playing, but if he's got baseball in his blood like you say, he'll settle into this new life." He looked at his watch. "I hate for us to have to run off, but I've got to get to St. Louis by day after tomorrow. You all be blessed."

Mrs. Paige hugged me again and then whispered in my ear, "You take care of yourself, little sister. And you can use that number to call me anytime. Especially if any of these little old kittens try to get at your man again."

"Yes ma'am," I said.

M.J. and I both watched as Mr. and Mrs. Paige left.

"Well," M.J. said. "What do you think about that?"

I smiled the first real smile since Granny was taken from me. "I think Granny took some time out of her first few days in heaven to be our guardian angel. That's what I think," I said.

M.J. put his arm around me and hugged me. "I think you're right. In fact, I know you're right because that's just the kind of granny we have."

We both hurried and got back inside Uncle Michael's car, anxious to get to Doc Henry's office so we could tell Cedric the good news. The drive there didn't take long, and when we pulled up to Doc Henry's, Mr. Tote and Doc Henry were sitting outside.

I hopped out of the car before M.J. could come open my door. I just wanted to see Cedric. When I got to the porch, Doc Henry smiled.

"He's resting, but I know he'll be happy to see you," Doc Henry said.

Mr. Tote stood up, the tears spilling from his eyes. "I'm sorry, Opal. I thought I could go to the funeral, but—"

I hugged him. "You don't have to say anything else, Mr. Tote. She loved you too. Thank you for staying with Cedric. This is where you were needed the most."

"Cousin, you go tell him the news," M.J. said, sitting down on the steps. "I'll just stay out here for a bit and give y'all some time alone."

I patted him on his shoulder and then went inside. Cedric looked to be asleep, but when I got close, he opened his eyes and tried to smile.

"Hey, pretty girl," he said. "You came back."

I bent down and kissed him. "Of course I came back. Where else would I go?"

"I should have been there with you today," he said. "I know it had to be hard on you burying Sister Birdie. I should have been there."

"You were right where you needed to be," I said. "I made it. It was hard, but everybody was so kind and loving, especially your mama and daddy. Don't you feel bad about not being there, because really, if the truth be known, you were there with me, Cedric. Every step of the way."

"Opal, this is just a lot. I've tried to figure out how I can be any good to you, but—"

I kissed him again. His face was cool to the touch. I silently said thank you to God for letting his fever break. "You listen to me, Cedric Perkins. Nothing about this scares me. Not that arm of yours. Not the feelings we're feeling for each other. Nothing. The only thing that scares me is you not loving me. That's it."

I watched as the tears rolled down his face. Normally, he was the one wiping my tears, but this time, I got to wipe his. This time, I got to be strong. I knew Granny would have scolded me and said I'd been strong my whole life, but sometimes it takes a body a minute to see what others have seen all along.

"I will love you for the rest of my days," Cedric said. "I just want to make sure I can take care of you. I just don't know what I can do with one arm, other than be a burden to you. You deserve better than that."

"You don't ever have to worry about being a burden to me.

Plus, you are still going to be able to have a job working in base-ball," I said, and then I told him about the conversation with Mr. Paige.

"For real?" he asked when I was done. "He really said that?"

"For real," I said. "We're going to be okay, Cedric Perkins. We're going to be okay."

He reached out with his good arm and pulled me close. For a time, that is where I stayed, until I heard the gentle sounds of him sleeping. I rose up slightly and looked down at his face. I didn't see the same worry lines that were there when I first arrived. His face looked relaxed and free of pain. I knew the pain wasn't gone for good, but I was thankful that for now, he was resting peacefully. I laid my head back on his chest and closed my eyes.

"Thank you, Granny," I whispered, and somehow, some way, it felt like I could hear her say back to me, "I told you I would always take care of you, Opal. Your granny will always be around looking after you."

And for the first time since she was taken from us, I truly believed those words to be true. I knew there would be some hard days ahead, but I also knew that in the midnight hour, when the stars looked like they were raining down from the heavens, it would always be a sign for me from Granny, letting me know that heaven was real and Granny was there, safe in the arms of Jesus. Safe from all harm and danger, but still looking out after me.

Acknowledgments

I often liken the act of finishing a novel to birthing a baby. Well, there were many midwives on hand to help bring this baby into the world.

First and foremost, I want to thank my amazing husband and partner, Robert L. Brown, for always being my "first reader-listener." For always giving great advice and always falling in love with the characters as much as I do. Thank you for keeping the home fires burning. Thank you for never making me feel guilty for leaving you behind as I visit these imaginary worlds. Thank you for knowing I will always come back to you. This book is as much yours as it is mine, Brown. I love you. I couldn't do me without you.

Thank you to my amazing son and first writing muse, Justin Bean. Son, you still make my breath catch inside my throat just like it did the first moment I held you. It is amazing to me that someone as phenomenal as you came from me. Thank you for being my constant cheerleader and inspiration. Thank you for seeing value in my words even before you understood their meaning, and thank you for embracing the writer who lives inside you. Your moment is coming.

Thank you to my dear friends and constant readers, Lauren Bishop-Weidner and Libby Filiatreau. You always give me such insightful comments. These characters are alive and breathing largely because of your feedback. Lauren, I especially thank you for sharing with me details from your childhood home. The Founder's Day celebration and the character Mr. Tote exist because of your memories. I hope I did them justice.

Thank you to all of my many relatives, especially those who call to check on me and encourage me on the days I feel discouraged. Thank you Aunt Lenoria, Aunt Brenda, Aunt Yuvonne, Aunt Gloria, Aunt Jean, Uncle Fred, and Kim. Your kindness and love inspire me so much.

Paw Paw Joel, thank you for standing in the gap and filling the parental void left open with the passing of my daddy, M.C. Jackson and my mother, Gwendolyn English. I would not have been able to walk through the fire those losses created without you.

Thank you to my sisters and my sister-friends who have talked me off the ledge many, many times: Renee, Joeli, Anita, Adriena, Alita, Julia, Honi, Crystal, Carrie, Colleen, April, Mijiza, TaMara, Elaine, Krista, Kiesha, Emily, Allyson, Patsy W., Patricia V., and so many more. Thank you for being my rocks. My tribe. My inner circle.

Thank you to the many Ball State students, past and present, who have become like children to me. Every day you remind me why I teach and why I work so hard to be an inspiration to you.

Thank you to the following books: *The Maid Narratives: Black Domestics and White Families in the Jim Crow South*; *Cooking in Other Women's Kitchens: Domestic Workers in the South, 1865–1960*; and *Telling Memories Among Southern Women: Domestic Workers and Their Employers in the Segregated South*.

Thank you to the Auburn Avenue Research Library on African American Culture and History in Atlanta, Georgia; the Genealogical Society of Henry and Clayton Counties, Inc. in McDonough, Georgia, and the staff at the courthouse in McDonough.

Thank you to the editorial and marketing teams at Thomas Nelson. I so appreciate you all for believing in this book and its potential to touch lives. Thank you to Kimberly Carlton, my editor extraordinaire. The first time we talked, I knew we were going to work well together. Our backgrounds are so different, but your willingness to get to know me and this world I created let me know that our differences were our strengths. I look forward to working with you again soon. I would also like to thank Amanda Bostic, Becky Monds, Savanna Carlton, Shannon Luders-Manuel, Jodi Hughes, Kerri Potts, Margaret Kercher, Nekasha Pratt, Matt Bray, and Marcee Wardell.

Thank you to my incredible agent and friend, Alice Speilburg. Alice, you and I have been through so much with this book. There were times when I almost gave up on writing it, but your unfailing belief in me kept me going. You encouraged me, you cheered me on, you commiserated with me, and then, when we got the offer, you got on the phone with me and celebrated. I am so happy our paths crossed and you said yes to me and my work.

Last but not least, thank you to the readers and booksellers. It is because of you my voice is more than a tree falling in the woods with no one there to hear it. You amplify my voice, and you allow me to keep writing because I know you are out there. Waiting. Thank you.

Discussion Questions

1. Discuss how the drought becomes an antagonist in the novel.
2. How does the absence of Opal's mother affect her relationship with the other women in the story?
3. In what ways does Opal struggle with the love between herself and her childhood friend, Jimmy Earl Ketchums, and her new boyfriend, Cedric Perkins?
4. Discuss the differences between how Opal views Parsons, Georgia, and her community known as Colored Town.
5. Opal often sees herself as weak. Explain your thoughts about her character. In what ways does she exhibit weakness and in what ways does she exhibit strength?
6. Discuss the role religion plays in the lives of the various characters and how they apply their beliefs to their everyday lives.
7. Miss Lovenia, the root woman, shares a different type of spirituality with Opal that eventually Opal rejects.

Can you imagine a time when Opal might renew her relationship with the elderly woman and the spirituality the woman tried to share with her?

8. Clear lines of separation exist between the races in the story, but some relationships seem to defy the color line, like Miss Peggy and her family's relationship with Birdie and Opal, and Doc Henry's relationship to the community, regardless of ethnicity. Discuss the significance of these uncommon alliances and relationships.

9. Opal often struggles with her faith, similar to the character Mr. Tote, but ultimately, Opal seems to find her way back to believing in God in some form or another. How does her wafting back and forth affect your perception of her?

10. Founder's Day has always been a day when the community could come together and celebrate the town and its inhabitants. This Founder's Day ends in violence and death. In what ways does this outcome mirror the racial unrest that was going on in the nation around that same time?

About the Author

Ankh Productions LLC - Photography by: Chandra Lynch

*A*ngela Jackson-Brown is an award-winning writer, poet, and playwright who teaches creative writing and English at Ball State University in Muncie, Indiana. She is a graduate of the Spalding low-residency MFA program in creative writing. She is the author of the novel *Drinking from a Bitter Cup* and the poetry collection *House Repairs*.

✳

angelajacksonbrown.com
Instagram: @angelajacksonbrownauthor
Twitter: @adjackson68